STRIPPING THE SUB

Book 6 of Stronghold Doms

GOLDEN ANGEL

Thank you so much for picking up my book!

Would you like to receive a free story from me as well? Join the Angel Legion and sign up for my newsletter!

ACKNOWLEDGMENTS

I have a lot of people to thank for helping me with this book.

Marie #1 for all her help with editing, catching small errors, and the continuity issues that I occasionally struggle with (I swear, she remembers all the things that I can't).

Marie #2 for catching my lack of commas, commas in the wrong places, and my excessive use of the word "that".

Karen for jumping in and finding all sorts of small errors, my mixed up words, and areas where I've written confusing sentences which need to be cleared up.

Katherine, for her ever-lasting support, encouragement and suggestions, which keeps me motivated throughout the entire writing process.

Michelle for her comments, questions, and suppositions, which always end up changing the way the plot and character development flows.

And Sir Nick for providing the much-needed male perspective, requests for clarification when my writing is confusing, and making me aware of continuity issues.

As always, a big thank you to all my fans, for buying and reading my work... if you love it, please leave a review!

PROLOGUE

14 YEARS AGO

Eleanor hugged herself as she got onto the noisy school bus, her head slightly tucked under, shoulders rounded. The bus ride home was always the worst part of her day this year. The ride to school wasn't nearly as bad because she was at the first bus stop, which meant she had first choice of seats. Unfortunately, for the ride home, she was always one of the last people on the bus because her seventh period class was so far away from the front doors of her high school.

No one wanted to sit at the back of the bus with the three jerks: Kevin, Ryan, and Lawrence. They were all sophomores on the football team and thought they were too good to be riding the bus. When they weren't tormenting their fellow passengers, they spent their time talking about what kind of cars they'd be driving next year and what position they'd have on the football team. All of them bragged to each other about how they'd be starting, even though starting positions usually went to seniors, not juniors. Reality didn't seem to matter to them.

Her steps faltered a little bit as she saw a new head sitting back there, in the very last seat, which Ryan usually claimed. Well, not new exactly, just unusual.

Mike. His head was tipped back against the seat, his eyes closed, and he looked like he was asleep.

A senior, he rarely rode the bus, but it happened every so often. Unfortunately, it meant there was no buffer seat between the terrible trio and the rest of the bus. Everyone else's gaze skittered away from hers as she walked down the aisle, her heart rising in her throat. She kept her eyes on the seat in front of Kevin, who always sat in front of Lawrence. With a choice of Kevin or Ryan, Kevin was definitely nicer. He was a little bit more of a follower, which meant he wouldn't immediately feel the need to start anything with the person sitting in front of him just for kicks. And, hopefully, being across the aisle and one seat up from Ryan would be enough of a buffer.

Even though he'd never done anything to her, she really kind of hated Mike in that moment. Couldn't he have sat in front of Ryan's usual seat? Did he have to sit in the very back?

Taller than anyone else on the bus, Mike had long, lean swimmer's muscles which looked good on him. He didn't play football like the other back-seat jerks; he was on the swim team when he wasn't the lead in the school show. Ryan had tried to make fun of him for the theater thing once and only once. Mike had stared at him, brown eyes completely focused, strands of long, brown hair brushing against his high cheekbones, until Ryan had cringed and turned away.

It wasn't like Mike was intimidating at first glance, but he was just so focused, so intense, and had the kind of self-confidence Ryan and the others only pretended to. Eleanor wished she could even pretend.

Sliding into her seat, Eleanor let out a quiet sigh of relief. Ryan had barely glanced at her, and Lawrence and Kevin had ignored her completely. She pulled out the book she was reading for English class - Ender's Game - and went to her bookmark. Maybe she could just read the whole way home and they'd ignore her.

That hope lasted until about two minutes after the bus started moving when Ryan snatched the book out of her hands.

2

"Hey, bookworm, whatcha reading?" he asked, not bothering to even look at the title as he held the book away from her.

Eleanor half stood, one knee on the bus seat. "A book for class. Give it back, please."

"Aw, she said please. That's cute," Ryan said, making a face at Kevin and Lawrence, who both laughed like the jerks they were. He tossed the book back to Lawrence, and Eleanor lurched forward trying to catch it, but didn't even manage to graze it with her fingertips. "Oops, too slow, Sandler."

She didn't know why Ryan called her by her last name, but somehow it always felt like an insult or a way of making her less than she was, and she hated it.

"May I have my book back please, Lawrence?" she asked, trying to keep her tone even though she couldn't stop the blush of anger rising in her cheeks. Getting mad just made them happy. Sometimes, if the person they were tormenting stayed calm, they'd get bored and leave their victim alone; so she always tried to stay calm, and most of the time it worked.

Unfortunately, it didn't appear that today was her day.

Lawrence looked at Ryan for a cue of what to do, but Ryan was still looking at Eleanor.

"Hey, Sandler, you're not bad for a freshman. How about you give me a kiss and we'll give you your book back?"

Ice slid down Eleanor's spine, spiking through her body and into her hands. Geezus... no.

It wasn't that Ryan was bad looking. He wasn't. None of the trio were. Blond haired, blue eyed, square jawed, and tall for his age; Ryan looked like he should be quarterback of the football team - and he might be in a couple years. Kevin was taller than him, with rich mocha skin, his curly hair shaved close to his head, and melting, chocolate brown eyes. The shortest of the three, Lawrence was also the most muscular; he had wavy black hair that was constantly falling in his hazel eyes and lashes which made every girl who met him sigh with envy. Put together, they were gorgeous. Unfortunately, their insides didn't even come close to matching their outsides, and Eleanor had absolutely no intention of kissing Ryan.

"No," she said in a low voice, keeping her gaze averted from all of them because if they saw how mad they were making her, they'd never stop. At least, she told herself it was just anger they'd see in her eyes. She glared at the textured green back of Kevin's bus seat, halfway between looking at him and Lawrence. "Please just give it back."

"What's the matter, bookworm? Too good for me?" Ryan moved closer, crowding her, and Eleanor fought her instinct to move away, because she could only move in one direction - further into her seat.

The other teens on the bus were noisy, talking to each other, ignoring or unaware of the drama taking place in the back. The bus driver was either too far away to care or just didn't care period. Everyone was used to the terrible trio harassing whoever was unlucky enough to sit closest to them. Everyone was used to the back of the bus being loud. If Ryan pushed her into the seat and made her kiss him - or worse - she didn't know if any of them would help, even if she started screaming.

Maybe if she started screaming someone would intervene, but then what? The terrible trio all lived in her neighborhood. They knew where she lived. Even if Ryan got kicked off the bus, it wouldn't make anything better. It would probably only make things worse, especially since then both Kevin and Lawrence would be pissed at her, and she would still have her last class in the farthest room from the bus pick-up.

All she wanted was her book back... but it wasn't worth whatever Ryan was leading up to.

"Forget it, keep the book," she said loudly, too loud in her attempt at sounding strong. She turned back towards the front, but Ryan grabbed her arm as she turned, setting her off balance. His fingers dug in, hurting her, and making her voice shrill with the fear she couldn't hide. "Let me go!"

"Let her go."

The deep, low tone was almost like a growl, and Eleanor whipped her head around to see Mike unfolding himself from the back seat, a pissed-off expression on his face. He grabbed the book Lawrence was still holding high in front of him. The bus lurched along the road, and Ryan's grip released as he stumbled back into his seat.

No one else on the bus seemed to notice or care as Eleanor sank into her seat, feeling completely breathless, her heart pounding so hard in her chest she could actually hear its rapid beating. It felt like she'd just run a mile at top speed.

A shadow loomed over her, and she looked up to see Mike standing over her, scowling.

"Scoot over," he said, jerking his chin at her. The bus seats on the left side where she was sitting could usually squeeze in two people, but Mike always seemed larger than the other teenagers on the bus and she wasn't sure they would both fit. Eleanor scooted anyway.

Then she was breathless for an entirely different reason as folded his body into the seat beside her, trapping her against the window and he handed her book to her. He had such a presence it almost seemed strange he could fit on the seat beside her. She took the book from him with nerveless fingers, hyper aware of the silence in the seats behind her, a strange counterpoint to the noisy chatter across the rest of the bus.

Mike leaned towards her, his voice low enough she doubted anyone else could hear it. "I'm going to hold your hand, okay?"

She couldn't find her voice, so she just nodded her head, still clutching her book, staring at the back of the seat in front of her. She wanted to just curl into a ball and shut out the rest of the world, but when Mike's fingers slipped through hers, his much larger hand cradling hers, suddenly she could breathe again. That simple touch made her feel less alone, less frightened.

"If they think you're mine, they'll leave you alone," he murmured into her ear.

Eyes wide, she couldn't stop herself from looking at him in shock. His? He didn't care if they thought he was interested in a freshman? She'd thought he was just trying to make her feel better not... not make *them* think something. But Mike just smiled at her, his brown eyes warm and encouraging.

"Thank you," she mouthed, too stunned to find her voice.

He leaned into her. "So, what're you reading?"

They ended up talking the entire way to the bus stop where he got off with her and immediately recaptured her hand. Behind her, she could hear Ryan, laughing and joking with Kevin and Lawrence, as they followed along. For the first time, hearing them heading home on the same route as her didn't make her feel tense or anxious. She felt completely safe.

Which kind of sucked.

"What's with the scowl?" Mike asked, looking down at her with a frown. "Should we stop holding hands now?"

She suddenly realized he thought there was someone in the neighborhood she didn't want witnessing their hand holding.

"No... it's just..." Her voice trailed off, because after he'd saved her, she didn't want to offend him.

"Just what?"

Eleanor couldn't help but glance back over her shoulder. The terrible trio didn't even notice, they were too busy doing their own thing, or at least pretending to. They hadn't even glanced at her when Mike had stepped out of the bus seat and gestured for her to go in front of him, keeping his body between her and them.

"It makes me so mad they couldn't just leave me alone," she said finally. "Thank you for stepping in, but it just..."

"It sucks that I had to," he finished for her when she struggled for a way to finish her sentence. Since he didn't sound offended, Eleanor nodded. "That's their problem, you get me? It does suck I had to step in, but that's because they're shitty and no other reason. If they weren't little jerks, they would have taken your no as a no, and they should have."

"So why didn't you just tell them that?" She couldn't stop herself from asking the question.

Mike raised his eyebrows at her. "Do you think that would have made much of a difference?"

She made a face, seeing his point. "Maybe for like, a day."

"Yeah. They're assholes. Eventually, hopefully, life will set them straight."

"Karma's a bitch."

"Exactly."

When he smiled down at her, his hand warm around hers, she had to remind herself he was just doing this to be nice. To protect her from the assholes. After all, she was just a freshman, and he was a senior.

But it still felt nice to hold his hand.

It didn't surprise Ellie that holding Michael's hand brought up a whole host of memories. Although they'd both changed a lot since high school, somehow holding his hand still felt the same. Like he was cradling her fingers against his, there for support and strength, there to protect her.

The whole rest of her freshman year, he'd ridden the bus, and every day she'd sat next to him. They'd become friends. He didn't have a girlfriend that entire year - and even though she'd had a huge crush on him, she'd still hoped it wasn't her fault. She would have felt pretty guilty if he'd missed out on having a girlfriend just to protect the little freshman girl on his bus; but she'd always been too scared to ask. Scared, embarrassed, whatever. He hadn't gone to prom, although she'd dreamed about him asking her, despite knowing it was a silly dream. When she'd asked if he was going, he'd just shaken his head, but his shoulders had stiffened in a way that made her think he was uncomfortable about the question, so she'd immediately changed the subject.

Then he'd gone off to college, and in the days before social media, they'd lost touch. Her cell phone plan in high school hadn't included texting or calls for a long-distance friendship. Besides, as a college student, would he really have wanted to keep in touch with a sopho-more in high school?

Although, if he had, maybe she wouldn't have made such stupid choices.

As if he could sense the sudden tension gripping her, Michael's thumb swept over her skin in a comforting manner. Out of the corner of her eye, she could see he was studiously watching the choral concert, but somehow he'd known.

Pushing thoughts of the past away, Ellie focused on the present. It was a pretty good present after all.

After college she'd become involved in the BDSM scene when she'd finally gathered the courage to step offline and try some real, in-person experiences. She'd ended up at Stronghold for one of their open houses and had ended up signing up for an Introduction Scene. One week later, she'd actually orgasmed with another person, for the first time, and they hadn't even been having sex. And she hadn't been even a little attracted to the Domme topping her, Ellie could appre-ciate an attractive woman but she was only attracted to men. Mistress Lisa *was* a sadist though, and it turned out Ellie was a masochist.

She'd played with just the Dommes at first, without much of a sexual component to her scenes since she was straight. After talking with them, the other subs, and finally feeling completely safe in the club (especially down in the Dungeon where there was always a monitor on-site and everyone could see everything), she'd tried her first scene with a Dom.

The only problem with scening with Doms was they knew she was straight, and so some of them became hopeful something more would come out of scening together. Unfortunately for them, she wasn't interested. And she didn't do scenes in private rooms until she met Andrew, and they had only clicked because neither of them wanted a relationship. He'd been safe, emotionally. Fun, outside of the scene.

Ellie had even started to make real friends at the club. She was friendly with plenty of the subs, but she hadn't been hanging out with them outside of work initially. First was Lexie, the sweet, extroverted receptionist, who seemed to take Ellie's standoffish demeanor as a personal challenge. Then Ellie had taken the self-defense class with Angel, a pretty brunette who now engaged to Adam – Adam also being a friend of Andrew's. Angel, unlike Ellie, drew people to her and, if she liked them, didn't let them go. Or, as Angel put it, decided to 'keep' them.

Not long after Angel showed up, so did Michael - all grown up and gorgeous, and the only person who called him Mike now was Angel. The first time Ellie had seen him, her past had come rushing back in an instant and she'd panicked. Immediately avoided him, even when he'd try to seek her out. The shame that had welled up inside her hadn't been anything new, but it had been something she'd thought she'd gotten past.

She wasn't the same girl he'd known back in high school. She didn't have the same positive outlook on the world, she didn't have the same courage, the same confidence. He'd spent so much time her freshman year, helping her build up all of that, and after he'd left, she'd held onto it for a while... until she'd fucked everything up. Now she was broken. She didn't trust. She didn't do vulnerability and openness. And she hadn't wanted him to see the new her. The fact that she was very much attracted to him didn't help her state of mind either. Ellie didn't *do* very attracted. Ellie did do scenes, but with strict boundaries, witnesses, and plenty of emotional space.

But when she'd tried to start pulling away from Angel, Lexie, and Andrew, somehow she'd found herself being pulled back. At one point, Angel, who was very close friends with Michael, had even told her, "I don't care what weirdness there is between you and Mike, I like you, so I'm keeping you."

It had warmed Ellie from the inside out. She still tried to keep herself a little separate from the group of friends, but... she liked having friends. So she'd tried to keep herself separate from Michael. And that had worked.

Until she'd gotten all pent-up and unable to hold herself together. Work had been crazy, being around Michael at the club had been driving her crazy, and she asked Andrew for a scene - which also stressed her out because he'd finally gotten back together with his ex-girlfriend. Not that she was asking for a sexual scene, they hadn't had one of those in months anyway, but she'd needed the pain... needed the release.

Andrew had agreed, as long as Kate could be there to watch, but he'd also included a fourth party to the scene. Even though Ellie had been blindfolded and the guest Dom never spoke and left before her eyes were uncovered, she'd known exactly who it was. But the blindfold had let her pretend, and it had been one of the most intense and satisfying scenes she'd ever done.

She'd tried to lie to herself that the high of the scene was because having two Doms working her over was an incredible experience, but deep down she knew that wasn't all of it.

Then, she'd been invited to come to Kate's choral concert. She couldn't say no. Not after Kate had been generous enough to let Andrew scene with Ellie. Besides, she liked Kate. She liked Andrew's group of friends. She liked being included. They were the first friends she'd made that she spent time with outside of the club as well as in it.

Ellie had seated herself in the front row with everyone else, in between Leigh and Sharon and had been enjoying herself, talking about Angel and Adam's engagement and whether or not they were going to end up being married before or after their baby was born. So far Adam was pushing for before, Angel was pushing for after. Ellie kind of thought Angel might just be pushing for after to get on Adam's nerves though. She was kind of a brat regularly, always looking for a spanking, and Adam's gentle handling of her since she'd become pregnant was grating on her nerves. She'd been turning down his proposals for a while too, until he'd finally snapped and taken her in hand. Now that he was back to treating her like glass, she was becoming contrary again.

Then, Jake had sat next to Sharon and she'd taken off, and Michael had taken her place. Sharon and Jake didn't get along. They were also both definitely attracted to each other, and didn't want to be - which was probably a big part of why they didn't get along. Not that either of them admitted to it, but Ellie liked watching people and figuring out what made them tick. She was pretty self-aware about her own hang-ups too, even though knowing what was wrong didn't lead to being able to fix it.

Which was why, when Michael offered to change seats, seeing how uncomfortable she was, when he said he'd stop approaching her at the club, and stop asking her to scene with him if that's what she really wanted... Ellie hadn't been able to answer right away. He'd sounded so sad. The lights dimmed before she could respond, and then Kate led the students out on stage, and Ellie did the only thing she could think of to do - she reached over to take his hand while listening to a choral version of *Bohemian Rhapsody*.

Okay, maybe there were other things she could have done, but she'd wanted to take Michael's hand. Even if she didn't really know what she wanted from Michael, she knew what she didn't. Maybe it was selfish, but she didn't want him to stop trying to reach out to her. She didn't want him to completely give up on her. She thought she'd given up on herself a long time ago, but hearing Michael say he would stay away if she wanted him to... every cell in her body rejected the idea.

The small smile on his lips indicated he was content with her non-verbal response. Which was a relief.

The music swelled as Ellie's thoughts skittered around her head. BDSM was supposed to be about communication, but, other than explaining her hard and soft limits, Ellie really hated talking. Doms that tried to get inside her head didn't get more than one scene with her. Inside her head sucked; she knew it, and she didn't feel like sharing her messed up thoughts with anyone else. She also didn't like having her boundaries pushed, and she'd known Michael wouldn't let her get away with that. Even in high school he'd been insightful.

There was so much of herself she didn't want him to see.

Maybe she shouldn't have taken his hand.

But she didn't like the idea of him leaving her completely alone either.

Indecisive much?

Rather than wallowing in her own issues, Ellie forced herself to focus on the music. The singing really was beautiful, and that was what she was here for after all.

THE FEEL OF ELLIE'S HAND IN HIS WAS A FAMILIAR ONE, BUT AT THE same time it felt completely different than it had in high school. Not just because they were older, but because in high school she'd been so trusting, so open. Now she was guarded, and holding her hand felt like a much bigger deal - because it was.

So it also didn't surprise him when she tugged her hand away from his to stand up, clapping along with everyone else at the end of the concert, and didn't return it. Disappointed him, but didn't surprise him.

Or when she quickly turned and followed Leigh out towards the aisle, without even glancing at him.

What did surprise him was that when she made it to the aisle, she glanced back at him, teeth sinking into her lower lip nervously. Granted, she was blocked from actually leaving by everyone else in the rows behind them, but he was still a little surprised she looked back at him.

"What are you waiting for? Go get her!" Jake whispered from behind him, poking his finger into Michael's back.

Michael was going to remember that for later.

But it wasn't bad advice.

He strolled to the end of the aisle, enjoying the way Ellie's fidgeting increased as he got closer. Anxiety was written in every line of her body, focusing him, making him more hyper-aware of her every movement. Yes, he got off on knowing he was causing her discomfort. After all, he enjoyed mental sadism as much as physical; a good mind fuck could be just as satisfying as a good flogging.

Seeing him coming, Leigh, Jared, Angel, Adam, Maria, and Rick - who had exited the aisle ahead of Ellie - all grinned. Internally, Michael sighed. It had become very apparent to him that the small group of friends was more gossip prone than high school teenage girls, and not just the women or the submissives either. All of them were guilty of it. Even the ones who claimed they tried to stay out of it, like Jared and Andrew.

It was just part of having friends though, and Michael liked having a stable group of friends again.

The aisle was clearing up by the time Michael made it to Ellie, but the others kept her trapped there by not moving, waiting for Michael's approach. Having nosy friends wasn't so bad when they were trapping a reluctant submissive for him.

Michael shoved his hands into his pockets to keep from reaching out and touching her. Even though she'd held hands with him, indicating she didn't want him completely taken out of her life, he wasn't going to rush in. He'd tried that when he'd first recognized her, and it had set him back months.

Slow and steady wins the race.

Catching her dark eyes with his, he held her gaze, ignoring the others. He stood close enough to her to loom but without touching her, making her aware of his presence without completely overpowering her with it.

"Play with me, tomorrow at Stronghold." He didn't phrase it as a question, but they both knew it was a request. Fear and excitement flared in her eyes. Still biting her lower lip, she nodded. Michael smiled at her. "Good girl."

Then, for the first time, *he* retreated.

He turned his ass back around returned to join Olivia, Justin, Jessica, Chris, Liam, Hilary, Jake, Lexie, Patrick, Andrew, and Sharon on the other side of the aisle. Justin, Jessica, Chris, Liam, and Hilary were standing ahead of the rest of their group, gathered in a small cluster and laughing about something. Spaced behind them, Lexie and Sharon had their heads together, allowing Sharon to pretend Jake didn't exist, while Andrew, Olivia, and Jake were involved in a conversation and Patrick was kind of staring off into space as he stood with his arms around Lexie. He looked like a guy who had something heavily weighing on his mind, but Michael wasn't going to ask. While he was definitely becoming friendlier with everyone in the group, he was closer to Andrew, Angel, and Leigh than any of the others. And sort of Adam and Jared by default, although Jared was a pretty quiet guy and hard to get to know, and Adam... well, it was hard for the two of them not to butt heads now and then. They did their best for Angel's sake, but Michael had been looking out for her for a long time, and Adam felt that was his job now, so they rubbed along uncomfortably, but Michael wouldn't call them close or anything.

As he approached, Sharon looked up at him and gave him a wink. "Good job. She's totally staring at you now."

Lifting her head, Lexie grinned at him too. "Please tell me you guys are finally going to hook up. Watching you two is torture."

"We're going to scene together," he said, keeping his voice casual at first, and then turning it stern for the warning. "Tomorrow. But you are not going to say anything to her about it. I don't want anyone pushing her."

Sharon rolled her eyes. Little brat. If she were more of a masochist, he would have been interested in playing with her when he first came back. She and Ellie even resembled each other a little; both petite and curvy with dark hair. Sharon's was much longer though and her skin was more olive than Ellie's pale cream. "Dude, we are so much more subtle than that."

Behind her, Jake snorted and then looked away as her head snapped around to glare at him. A small smile played on Lexie's lips. Luckily for Jake, the line of people was finally clearing up and they started moving up the aisle towards the lobby, where Kate would come out to meet them. Sharon flounced ahead with Andrew, her nose in the air, completely oblivious to Jake checking out her ass from behind. Michael noticed, but he didn't say anything. She did have a cute, curvy ass after all.

"Want to go get a beer after this?" Jake asked, turning his head as he asked the question to include both Patrick and Michael.

Michael shrugged. "Sure."

His day job wasn't particularly demanding - Adam had hooked him up with an administrative assistant position through his temp agency - and he was between shows right now, so he had plenty of free time.

As they waited for Kate, he couldn't help but think he felt a bit at loose ends. He'd come back to DC because he wanted something more permanent. He'd gotten tired of always being on the road for theater, always traveling and living out of a suitcase. It had been an incredible ride, but over the years, the enjoyment had started to pale. Now that he was here, he was still feeling restless and unsatisfied. Maybe it was the theater life in general that was starting to pale.

It was a lot of hard fucking work and not a lot of pay. Anyone who got into theater wasn't doing it for the money.

Maybe he was just getting old. There were plenty of other actors who were older than him but... it just didn't appeal the way it used to. He just didn't know what else he wanted to do. Definitely not be an administrative assistant full time. He couldn't see himself *not* working either. But he wasn't happy with where he was. Especially since a few months ago a great-uncle had passed away and left Michael with an inheritance. He didn't have to work anymore, he just didn't know what else to do. The feeling of being unsettled had been growing stronger every day he'd gone to work at a job he didn't actually need. Being unsettled by Ellie hadn't helped either.

Hanging out with friends helped.

Ellie turned down the invitation to go out and practically fled the lobby after giving Kate a quick hug, but the flushed look she gave Michael before she ran made him feel incredibly impatient for tomorrow. She was on edge and needed some time to regroup, and he was okay with that, even if he wished she had come out. Angel and Adam also headed home, Angel yawning her way through the goodbyes, and Jared and Leigh weren't far behind them. Although Kate tried to talk Sharon into joining them, Sharon had gotten a text on her phone and was off to meet Brian, one of the newly trained Doms at Stronghold.

Standing next to Olivia, Michael was surprised to see her frowning as Sharon trotted off.

"Everything okay?" he asked the fiery-haired Domme. He liked Olivia, although he sometimes felt like she was still holding back her judgment on him.

"Yeah. I'm just having a hard time picturing Brian and Sharon together. He's... definitely not the Dom I would have chosen for her." Olivia had taught the new Doms class, so she was well acquainted with the Doms and their preferences.

The others teased her about being a mother hen, and Michael could see why. "Maybe they're stepping outside of their comfort zones."

"Mm," Olivia replied, noncommittally, making Michael laugh. She tilted her head towards him, laughter in her silvery eyes. "I'm just saying. They're not going to last."

"I'm sure you're right," he said agreeably. Truth be told, his only interest was because he wanted to see if things would ever shake down between Jake and Sharon.

Damn.

He was getting as nosy as all the other gossip-hounds in this group.

"So I hear you're scening with Ellie tomorrow." Chris' dark eyes gleamed with amusement as Michael let out a resigned huff of air. They'd gone to a bar not too far from Kate's school which wasn't too loud but was also kind of full. They'd ended up scattered around separate tables by necessity.

It was a big group of friends.

A big, nosy group of friends.

"I literally asked her to scene with me about half an hour ago, and I'm pretty sure everyone in this group already knows," Michael said dryly before taking a long sip of his beer.

"That's just how we roll," Patrick said. Before Justin had come up, Patrick, Jake, and Lexie had all been chatting with Michael, thankfully not about Ellie. He wasn't entirely pleased with the conversation turn.

"It's not my fault," Chris protested, although he was still grinning. "Jessica wanted to know."

"And yet you don't see Justin over here," Lexie pointed out, teasing.

Justin, Chris, and Jessica were in a poly relationship centered around Jessica since both Justin and Chris were straight and dominant. They also looked alike, having the same height, broad-shoulders, and dark hair and eyes, but in personality they were fairly different. Justin tended to be much more serious whereas Chris was more playful; outside of the bedroom, Justin tended to lead - and from what Michael had witnessed of their public scenes, he tended to lead in the bedroom as well, although Chris had no problem dominating Jessica on his own. Justin was just as big a gossip as the others in the group though, even if he wasn't nearly as blatant about it as Chris.

"Yeah well, I'm nosy," Chris said cheerfully.

At least he admitted it.

A smile on his face, Michael turned his head towards Jake, and was immediately distracted by the way Jake was looking at Patrick. Turning his head to face the other man, he was a bit surprised to see Patrick staring off into space again with his forehead wrinkled so much it was pulling at the scar next to his eye. Group gossip said Jake had accidentally given him that scar when they were teenagers.

"What's up man?" Jake asked, reaching across to slap the table in front of Patrick and making the big man jump. As Patrick scowled across the table at his best friend, Lexie placed her hand on Patrick's chest and looked up at him in concern.

"Are you thinking about the club again?" she asked, her tone worried, which of course made everyone else standing at the table worried. Chris straightened, the grin gone from his face, and Michael felt a trickle of alarm go up his spine.

Patrick owned Stronghold, which was open five days a week, and operated mostly as a kink-club. On Tuesdays, it was open for swingers; on Wednesdays, they'd added classes (women's self-defense, along with BDSM 101 for new subs and Doms); and Thursday through Saturday nights, it was a full on BDSM club. It was where they all spent most of their time when they went out. Michael hadn't thought it would be in trouble; it was always packed, especially on Friday and Saturday nights, and there was always a wait to use the equipment and the private rooms.

"What's wrong with the club?" Chris asked, sounding as alarmed as Michael felt.

"It's too successful." The tone Patrick used was the complete opposite of his words. Usually people didn't talk about being successful like it was some kind of horrible outcome.

"What do you mean?" Michael asked, while Jake and Chris stared blankly at Patrick.

"We've had to start turning away newbie applications," Lexie explained. "We're running at full capacity, but we can't expand without either getting rid of the gardens or buying land on either side, but those warehouses aren't interested in selling."

Patrick's arm tightened around Lexie, his dark fingers stroking her pale cheek, although the gesture looked more like it was to comfort him than her. "I've also been getting some pressure to make the club more select. We have some members who want more privacy and security because of their positions in the real world. I've thought about opening a second location, but I'm not sure I want the hassle. Honestly, I never thought the club would be this successful. I don't really like the idea of opening another club all on my own."

"You have me," Lexie pointed out, scrunching up her nose at him. They all knew she was just doing it to make him smile, and it worked. While Lexie did help immensely with running the club, they all knew there was no way Patrick would be okay with letting her run a club in a separate location from him. Out of the whole group, their relationship was the closest to being a 24/7 Master/slave dynamic. It worked for them, but it also made Patrick extremely overprotective and intent on having her nearby.

"Yes I do, Pixie," Patrick said, a wide grin splitting his face as he looked down at her, the stress dropping away for just a moment.

Huh. The possibilities spun around Michael's head. A second Stronghold location? A more private location. Probably something ritzy since the people looking for more privacy and security would also have more money. Something more dramatic than the comfortably elegant main floor of Stronghold. Not just dramatic in looks either; Michael felt the stage at Stronghold was severely underused.

"What if you had a partner?" Michael asked, the question popping out of his mouth before he had a chance to really think it through. He wasn't often an impulsive person, but... it had just come out.

Patrick blinked in surprise. "A partner? To run the place?"

"Not just run it, but invest too," Michael said, a thread of excitement started to curl through him. It was a spontaneous, almost silly, idea, that came out of nowhere and yet... he could picture it. Want it. Now all four of the others were staring at him in surprise. "I inherited some money a little while ago and, other than paying off my mom's house, I haven't done anything with it. I could live off of it, but..." He shrugged. He'd actually wanted to buy his mom a new house but she'd liked her neighborhood and her house, and insisted she didn't want to bother with the care of a larger place. Which Michael could understand since he was still living in the same small one bedroom apartment he'd rented when he'd first returned to DC.

"I'm sorry," Lexie said, her eyes filled with sympathy. "I didn't realize you'd lost anyone."

Feeling a bit uncomfortable, because he knew he was about to sound callous, Michael ran his hand through his hair and smiled a little sheepishly. "My great-uncle... I actually hadn't seen him in years. He was kind of estranged from the family, but... I guess he didn't have anyone else to leave it all to. It's... well, let's just say I have more than enough to invest in a business if that's what I want to do."

Leaning forward on the high table, one arm still looped around Lexie, Patrick's gaze was entirely focused on Michael. "What would you want to do with it?"

"Well, I'm the first to admit I've never actually run a club, but I've worked a lot in restaurants, and I definitely know how to manage people," Michael said. "It would need to be similar but different from Stronghold. Put it in a more central location in the city but with a discreet entrance. If people want more privacy and security, they're going to have to pay more for it, so might as well go ahead and make it upscale in every way - food, drinks, decor." He could feel his enthusiasm growing as he started to really warm up to the idea. "Make it kind of like a classy speakeasy - you can't get in unless you're in the know."

"I like it," Lexie said, before Patrick could reply, her bright blue eyes shining. "Not that I don't love Stronghold, what you're describing sounds like a snobby version, but in a good way."

"Why food?" Patrick asked. "That's a lot more work."

"Yeah, but it also makes it more than a kink club, and if the new target clientele is people with money to spend, they'll like the extras. It could be like a speakeasy, restaurant on one level, then the rest of the club on the others. Or behind a door. The restaurant takes the place of the lobby, and that way people can hang out before or after. Food could still be served at the bar in the club area, but it wouldn't be the focus there. Hell, make it into a hotel... have some rooms where people can spend the weekend if they reserve the rooms, fully immerse themselves into the BDSM experience."

Interest was alight in Patrick's eyes, tempered just a bit by caution. "That doesn't sound anything like what I was originally thinking, but I *really* like it. Keep talking."

"Okay, well while you guys do that, I'm going to go talk a walk over to the bar," Jake said, picking up his near-empty beer glass. "There's a seriously hot blonde over there who could definitely use my company." Lexie made a faux-gagging noise as her brother walked away, but the others just chuckled before turning back into the conversation, just as interested as Patrick and Michael at brainstorming ideas.

It didn't take long before the entire group was squeezed in around their table, suggesting ideas for what a new Stronghold club might look like while Lexie scribbled frantically on the back of a paper coaster.

⚜ 2 ⚜

"How can I have so many clothes and nothing to wear?" Ellie muttered under her breath. She shot a glare at Watson who was sitting on her bed. "And, of course, *someone* had to shred the exact corset I was planning on wearing."

Completely unperturbed by her annoyed tone, Watson lifted his leg in the air and proceeded to lick his nonexistent balls. She made a face at him.

"So helpful."

Furry little bastard. At just one year old, he still had a lot of playful kitten left in him and, unfortunately, one of his favorite things to do was play with corset strings, which often led to shredding the actual corset. Normally, she left the closet door closed, but if she accidentally left it open even a crack, her nosy cat was in there in a flash. That's probably what she should have named him, but she'd gotten him right after she'd started watching Sherlock and he'd had a limp just like Watson in the first episode... His leg was all healed up now, just like Watson's.

"Well at least you didn't get fur on everything," she muttered under her breath. He was short haired, but his orange and cream fur tended to stand out, especially on her club wear, which had a lot of black in it.

The doorbell rang and Ellie let out a sigh of relief. Thank goodness. When she'd realized Watson had shredded her corset, she'd done something she'd never done before... she'd reached out for help. Ellie usually wore whatever she wanted to the club; she'd definitely never dressed for a particular Dom before. She didn't know why she'd gotten so hung up on the idea of wearing her purple corset tonight, but now that it wasn't possible, she'd turned into a total twit, unable to make a single decision for herself. So she'd texted Lexie, begging for help getting dressed.

Hurrying to her front door, Ellie tried not to feel like a failure just because she couldn't do something as simple as picking out an outfit. This was what friends were supposed to do in the event of a wardrobe crisis. She'd seen it in movies and read about it in books. Just because she'd never had a friend to do this with didn't mean anything... she'd also never had a wardrobe crisis before. Lexie had been the first person to spring to mind, and, thankfully, she'd also seemed thrilled Ellie had reached out to her.

None of this felt like Ellie. Being so nervous she became indecisive... reaching out to a friend for help because she couldn't make up her mind... yeah, she wasn't used to any of this. It felt like she was in high school all over again. She hadn't felt like this since she was a teenager... because nothing had mattered enough to fluster her like this since she was a teenager.

"Helloooo...." She said as she opened the door, but her voice trailed off as her eyes widened with shock.

"Hello!" chorused the group of women outside of her apartment. Lexie surged forward to wrap her in a hug, which Ellie returned even though she felt like she was having an out-of-body experience.

Giggling, Angel pushed her way into the apartment, a plastic bag swinging from her arm. She was followed by Leigh, Sharon, and Maria.

"I brought reinforcements," Lexie said impishly as she let Ellie go.

"I see that," Ellie said uncertainly.

It wasn't that she was upset with all the company, she was just kind of surprised by it. All of them looked excited as they looked at her with anticipation, which started to make her feel all warm and gooey inside. Yeah, she definitely wasn't upset.

"Sorry to just invite ourselves over," Leigh said, almost managing to sound apologetic. "But when you texted Lexie, she texted Angel about getting a corset from her, and we were all hanging out together...."

"And we figured we might as well come along for the ride," Sharon said, her dark eyes sparkling.

Maria snorted and shook her head, her trademark messy bun wobbling but ultimately staying in place. "By which she means a stampede of horses couldn't have kept her away."

"Oh yeah, cuz you were so reluctant," Sharon shot back, grinning.

"Well... thank you all for coming," Ellie said, nervously rubbing her hands on the yoga pants she was wearing and hoping she didn't sound as awkward as she felt. It was really nice of them to show up, but Ellie just... wasn't used to this.

"We come bearing gifts and many opinions," Angel said, holding up the bag she'd been carrying. "I brought a couple of corsets I think will look fabulous on you."

Like Ellie, Angel worked from home for the most part, but her work was very different from Ellie's. Angel had her own Etsy shop where she sold a lot of handmade pieces, although currently her business was really booming from the number of custom pieces subs and Dommes at Stronghold were commissioning from her. Ellie had actually designed the business cards Angel handed out there.

She was doing just fine with her graphic design freelancing, but she didn't really have enough extra budget for the kind of corsets Angel made. Ellie got most of hers through clearance sales on big websites - three corsets for $100, that kind of thing. As far as she knew, Angel didn't sell a single corset for under $100.

"Ummm..." Ellie tried to find the right words to say 'that's really sweet but there's no way'.

Correctly interpreting the look on her face, Angel shook her head. "Oh no, no payment necessary. You're finally scening with Mike, and that's payment enough for me."

Ellie knew Michael and Angel were good friends, but she didn't really understand why Angel would consider that payment. Fortunately, Maria asked the question for her.

"How do you benefit from Michael scening with Ellie?" Maria asked, sounding amused. Even though they were all around the same age, Maria often seemed like the big sister of the group to Ellie.

"And why does that make me feel kind of like a prostitute?" Ellie muttered. Only Lexie seemed to hear her thankfully, and she snorted into her hand so as not to draw attention to Ellie's comment.

"Because if Mike hooks up with Ellie, then Adam will stop being so overly possessive about Mike and me hanging out, because it's obvious Mike's really into Ellie," Angel said gleefully.

Ellie opened her mouth and closed it again without saying a word, because she couldn't really think of what to say. She wanted to protest that Michael didn't like her *that* much, but he obviously did like her enough to pursue her, and Angel would probably know better than Ellie exactly how much he liked her since they were good friends.

"It would also probably help if you stopped calling him 'Pretty Boy' and playing with his hair," Leigh teased.

"Well, he is pretty and so is his hair. If Adam grew his hair out I would want to play with it more."

"Then he'd really look like a Viking," Sharon mused, her eyes going a little unfocused.

Angel elbowed Sharon in the side. "Hey, no fantasizing about my man while I'm present. You keep that shit to yourself."

"Okay ladies, focus," Maria said, cutting into the banter. She smiled at Ellie. "Let's take this to the bedroom."

"Hopefully that won't be the last time Ellie hears that today," Lexie joked as she grabbed Ellie's hand and led the way down the hall.

This was not at all what Ellie had expected when she'd texted Lexie earlier... it was so much better. If this was what happened when she let people in a little, maybe dropping her guard wasn't so bad.

FUCK ME SIDEWAYS.

Ellie looked like submissive sex on a stick. The violet and black corset she was wearing set off her creamy skin, black hair, and dark eyes, and pushed her breasts up like an offering platter. Black lace trimmed the top of the corset, matching the lacy, black mini-skirt she wore with it. Her legs were bare, pale against the dark skirt, and she was wearing strappy high heels which gave her several extra inches of height and added a seductive sway to her walk as she moved into the main room of Stronghold. Her hair was pulled back from her face but was otherwise down, curling around her shoulders, and her dark eyes looked huge in her pale face.

Trailing behind her, like a brood of ducklings, were Angel, Leigh, Sharon, Maria, and Lexie, all of them with excited expressions of expectation on their faces. Nosy little subs. They'd all dressed up for the club, but none of them were nearly as all-out dolled-up as Ellie. They waved at him and trotted over to the bar, with wide conspiratorial grins on their faces.

When another Dom, Leo, stepped in Ellie's path to talk to her, Michael was moving before he could even think about it. Leo was another sadist, with a liking for wax play, and someone Michael knew Ellie had played with in the past, although not recently. Michael had planned to make Ellie come to him but...

Oh well. It wasn't often Michael allowed his impulses to affect him so greatly, but he wasn't about to miss out on his chance to play one-on-one with Ellie now that he'd finally gotten her to agree.

"I'm sorry, Master Leo, but I've already made plans to scene with Master Michael tonight," Ellie said, with a smile on her face to soften the blow, just as Michael came up behind Leo. Gratification and relief slid through him; she wasn't trying to run or use Leo's advances as a shield. Her eyes flicked past Leo and she smiled, causing the other Dom to turn to see what she was looking at. With Michael only a few feet away from him, he nodded in greeting.

"Maybe some other time then," Leo said to Ellie with a half-smile, stepping back and away, before pivoting to head towards the Lounge area where other unattached submissives gathered.

Michael's acting skills came in handy, since he wanted to scowl at the other man's comment. Of course the other man would assume Ellie would still be available to play on another night - she rarely scened with the same Dom twice in a row and she never made any kind of commitment, even in the club. He hoped to change that, but he wasn't stupid enough to say so now, even if the idea of her going from playing with him to playing with Leo sent a hot, possessive feeling surging through his chest.

If he showed any of that, he was afraid Ellie would run again.

She was skittish, like a wild animal... while they hadn't spent much time together, he'd spent enough time watching her to know that the sweet, generous, giving girl he'd protected had grown up into a sweet, generous, giving woman. She just now also had walls as big as the Great Wall of China, and he wanted to strip back those defenses and claim her. It was a primitive emotion and strange to him because he'd never felt like this before, and it didn't make any logical sense since they hadn't actually spent time together in over a decade... but there it was. The protective feelings she roused in him now weren't nearly as innocent as they had been in high school. He'd known she'd had a crush on him then even though he'd never considered her anything more than a cute, sweet kid — and now he wanted to do terrible, perverse things to her until she was screaming his name and begging for more.

But he had to hold back, play by her rules for now... show her he could be trusted and wait for her to come to him. The slow route was frustrating as hell... but it also worked, as evidenced by her finally agreeing to do a scene with him. Chase her, but not too fast and not too hard... and then let *her* catch *him*.

Which meant he had to smile and act like it didn't bother him at all that other Doms were thinking about playing with her in the future.

Fortunately, for his peace of mind, Ellie didn't agree to a future play date, even though she smiled at Leo before he turned away, her gaze went back to Michael and her focus remained there. Big, dark eyes full of a mix of anxiety and eagerness - exactly the combination a Dom like him liked to see. Needed to see.

All for him.

"Hello there, beautiful," he murmured, holding out his hand. The sensation of triumph surged through him when she barely hesitated before taking it.

"Hello, Master Michael," she said almost shyly.

As much as he liked hearing his title and name on her lips, it also felt a little wrong, like she was using it to distance herself from him. He kept himself from frowning, but he shook his head.

"Just Michael," he said firmly. Slight consternation flickered across her expression, confirming his suspicion. She called all the Doms by their titles. This would differentiate him; she wanted to say no, but obviously protesting such a little thing would seem silly, so she didn't.

A second victory for him, following behind just getting her here to scene with him.

He could see their friends out of the corner of his eye, hanging out by the bar like they usually did, all of them pretending they weren't watching him and Ellie. No doubt their respective significant others would be arriving soon, which would either distract them or double the number of people pretending they weren't watching.

"I have the School Room reserved, unless you'd prefer to play in the Dungeon," he said, keeping his tone casual.

Other than with Andrew, he'd never seen Ellie play in the private rooms. He wanted her all to himself, but for this first scene, he'd let her choose her comfort level.

Ellie blinked.

Opened her mouth.

Hesitated.

Hope rose in his chest.

"The School Room?" she asked, sounding wary but curious.

Michael grinned mischievously at her, reaching out with his free hand to tug a tendril of hair resting on her shoulder. "I thought it might be fun, considering how we know each other."

So what if he hadn't had fantasies about her in high school? Now that they were older and it wasn't perverted for him to be attracted to her, he'd had a few classroom fantasies. And he'd hoped the school room would tempt her, considering he'd been aware she definitely had harbored a crush on him in high school.

It looked like it was working too. Ellie might not normally utilize the private rooms, but the idea of being in a classroom with *him* had her considering it.

She stared up at him, her eyes slightly unfocused; he could practically see her thinking. Hesitating. He waited patiently, ignoring the hum and conversations happening around them, the people walking past, the distractions, and just looked down at her. Letting her take her time.

"Okay," she said finally, despite the apprehension clear on her face. "We can do the school room."

"Thank you for trusting me," he said, smiling down at her. Keeping his hold on her hand, he turned and began to lead her towards the stairs.

Victory tasted sweet.

***

Thank you for trusting me.

Michael's voice echoed in her head, nearly making her stumble as she followed him blindly, hand tucked trustingly into his.

How had he struck so close to the heart of the matter so quickly?

She trusted him. Despite her actions, despite how she'd run from him, she trusted him. Hell, part of the reason he scared her so badly was because she trusted him far beyond any of the other dominants she had scened with. That and his connection to her past and all the things she didn't want to think about and definitely didn't want him to know.

But she went along with him anyway, hand in his, heart pounding, body thrumming with anticipation. As they passed by the bar, Angel and Lexie both gave her a thumbs up, and Ellie smiled, even though she was definitely feeling a little apprehensive.

When was the last time she'd been in a private room with a dominant who wasn't Andrew or a sadistic Domme? Whenever it was, she knew the door had always been left open when during all of those scenes, at her request. She already knew she trusted Michael enough to let him close the door, which made her feel panicked for a whole slew of other reasons.

When was the last time she'd actually wanted to have sex with the person dominating her? Sex was definitely not a required part of BDSM, and Ellie had found it was easier to keep the Doms at bay if she made sex one of her hard limits for the scene. It wasn't one of her club hard limits because sometimes she did want sex, but those times were more about how long it had been and definitely not about the particular dominant.

But she wanted to have sex with Michael.

Would he even want to have sex with her? Or did he only want to scene with her because she'd been running since the day he stepped into the club and he took it personally?

That's your anxiety talking, Ellie. If you're nervous, ask, but don't build up something in your head without any evidence.

The voice in her head always sounded like her therapist, Dr. Amy Evanko. She'd been going to Dr. Amy for years now, so that made sense.

Not that she was going to ask Michael, because deep down she already knew the answer. It was just... sometimes the thoughts in her head got away from her and came up with all sorts of ridiculous scenarios that had the ability to panic her. Like, actually panic - shortness of breath, rapid heart rate, and gut-churning nausea. Dr. Amy worked with her on talking herself down from the ledge whenever she got like that.

Stopping outside of the door to the School Room, Michael frowned down at her. "What's wrong?"

This is why she knew he wasn't just into her for the chase. That just wasn't the kind of guy Michael was. At least, he hadn't been in high school, and she hadn't seen any evidence that part of his personality had changed since then.

"Just nervous," she said.

The smile he gave her was gentle. "We don't have to do this unless you want you."

"No! I mean yes," Ellie said hastily, stumbling over her words, feeling like a little kid who was afraid her treat was about to be taken away. "I want to do this... I'm just... nervous." She sighed. She sounded like an idiot. A total newbie. Nothing at all like the confident persona she strove for. "Are we going to have sex?"

The smile on Michael's face shifted to something more predatory, making her nipples pucker beneath the corset Angel had insisted was now hers. He really was ridiculously hot. It kind of wasn't fair. All he had to do was smile and she creamed her panties. Add in his sweetness, his protectiveness, and his persistence in reaching out to her (without being creepy or stalkery about it), and how was she supposed to have kept resisting? She wanted him.

"We'll decide that during negotiations," he said, opening the door and ushering her into the room with his hand on the small of her back. She swore she could feel the heat even through the corset.

"Negotiations?" she echoed. There was no way he'd skipped looking over her play sheet, which had all of her hard and soft limits on it. Especially since she knew he had to be the Dom who had joined in the scene with Andrew. Maybe he was just trying to make her wonder whether or not he really had been?

Giving her a gentle push towards one of the desks in the first row, Michael moved to the teacher's desk, standing in front of it and leaning back against it with his arms crossed as Ellie settled into her chair. With her sitting and him standing right in front of her, she could already feel herself settling into a submissive mindset, and it made her feel calmer emotionally, even as her body tingled with growing excitement.

"I've already looked over your limits, but I still want to talk about them first, since this is our first scene together," he said, although one side of his mouth hitched up into a little half-smile when he called it their first scene. Yeah, he was definitely the "mystery Dom" from her scene with Andrew. "You have some unusual limits."

Immediately, Ellie's body tensed, the calm she was feeling retreated as she scrambled for the walls which normally kept her from feeling vulnerable. It was a long moment before she realized Michael was still standing there, watching her reactions, and she had to force herself to release her white-knuckled grip on the sides of the desk. She pressed her palms flat against the desk, spreading out her fingers. Tilting her head back, she looked up into his eyes, somewhat defiantly.

He just raised his eyebrow at her.

Damn observant Doms. He was probably reading all sorts of things into her reaction. Maybe even hitting somewhere near the truth.

"I haven't had anyone complain before," she finally said, unable to bear the silence and his measuring gaze.

"It's not a complaint, but we're going to talk about them," he said, his tone calm and even.

If she wasn't sitting in a desk, she might have tried to run then and there. Worse, she was pretty sure he knew it. Which was why he'd maneuvered her into this particular room and this particular situation. He could be on her before she even finished standing up, much less before she tried to bolt. Of course, she could always say 'Red,' the club safe word, and she knew he would honor it... but her pride balked at using a safe word just because he wanted to talk.

Especially because her friends downstairs would immediately be all over her the second they saw her, and then she'd have to explain to them why she was back downstairs so quickly.

Realizing she was trapped actually helped, even though she knew that would be strange to most people. Kind of like when she was in bondage. When there was nothing she could do about her situation, when all her choices were gone, she could actually relax.

Still, she couldn't quite keep herself from sounding rebellious and a little bratty when she responded. "So what do you want to know?

She leaned back against her seat, crossing her arms over her chest. It wasn't the most comfortable position in the world because of the corset, but she'd live. Michael stared down at her, scrutinizing her. Assessing her. Making her want to squirm.

"Let's start with the soft limits. No need to ask about multiple play-partners, I have no interest in sharing you for this scene. Blind-folds - I'd like to use one today. Are you okay with that?"

"Yes," she said, relaxing just the tiniest bit. Soft limits were much easier. She'd trust Michael to do any of them. It didn't surprise her that he was reciting her limits by memory either; she'd have been more surprised if he hadn't. He was thorough like that.

"Anal play?"

"Yes." Her anus clenched in anticipation. Ellie actually loved anal play, but she didn't trust too many people to do it right. She might be a masochist, but that didn't mean all pain felt good, and anything anal made her feel incredibly submissive, which wasn't always how she wanted to feel when she was playing. Especially with someone new. But with Michael? Yeah, that was fine.

"Fisting?"

Her pussy fluttered, her chest tightening. "I'm... open to it, but I've never done it before."

In fact, the first time she'd heard of it she'd been horrified, in a completely fascinated kind of way. She'd watched videos of it online, peeking through her fingers, completely enthralled even as her stomach churned in panicked terror. To say her feelings were mixed was putting it lightly. Especially when she looked at Michael's long fingers and large hand.

"We can work up to it, in the future."

Relief warred with disappointment, followed by a flutter of apprehension as she realized he was already planning future scenes for them. That was... good? Scary? Exciting? Nerve-wracking? ... All of the above?

"Now, hard limits."

Ellie's insides twisted.

M ichael didn't think he'd ever scened with a submissive so reluctant to just talk. Even the impatient ones would concede, although they might try to get it over with quickly. In contrast, Ellie's expression turned stubborn, and he knew he wasn't going to get all the answers he wanted today.

That was fine. He could be patient.

He also wasn't going to let her get away with completely avoiding answering his questions.

"Hair-pulling seems the most problematic for me," he said, keeping his tone light and conversational. "I like to touch a woman's hair, run my fingers through it." He let his gaze slide to her raven-locks, making it clear he'd like to play with *her* hair, and was pleased when her cheeks flushed pink. "Can you clarify your limits with your hair?"

The question set her off balance, as it was meant to. She obviously hadn't ever been challenged on any of her limits. Michael wasn't going to push her past them, but he also wasn't going to let her remain comfortably within them without at least examining their boundaries.

Her left hand rose, seeking out a lock of hair to wind about her fingers as she thought for a moment.

"Running your fingers through it is fine," she said, almost shyly. "Even a little pulling that's not too hard, just... just not wrapping it around your hand or um... Yeah. Just not wrapping it around your hand."

Michael rewarded her with an approving smile. "Thank you. I have to admit, I would have been disappointed if I'd been forbidden from playing with your hair at all." The smile she gave him in return was still shy, but gaining in some confidence. "You left breath play blank on your form, it's not a limit, but you didn't indicate an interest in it either. Would you be open to trying some breath play?"

Her teeth bit down into her lower lip, dragging across the surface as she considered. Michael didn't miss the way her legs pressed together under the desk. Something about it appealed to her, but she was even more unsure about it than the hair pulling. Still, he wanted an answer, so he waited patiently for her to think through it.

"I... yes. I'd want to use 'yellow' as a slowdown word and... only with you."

"Thank you, sweetheart," he murmured, touched - again - by the trust she was showing in him.

It soothed some of his angst over the way she'd avoided scening with him for months. At least now he knew it wasn't something he'd done. It couldn't be; she was already showing far more trust in him than she had for anyone but Andrew. Hell, perhaps even more than she had for Andrew, since Andrew had definitely never pushed her emotional limits even though he might have done so with her pain threshold.

There were a couple other items he wanted to address, but she'd tensed up so much when he said he wanted to talk that he didn't think pushing even more now was the best course of action. It could wait until she was more comfortable with him. Wait until after she'd played with him a few times and was feeling more confident.

"Alright, Ellie... now... we're back in high school, what do you think we should do with this empty classroom?" he asked, giving her a wink.

Ellie gaped at him, a flash of relief flickering across her expression, immediately followed by wariness. "That's it? What about my other limits? What about sex?"

"Your other limits are unimportant for today's scene," he said, and was pleased when she immediately relaxed, looking only a little troubled. Probably because she was already thinking to the future and having to talk about her hard limits then, but Michael was sure he could distract her. "As for sex, how do you feel about it?"

"Yes."

"Yes what?" he asked, a little surprised at the alacrity of her answer.

"Yes, I would like sex." Her voice was a little breathy, definitely eager. Michael's cock jerked in anticipation.

But he shouldn't read too much into her eagerness. Ellie scened a lot with a lot of different Doms and sex didn't necessarily mean anything emotionally. Although, it would certainly be enjoyable.

"Then sex will be left up to my discretion as the Dom."

She made a face of disappointment that almost made him smile. But he held it back, since it wouldn't fit his plans for the scene.

Stepping forward, he leaned down and placed his hands on either side of the desk she was sitting at, placing their faces only inches apart. "So, Ellie... are you wearing any panties today?"

Her face flushed immediately, and the presence of her legs close to his suddenly disappeared as she pressed hers together underneath the desk. Michael grinned.

A little spark rose up in her eyes at his reaction, and then a foot was pressing against his inner calf and gliding up the inside of his leg. "Wouldn't you like to find out?"

"I absolutely would."

Straightening back up, he stepped back and glanced down at her legs, which were slightly parted, although the desk blocked the view of her short skirt. Ellie giggled at the mock-disappointed noise he made.

"You should stand up so I can find out," he said, just a hint of an order in his voice.

"Maybe you shouldn't have had me sit down if you really wanted to know," Ellie sassed back, making him grin.

This was the Ellie he remembered from high school, and apparently it was a side she didn't show too often. From what he'd seen, she was pretty quiet, even among her friends. While he remembered her being shy, she definitely hadn't been reserved once he'd gotten to know her. He'd thought maybe she was just quiet in comparison to the more exuberant of their friends - Angel and Chris could make anyone except each other seem quiet by comparison - but no... this sassy little sub with the sparkling eyes had definitely not made an appearance before, at least not that he'd observed. And he'd been watching closely.

"Are you trying to sass me into spanking you before I even know what you have on under your cute little skirt?" He was teasing, but still allowing just a hint of threat to deepen his voice.

The flush in her cheeks and the hitch in her breath said Ellie was enjoying flirting with danger... and he was enjoying seeing this side of her personality come out to play. None of the Doms had ever mentioned her being a SAM - a Smart-Ass Masochist - which meant she might not have allowed herself to relax enough with any of them to fully be herself.

"Sass you into spanking me?" She asked, sliding sideways out of the desk and getting to her feet. She turned around, peeking back at him over her shoulder as she flipped up the back of her skirt to show off her completely bare bottom. "Right on my bare butt?"

ELLIE SQUEALED AS MICHAEL DARTED FORWARD, CATCHING HER around the waist with one arm as his hand smacked down on her butt cheek with a fiery slap. A giggle worked its way up out of her throat, the sound so strange in their current location that she almost wondered who had made it.

She felt almost giddy. Aroused, excited, apprehensive... and giddy. It wasn't exactly a mix she was used to. Arousal, apprehension (in a good way), relief to be scening... those were all things she was used to. Sassing and playfulness? Yeah, not so much. But, with Michael, it felt almost natural.

Fun too. Daring. Which made her apprehension rise, but also her excitement. She'd been so anxious when he'd wanted to talk about her limits; having him end the conversation before she'd anticipated had felt like a giant weight being lifted.

"Feels like no panties to me," Michael growled in her ear, his hand rubbing over the bare skin he'd just spanked, her skirt brushing against her ass around his hand.

She was also more aroused than she'd ever been by just a single swat to her bottom. Normally, it took at least a full on glowing, red ass before she was really turned on, but right now she was wet just from teasing him and the tiny little sting. Yeah, she wanted more where that came from, but her level of arousal was still surprising.

"Perv," she said, arching her back to stick out her bottom more.

Michael just laughed and turned her around to face him rather than giving her another spank. He laughed again as she pouted up at him in disappointment, inwardly wondering where this flirty playfulness of hers had come from. If she'd been doing it on purpose it would have made more sense, but it just seemed to be flowing naturally, even if it felt a little strange.

It seemed like he was enjoying himself too; the mock-stern expression on his face didn't hide the way his lips tilted up at the edges or the amusement dancing in his eyes.

"Are you trying to rush me, Ellie?" he asked, teasing through his flinty tone. "Topping from the bottom?"

"Umm... no?" It came out as a question.

Topping from the bottom wasn't something she did in a scene. She just accepted whatever she was given. If she needed more, she asked for it outright, she didn't taunt or challenge her dominant... but that was kind of what she was doing, wasn't it?

Michael chuckled. "Show me how good you can be then," he said, giving a tendril of her hair a tug before turning his body to give her room to move around him. "Go bend over the teacher's desk."

Anticipation thrummed through her as she passed by him, so close she could have touched him... but he hadn't told her to. And she really wasn't trying to top from the bottom. Ellie liked pain she had earned from being a good girl, she wasn't really into punishments. Besides, if Michael was anything like Andrew - and she suspected he was - punishments usually meant not getting a special treat rather than receiving extra blows.

Damn devious sadists.

Ellie bent over the desk.

The back of her skirt fluttered against her pussy lips; it was short enough that she was sure Michael had a very nice view. Her breasts, plumped up by the confines of the corset, flattened against the desktop, nearly spilling out. Widening her stance a little to help her balance, she turned her head to lay her cheek against the cool wood, her hands on either side of her head.

"Very pretty, Ellie," Michael said approvingly, his hand sliding up the back of her thigh and flipping up her skirt to bare her ass completely. "Good girl."

The accolades made her blush happily, filling her with warmth, right before -

SMACK! SMACK!

Two quick, hard swats, one to each ass cheek. The initial impact like a sharp sting, followed by a slow burn that made her want to moan.

It wasn't that masochists didn't feel pain. It was that the pain could feel good. It hurt... but that hurt would evolve into endorphins and adrenaline and sexual pleasure. If it was administered correctly.

And Michael knew exactly what he was doing.

His hand rubbed against the two spots.

Not soothingly. Not to rub away the burn.

No, he rubbed her tender skin roughly.

Ellie squirmed.

Michael lifted his hand.

"Have you thought about what kind of scene you would like, Ellie?"

Thought about? No. Fantasized about what Michael might do, based on past experiences, sure, but right now it felt like he was asking if she wanted anything specific.

She shook her head. "Just make me hurt."

The plea in her voice would have embarrassed her at one point in her life. No longer. She had accepted she was wired this way a long time ago. Begging for pain at Stronghold didn't bother her, not even in front of someone from her past.

Whatever he wanted to do to her... that was what she wanted.

"Hmmm." The low hum of his voice was accompanied by a sensuous stroke of his fingers over the tender places on her ass. The light touch was a tease to her senses, and Ellie had to remind herself not to arch her back again, not to try and force his hand just because she wanted more. *Bad Ellie, no topping from the bottom.*

Definitely not something she'd ever had to remind herself before.

She bit her bottom lip as his hand continued to stroke.

Gently.

Like he was just waiting for her to protest. To be bad. To try and tip his hand.

A test.

And for some reason, it got her hot even as she wanted to scream at him to just spank her already.

Mental sadism? Was that a thing?

She wasn't used to having to wait. Most scenes started with her being tied up, moved on to whatever implements the dominant wanted to use, and ended with her being untied, and sitting in the women's locker room while she came down from her scene high. Unless she was scening with Andrew, he always insisted on her receiving some kind of aftercare from him - or from Jared if he couldn't for some reason.

This was... what was it?

What was she doing?

Was she *flirting?* Unease sparked.

SMACK! SMACK! SMACK! SMACK!

Ellie gasped as Michael's hand came down hard on the exact two spots he'd already spanked, reigniting and building on the sting. Her body hummed. Her thoughts tripped.

"You're thinking too hard, Ellie," he murmured, rubbing those same spots roughly, squeezing her cheeks and sending a rush of hot warmth straight through her core. Ellie moaned. "I don't want you able to think."

"Then maybe you shouldn't leave me waiting," she muttered saucily.

Michael made a tsking noise. "Just for that comment, you're only going to get my hand, not a paddle."

Dammit.

SMACK!

SMACK!

The two red spots on her ass had apparently turned into targets, because Michael was focusing on them to the exclusion of all else. Her focus narrowed to those two spots, knowing exactly where the next blows were going to land.

SMACK!

SMACK!

Her breath caught in her throat. Even without the paddle, each smack of Michael's palm against her flesh was a jolt of growing pain, like fire had set in her skin and was being stoked higher and higher. Her pussy throbbed with need as she whimpered, wanting more... and only being touched in those two exact spots.

Over and over again.

SMACK!

SMACK!

It was like an unending rhythm, one she kept thinking he couldn't keep up... but he did. The two spots were like a conflagration - burning, pulsing, throbbing as he spanked them over and over again.

She felt her pussy spasm.

Her muscles clench and release.

Tears sparked in the back of her eyes.

There was something about the intensity of having all his focus on those two spots, of having all the pain congregated right there... his hand must be smarting by now. But still he continued.

When he suddenly stopped, Ellie's body jerked in response to a swat that didn't land. She sucked in a breath feeling almost light-headed. It wasn't the harshest spanking she'd ever received, especially since the majority of her buttocks were left blemish-free, but she knew she'd be feeling it for a few days.

So far, this scene with Michael had been nothing like she expected... what was he going to do next?

EACH OF ELLIE'S BUTTOCKS NOW SPORTED A DARK, PURPLISH-RED spot right in the center of the creamy mound, and Michael's palm was tingling with stinging fire from such a concentrated spanking. Her cheeks quivered, clenching and relaxing, the pink pucker of her anus winking at him. Just below, her pussy lips were plumped, swollen, wet, her clit peeking out from underneath its hood as proof of just how aroused she was.

He wondered if she realized just how much her body language told him in the moments of stillness.

Before, when he'd made her wait, she'd gone into her head and he'd practically been able to watch the tension knot itself through her body. Now, her attention was on her body... on her pain and arousal, and she was completely relaxed.

Waiting.

Submissive.

Perfect.

"Good girl," he said, his voice deep, low. A shiver went down her spine, mostly hidden by the corset she was wearing and her hair, but he saw the movement in her upper back. A good kind of shiver.

Ellie deserved a reward.

Walking around the desk, he chose the side she was facing so he could see her expression. She smiled at him, her eyes dreamy, cheeks flushed. Nowhere near subspace, but she was in a good place. Interest and excitement sparked as he opened one of the desk drawers.

The desk held a veritable banquet of treats. Michael grabbed one of the individual bottles of lube and a medium sized vibrating plug. It was the same reddish purple he'd just spanked into her cheeks, and after they finished playing tonight it would be hers. If he could convince Ellie to play with him again, he'd buy some toys just for her before their next scene... he hadn't wanted to do so for this one. Maybe he'd been afraid of jinxing it.

Anal was on her soft limits.

He was going to push her, but she was going to like it.

When she felt the tip of the plug, slick with lube, against the crinkled rose of her ass, she tensed.

"Relax, Ellie, it will make it easier," he said.

"Easier for you," she muttered.

Not that he particularly wanted it to be easy. He pressed. She resisted. Not because she was trying to, but because she was uncomfortable.

It didn't matter.

He'd used enough lube so she couldn't keep the toy out. Michael didn't bother trying to work it in and out; he just pressed, and her bottom strained. Stretched. Opened.

Ellie groaned as he pushed it in, very slowly but firmly, a long, slow slide into her resisting body.

"It hurts," she said, the slightest hint of a whimper.

Hurting didn't bother her. Having her ass filled did. His cock jerked against the front of his pants at the seductive quaver in her voice. Seductive to him because he liked hearing her discomfort.

"You'll get used to it," he said. Her breath caught as her hole stretched over the widest part, and then she sighed as it sank fully in, her tight muscle settling around the narrow neck between the plug and the flange. For a moment, she relaxed, and then she squirmed a little, as if trying to get comfortable.

Grinning, Michael tapped on the base of the toy, enjoying her reaction as she squirmed again. Reaching up, he undid the knot in her corset laces, loosening the tight hold.

"Stand up and turn around, Ellie. Hands behind your back."

She made another little sound of distress as she obeyed, shifting her weight back and forth on her feet, her nose wrinkling as the plug was moved around by her changing stance. Gorgeous. Adorable. Unsure but eager.

Big, dark eyes blinked up at him, filled with interest and tinged with a touch of apprehension. Her tongue flicked out to lick her lips, immediately making him think of putting her on her knees. Unfortunately, that wasn't part of tonight's plan.

Slow and steady wins the race.

"The corset is beautiful," he said, tracing his finger along the top of it, just barely brushing against the soft skin of her breasts. "But it's going to have to come off."

Another little hitch of breath and a sweep of her tongue over her bottom lip in were her excited response. Michael grasped the front of her corset and pushed it together, undoing the clasps, and then pulled it free from her body. Pink grooves were set into her creamy skin where the boning had pressed in, creating an even more exaggerated hourglass shape than she naturally had. The tips of her nipples were hard, a darker pink than the grooves on her skin, begging to be touched.

Cupping her sensitive breasts in his hands, Michael leaned down to suck one hard nipple into his mouth. Ellie gasped at the sudden movement, her back arching as she leaned back against the desk, her hands still locked behind her. During the scene Andrew had shared her with him, Michael had discovered she had very sensitive nipples and the undersides of her breasts, something he was eager to exploit now.

Reaching into his pocket, he pulled out a square of burlap. It wasn't particularly rough burlap, but it was well textured and wouldn't actually prick. Perfect for abrading skin.

With his right hand, he began rubbing the burlap all over her right breast while he sucked on the nipple of her left. Ellie whimpered and squirmed, and he could practically feel her confusion as her skin began to turn pink under the rubbing of the cloth square. Smiling, he switched breasts, and she let out a little shriek as his mouth closed around her nipple, which would be feeling much more sensitive after being worked over by the burlap.

The rough cloth abrading her skin would make her that much more tender, that much more sensitive, and would make the sting of the lash that much more effective.

He sucked hard on her nipple, long pulls on the turgid bud as she squirmed and trembled, her breath coming faster as she struggled to hold her position. Releasing the little bud from his mouth with a pop, Michael straightened and looked down at her. He grinned. The surface of her large breasts was now pretty and pink, her nipple glossy and plump, completely primed to be tormented by him.

"Up on the desk and lie on your back," he ordered her as he went to one of the cabinets which he knew stored an assortment of impact instruments. "Hands by your head, feet flat on the table and spread apart." Michael picked out a crop with a leather flap and a small pussy whip made of thin rubber strands. When he turned around, Ellie was laid out on the table for him, her pink breasts slightly flattened by the position, her skirt a mere strip of cloth around her waist, and her thighs spread wide.

She really did look like a school boy's fantasy. Well, a kinky school boy's.

He positioned himself on the side of the desk, looking down over her, and placed the pussy whip down near her legs.

"Good girl," he said again as he brought the crop down on her breasts.

⚘

A LINE OF FIRE, MUCH STRONGER THAN SHE'D EXPECTED, STREAKED across the underside of Ellie's breasts, making her suck in a gasp of air as her pussy clenched. The plug in her ass jostled around, reminding her of its presence - as if she could forget - and it felt like her entire body pulsed in response. Anal wasn't on her soft limits because she didn't like it, but because it felt so intimate to her, but she loved the way it felt to be filled. The coolness of the wood was heating fast under her ass, where the twin spots he'd spanked throbbed under the weight of her body lying on them.

She felt spread out. Vulnerable. On edge.

This scene wasn't anything like what she'd expected and it made her feel more alert all over, her senses heightened, constantly trying to anticipate what he was going to do and never managing it. She'd been expecting something like her scene with Andrew.

She was left off balance, but she was also more turned on, more into the scene than she'd felt during a scene in months. Maybe years.

Michael's hand slapped against the underside of her breast, over the welt he'd just laid down with the crop, and she cried out, arching upwards. His hand felt hot on her sensitized skin, rougher than before, uncomfortable just from contact, and she finally understood what he'd been doing with the rough cloth. It hadn't hurt when he'd been rubbing her with it, but it made her so sensitized that everything else he was doing now hurt more. His hand lifted and came down on her other breast, rubbing and squeezing the same way, and Ellie writhed.

The sensations assaulting her were confusing and arousing. Her ass was full, uncomfortable, and just the memory of the long, slow slide of the plug into her made her feel breathless. It hadn't hurt enough to make her say 'red' but the long burn had been completely new to her while the slow filling had made her pussy throb.

Now, her breasts were beginning to burn too, as he lay down another streak of fire across the tops of her breasts, and followed it up with slaps and more rubbing.

Her ass was full, throbbing, and burning with discomfort. Her breasts were tender, tingling, and licked with fire. But her pussy, her needy, quivering pussy, was left quiet and empty.

THWAP! THWAP! THWAP!

Michael started to rain little strikes down across her breasts and stomach, using just the leather flap on the end of the crop, and Ellie arched as she fisted her hands by her head. Not being bound actually made it harder not to move as the little, stinging slaps bit into her flesh, sparking pain with every blow.

The sudden start of vibrations in her ass had her hips jerking upwards, and she cried out as her anus spasmed and tightened around the plug, making it feel even larger as it buzzed inside of her. Her pussy throbbed, emptier and needier than ever.

"Please," she begged, arching her back but otherwise managing to hold the rest of her body in place. "Please... more..."

The small strikes of pain mixed with her growing pleasure, adding to her need as the pressure inside of her began to build.

"More?" Michael asked, with a sadistic smirk as he laid down the crop. "More here?"

Ellie nearly screamed with frustration and the explosion of pain and pleasure as his hands closed over her breasts and roughly caressed. Her sensitive skin flared and burned at his hot touch, the welts throbbing and stinging. When his fingers closed over her nipples and pinched hard, crushing the tiny buds like tight clamps, she cried out as she nearly orgasmed from that alone. Her pussy convulsed, so empty, so needy... stimulated only by the vibrations in her ass.

"Please," she begged breathlessly, practically tearful from the aching need to orgasm. She was so close... so very, very close. "Please whip my pussy."

Leaning over her, Michael brushed his lips over hers, very gently, a complete contrast to the way his hands were mauling her aching breasts. "As you wish."

Even when he released her breasts, they didn't stop hurting. Blood rushed back into her crushed nipples, the lingering ache of his roughness tingled on her skin, and the cool air felt even colder against the warmth of her skin. Her knees fell to the side, opening her even further, as he moved down to the other end of the desk, picking up the small whip on the way.

"Very pretty, Ellie," Michael said approvingly. His free hand caressed her ankle and calf, warm and gentle. She closed her eyes for just a moment, taking in all the sensations, feeling every inch of her body, her ass tightening around the plug inside of it.

Pain and pleasure exploded as tiny rubber strands snapped against her pussy lips and clit. She cried out, her knees involuntarily coming together.

"Open, Ellie," Michael said, his voice firm as his hand slid up her calf, exerting pressure to make her legs fall open again.

She obeyed, her hips tilting to offer her pussy up for more abuse.

Her body arched and writhed as the whip landed again on her most tender parts, her pussy and ass spasming. The vibrations in her ass felt more intense than ever... she was so close to cumming...

Another snap of rubber tendrils stung her lips and clit, and she cried out... and then screamed as Michael's hot mouth suddenly closed over her abused clit. He sucked hard, and Ellie's orgasm went from good to overwhelmingly intense in a heartbeat. She sobbed as her body pulsed, bringing her hands down to tangle them in Michael's hair as his tongue flicked against her swollen clit.

It was the most satisfying orgasm she'd had in months.

TAKING LONG, SLOW LICKS OF ELLIE'S CREAMY SLIT AS SHE CAME down from her orgasm, Michael adjusted his cock in his pants, trying to keep his fantasies under control. Tonight was about her, not about him.

Keep her coming back for more.

Hopefully.

He shut off the vibrator in her ass, letting it go quiet. Although, he wasn't going to remove it. He wanted to send her home with it.

When she let out a long sigh and her hands relaxed in his hair, Michael reluctantly straightened. The tart, sweet taste of her filled his mouth, and it was all too easy to imagine grasping her by the hips and pulling her to the edge of the desk so he could fuck her senseless while sharing the taste of her cream with her.

Opening her eyes, Ellie looked surprised as he helped her sit up, holding her corset in his hand.

"What about you?" she asked, looking a little dazed. "What about sex?"

"My decision as the Dom, remember? I'd like to do another scene with you though. Next week, same time?" he responded as she slid to a standing position. He pulled the corset around her. With the loose laces, the front clasps easily slid into the place.

She stayed silent as he turned her away from him so he could tighten the laces just enough for the corset to stay in place, although not nearly as tight as they'd been when she'd arrived at the club. When she faced him again, her expression was wary but thoughtful.

"Okay," she said quietly.

Triumph surged through him, far more satisfying than a mere orgasm would have been.

"Good girl," he said, cuddling her under his arm. "Now let's go to the aftercare couch."

"I don't need aftercare," she said. It sounded like an automatic response, and Michael was fairly sure that it was.

"But I need to give it, and I'd appreciate it if you let me," he said evenly as they exited the room. He gave a nod to one of the subbies on duty, hanging on the side of the Dungeon, letting him know the room was ready to be cleaned. As he'd suspected, Ellie's need to please him in some way after the scene meant she allowed him to lead her to the aftercare corner, wrap her in a blanket, and snuggle her on the couch.

It caused a few stares since Ellie only ever accepted aftercare from Andrew or Jared... but she snuggled right into him and allowed him to hold her on his lap, her head resting on his shoulder. Most people wouldn't call it a 'happy ending,' but for Michael, it was exactly the ending he'd been aiming for.

No matter how much his cock ached.

🕊 4 🕊

After walking Ellie out to her car, Michael wasn't really into hanging out around the club and dealing with the inevitable gossip, so he went home too. His apartment seemed emptier than ever, although the solitude was usually a relief. The sparsely furnished one bedroom was basically just a place for him to hang his hat; he hadn't really done anything to make it into a home yet.

He'd gotten too used to being on the move, needing the ability to pack up and go easily; settling in one place had felt foreign. Even though he wanted to make it look more like a home, whenever he went into a store with decorations and knick knacks, he had trouble convincing himself to buy anything. His brain kept asking what he would do with it if he got into a show and went on tour again. It didn't matter that he didn't plan to go on tour again, it was still the mindset he was most comfortable with.

Now, he looked around and wondered what Ellie would think if he ever managed to convince her to come to his place.

Just thinking about her possible reaction reminded him of how gorgeous she'd been tonight... how surprisingly sassy and fun before submitting beautifully. His cock, which had never fully gone down, rose up again as he ran his tongue around the back of his teeth, the taste of her still lingering. With a groan, he headed for the shower.

Not a cold one either.

With the hot water pounding down on his back, conditioner coating his hand, he closed his eyes, fisting his hand around his dick as he started to pump, his mind already reaching for the memory of Ellie's voice as she whimpered and moaned... the tiny noises she made in the back of her throat when the leather tip of the crop had landed on her breasts, inflicting little sparks of pain, but not the welts the full length of it had created.

Her creamy skin had marked up beautifully - the two large prints he'd left on her ass, the welts and peppering of small marks on her breasts, even her pussy lips had plumped and pinked under the small whip. Tomorrow, she'd feel his marks and remember every time she touched her breasts, every time her clothing moved over her skin... the two long welts would last till then and the abrasion from the burlap would make her more sensitive. She'd think about him every time she sat down, feeling the two spots where he'd focused her spanking.

And she'd agreed to scene with him again.

His balls tightened as he started thinking about all the perverse, sadistic things he could do to her.

Clamps and weights on those sensitive nipples. She'd make those little moaning noises in the back of her throat every time the weights swung, and he'd make sure they swung a lot.

Clamps on her pink labia. Maybe he'd connect them to the ones on her nipples, forcing her to hold a position or pull on the clamps... clover clamps, which would tighten with each tug.

Turn her ass pink with his hand and then setting lines across her blushing cheeks with a cane.

Flogging her from head to toe until she was begging to cum.

And once she was reduced to a mass of sensation, a seething mix of passion, pleasure, and agony, he'd sink his cock into her and finally sate the need which had been building since she'd come back into his life. He squeezed his cock, gasping as his orgasm hit him hard and fast, Ellie's face standing out in his mind, her cries filling his ears.

"Fuck..." he muttered, leaning his shoulder against the tile of the shower wall. It felt cool against his skin as he straightened his knees, his cock throbbing and slowly softening in his hand.

It wasn't the first time he'd jerked off while thinking about Ellie - and it probably wouldn't be the last - but it was definitely one of the more potent. Sharing her scene with Andrew, when she had been blindfolded and hadn't actually been submitting to him, hadn't been nearly as emotionally satisfying, and, while it had fueled his fantasies, hadn't had quite the same impact.

Waiting for next Saturday was going to be an exercise in patience.

Well, at least he'd have the planning of the new club to keep him occupied. There was a lot to do; sign contracts with Patrick, search for a space, start looking for employees, and he should probably put in his two weeks to his current job.

It seemed like his whole life was starting to move forward in an unexpected way now. Apparently when it rains, it pours.

EVERY PART OF ELLIE'S BODY ACHED DELICIOUSLY.

"MROW!!!"

"Yes, yes, I see you," she said, exasperation filling her voice. Watson darted forward, winding his furry, orange body around her boots, obviously not accepting of her reassurance that he was totally and completely visible to her. While he was a shy cat with strangers, with her, he was a complete and total attention whore. "Needy cat."

"MROW!!!"

He sat down, looking up at her expectantly.

Ellie sighed as she leaned over to scoop him up. Her anus clenched emptily, her corset shifted over her sensitive breasts, and she shuddered. Yeah, she was going to be feeling the aftereffects of tonight's scene for a while.

What she really wanted to do was just sit on her couch and decompress by herself, settle into the aftereffects of the scene, but Watson needed attention and when Watson needed attention, Watson got attention. Because otherwise he annoyed her until he did.

He purred happily as she cradled him like a baby, belly-up, his little, white paws coming up to try and bat at her face. Kissing the bottom of his paws, she moved towards her bedroom. Pajamas first, then to the couch with the little monster. She needed to just chill out for a while.

Sit.

Think.

Despite the satisfaction she'd felt after the scene, she'd started feeling unsettled. Maybe it was sub drop, but she didn't think so. She was pretty sure it had more to do with Michael.

Watson grumbled as she put him on the bed, watching her with narrowed eyes as she stripped out of her clothes and pulled on comfy sweats. She knew from experience that if she tried to leave the room without picking him back up, he'd let out an ear-splitting yowl.

"I see you, I see you," she muttered, scooping him back up.

Okay, it was kind of nice to have a sweet, furry animal to cuddle with even though she wanted to be alone with her thoughts right now.

"After all, you don't really count as people, do you?" she asked, tickling Watson under the chin while he purred ecstatically, his little paws waving and kneading the air. "Even if you do demand my attention when I just want to focus on me for a minute."

Gingerly, she sat down on the couch, hissing slightly as the cushions didn't totally protect her bottom from the throbbing, lingering soreness. Absently stroking Watson's belly, she leaned her head back and let out a long sigh as her body relaxed.

She felt so good.

Sated. Loose. Relaxed. The way she felt after the best kind of scene. And she hadn't felt this way in a while.

Which didn't really make sense because, as intense as the scene had been, she'd had scenes that involved so much more... more pain, more implements, more orgasms. This scene... even though she felt sated, she still wanted more. She didn't want a scene with someone else, she wanted to go back to Michael.

Which was a really scary feeling.

Even more so because she hadn't exactly been acting like herself. Although, that seemed to be the theme of the day, from calling Lexie because she was freaking out over what to wear, to sassing Michael, to agreeing to another scene with him. That last one made her feeling particularly antsy because she knew everyone at Stronghold was going to read all kinds of things into it... but she still wanted to do it.

As if sensing her anxiety, Watson let out a particularly loud purr, his paw coming up to bop her on the underside of her chin.

"Yeah, your momma's got issues," she said, tilting her head down to kiss his foot. Watson liked having the pads on the bottom of his feet kissed and nuzzled, the little weirdo.

Trust and relationships were two things she didn't even try to do anymore. She'd made the attempt twice since her first disastrous high school boyfriend, and neither time had worked out well. Her college boyfriend, Steve, had tried, but having a damaged girlfriend wasn't a lot of fun for a horny guy with a high sex drive, and eventually he'd given up on her. The next guy she'd almost dated had been in the scene, but then he'd ignored her safe word the first time they'd scened alone. She'd had to scream it over and over before he finally gave in, pouting the entire time like she'd been unreasonable about having her hair pulled. If he'd ignore it for a small thing, he would have ignored it for larger ones too and she'd immediately stopped seeing him. After that, Ellie had kept everything in the club where there were Dungeon Monitors and lots of witnesses to everything and she didn't see anyone regularly. It was why she only did private room scenes with Andrew, and she'd taken months to get to that point with him.

But with Michael...

Everything was different, just as she'd known it would be from the very beginning. Yeah, she'd spent months running from him, but once she'd agreed to scene with him, she'd immediately trusted him enough to go into a private room and close the door. And she'd been... herself. Uncensored. Unguarded. Vulnerable in a way she hadn't been in so long.

No wonder she'd been running from him for so long. She wasn't used to letting herself be that open. Even with her friends. But a few minutes with Michael and she'd found herself not just talking, but sassing... almost flirting.

She'd given in because...

Because she was envious. Because she'd known her time with

Andrew was coming to an end. He was the Dom she trusted the most, but she'd hated herself for needing to ask him for a scene when he and Kate were back together. Not all scenes had a sexual component to them, but since she and Andrew had had sex in the past and his second chance with Kate was pretty new, she'd still felt weird about it. Especially since he wasn't scening with anyone else. And while she hadn't begrudged his attention to Kate, and he certainly hadn't held back during the scene, she'd known his full attention wasn't on her.

And she wanted someone's full attention on her.

Admitting that to herself had been hard. Admitting to herself that the only person whose face she pictured, when she fantasized about having a Dom's full attention, was Michael's was even harder.

But if she wanted to try for a relationship, where better to start than someone she already instinctively trusted? Even if it didn't work out, she knew it wouldn't be because he treated her horribly. Maybe she really was too damaged to salvage, which she suspected sometimes, but if anyone could be patient enough, understanding enough, it would be the man who had been pursuing her for months. She'd seen him doing other scenes at the club and knew his patience bled into his style of domination as well.

He'd probably need every last bit of it to put up with her.

Watson's paw bumped her chin again and Ellie smiled. Somehow he always knew when she was spiraling and distracted her. She'd told her therapist Dr. Amy that he was like a little therapy cat, always interrupting her thoughts when they became too anxious or self-loathing.

"Such a good kitty," she said, baby-talking to him as she rubbed his belly. Watson stretched, giving her more access, and purred like a little motor. "You think I should try to have a relationship, don't you?"

Actually, probably not. Watson was not a big fan of men. When her brother, Austin, had come for a visit and spent the week on her pull-out couch, Watson had hidden the entire week. Her brother claimed he hadn't even caught a glimpse of Watson the entire time he was there.

Still, unless Ellie wanted to spend the rest of her life alone...

Other people were getting together. No one had ever thought

Adam would find a sub he could tolerate in a long-term relationship, and now he was going to be a daddy soon and begging the sub in question to just hurry up and marry him already. Everyone had bet Patrick would never actually make a move on Lexie either, but now they were together and glowingly happy. Even the most unlikely-to-be-in-a-relationship, commitment-phobic Andrew, was in love and completely exclusive with his second-chance love.

It was enough to make even an ultra-cynical pessimist like Ellie start to feel hopeful. Especially when she managed to get through an entire first scene with a man without even a tiny moment of panic, and ending it feeling like she wanted more from him... something she didn't think she'd ever allowed herself to feel before.

๑๑๑

"SO WHAT DO YOU THINK?" CLAUDIA, ONE OF THE SUBS WHO CAME to Stronghold regularly with her husband and Master, asked proudly, waving her hand around to indicate the full space.

Apparently, when Patrick decided something, he *decided* something. Michael probably shouldn't be too surprised; after all, he was pretty decisive himself, but he still hadn't expected Patrick to move quite as quickly as he had. They'd hashed out an agreement for going into business together on Monday, signed it on Tuesday, and now here they were looking at properties on Wednesday. It just so happened Claudia was a real estate agent specializing in business properties, and Patrick had contacted her on Monday as soon as they'd agreed to open the second club.

They were now in the third space Claudia had lined up for them. Originally, it had been the fourth on her list, she'd told them, but after getting their impressions from the first two, she'd bumped it up.

She was good too... because Michael thought it was pretty fucking perfect.

Completely different from the warehouse district where Stronghold was located, this building was right in the center of downtown. The entire four-story building was now available, although it needed a bit of fixing up. The main floor used to be a speakeasy restaurant, while the upper floors had held offices. The main restaurant area wasn't very large because the main floor was divided between the front restaurant and the "speak easy."

"What do you think?" Patrick asked, turning to Michael after a careful look around. They were back in the main dining area after having explored the upstairs.

Michael raised his eyebrows at the other man.

"Sure you don't want to tell me what you think first?" he joked. Patrick just grinned back at him, arms crossed over his chest and totally at ease. He knew he was a bossy bastard. Fortunately, Michael was pretty easy-going in most ways.

"I think it's fucking perfect," Patrick said. "But since you're the one who'll be running it, I'll let you have a say."

Claudia giggled as Michael barked a laugh. Watching the two doms, she jumped up to sit on one of the high barstools while she awaited the verdict. Those stools would have to go. They were cheap looking plastic trying to be something it wasn't. Whoever had had this place before had tried to scrimp and save on small things, but people didn't want to spend money in a cheap looking place. The speakeasy would have been a cool idea if it had been done right, and it was also what made both the location and the space so ideal.

Looking around at the front space, Michael found it easy to picture exactly how he wanted things set up. It really was perfect. The speakeasy area was accessed through the back hall. There was another bar back there with little alcoves already set up along the walls, and a small raised platform in the center of the room, which would be perfect for demos. The upstairs floors could be turned into private rooms, like the upstairs rooms at Stronghold. Theme rooms. He'd have to think of some new themes though, he didn't want to do repeats. A spa/massage room perhaps? A small medieval Dungeon room... maybe a pet room or and an age play room for the fetish players... Excitement curled inside of him as the place came together in his head.

It would be easy to keep regular restaurant patrons out of the "private dining" areas, and the main restaurant and bar would make a good front for the members who didn't want their activities known. Especially since the entrance was tucked back from the main street, so they wouldn't get a lot of foot traffic anyway.

They also didn't plan to advertise. From what Patrick said, they were going to have more than enough business just through Stronghold. The sister clubs would each offer something different. Stronghold would be the starker, darker side of BDSM. It had the Dungeon, after all. This club would be more centered on performance in its main room, with private alcoves for voyeurs to play in while they enjoyed the main show, as well as private rooms upstairs. Everything about it would be more discreet and private, the focus on already established couples and play partners, since it wouldn't have the Lounge area for single subs like Stronghold, although Michael would definitely have club submissives and dominants available for sessions.

Looking back at Patrick, Michael smiled. "It'll do."

"Yay!" Claudia said, clapping her hands excitedly. "I knew you'd like it. Okay, let's go talk paperwork."

Suppressing a groan - because this was definitely the boring part - Michael followed Claudia and Patrick back to the car. There was a garage right next door, which would be convenient.

But, as he glanced back over his shoulder down the side street where the entrance was, he felt a surge of excitement. This was going to be a lot of work, but he had a feeling it was also going to be a lot of fun. Plus, he could still scratch his performing itch if everything went as planned. He wondered if Ellie would be down for doing some demos with him.

STARING AT HER COMPUTER SCREEN, ELLIE MADE A FACE.

Not because the current design she was working on looked bad - it didn't - but because she was having serious trouble focusing for the fourth day in a row. Fortunately, she didn't have anything urgent this week, but since she was a freelance graphic artist, the faster she worked the better. After all, she couldn't take on new projects if she was already working on too many unfinished ones.

This week she was working particularly slowly. Her mind kept wandering, back to the weekend and her scene with Michael and forward to this upcoming weekend and fantasizing about what this scene might be like. What he might do. What he might try to surprise her with. How she might act.

Whether or not they'd have sex this time.

It was weird; before scening with him, she'd fantasized, of course, but it hadn't made her so antsy. Hadn't made her feel so impatient and needy. Scening with him had awoken some kind of itch inside of her, and she couldn't scratch it, not with a regular dildo, a vibrator, a plug, her Hitachi, or even a combination of toys. She just stayed... itchy.

When her phone buzzed with an incoming text message, it was a relief to turn away from the computer screen.

Angel - *I'm bored at home. Wanna go to lunch? Olivia's in the area so she's coming too.*

Ellie grinned. Distraction? Yes, please! Plus she could give Angel the present she'd ordered for her last week, which had come in yesterday.

Sure, where?

Murphy's Meals in half an hour?

The restaurant Maria was the day manager of... duh. She should have guessed; Murphy's was the go-to place for all of the girls in the group if Maria was working. Fortunately, it was also really good food and affordable.

Sounds good, see you there.

Strangely, having a new distraction in the form of going out to lunch actually helped her get some work done in the fifteen minutes before she had to leave, which meant she didn't feel so bad about going out to lunch. When she got to the restaurant, Angel was already sitting in a booth with Maria and Olivia, all of them chatting animatedly. As soon as Angel saw Ellie, she perked up and waved, making the other two turn.

Olivia was dressed in a red power suit that somehow managed to not clash with her red hair, which was pulled back into a neat bun. Next to her, Maria's messy bun of curly hair looked even messier, although just as cute; she was wearing a basic teal-blue, button-down shirt, the sleeves rolled up to her elbows. As always, the most casually dressed was Angel, whose purple t-shirt featured a white, maniacally laughing bunny running with a chainsaw in each hand and the words "My Spirit Animal" emblazoned above the bunny's gleeful countenance. Ellie's lips twitched. The t-shirt was definitely getting a little tight over Angel's bump, which was starting to become too big for her to wear her regular clothes.

Grinning, Ellie handed over the plastic bag she was carrying to Angel as she slid into the booth next to her.

"Hey guys."

"Hey Ellie! I'm so glad you could make it out!" Maria said, with a warm smile of welcome. Olivia smiled at her too, although she was more interested in the bag Angel was peering into.

"What's this?" Angel asked, pulling out the shirt.

"A pregnancy present," Ellie said, feeling her lips spread even wider as she waited for the revelation.

Angel pulled up the shirt so the back was facing Olivia and Maria, and cackled with gleeful amusement. "Oh my god, it's perfect!"

"What does it say?" Olivia asked, already sounding amused just from witnessing Angel's reaction. They all enjoyed Angel's continued torture of Adam, who was not always a fan of her t-shirts. He wasn't uptight exactly... except he kind of was.

Angel flipped it around so Olivia and Maria could see the Death Star on the stomach of the t-shirt, right where her pregnant belly was rapidly expanding and the words 'That's No Moon' floating in space above it. It was meant for a pregnant woman, so it was both large and stretchy, and the material was super soft for comfort. Maria snorted with laughter as Olivia cracked up.

"Thank you, Ellie!" Angel practically sang out as she put the shirt back in the bag and turned to hug her.

"You're welcome," said Ellie giggling. "I just saw it and thought of you." And now she was basking in the glow of how nice it was to have friends and to be able to give a simple gift in exchange for such a happy reaction.

"It's perfect," Angel said happily. "Adam might even face palm."

Maria shook her head. "You two have the weirdest relationship."

"Nah, she's perfect for him," Olivia said. She rolled her grey eyes expressively. "Adam needs regular shaking up and someone to make him smile."

"Smile. Sigh. Face palm." Angel stuck her tongue out at Maria. "Like you don't try to find ways to get under Rick's skin."

"Yeah, but he's not bothered by *t-shirts*."

"I bet I could find a t-shirt that would bother him. But in order to prove it, you have to wear it for his reaction, you can't just show it to him."

Maria opened her mouth to respond... and hesitated.

"I wouldn't accept that challenge if I were you," Ellie murmured, picking up her menu to hide her smile. Next to her, Angel was practically quivering in her seat, obviously hoping Maria would fall for the bait.

Sitting back in the booth, Maria crossed her arms over her chest. "So what's everyone eating?"

Slumping in disappointment, Angel elbowed Ellie, obviously blaming her for Maria's retreat. Ellie just giggled. When she looked up from the menu, Olivia was studying her from across the table, a contemplative expression on her face. Uncomfortable, Ellie looked back down at her menu, but when the server came over to take her drink order, Olivia was still looking at her with that piercing gaze. It wasn't judgmental, but it was just a little too focused for Ellie to be able to relax. Everyone ordered their food, and Ellie ordered a glass of wine at the same time.

She spread her fingers across the edge of the table nervously, concentrating on the smooth wood it was made out of. Angel and Maria started chattering, with Olivia's occasional interjections, but Ellie could still feel Olivia's focus on her. Which made her feel nervy. The Domme had the same kind of penetrating gaze Michael did, like she could see more than a normal person. Not exactly a comfortable feeling.

"... new club."

"New club?" Ellie asked, echoing Angel's last words.

"Yeah, apparently Michael and Patrick are going to be business buddies," Angel said, playing with her straw wrapper. "Patrick can't fit any more people into Stronghold, but new applications are still coming in, and there are some people who want to come and would be willing to pay big bucks for a more discreet location."

"So the new club is going to be more expensive?" Maria asked.

"Only for people who want membership exclusively there or to be able to visit as often as they want," Olivia said. Ellie dared to look up and was relieved to see Olivia's focus had shifted to Maria. "Regular Stronghold members will be able to visit there four nights a month with their Stronghold membership, and it'll be open Wednesday through Saturday every week so they'll have plenty of chances. Or they can pay more for more visitation days, etc. if they want to, or even apply for a full membership to the new club, but the regular membership dues to Stronghold aren't going to change."

"That's pretty cool," Maria said, resting her hand on her chin. "I bet it's going to get slammed when it first opens though. Everyone's going to want to check out the new place."

"The smart people will take advantage of Stronghold being emptier to get the reserved rooms they want," Angel said. "Lexie said it's getting harder and harder to manage the reservations... especially when people go over their time."

Olivia snorted. "Don't remind me. I had to kick Mitch and Caroline out of a room on Friday night because he was taking his sweet old time. Not the best way to end the scene, but my Baby Doms are going to have to learn to play by the rules."

Pressing her lips together, Ellie tried not to laugh. Only Olivia could manage to sound like a mom when talking about a group of very dominant, alpha men. Calling the newly trained Doms 'Baby Doms' made them sound like something they definitely weren't. Ellie had helped out as a subject for the classes, so she'd gotten to know them a little, and none of them were what she would call 'babies' in any way, shape, or form. Even if Mitch liked to try and bend the rules sometimes, he was all alpha male when he wanted to be.

"Speaking of Michael and room reservations, I heard he's got another room reserved for this weekend," Angel said wickedly, turning her head to Ellie. "Know anything about that?"

"Maybe," said Ellie, keeping her voice even and smiling at their server, who had arrived at the table with their food.

Pretending to gasp, Angel put her hand over her heart and leaned back as her chicken risotto was placed in front of her. "Oh my goodness... Ellie, are you teasing me?"

"Maybe." This time it was more of a struggle to keep her face straight.

Maria snorted laughter as Angel shook her head. "Michael's already been a terrible influence on you. Just horrible."

"Take that sass into the club and the Doms aren't going to know what hit them," Olivia said, sounding amused as she picked up her fork to dig into her salad. Ellie just shrugged, but a little smile played on her lips.

"If you tell me whether or not Michael's scening with you, I'll tell you what room he's reserved."

The offer had Ellie straightening up with interest and speaking without thinking. "You know what room?"

"Ah HA!" Angel pumped her fist. "I knew it! You're scening with Michael for a second week in a row!"

"So?" Ellie said, shrugging her shoulder like it wasn't a big deal as she picked up her chicken club sandwich.

"So? So?!" Angel shook her head, sharing disbelieving looks with Maria. She tried to catch Olivia's eye too, but Olivia was already focused back on staring at Ellie like she was trying to crawl inside her head. "You never scene with the same Dom two weeks in a row. Not even Andrew. And you never scene in a private room with a Dom other than Andrew. But now you're breaking both rules for Michael. That's big!"

"I'm pretty sure she knows it's big," Olivia said dryly. "However, the bigger a deal you make it, the more pressure it is on both of them."

"Oh... Right, sorry," Angel said a little sheepishly. "I just get excited. I love Michael, and I really like you, and he obviously *really* likes you and... well... I just want him to be happy..."

Alarmed, Ellie froze as Angel teared up. What the- what should she do?

"Pregnancy hormones alert!" Maria passed a tissue over to Angel, who took it.

"Thanks... ugh... I don't even know why I'm crying. I know I said I love Michael but I don't love him enough to cry over him. Oh my god, please don't tell Adam I cried about Michael. And definitely don't tell Michael I cried about Michael. I will never hear the end of it."

"I won't tell if you don't bring up my scening with Michael again," Ellie said quickly, making sure to make it clear she was teasing by her tone of voice.

They all stopped and stared at her, Maria's jaw dropping a little. Then Olivia held up her hand for a high-five.

"You tell her, Ell."

Grinning, Ellie slapped Olivia's hand. Okay, so maybe the Domme wasn't so scary. Well, actually, she really was, but she was pretty cool too. Happily, Ellie dug into her sandwich while the conversation turned back to Patrick and Michael's new business venture, which she was happy to hear all about. Part of her was a little sad she hadn't heard about it first from Michael, but... it's not like he even had her phone number. And they didn't hang out or anything. They just saw each other at the club.

Maybe she'd ask him about it this weekend. If they had time before their scene.

$$\mathfrak{F} \quad 5 \quad \mathfrak{F}$$

Walking into Stronghold, thinking about how they were going to do the new club differently, made Michael look at the whole place with new eyes. He tried to ignore that though, because he wasn't there to think about the new club (they really needed to think of a name), he was there to scene with Ellie.

Focus.

He didn't want to mess things up with Ellie just because he now had a new thing going on with his work life. Plus, it wasn't like the new club was going to be ready to be open for a couple of months. Even though their offer on the building had been accepted (thanks, in large part, to the substantial down payment Michael had been able to provide), there were a lot of renovations needed - and some of them needed to be done discreetly. Fortunately, Andrew had already offered to help on those, and the rest of their friends would probably step up to help too. Obviously, if the club was going to be discreet, they didn't want an entire group of contractors to know what it was being used for. However, they'd be able to take care of setting up the entire restaurant and doing some of the basic work on the private rooms before Andrew and the rest of them came through and added all the kinkier elements.

But, as excited as he was about this new business venture (especially after putting in his two-week notice to his less than stimulating day job), he didn't want to let it distract him from Ellie. She deserved his full attention. Not only that, but he probably wasn't going to get what he wanted from her unless he gave her his full attention. She had a lot of practice at holding herself back and keeping herself apart from the Dom she was scening with.

Angel waved at him from where she was standing next to Adam at a table in the bar area. Adam had her tucked under his arm, and Michael grinned when he moved towards them as Ellie's shorter head came into view around Jared's shoulder. Sharon was the shortest of their group of friends, but Ellie and Lexie were close behind in the petite stakes, even when wearing heels. Seeing him, Ellie smiled nervously but with a light of anticipation in her eyes, which just made him grin even more broadly. Leigh and Jake were also at the table chatting together, and Ellie looked relaxed, surrounded by people she was comfortable with.

"Hello, pest," he said, ruffling Angel's curls as he slid in next to Ellie. From the other side of her, Adam narrowed his eyes at Michael in warning.

Of course Adam didn't really think there was anything going on between Michael and Angel, it was just in his nature to be possessive, and it was just in Michael's nature to want to rile him.

"Hello, beautiful," he said, turning his attention to Ellie, who flushed a very bright red and stared at her drink.

"Hi," she said, her voice wavering a little although she struggled to keep it normal. The way grins were popping up around the table, it was probably a good thing she was focusing on her drink and not on their friends.

"Hello, everyone else," he said grinning at Ellie's reaction.

He wasn't just calling her beautiful to compliment her though, she really did look lovely, wearing a black leather halter-top that dipped low in front before being tied together with laces. Her entire upper back was left exposed, creamy skin just begging for a whip or flogger. The black leather mini-skirt hugged her ass, curling around her curves invitingly and barely covering them. The strappy shoes on her feet looked more like torture devices than footwear, but they also made her legs look incredible.

Michael wanted to touch her, the way Adam had his arm around Angel's waist as she leaned against him, or the way Jared had Leigh tucked between his legs, but he didn't want to scare her off either. Slow and steady. Instead, he just stood close enough to her so he could feel her body heat, so she couldn't move without brushing against him; invading her personal space but not actually claiming her the way he wanted to.

Across the table, Jared lifted his beer glass to his lips to hide his slow grin as he watched. Leigh was more interested in Ellie, coming to Ellie's rescue when it appeared she was continuing to pretend unnatural interest in the bubbles of her soda.

"So uh," Leigh cleared her throat. "I heard about this thing on the radio today, which I can't believe I'd almost forgotten about, that I think we definitely need to revisit. Push presents."

"Push presents?" Ellie asked, obviously jumping on the new topic to distract from her reaction to Michael's arrival. The color in her cheeks was still high, but fading a little. "What on earth is that?"

Leigh's eyes slid over to where Adam and Angel were canoodling, smirking slightly. She brushed her long, brown hair back from one shoulder, and shooting Jared a smile when he began running his hand through the long strands. "Apparently, it's a fad for having a baby; like a thank you from the father to the mother for carrying his progeny for nine months..." She looked meaningfully at Angel.

"And then pushing it out of her!" Angel said, finishing the sentence as she cracked up. She looked up at Adam, almost gleefully. "I can't believe I forgot to tell you about this. But now you know, after I give birth to your baby, I expect a 'push present.'"

"It should probably come in a Tiffany's box," Michael added helpfully, earning another glare before Adam's narrow-eyed focus returned to his fiancé. Next to Michael, Ellie giggled, covering her mouth with her hand. Jared, Leigh, and Jake were a lot less discreet about their own amusement.

"I don't know how we would fit me-not-leaving-you into a Tiffany's box," Adam said dryly.

Angel's mouth dropped open as everyone else burst into laughter at Adam's unexpected response and her reaction. Jake looked like he was choking on his drink, laughing so hard he finally gave up and just put his head down on the table.

"You're expected to not leave me!"

Raising his left hand, Adam wriggled his fingers at her, his expression completely serious but his blue eyes were dancing. "No ring, no guarantees."

Leigh was holding onto Jared for support she was laughing so hard. Michael would be laughing a lot harder, but he was distracted by Ellie leaning into him as she giggled incessantly, trying to hide her face against his arm. To put his arm around her, or not to put his arm around her... that was the question...

Fuming, Angel raised her own hand, where her diamond engagement ring glittered, her chin jerking up with a challenge. "You already put a ring on it, you're stuck with me."

"If you liked it, *you* should have put a ring on it," Adam said, as seriously as he could while reciting Beyoncé lyrics.

Their dynamic always entertained Michael. Adam was good for Angel in so many ways; not in the least that he could sometimes actually get the better of her when it came to teasing. Most of the time, he either ignored her attempts at riling him or spanked her for them, but sometimes he gave as good as he got, and watching Angel flounder when it happened was phenomenally enjoyable.

"Oh no, Mommy and Daddy are fighting," Leigh managed to choke out between spurts of laughter. "Oh dear, what have I done?"

"Mommy and Daddy are engaged in foreplay," Michael responded, draping his arm around Ellie's shoulders with a casualness he didn't feel. To his relief, she didn't pull away; instead, she leaned into him, and his spirits lifted even higher, although he didn't dare show any outward reaction. "They'll probably thank you later."

Angel's head whipped around so she could glare at him. "You annoy me."

Solemnly, Michael looked over her head at Adam. "She's switching targets; that means you won the argument."

The feisty little noise Angel made sounded an awful lot like a growl. Pulling her back against him, Adam gave her ass a little swat as he started whispering in her ear. Probably something dirty and distracting, going by the changing expression on her face.

⚜

Leaning against Michael, tucked under his arm as he teased Angel and Adam alternatively, felt weird but nice. Weird because she'd never allowed this kind of intimacy from another Dom - actually from another man in a really long time - and nice because... well, because his arm felt strong, and secure, and protective. She especially appreciated the last feeling because she was getting a few dirty looks from the Lounge area where the unattached submissives were gathered.

It didn't take a genius to figure out why they were so pouty - Michael was hot, sweet, and excellent with a whip. A lot of the subbies had crushes on him. A lot of them had had crushes on Andrew too and had somewhat resented she'd been his only regular play partner. That resentment had been ameliorated when nothing more than play came from it, especially after Kate showed up, but now that she was playing with Michael for a second weekend in a row, she wasn't entirely surprised some of the other submissives were a little disgruntled.

There were others who were cheering for her though. Tori gave her a thumbs up and a wink. They weren't friends outside the club, but they hung out sometimes at Stronghold, and Tori had always been urging Ellie to do more than just play with the Doms. A few of the other submissives smiled encouragingly at her. So it wasn't all jealousy and resentment, but she still liked having Michael's arm around her.

Warm.

Secure.

The last time she'd felt like this...

Ellie stiffened as her breath caught in her throat. Choked her.

Fear and adrenaline surged as her heart jumped, pounding, white noise roaring in her ears as spiders crawled across her skin. Phantom fingers slid through her hair, gripped, and she jerked.

Jerked away.

"Ellie!"

"Step back, let her breathe!"

"Ellie? Honey, are you okay? Ellie?"

"I'm okay," she said, gasping slightly, blinking rapidly as her sight started to clear.

Notice what's around you, Ellie. Dr. Amy's voice in Ellie's head was calm, grounding, beginning the familiar routine she'd made for herself to help with her anxiety and panic attacks. *What do you hear? What do you see? Where are you? Focus on what's actually happening.*

Music was playing.

She was sitting on a barstool, two arms around her back holding her stable, one coming from either side. The hard body of a man on her left, the soft press of female curves on her right. She leaned right, towards safety and the smell of vanilla.

On her left, a hand wrapped around hers, fingers sliding into hers, and Ellie immediately relaxed.

Safe. I'm safe.

She took in a deep, shuddering breath as the awful band around her chest dissipated, her fingers gripping the hand holding hers hard. It took her a moment to realize the person whose hand she had in a death grip was Michael's, while she leaned on Leigh. Across the table, Angel looked like she was about to jump out of Adam's arms to get to her.

Jake reappeared beside Adam, a short glass with amber liquid in his hand. He put it on the table in front of her. "Here, have a bit of a drink, you're pale as a sheet."

"Thanks," Ellie said, her voice sounding slightly cracked. She blinked back sudden tears as humiliation swamped her.

She hadn't felt like that in years.

Years.

Then Michael put his arm around her and...

And everything went to hell because her head was all fucked up.

Because she was embarrassingly, horribly damaged. Yeah, this was why she avoided doing the whole 'more than playing' thing. All her new friends staring at her with concern, all of them thinking the same thing - 'What's wrong with her?'

Ellie drank the entire shot of whiskey in one gulp. At least, she assumed it was either whiskey or bourbon by the tiny bit of flavor she managed to taste. The burn went all the way down her throat, spreading some warmth through her chest. Her fingers tingled. Unfortunately, it didn't do anything about all the people still staring at her.

Her shoulders hunched forward, as if to ward them off.

"Master Michael? Master Michael, your room is ready." Ellie recognized Glory's voice, coming from behind her. Glory was one of the submissives who paid a discounted membership rate to Stronghold in exchange for shifts taking care of the private rooms, helping out Doms after scenes, and cleaning equipment in the Dungeon.

"We're not going to need it tonight-" Michael started to say, and Ellie immediately interrupted.

"No! I mean, yes, we still want the room." She spun in her seat, towards Michael, still holding his hand, so she could see Glory. The blonde submissive looked confused. Looking up at Michael, she could see the concern and hesitation in his face. "Please? It will help, I swear it will."

Not only would it give her some privacy, but she'd found a play session really could help her regain her lost equilibrium. The pain helped focus her mind on the present rather than the past, and she always felt cleaner afterwards. Calmer. More in control. Sex was easy, especially in Stronghold where she had the final say in everything. She needed that.

If he didn't play with her tonight, she'd have to go find someone else. Her little... episode... had left her shaken and anxious, and if she didn't find some way to burn off some energy, she'd have nothing but nightmares tonight and possibly for days to come. It wasn't just about wanting to do a scene now, she *needed* it. And she'd much prefer it be with him, because even now, he made her feel safe.

Even though being held by him had triggered some kind of sensory memory and her episode.

Well, she'd never claimed her head made any sense.

Studying her face, she could tell he was hesitant, and she squeezed his hand. "*Please*, Michael."

Slowly he nodded. "Alright." Looking up, he glanced around the table. "We'll see you guys in a bit."

Ellie barely glanced at the others, hating the conflicted, concerned expressions on their faces. Hating being the center of attention.

As she started to slide off the bar stool, Leigh's arm tightened around her for just a moment.

"If you need *anything*, we're here," Leigh whispered, before releasing her.

Warmth flooded Ellie, chasing away some of the humiliation. Leigh didn't sound judgmental or disapproving, just fiercely protective. She accepted Ellie knew what she was doing, but wanted to make sure Ellie knew Leigh was there for her if she needed. Even though Leigh had known Michael for longer than she'd known Ellie, she was ready to come to Ellie's defense if needed.

Suddenly, it wasn't so hard to look at everyone anymore as she realized she didn't need to be embarrassed. Not about her episode, and not about her need for a scene after it.

Concern is not necessarily a bad thing. It doesn't mean they're thinking you're crazy.

Thanks, Dr. Amy.

Forcing a smile onto her face didn't take as much effort as she thought it would, and she managed to look at everyone around the table before turning away, her hand still in Michael's. There was concern on his face too, but he wasn't looking at her like he thought there was something wrong with her, just like he was worried about her.

There is a difference. Keep remembering that.

This was not a group of people who liked to cast stones. They didn't judge. They didn't think they knew better than her. They were just there... just in case.

They were pretty awesome.

Ellie could have really used them earlier in her life.

HOLDING ELLIE'S HAND IN HIS, MICHAEL WAS MORE RELIEVED THAN ever that the Interrogation Room - the room he'd originally wanted to reserve - had already been completely booked tonight. While she seemed eager for a scene, after seeing her go completely pale, blank, and unresponsive - and not knowing why - he wasn't up to pushing her as much as he'd originally planned.

"Are you sure you're okay?" he asked, giving her hand a small squeeze as they headed down the stairs.

The smile she gave him was a little manic and didn't quite reach her eyes. "Yep. I'm fine."

He reviewed all the ideas he'd had for tonight's scene in his head, rapidly revising his plans as they descended into the Dungeon.

Since the Interrogation Room hadn't been available, Michael had reserved the Doctor's Office instead. He could definitely work with that. In fact, the medical surroundings might even offer up some fun the other room wouldn't have. It wasn't his usual, but...

As he led Ellie to the open room, he caught the jealous glances of several Doms who saw them and couldn't help but smirk a little. Yeah, two weekends in a row with Ellie, something none of them had managed before. It was also a good reminder not to fuck this up, since he was already getting a chance no one else had.

Glancing up at him, the smile on Ellie's lips looked a little more real now.

"So we're going to play doctor, huh?"

"We can if you'd like to," he said, smiling back at her, trying to inject as much warmth into his smile as he could so she wouldn't see his concern and anxiety about doing a scene with her right after she'd had what looked like some kind of PTSD episode or something. The desperation in her voice when she'd begged for the scene had been the only thing which had convinced him to give in to her, and his acceptance had immediately calmed her, so it was probably the right thing to do... but he still felt pretty unsettled about it. "I'm not really into improv, so I'm not always great at role play past the first few lines."

Ellie's smile widened. "You didn't do so badly last week."

"Thank you," he said, a bit dryly. "Now be a good patient and take off all your clothes."

She started laughing, chasing the rest of her tension from her expression and body, and Michael was finally able to relax a little too. Closing the door behind them, he turned to see Ellie pulling off her halter top, letting her breasts gently bounce as they were freed from the confining fabric. Crossing his arms over his chest, Michael leaned his hip against the counter, enjoying the show.

"I'm pretty sure doctors are supposed to leave the room while their patients undress," Ellie teased.

"I knew there was a reason the medical profession had no appeal for me."

Giggling, Ellie turned her back to him and wiggled her hips as she started peeling off her mini-skirt. She peeked over her shoulder at him, mischievously. "So, theater must be nice, with all the costume changes."

"The quick changes on the side of the stage are the best," he said, enjoying the way she carefully stepped out of her skirt, not even wobbling in her high heels. She seemed completely past whatever had happened upstairs. He still felt discomfited, but he didn't want her to know that. "Whoever's around gets to lend a helping hand the first dress rehearsal, and then that's their job for the rest of the show. Although, just standing back and watching can be quite nice."

She preened under his attention as his eyes traveled over her naked body while she bent over to unstrap her heels, turning to the side so he could see her hanging breasts and the curve of her form. Damn she was gorgeous.

Michael wanted to step forward and pull her into his arms... but he kept holding back. He didn't want a repeat of upstairs. Which was also why he was hesitating on really getting the scene going.

"Ellie..."

She straightened up, wariness in her expression as she heard the change in his voice. "Yes?"

"Are you sure you're up for scening?" When her expression turned mutinous, he held up a placating hand. "I've never had anyone safe word in a scene with me, and I'm quite proud of that. I'm asking because I didn't mean to do anything to upset you upstairs, and yet I managed to anyway. I'd like to avoid upsetting you down here."

Hugging her clothes to her front, it was obvious she felt vulnerable. Her eyes flicked to the door, but to get to the door, she'd have to pass him. Michael didn't want her to feel trapped, and he certainly wouldn't block her, but he didn't regret positioning himself to make it harder for her to run either. Ellie took a deep breath and let it out, like she was steeling herself against something.

"If you stick to my hard limits, I should be fine," she said. "I need this. I really do... it... I feel back in control when I'm doing a scene. I *know* that if I say 'red,' you'll stop. I need that right now. I need to lose myself in a scene and know I can trust you."

He moved forward, quickly, to cup her face in his hands. "You can always trust me," he said softly. "If you need even a breather tonight, just say 'yellow,' and I'll pause and we can talk."

Something flickered across her expression. Yeah, she didn't like to talk. Too bad. They were going to have to eventually. But he wasn't going to push her tonight. He wasn't going to try to dig deeper into her psyche when it had already taken a hit tonight. The confession of what she needed was enough for now.

He was going to give her what she needed, pleasure her, and show her she could trust him.

Taking her clothes from her, Michael stepped back. "Alright then. Up on the table, Ellie."

❧ 6 ❧

Heart pounding in her chest with relief and excitement, Ellie hopped up onto the doctor's table while Michael put her clothing on the counter. There was something hot about being completely naked while he was completely clothed. Sure, she felt vulnerable, but in a good way. Sexually vulnerable, physically vulnerable... not emotionally.

Emotionally, she was still a little off-kilter, but she was already feeling better. Leigh's words had helped a lot, Michael's understanding and his lack of pushing for more answers had helped even more. Plus, she was going to get her scene. Just the anticipation helped make her feel more centered, more calm.

"Lay back, hands above your head," he said, his voice deepening, making her shiver as she raised her arms above her head, spreading her legs for balance as she lay back.

Michael moved around her, his gaze sliding over her naked body with appreciation as her nipples hardened. She could see he was still a little concerned, but at least he wasn't stopping.

At least he wasn't questioning.

That would be a serious mood killer.

Wrists went into leather straps, feet went into stirrups, and then leather straps secured her ankles. Michael ran his fingers up the inside of her leg, making her squirm a little as his fingertips brushed over her sensitive skin. She also felt a trickle of dread as he neared her pussy, but she trusted he remembered her hard limits.

No touching the top of her mound.

For just a moment, she felt dragging fingers pulling on hair that no longer existed, and she shuddered as her skin crawled, fear welling in her chest. Michael stilled immediately, his fingertips soft against her inner thigh.

"What is it?"

Dammit.

"Just..." She hesitated, wetting her suddenly dry lips with her tongue. "You're getting close to my mound."

His eyes softened. "I remember your limits, sweetheart, it's okay."

"I know that... it was just a physical reaction."

Tilting his head to the side, Michael studied her, and Ellie flushed, suddenly feeling vulnerable in a not very good way. She was on the verge of saying yellow when he spoke again.

"Would a lighter or firmer touch make you more comfortable?"

"Firmer," she said immediately, her words almost a plea. Anything but dragging fingers. It was too close to feeling like her skin was crawling.

Watching her closely, Michael immediately dug his fingers into her thigh, massaging the muscle, and Ellie closed her eyes as her body relaxed.

"What color are you, Ellie?"

"Green," she said, with a little sigh. She'd prefer not to spend their entire scene saying colors, but she understood why he needed a little reassurance right now, and she was happy to give it to him, especially if he kept massaging her legs. Slowly, his hands moved higher, bringing them closer together, but that didn't bother her at all.

The firm, stroking motions of his fingers felt good, even as he neared her mound, and she didn't have a single moment of dread or even trepidation, not a single flicker of memory. Just pleasure. She sighed happily. This was good.

His hands curved over her hips, sliding up her body to her breasts, and Ellie arched a little. Part of her was almost sad he hadn't continued the firm kneading onto her mound... she thought it actually might not have bothered her as long as he'd continued the motions he'd been using, which were nothing like scrabbling fingers. As he cupped her breasts, kneading the soft flesh, the bad memories slid even further away, and Ellie relaxed further, moaning a little as his fingers plucked at her nipples.

"I know blindfolds are on your soft limits, but how would you feel about wearing one this evening?" Michael asked, his voice deep and almost hypnotic as he continued to massage her breasts, which were starting to feel swollen and achy. "I'd like to indulge in some sensory play with you."

Curiosity rose. Ellie hadn't ever really been interested in sensory play. Impact play was what she was used to and what she enjoyed, but... well, it was Michael.

"Will you still whip me a little?" she asked, her voice almost wistful as she opened her eyes to look at him.

Chuckling, Michael pinched her nipples and made her squirm. "If you're a good girl."

This time her wiggle was deliberate and provocative, lifting her chest further into his hands.

"I can be a good girl."

"Okay then, good girl, I'll get the blindfold."

Not being able to see didn't bring up any bad memories, she just didn't usually like feeling quite so vulnerable. She liked being able to see what was coming. But, with Michael, she felt vulnerable in a good way. It was a little scary, but the kind of scary that made her heart beat just a little faster, her nipples pucker, and her breathing become more shallow in anticipation.

The blindfold was a good one, it shut out all of the light even under her eyes, leaving her completely blind.

Soft lips pressed gently against hers. "Thank you for trusting me."

She blushed. "Not like I haven't been blindfolded with you before."

"I thought we were pretending you didn't know it was me," he teased, and then his hands closed around her breasts, warm and firm, but somehow rubbery, as he kneaded her soft flesh, avoiding her nipples. It took her a moment to realize the rubbery texture of his hands was because he was wearing plastic gloves. To give the medical thing more realism?

Ellie moaned. His palms felt warm - warmer than before or was the blindfold tricking her into thinking her senses were already heightened?

"I smell cinnamon," she said in surprise, as the spicy scent wafted around her.

"Cinnamon warming oil," Michael said, amusement tingeing his voice. "You should be feeling it too."

Oh... that's why his palms felt so warm. And why her breasts felt so warm. And like they were getting warmer. Ellie squirmed. It didn't feel bad, and it didn't hurt exactly, but it wasn't one hundred percent comfortable.

Michael's hands moved away but the warmth stayed, tingling and hot on her flesh, her nipples aching from lack of stimulation even as her breasts throbbed from it. She'd never really been interested in oils before, never thought it could do much for her, but the cinnamon stung her nose and was starting to feel like little pinpricks stinging her breasts. It was a more subtle sensation than impact play, but it wasn't bad.

In fact, it was really good.

Fingers closed over her nipples, rubbing. *Just* her nipples. Deliberately not touching the rest of her swollen breasts.

"Now this is mint."

She gasped, arching, as the oil was rubbed into her skin.

Mint was *cold*.

It felt like he was rubbing her nipples with ice cubes, almost. She hissed out a breath, her body writhing, but because he was using oils and not ice, there was no way to get away from the cold. The contrast between the cinnamon and mint, the heat and the cold, had her panting for breath as her pussy throbbed.

The pain wasn't hard or deep like she was used to, but it was maddening, like an itch she couldn't scratch... and the sensations didn't go away, there was no rest period between lashes, she just burned - hot and cold - and there was no escape. Ellie hadn't realized just how effective the oils could be. She'd been missing out.

When his fingers moved away, her nipples still burned cold, and his finger trailed down the center of her stomach, leaving a trail of tingling coolness.

"Which do you think I should use on your pretty pussy?"

Ellie whimpered again as the portion of her anatomy in question spasmed. His finger moved away from her body when he reached her belly button, and she heard the sound of at least one of his gloves being replaced.

Did she want her pussy to burn hot or cold? Not that he was really asking her. His question had been completely rhetorical, meant to mess with her mind, because now she knew where his next target was, but she didn't know which oil he'd use. Anticipating the delicious burn, her pussy was already fluttering, her mind torn as to which she wanted, or if she wanted neither – but she wasn't anywhere near safe wording.

"Which do you think I should use on your ass?"

Fingers pressed against her anus, and Ellie squealed in surprise as her tight hole stretched to admit them. Her muscles burned as his fingers slid into the narrow orifice.

"Neither?" she said, phrasing it like a hopeful question.

Michael chuckled, thrusting his fingers in and out, fucking her with them. "Too late."

It must be the cinnamon, because she didn't feel the immediate coolness like she had with the mint. As her anus continued to burn, getting warmer with every thrust of his fingers, she knew she was right. Panting, she squirmed, unable to stop herself from trying to writhe away from the oils tormenting her sensitive parts.

Two cool fingers slid into her pussy, and she moaned, arching upwards as the mint oil covered digits spread their offering over her sensitive tissues. Now she was burning inside and out, fire and ice, her holes spasming around his fingers as her body writhed for him.

It hurt so good.

When he slid his fingers out of her, she cried out in disappointment and also in renewed discomfort. The friction of his thrusting fingers had actually helped relieve some of the itching burn; now she had nothing to focus on but the fiery torment of the oils.

"Please," she begged, her body quivering, her pussy shuddering. "I need more..."

"More?" Something in his tone made her try to cringe back against her restraints, she heard the sound of him switching gloves again. "Well, since you asked so nicely. This is pepper oil."

His fingers pressed against her clit and rubbed. Ellie howled, more out of fear than actual pain, although a moment later she was crying out in in pain too.

It *burned*.

Far hotter than the cinnamon. And his fingers were rubbing the oil relentlessly into her most sensitive bundle of nerves. Needles of red-hot agony pierced her, followed immediately by inexpressible ecstasy as an orgasm suddenly blew through her.

Ellie screamed, her tears soaking into the blindfold as the exquisite mix of pain and pleasure wracked her.

<hr />

WATCHING ELLIE WRITHE IN ORGASM, HER BODY BOWING AND thrashing, Michael pressed his free hand - his ungloved hand - against the front of his leathers, against his cock which was throbbing painfully. Fuck she was gorgeous. He rubbed her clit with his other hand, using firm circular motions to both rub in the tiny drop of pepper oil and to stimulate the sensitive bud.

The sensations of the oil would fade, although he'd use some olive oil at the end of the scene on her clit to soothe the effects of the hot pepper oil.

For now, he'd give her the whipping she'd requested.

Her pussy was soaked with juices, her clit hard and swollen, peeking out from between her puffy lips, and he could tell from the expressions on her face as he'd used the different oils that she hadn't been expecting the effects to be so intense. Thankfully, Patrick kept the medical room fully stocked for the people who wanted to play. If Ellie wanted to play with chemicals again, there would be other options - even pervertibles at home like Tabasco sauce, toothpaste, and Icy Hot.

Pulling off his gloves, Michael tossed them in the trash can, enjoying watching Ellie pant and squirm as the oils worked on her without any need for further stimulation by him. She'd be burning, hot and cold, all over on her most sensitive parts, although the effects on her breasts were probably starting to fade a bit.

So he'd start there.

The leather strap he chose was like an old-fashioned Victorian tawse; about a foot and a half long including the handle, and it could be used for a thuddy or stinging sensation depending on how he wielded it. Standing to the side, he wasn't going for anything too heavy, but the impact play would add to the hot warmth of the oil, and would particularly sting her budded nipples.

"What color are you, Ellie?"

"Green," she said breathlessly, immediately, a bit of a plea in her voice.

Such a beautiful masochist.

WHAP!

She screamed as he brought down the leather strap across the top of her breasts, the blow surprising and paining her. Panting, she jerked at her restraints. Michael only gave her a moment, admiring how the tops of her breasts went from creamy to bright pink, before laying down a second stripe.

WHAP!

This time, he practically skimmed the leather along her stomach, landing it against the undersides of her breasts and making the large mounds shake and bobble.

Ellie sucked in a breath before crying out again, less noisy this time as she'd expected him to continue to torment her breasts.

WHAP!

The leather landed flat atop her nipples, biting down into the flesh of her breasts, and she screamed, arching upwards as the pain shuddered through her. Michael's cock throbbed.

He wanted nothing more than to don a condom and shove himself into her creamy pussy, hands on her breasts, tormenting her even more as he pounded between her legs. The sensation of his body against her swollen, burning clit would only compound the pleasure for her.

Instead, he focused on whipping her breasts, ignoring his cock, as he turned her skin from cream, to pink, to an angry, bright red. It didn't take long, using the wide leather strap, even if he wasn't beating her full force, but the effort left both of them panting and horny. When he moved back down where Ellie's legs were spread, he could see a small puddle of wet juices on the table beneath her, her labia were dark pink and slick with her cream, and her clit was bright red and completely erect.

She was temptation incarnate.

"Please, Master Michael, please, fuck me," she started to beg, as if sensing his desire, his wavering resolve. Only the fact she'd called him Master Michael, rather than Michael, allowed him to keep his head.

Michael had noticed Ellie used calling all of the Doms by the honorific and their name as a tactic to distance herself from them. His name or Master was too intimate for her, apparently. Which sucked, but also helped him hold onto his self-control.

"Not tonight, Ellie."

The chains on her wrist cuffs rattled as she jerked them angrily. "Dammit, it's fine, just fuck me!"

Her sudden ascent into anger proved everything was definitely not fine. Whatever had happened before they came down here, it was still affecting her, and their first time was not going to happen when she wasn't totally into the scene.

So Michael slapped his hand against her pussy, spanking the puffy lips. The wet sound cut off her angry begging, her honey clinging to his fingers when he pulled them away.

SMACK!

He slapped her pussy again, but this time, instead of pulling his fingers away, he kept them pressed against her wet flesh and rubbed. Ellie moaned as he did so. It was doubtful she was feeling much stimulation from the oils now, although she'd still be sensitive,

"Who is in charge, Ellie?" he asked softly, his voice laced with steel.

"You are," she said, with a breathy little sigh of disappointment. A sad subbie who'd already realized she wasn't going to get laid. Michael's lips twitched in amusement.

"Good girl," he said, and slapped her pussy again as a reward.

Ellie arched against his hand, moaning, and she cried out as he pushed his fingers into her tight hole. Her hips moved, working up and down, her body undulating, and Michael grinned as he realized she was putting on a little bit of a show for his benefit.

Trying to tempt him.

Naughty subbie. But adorable.

Pumping his fingers in and out of her pussy with his right hand, trying to ignore his aching cock as her wet muscles shuddered around his fingers, he reached up with his left to play with her breasts. Now, her writhing became more real as he reignited the torment from her whipping, his fingers roughly handling her soft flesh, kneading and squeezing.

His own breathing became ragged as he fucked her with his fingers, watching her move, memorizing her reactions, all the better to jerk off to his memories later.

"Oh fuck... Michael... oh... oh fuck... Fuck... Michael!" She screamed his name as she came again, and he nearly came in his pants as her pussy squeezed his fingers, the muscles spasming as she climaxed.

Thrusting hard and fast, he pinched her nipples, tugging the sensitive buds, watching her writhe as agony and ecstasy collided. Sadistically, he ground the heel of his palm against her clit, tormenting the already tortured nubbin even as he drew out her pleasure.

He wrung every last bit of pleasure he could get from her before he finally slid his fingers from her sopping, quivering body. It was the best kind of satisfaction he could get from this scene.

FEELING COMPLETELY BONELESS, ELLIE LAY LIMPLY AS MICHAEL cleaned around her, her mind foggy and slow. She couldn't say how long it took him, but one minute he was sliding his fingers from her, praising and stroking her, then she was all hazy, and he was picking her up and carrying her out to the aftercare corner of the Dungeon. She knew he'd taken care of the room and her clothes and everything, but she didn't really remember him doing it because she was so out of it. Nuzzling her face into the crook of his neck, she inhaled deeply as he wrapped a blanket around her and settled her onto his lap.

He smelled good.

Even though she was muzzy, she knew this kind of reaction wasn't like her. She normally didn't let down her guard enough to be so complacent... but she'd known Michael would want to do aftercare, and so she'd just kind of let herself go when the scene was over.

Let herself float.

Let herself just enjoy.

It felt nice.

Although, the hard cock digging into the soft flesh of her ass reminded her of a bone she had to pick with him.

"Why wouldn't you fuck me?" she asked, lolling her head back on his shoulder.

The question came out more curious than anything, with just a hint of pout.

Stroking her hair, his fingers gently running through any knots, Michael thought over her question for a moment. She really did like him playing with her hair. It felt so good, in a completely vanilla way. Maybe she should have been more specific about her hard limits years ago. Or maybe it was just okay because it was Michael.

"I'm not ready to yet," he said finally. Which really wasn't an answer at all. Ellie narrowed her eyes at him.

"Why not?"

"Because if I have sex with you, I don't think I'm going to want to let you go afterwards, and I don't think *you're* ready for that." He added a rueful smile to his statement, to take some of the seriousness out of it, but Ellie's eyes still went wide and her jaw snapped shut.

Cuz, okay, maybe she wasn't ready. Her little freakout just from having his arm around her had proven she wasn't.

But... but she wanted to be ready. At least, she wanted to try. She'd never wanted to try before, but Michael made her want to try.

The way he was with her made her want to try. Not just when they were in a scene, but outside of the scenes too. She'd pushed him away for a really long time, maybe it was time for her to put herself out there a little. Push past her comfort zone a little more. Even more than just scheduling a new scene with each other every time they saw each other.

"Maybe we could have a club relationship," she heard herself saying. And then she froze, her heart pounding, not sure if she wanted him to take her up on it or not.

His expression was thoughtful, but otherwise blank as he studied her expression. Probably seeing all sorts of things she didn't want him to. Reading all sorts of things into her reaction she'd rather remain hidden. Summoning up some bravado, Ellie forced herself to relax, pretending she was totally at ease with what she'd just suggested.

Pretending she was totally fine with the idea of something she'd avoided ever since joining Stronghold.

She could do this.

A club relationship wasn't a real relationship, after all. It was strictly confined to the club. There would be set boundaries, an agreed upon contract, and all it really meant was she was going to keep playing with him and only him, and he would keep playing with her and only her. She could handle that. Sure, the level of commitment was unheard of for her, but this was Michael.

This was a step. A small one. Really a tiny one, she told herself, concentrating on taking deep, even breaths, because there was no reason to panic.

"I don't want you to make this decision while you're still high off the scene," he said eventually, his voice soft. "If you still want to sign a club contract with me in a few days, I would be happy to negotiate terms with you."

"In a few days?"

"Yes," he said, a slow smile spreading across his face, like a challenge - and also like he was enjoying her discomfort. Sadist, right? "You'll give me your phone number and I'll call you to talk about it. I'll need it anyway if we decide to sign a contract."

Right. Phone number. Ellie could do that.

She nodded, closing her eyes and leaning her head back against his shoulder so she didn't have to look at him. Instead, she concentrated on the pleasant aching between her thighs, the way her breasts, pussy, and anus still tingled, the slight throbbing of her breasts from their strapping, and the warmth of Michael's arms around her in a protective hold. A club contract would mean doing this regularly.

Yeah. She could definitely do that.

7

What had she been thinking? She couldn't do this. Ellie paced around her coffee table, whatever confidence she'd had before being shaken by her doubts. Although the television was on, she hadn't been able to pay attention to anything she put on.

It was now Wednesday, Michael was calling in an hour, and Ellie was falling apart. Ever since their scene, she'd been flip-flopping back and forth on whether or not she could be in any kind of relationship, even one with contracted boundaries and which only existed in a club. Especially with someone who was going to push her, not just physically, but emotionally.

They'd been talking over text every day since she gave him her number. Not long conversations or anything, but just... checking in. Seeing how she felt the day after the scene, asking if she had any bad after effects from the oils. Texts just saying hi. She'd sent him several pictures of Watson being particularly cute, and instead of being put off by cat photos, Michael had encouraged her to send more. He'd sent her photos of the space where the new club would be going. Told her about his impatience with working through the last two weeks at his

89

current job when all he could think about was what he wanted to be doing with the club.

It felt remarkably like high school again, but with higher stakes. In high school she'd never hoped her crush would be reciprocated. Now, the tables seemed to have turned.

Ellie wasn't dumb. She knew he liked her. She just wasn't sure how much of her issues he'd be willing to tolerate.

Hope warred with fear, optimism with anxiety, and she vacillated back and forth on an hourly basis whether or not it was really worth risking getting involved with him, even in this minor way. Not because she thought she would be satisfied with a club relationship, but because she thought she wouldn't. She was pretty sure she was going to want more.

But she was really scared to want more.

Her phone buzzed, making her jump. Text message. She glanced at the clock. Shouldn't be Michael. Unless he was texting to say he wasn't going to be able to call.

Ceasing her pacing, she picked up her phone from the coffee table. Text from Angel.

Can you come help out with the class tonight? I need someone to walk around and help critique. Baby is giving me issues.

Wednesday nights at Stronghold, Angel held self-defense classes for the submissives, something which Ellie had already participated in. This wasn't the first time Angel had needed an extra hand, although last time it had been because her morning sickness hadn't exactly been confined to the morning.

Yeah, definitely. I'll be there at 7.

Class wasn't till 7:30 pm, but Angel was always there half an hour beforehand, so Ellie would be too. Plus it would mean some girl time tonight. Which would be good. Whether she said yes or no to Michael, she would definitely not mind some girl talk.

Although... would Angel be mad if she knew Ellie said no?

Ellie didn't even know if Michael had told anyone she'd been the one to bring up having a club relationship. Maybe no one knew. Maybe if she said no when he called, no one would have to know.

Except she kind of wanted to talk about it with someone.

"Meow."

Watson's warm, furry body wound around her ankles.

"I didn't mean you," she muttered, bending down to pick him up. Silly animal. "Talking to you isn't super helpful."

Purring, he rubbed his cheek against hers, his paws kneading the collar of her shirt with happiness at being held. It was a good thing he was a one-animal-in-the-house kind of pet, or she'd probably be a crazy old cat lady by now.

"And I really don't want to be a crazy old cat lady," she told him.

But if she didn't want Watson to continue being the number one male in her life, at some point she needed to let another one in. Preferably a human one. And Michael was already more in than any other man ever had been.

When she was in the moment, she just wanted to be with him. It was only when she was able to overthink everything that she started having issues... so, maybe she should just trust her instincts.

She'd once been able to convince herself into a relationship which had turned out to be a disaster, ignoring the instincts and evidence telling her Lawrence couldn't be trusted. Now the evidence and her instincts were telling her she should let Michael in... maybe she should stop trying to talk herself out of it.

PARKING HIS CAR, MICHAEL LEANED BACK AGAINST THE SEAT, glancing at the clock. Two more minutes and then he was going to call Ellie and find out whether or not they were going to take a step forward. Even if she'd changed her mind now that she'd actually had some time to think, he wasn't going to be dissuaded from pursuing her, but it would be good to know where he stood.

No matter how frustrating it would be if she'd changed her mind about a club contract after getting his hopes up.

It had been clear from the beginning she wasn't going to be an easy submissive, so he was just going to have to be patient. After all, she'd warned him and so had everyone else.

As soon as he was done talking with her, he'd be headed into

Marquis... which was what they'd decided to name the new club. He'd been stopping by every night ever since renovations started, just to see what had been done. Not because he didn't trust the contractors or Patrick, but because he liked to see the club coming together and being there just made it more real. More tangible. Pictures didn't really do it justice, especially since some of the daily changes weren't obvious at first glance.

So, if Ellie hadn't changed her mind about a club contract, visiting the club site would be a nice cherry on top of the day; if she had changed her mind, visiting would hopefully cheer him up.

It was time.

Pulling up her number on his cell phone made him feel awkward, like a gangly, unsure teenager. Definitely not a fun way to feel, but one he'd become somewhat accustomed to while pursuing Ellie.

She picked up on the second ring and, as a sop to his ego, sounded just as nervous as he did.

"Hello?"

"Hello Ellie," he said, keeping his voice smooth, glad of his theatric training which, hopefully, allowed him to sound a lot less nervous than he actually was. Strangely, hearing the slight tremor in her voice made him feel calmer and less anxious. "How was your day?"

"Pretty good. Long." She paused for a moment and he could imagine her fidgeting. Poor little subbie wanted him to get right to the point. He'd thought maybe a bit of mundane conversation might help ease her, but apparently not.

"Well, you know why I'm calling," he said, and he thought he heard her let out a quiet sigh of relief. He modulated his voice, trying to keep his tone completely neutral so she wouldn't feel pressured or like she was disappointing him if she had changed her mind. "Would you like to sign a club contract with me this weekend?"

The pause before her answer had his chest tightening in anticipation. *Please say yes, please say yes...*

Her voice was a mere whisper when the answer came, her words spilling out so fast they practically ran together. "YesIwouldliketosignaclubcontract."

The grin that spread across his face stretched his muscles so much they actually hurt. If he hadn't been in his car, he would have done a victory dance - or at least jumped up and down. As it was, he punched the ceiling of his car when he pumped his fist, and had to cough to cover the inadvertent exhale in pain.

"Great! That's... that's great!" Good job with the vocabulary Mike. Very impressive. Clearing his throat to give himself a moment to collect himself - all he needed was his voice cracking to complete feeling like an inept teenage boy - Michael shook himself. *Get it together, grouch. You. Are. A. Dom.* "I'll email you the contract tomorrow so you can read it over. Let me know if you want me to make any changed and I can edit the contract before this weekend. Can you be at the club on Friday to sign it?"

"Yes... yes, that sounds good." Her voice sounded small, breathless, but also excited. Which was a relief.

The contract was already ready, but for some reason he didn't want to admit that, which was why he was going to send it to her tomorrow. Plus, this way he could give it one last look over before he actually sent it.

"What are you up to this evening?" he asked, suddenly cheerier than he'd been all day. Maybe she'd like to come see Marquis in person instead of just the photos he'd been sending her.

"Oh, I'm going over to Stronghold to help with Angel's class. Actually, I should probably get going, I need to change and head over early to help set up."

"Ah, yes. Well, have fun. I'll talk to you later." He didn't bother keeping his regret out of his voice, even though she hadn't expressed any at already having plans.

It was probably better this way anyway. Trying to push Ellie to come out with him, right after she'd agreed to a club contract, probably wasn't the best way to go. But he still wanted her to know he would have liked to spend time with her.

Baby steps.

Frustrating, tiny, baby steps.

Necessary steps.

Letting out a deep breath, Michael shoved his phone back into his pocket and got out of his car. The August night was hot and muggy, but it would be turning cool soon enough. He and Patrick had agreed they wanted Marquis opened with a New Year's Eve party. Everyone from Stronghold would be invited. People were already applying for memberships, despite the hefty fees. Just as Patrick had predicted.

Walking into the front door, Michael flipped on the lights and grinned. The main room was really coming together. Hardwood floors, walls painted a dark burgundy red with white trim. The booths along the wall had been put in today; they were padded leather with black seats and white backs, curved so anyone from two to six people could comfortably sit in them and still see everything happening in the rest of the restaurant. Eventually, there'd be curtains hanging from the ceiling, which could be closed, so they could also be more private if they desired.

It looked good.

The bar was a wooden antique and had been brought all the way up from Savannah, Georgia. They'd picked it out online and it looked perfect in the new space. The wood had been polished to gleaming, and it tucked neatly along the side of the restaurant across from the booths. Matching wooden stools would eventually be installed in front of it, but they were still going through a little bit of refurbishing. The bar and stools were in great shape, but Michael and Patrick wanted them to be perfect.

Walking through the large, empty space, Michael headed to the back hall, past the bathrooms, to the staircase and went upstairs. Not much had been done up here yet, but Michael was possibly the most excited about this room and its stage. He'd already started talking to some of the dominants with specialties about doing demonstrations on the stage.

Rigging, fire play, cupping, whip demos... he wanted it all showcased here. Erotic but without sex. Instructional, but fun. The Dungeon at Stronghold was great for the exhibitionists and voyeurs, and Patrick occasionally used the stage at Stronghold to give demos, but that wasn't what Michael was going for.

No, he wanted people to walk into this room, with dim lights barely reaching the alcoves where they would sit. He wanted all the focus on the demonstrations, on the circular stage in the middle of the room. Like performance art. Something to focus on, unlike the chaos of the Dungeon. A more intimate and close-up experience than Patrick could provide at Stronghold's stage.

It wouldn't appeal to everyone, especially not all the time, but Michael thought it would be a nice addition to what Stronghold already offered. Marquis was going to be smaller by necessity; besides, he wanted this club to offer something unique. He didn't want it to just be an overflow space for Stronghold members, and Patrick agreed.

Where Stronghold was sex, Marquis would be seduction.

⌘

"Hey, we're gonna hang out here for a bit, wanna join us?" Angel asked as Ellie wiped a towel across her face, cleaning off some of the sweat.

The self-defense class had been a bit more of a work-out than she'd been anticipating. She'd spent as much time chasing Angel around and trying to get the pregnant woman to *stop* being so physically involved in the class as she did demonstrating the moves Angel asked her to.

Ellie narrowed her eyes at her friend. "I'm starting to wonder if you asked me to come help with this class under false pretenses."

"Would I do that?" Angel quipped, making her voice nasal as she batted wide eyes and gave Ellie such an innocent smile there could be no doubt of her guilt. "Jessica and Kate are coming too. And obviously Leigh and Lexie since they're already here."

"You could have just asked me to come out tonight," Ellie said, trying to sound stern although a laugh kept trying to bubble up. She put down the towel and went to grab the last of the equipment which needed to be stacked in Stronghold's storage closet.

"Yeah, but I really did need the help, so it worked out."

Giving her a look, Ellie shoved the arm pads into the closet. Angel might be pregnant, but she still seemed to have twice the amount of energy Ellie did. She'd sat down a few times during the class - mostly when Ellie or Leigh insisted.

Turning around, Angel yelled across the room to Leigh, who was just coming out of the ladies' locker room. "Ellie's hanging out with us!"

"I never actually said that," Ellie complained as she closed the closet doors.

"You didn't say no either, so that's a yes in my book."

"You realize you sound kind of super rapey, right?" Leigh asked, laughing, as she came over to join them.

"Hang-out-rape?" Angel asked, musing. "That seems okay."

Leigh threw her hands up in the air and even Ellie dissolved into giggles with them.

Five minutes later Kate and Jessica had arrived and Lexie had come out of Patrick's office and they were all hanging out in the Lounge area after getting some drinks. Ellie and Leigh chose simple rum and cokes to imbibe, Kate made herself some kind of blue mixed drink, Jessica just grabbed a beer, and Lexie poured herself a glass of Baileys on ice. Patrick had taken one look at what was going on and turned straight back around, retreating quickly into his office.

"He still has more work he can do," Lexie said. "We've probably got about an hour before he decides I've had enough fun and drags me home."

"Where you'll have a totally different kind of fun," Angel said, lifting her glass of water to Lexie. She was sprawled out on her chair entirely inelegantly, slouched down with her legs apart and her baby bump sticking straight up, her head resting on the back of the low armchair.

Leigh, who was sitting on the floor with her back against Angel's chair, in between her legs, grinned. "Naughty fun."

"Yes, that would be what I was implying." Angel nudged Leigh's shoulder with her leg. Across from them, Jessica and Kate stifled laughs. Jessica was in the chair directly across from Angel, and Kate was directly across from Ellie, so it wasn't like trying to hide their laughter really worked. Lexie, who was sitting on the floor between them with her back against their recliners, didn't bother to hide her giggles.

"You two are like an old married couple sometimes," Jessica teased.

It was kind of weird sitting around in the Lounge area with a bunch of subs who were all dressed in regular clothes. Ellie was still in her workout capris and a tank top, like Angel and Leigh, while Jessica and Kate were both wearing jean shorts and casual shirts. Jessica's hair was pulled back in a ponytail and Kate had hers wrapped in a neat bun on the back of her head; whereas during usual club time, they both often had their hair down. Only Lexie was dressed as she often was in the club (at least when her brother was present); wearing nothing but one of Patrick's large shirts, which covered her completely. She'd probably been totally naked while she was in his office.

"Speaking of getting married, how are the wedding plans going?" Kate asked, turning her attention to Jessica.

Even though Jessica's upcoming ceremony wasn't going to actually be a legal wedding, since she'd be "marrying" two men, they all called it that anyway. After all, it wasn't Jessica, Chris, and Justin's fault the government hadn't caught up on poly relationships. Fortunately, they were able to do some legal maneuverings with trusts and wills which would give them pretty much all the rights of spouses... just without the tax breaks every April.

"Good! We decided on a spring wedding. We've started searching locations, although there'll definitely be some kind of exclusive kinky after party, either here or at Marquis since it'll be open by then," Jessica said with a wicked smile.

"Like a collaring ceremony?" Ellie asked. Stronghold had hosted more than a few of those since it had opened.

"Yup, although we haven't worked out the details. Suffice to say, it won't be family friendly. Definitely stuff our parents would rather not hear about," Jessica said. She sighed. "My parents have gotten a lot better about me being with both Justin and Chris, but I'd rather not push it and make us all uncomfortable again."

"What about Justin and Chris' families?" Angel asked.

"Justin's mom is the best," Jessica said, her face lighting up for just a moment before darkening again. "Chris' family... he and his brother email each other sometimes, but that's about it. They haven't actually talked since we all got together. We're going to send them an invite but..." She bit her lip, her eyes darting around even though they knew they were completely alone in the club.

"You kind of hope they don't come if they're going to be awful," Leigh said, her voice gentle. "Totally understandable."

"I still feel like a jerk for thinking it," Jessica muttered, looking guilty.

"Don't," Angel said. "I'm still freaking out about Adam's parents both being here when the baby is born. They haven't seen each other in over a decade, they might be perfectly fine, but I kind of wish they weren't coming just because it's an additional stress. It's human nature to not want more stress piled on top of an already stressful situation. It's also human nature not to want anyone raining on our parade."

Leigh twisted around slightly so she could look at Angel. "That's what I'm here for. If anyone starts upsetting you, I'm kicking them out of the room. I don't care if they're Adam's parents."

"And if she's not there, one of us will do it," Lexie said, nodding decisively. "You and Adam won't have to deal with that crap at all."

Despite her small size, no one doubted for a moment Lexie would be just as effective as Patrick at bodily dragging someone from the room if someone was upsetting her friends. For that matter, Ellie didn't doubt even mild-mannered Leigh would. While Leigh tended to be nearly as quiet as Ellie, if someone was messing with one of her friends she changed to an angry bulldog in an instant.

"Or you could sic Olivia on them," Ellie said. Although she would love to see Lexie or Leigh's version of a smack down, but Olivia was really good at preventing the need for one.

"Ooo, yeeeees," Kate said, her voice almost a hiss of satisfaction. "Feed them to the Domme."

Everyone cracked up at the description, which was kind of super on point. There weren't a lot of people whom Olivia couldn't eat for breakfast - even here at Stronghold. She had the evilest of evil eyes.

"So Ellie... you're awfully quiet over there," Jessica said, as the laughter faded, an almost mischievous smile on her face. Everyone turned towards Ellie, making her want to squirm. "Feel free to tell us to mind our own business, but we're all dying to know about you and Michael."

"Shhh, don't tell her she can ignore our questions," Angel protested. "I want answers!"

"You're so nosy," Leigh shot back at her, pinching Angel's leg. The two of them had a mini-tussle which everyone else ignored other than looks of amusement. They were still focused on looking at Ellie, rather than diverting their attention.

"Oh um... things are good?" Ellie answered, her voice lilting up as though she was asking a question. She knew that wasn't enough information for them though. "Um, we're going to sign a club contract."

"Whoo-hoo!" Lexie pumped her fist in the air with excitement, which made everyone laugh. Kate clapped her hands together in delight while Angel leaned over even further – which helped her avoid Leigh's fingers – to give Ellie an enthusiastic one-armed hug. Jessica grinned, looking thrilled, and she gave Ellie a thumbs up when she saw Ellie looking at her.

"What's a club contract?" Leigh asked, looking confused as she finally stopped trying to pinch Angel.

"Something you'll never have to worry about," Kate quipped, giggling.

"It's like an in-club relationship," Lexie explained. "It sets out all the boundaries and limits of the relationship, including whether or not it's exclusive, and there's often a time limit."

"But it's only for when you're actually at Stronghold?" Leigh still sounded a little confused and it made Ellie want to squirm.

Normally club contracts were between people who were only inter-ested in seeing each other at the club, whereas she and Michael already saw each other outside of the club quite often. Which meant it was already going to be different for them. But it's not like they were going on *dates* outside of the club or anything. And this was already a huge step for her.

"Unless the contract specifies activities outside of the club, but I don't think I've ever seen a club contract that does," Lexie said.

"So what's the time limit?" Angel asked curiously, looking at Ellie.

Ellie shrugged. "I don't know yet, Michael's sending me the contract to look over tomorrow."

"Five bucks he doesn't put in a time limit!" Angel said immediately, her head whipping around to look at the others.

"I am so not taking that bet," Jessica retorted. Ellie blushed.

Should she want a time limit already in there? Would it be easier to renegotiate at the end of a month? Two months? A year?

The idea of a year made her feel a little panicked. A year was such a long time. A month seemed so short. But what if things started to get weird after just a month and a half and she was still locked in for two more weeks? She'd feel honor bound to just get through it, which didn't sound appealing at all. Michael would be the same way, and she hated the idea of him spending time with her just because he said he would.

An open time frame for a contract sounded better. It could end when it needed to. No need to trap herself, even in just a club relationship.

"You look kind of panicky, hun, are you okay?" Leigh asked, reaching out to gently touch Ellie's knee. "We can change the subject."

"No, it's okay... I'm okay," Ellie said, although now that Leigh had said something she realized her chest was feeling kind of tight. She hated how sometimes her body just reacted without any real reason. "I'm just..." She let out a long sigh. In the back of her head she could hear Dr. Amy's voice again, encouraging her to open up. To let people in a little. "Anything to do with relationships makes me nervous."

"So it's not Michael, specifically?" Angel asked, leaning on the armrest towards Ellie, her hazel eyes sharpening with interest.

"No, definitely not. I feel safer with him than with anyone."

"When was your last relationship?" Jessica asked.

"High school." Ellie's teeth snapped shut as she practically bit off the last word. She didn't like to think about it. Didn't like to think about *him*.

On her knee, Leigh's fingers tightened in a supportive way, just as Angel reached out to put her hand over Ellie's, which was when Ellie realized she'd clenched her hand into a fist.

"It's okay, Ell. We... well, we all kind of figured out something really bad happened to you. You don't have to talk about it," Angel said softly, her voice full of compassion and understanding. "You've taken my class. We all know there are way too many women out there who have had something happen to them."

Leigh shivered. Ellie only knew because she felt it. Her eyes were downcast on her own lap, the familiar feelings of shame and humiliation rising up. It was one thing to think people might have guessed, another to realize they actually knew.

"I was attacked in the parking lot here," Leigh said softly. "If Kate hadn't come to my rescue, I know I would have been hurt. Maybe raped."

"My prom date in high school shoved me up against the wall at the after party we were at when I told him no," Kate said, her voice faraway. Ellie peeked to see the gorgeous blonde staring off into the distance. "Grabbed my boob and almost tore my dress. I started screaming and my friends came running. He apologized later, said it was just because he was drunk, but I never spent any time with him again after that." Her voice hardened at the end.

"I only ever played Seven Minutes in Heaven once, when I was fourteen," Lexie said. "The guy shoved his hands down my pants and touched me. I bit him and kicked him in the balls." She sounded so proud of herself that the sad tension, which had been growing in the room, broke and everyone started laughing. Even Ellie. She looked up to see Lexie shrugging, although her cheeks were pink and her smile wasn't entirely genuine.

"A guy tried to follow me from a party back to my dorm when I was in college. He kept catcalling me and asking me why I was being a bitch by ignoring him. I kept walking faster, but having to chase me just made him angrier," Angel said, giving Ellie's hand - which was no longer a fist - a little squeeze. "I was lucky, I found a campus security guard on the way and she chased him off. She's the one who told me about the self-defense course the campus offered."

The words bubbled up inside Ellie and it felt like her chest hurt from all the years she'd spent pushing them down, holding them in. Her gaze dropped back down to her knees where Leigh's hand was still resting. Where she could see Angel's hand gripping hers out of the corner of her eye.

"My high school boyfriend raped me at a party," she said, choking off the words as a sob rose in her throat. Her shoulders hunched forward, waiting for the blow. The questions. The disbelief. The judgment. The usual reactions.

Angel's hand gripped her harder.

"Oh honey...." Kate's voice was so much closer and Ellie looked up in surprise as the light around her dimmed and she was suddenly in the center of a protective circle of support and love. They were all around her, someone perched on her right, Angel leaning in from the left, hands on her shoulders, her legs. Tears rose. Hope, almost too painful to bear, slid through her.

"We were both drunk, but I didn't want it... I *didn't*. I said so. I'd told him maybe we could, before the party, but when he started pushing me *I said no*." Her voice hitched as the tears slid down her cheeks. They swam in her eyes, making it impossible to see.

"We believe you," someone murmured. She didn't know who, but it didn't matter, because everyone else was immediately saying it too, their voices full of concern without an ounce of doubt or disbelief.

Not one of them asked if she hadn't been clear. Not one of them asked why she'd told him 'maybe' if she was going to change her mind later. Not one of them tried to get her to 'see his side.' They just surrounded her with complete and total support and love.

They were on *her* side.

Ellie dissolved into sobs as she leaned against someone's arm, both her hands clutching others, and what felt like years of resentment, anger, self-doubt, and self-recrimination flowed out of her.

8

"So a club contract, huh?" Angel asked, plopping down on the couch next to Michael and peering at the laptop he was using.

Michael sighed inwardly. This was what he got for coming over to Patrick's to work on Marquis stuff. He'd called out sick, not really caring whether or not he'd get a good reference from the job. They didn't really need him at this point anyway, he was just sitting around doing nothing, so he might as well be at home working on something for his future. He hadn't realized Angel and Lexie would be there as well and, while some of their observations were welcome, they kept dropping hints which he recognized as avenues to open a discussion about him and Ellie.

Apparently Angel had now lost her patience with the hints and his luck had run out, because Patrick had gone into the kitchen to help Lexie make lunch. No chance of ignoring her by talking about business with Patrick anymore, unfortunately.

"Yes, pest, a club contract." He tapped the mouse pad, pretending to be totally engrossed in the design sketches on the screen.

A pointy finger in his side had him yelping and swatting at her hand. "Don't ignore me."

"As if I could," he muttered.

"Why a club contract? Why not just ask her out on a date?"

"Do you think she'd go out on a date?" Curious, because he hadn't expected that suggestion, he stopped pretending the screen had all his focus and turned towards his favorite pest. She was leaning back against the back of the couch, her hair piled in a messy bun, with one hand on her baby bump. Today's t-shirt was a Star Wars themed one, with the Death Star over her bump and the words "That's No Moon" with a background of stars. While her stomach wasn't big enough to really fill out the Death Star yet, it wasn't hard to imagine it getting there. Which was both weird and wonderful, knowing she was growing a tiny human being inside of her. Sometimes he wondered what their lives would be like now if he hadn't dated one of her best friends and they'd ended up dating instead... but he knew it wouldn't have worked. Angel liked pain with her pleasure, but not to the levels Michael enjoyed giving it.

"I have no idea," Angel answered matter-of-factly. "I just want to know why you didn't bother to try."

"Because I'm pretty sure she wouldn't have said yes and I'm trying not to push her or scare her off," he said. "And I didn't suggest the club contract, she did." The expression on Angel's face made him laugh. "Oh, didn't know that, did you? Nosy thing."

He poked her back, but he poked her thigh, and a lot more gently than she'd dug her finger into him.

"But you like her right? You want more than a club contract?"

"Why the third degree, pest?" he asked, rather than answering her questions. Angel really was a nosy thing, but she usually wasn't this bad. She might ask, but she didn't usually shoot questions at him like he was under interrogation, or with such an accusatory tone in her voice.

Angel crossed her arms, resting them between her breasts and swelling bump as she frowned at him. "Because I think she likes you. And she deserves a real relationship."

"Well I like her too, and I agree," he said, raising his eyebrow. "Is that all?"

A strange look came over her face, almost like hesitation and a little bit of doubt. "You're... you're careful with her right?"

There was a strange note in her voice, alerting Michael to another unexpected shift in the conversation. Hesitant and doubtful were not adjectives often applied to Angel. In fact, he'd say they almost never applied to Angel.

"What's going on, Angel?" he asked, turning more fully towards her.

She bristled defensively. "Nothing. I'm just asking a question."

Asking a question and worrying about it. Michael tilted his head, studying her, and Angel blushed. They'd done a lot of theater together and Angel was a very good actress, but she wasn't great at hiding her own emotions without putting some real effort into it, and he could tell when she was doing it. Something had riled her protective instincts with Ellie, which Michael didn't have a problem with, but now he was curious exactly why. It didn't seem like just the club contract.

Ellie had been at the self-defense class last night, helping Angel out...

"Did something about Ellie's past come up last night?" he asked. Whatever had happened to her, it seemed like the class would be a likely avenue for something to actually come out.

"I can't talk about that," Angel said immediately, her face going neutrally blank. Which, of course, was an answer in and of itself.

"I don't expect you to betray her confidence," he said, giving her a look. Really, she should know him better. "I know something happened to her though. Her hard limits make it pretty clear."

"Really?" Angel's natural curiosity perked her up a bit and Michael just had to shake his head in amusement.

"And you know that's confidential information too, unless she chooses to share it with you."

Pouting, Angel stuck her tongue out at him. "I wasn't being nosy, I just didn't realize you could tell someone's experiences from their hard limits."

"Well, you have to be particularly wise and insightful... Ouch!" Damn her elbows were sharp. And she'd somehow managed to get him in almost the exact same spot she'd poked him earlier. Considering she was both pregnant and not his, he didn't have much in the way of recourse either, unless he wanted to tattle on her to Adam, and he had way too much dignity to stoop so low. Not to mention, he wasn't entirely sure Adam wouldn't just reward her. The two of them got along fairly well, but Michael liked to needle the other man just for fun sometimes. His best defense was probably to just distract her. "So she talked about it with you, huh?"

"Not any details, but yeah a little," Angel said, making a sound halfway between a sigh and a growl. "We all did."

Michael frowned. "What do you mean you all did?"

"We all shared our bad experiences," Angel said with a shrug, although he could tell she was feeling uncomfortable saying so. Which was unusual because not much embarrassed Angel and finding a topic she was uncomfortable talking about was kind of like finding a unicorn. His frown deepened, a surge of protective anger rising inside of him.

"What bad experiences?"

"Oh geez, you had to go and get him going too?" Lexie asked, walking back into the room, followed by Patrick. She was wearing her usual attire for home when there was company - one of Patrick's big shirts. Michael was fairly certain Patrick just kept her completely naked all the time when no one else was around.

Smart bastard.

Patrick, on the other hand, was fully clothed in jeans and a t-shirt, his dark eyes appreciatively wandering over Lexie's exposed legs. He had the smug look of someone who was feeling very satisfied at the moment. No wonder they'd been taking so long in the kitchen. Michael just hoped they hadn't done something horribly unhygienic, because the sandwiches Lexie was setting down on the coffee table looked delicious, as did the fruit salad Patrick was carrying.

"What?" Angel asked, looking defensive as she pushed herself into a sitting position. "It's not my fault they all flip out as soon as they hear something bad once happened. News flash guys, bad things happen to everyone. I didn't even get to the part where we deal with this shit on a daily basis."

"What?"

"Not, like being molested," she waved her hand at him, as if that was going to help him calm down. "But walking down the street, the cat calling, the guys pulling over their cars to try and talk to us."

"They *what?*"

"Yeah, they're the worst, cuz that's actually scary rather than just annoying. You'd think the baby bump would put them off, but I still had a guy pull over and try to get my number the other day." Angel looked down at her belly and poked it. "You are not the man-deterrent I thought you would be."

Michael was practically hyperventilating. He didn't know what was worse – hearing his pregnant friend was being harassed on the street, or that she didn't see anything out of the ordinary about men actually stopping their cars to try and talk to her. Honking was one thing – although now that he thought about it, he didn't particularly like that idea either. Why should Angel and the others have to put up with being leered at by guys driving by? Fuck guys who honked at women on the street.

"Calm down, Michael, there's nothing you can do about it. Heck, there's nothing *we* can do about it," Lexie said, popping a grape from her fruit salad into her mouth. Her expression was a little resigned but just as matter-of-fact as Angel's. "I've had guys pull over when I was out for a run, wearing sweatpants, and looked and smelled like ass. Some guys just suck. But not all guys act like that and we all know it. Unfortunately, those who exist tend to spread the bad. We're used to dealing with it."

"Yes, but you shouldn't have to," Patrick said, his voice a deep growl as his eyes flashed. Obviously he had the same feelings on the subject Michael did – which probably their entire group of friends would.

"Agreed, we shouldn't," Lexie said, rolling her eyes, in a tone which indicated she'd already repeated this sentiment multiple times. "And yet, we all have a story. Granted, some stories are way worse than others, but that's what it's like to be a woman unfortunately. Why do you think Angel manages to stay employed?"

When she wasn't making items to sell on her Etsy store, Angel taught self-defense classes, both part-time at a local community college and at Stronghold. Michael had always thought they were a good idea, but he'd seen them as a 'just in case' kind of thing, not something he thought all of his female friends would actually need to use at some point. The idea that every single one of them had a story made him want to stand up and rage, and then go hunt down every man who had ever hurt them and cut off his balls.

Despite Patrick's controlled movements as he set down the bowl of fruit salad and handed out the plates stacked beneath, the fury in his eyes absolutely reflected the same sentiment. He looked like Michael felt - helpless. And even more infuriated that both Angel and Lexie acted like this was somehow normal, even expected, that they'd at some point had a man either threaten or hurt or... ugh, Michael's imagination was coming up with all sorts of awful scenarios.

"Look, the point is, we're fine. Some men are shitty. I was lucky, in my situation I was just scared," Angel said. "A guy tried to follow me home and he was really loud and threatening, but I found a security officer and my story ended happily. I'm safe. That's when I started taking the self-defense classes and decided I wanted to teach them too."

Even the thought of Angel being threatened by a man had Michael grinding his teeth. What if she hadn't found the security officer?

"How did I not know about this before?" he demanded.

Lexie and Angel exchanged a look which spoke volumes as Lexie sat down on the floor between Patrick's legs as he settled onto the armchair. The kind of look that left the two men out and Michael didn't like it. Angel hadn't had a whole lot of female friends, other than Leigh, before she'd started going to Stronghold. It felt weird to be left out, to see the connection between the two of them, an understanding he didn't, and couldn't, have. It was disturbing and upsetting, considering the reason.

"It's not really something I like to talk about," Angel said. "None of us do. People can be kind of judgmental. When I told the girls in my dorm what had happened, most of them were sympathetic, but some of them wanted to know if I had talked to him at some point, if I'd smiled at him or something - as if that would somehow mean it was okay for him to follow me. Guys were even worse. They wanted to know where I started from, if I was at a party or a bar, if I'd been drinking, what I was wearing, why was I walking alone… and more of them were looking for some kind of explanation which would blame me instead of being sympathetic or angry on my behalf."

What hit Michael hardest, in that moment, was that part of his brain pinged, acknowledging what seemed like legitimate questions, until Angel pointed out how looking for an explanation shifted some of the blame to her. Which was bullshit. Obviously it wasn't her fault. He just couldn't help but think maybe if she'd been wearing something sexy, it might have drawn the guy's attention… but women in Stronghold could strip naked and expect to be treated with respect. Women on the street should be able to have the same expectation. Saying a woman should dress less sexy just shifted the blame to her, the advice meant shifting the predator's attention to a different woman, a woman who was dressed more sexily, rather than focusing on the man, who was really the only one at fault.

He wanted his friends to be protected, but staying safe shouldn't mean changing what she was wearing or not going out to parties or anything other change to her behavior. Even if it seemed like a legitimate question, he could see how it came off as pointing a finger.

"Plus, you feel super alone. I think that's what finally helped Ellie to talk a little last night," Lexie said, her head leaning against Patrick's knee. She had one arm wrapped around his leg, her fingers stroking his ankle, almost as though she were consoling him. One of his big hands was on the back of her neck, the chocolate color of his fingers standing out against the pale cream of her skin. He was leaning forward, almost protectively hovering over her. "Hearing she wasn't the only one who had been through something."

"Who else was there last night?" Michael demanded. Even though he couldn't do anything, he suddenly had the overwhelming need to know. Patrick shot him a look of sympathy, at the same time Angel and Lexie both shook their heads.

"Don't worry about that," Angel said, reaching out to pick up a sandwich. "Mmm, these look amazing."

He made a noise of frustration. "I just don't understand how you can act like this isn't a big deal!"

"It's not," Angel said, shooting him a glare. "I mean, it is and it isn't. We know it shouldn't happen, it fucking sucks when it does happen, it affects us, but we rise above it. We find ways to guard ourselves and defend ourselves and we watch out for each other, but we don't wallow in what happened to us, or we'd be walking around scared all the time instead of just aware and on guard. Although, even then, we're a lot more likely to be hurt by someone we know than someone we don't. Which is why it's nice to belong to a group of friends like ours where the guys are *all* decent and trustworthy. Even if you occasionally do stupid things."

As she sat back, happily munching on her sandwich, Michael was struck by two things.

One - he and Patrick were definitely having a much harder time dealing with the women's reality than the women were.

Two - he was pretty sure Ellie had the worst story. Because she was the most guarded. And that made him want to run around hitting things all over again.

But he couldn't.

With Lexie and Angel's determined help, somehow they managed to get the conversation back around to Marquis and what kind of decorations they wanted, which was what they'd been talking about before Lexie and Patrick had gone to make lunch. Both Michael and Patrick remained distracted for the rest of the afternoon though. Distracted and agitated.

When Michael got home he immediately headed out for a run to clear his head. It was still hot and humid, but he didn't care. Being in his apartment made him feel confined; he had too much energy running through him to sit still and concentrate on anything.

He didn't often go running, he really had to be in the mood for it, and today was definitely one of those days. It hadn't escaped his attention Lexie didn't share what her story with the others had been. He assumed it was too personal. Or maybe too upsetting. Although he was willing to bet Patrick now knew the details.

Were the details something he needed to know? With the others, no... it didn't seem to affect them the same way whatever had happened to Ellie still affected her. With her, considering her hard

limits, she was still dealing with the impact. Which meant it was probably really, really bad.

Michael's leg muscles burned as he pumped them harder, running
faster, as though he could outrun the rage and feeling of helplessness
assaulting him. It took him a moment to also realize he was a little
upset Angel and Lexie obviously knew more about what had happened
to Ellie than he did.

He'd known Ellie for longer, dammit.

Slowing his pace, because his lungs were starting to burn and his
legs felt like they were on fire, Michael forced himself to take deep
breaths of the muggy air - which wasn't easy. This had to be one of the
worst evenings he could have chosen for a run; the air was so thick he
practically felt like he was trying to breathe in water.

He knew it wasn't personal. Lexie had even said Ellie had probably
only opened up because the others had. Michael didn't have any kind
of life experience that really compared. Before, he would have said he
could imagine what life was like for women, but... he hadn't. He'd
never even known how Angel had gotten into teaching self-defense
classes.

Which made him think about what Lexie had said about being out
for a run. He looked down the street in the dimming light, with all the
cars passing. Some of them already had their headlights on, some of
them didn't. He tried to imagine what it would be like to have the cars
honking at him while he was trying to run. To have someone hanging
out the window at him.

To have someone pull over their car to talk to him.

He considered himself an aware kind of guy; he knew he ran a bit of
a risk going out running alone, especially after dark, but overall he wasn't
scared when a car stopped. He just assumed someone needed directions.
What would it be like to be petite, lightweight Lexie, and have a car
stop... she wouldn't know if they were looking for directions or her
number. Whoever was in the car was likely larger and stronger than her.

Self-defense moves could only count for so much. Michael had
helped out at the class final exams before, letting himself get beat up
by the students... but he was always covered in pads which made him

move slower and he definitely never used his full strength. Which, now that he thought about it, might not have done them any favors. Although Angel always said a big part of self-defense was confidence.

Sweat poured down his face as he slowed to walking, his damp hair getting in his eyes and he pushed it back impatiently as he brought his water bottle up to take a drink.

He was seeing the world through a slightly different lens and he was not a fan.

The beeping of his phone distracted him and he unzipped the pocket on his runner's belt, thankful for the distraction - especially when he saw it was an email from Ellie. A grin spread across his face. She agreed to everything in the club contract and was looking forward to signing it tomorrow.

So there was something to be happy about.

Just that response lightened his entire mood. This was really going to happen. It might only be a tiny baby step for him, but he was coming to realize it was actually a huge step for Ellie. He had her trust.

And he was going to do everything in his power to make sure he kept it.

DR. AMY'S OFFICE NEVER CHANGED.

Ellie had been seeing her for years, although now she only went once a month unless she felt like she needed to come in sooner, and the office had remained exactly the same. There was something soothing about consistency, and Ellie always wondered if that's why Dr. Amy didn't bother updating.

There was a big desk and computer, which Dr. Amy only sat behind at the end of the appointment when they were making a new one. Two couches in an L shape with a coffee table in front of them and a comfortable armchair set across from them provided plenty of seating for any number of people, just in case there was family counseling. Before Ellie's parents had moved to California, they'd come with her more than once.

Her mom had been concerned about her lack of relationships and the fact Ellie had been seeing a therapist for such a long time and still wasn't *fixed*.

Sometimes Ellie didn't like her mom very much.

The couch Ellie was sitting on was dark brown leather with huge, soft cushions. She always sank right in and felt immediately comfortable, one arm resting on the arm rest to her left. She liked the corners of couches, especially big ones like this. They felt secure.

"So, you've gone from avoiding Michael to now agreeing to a kind of relationship with him," Dr. Amy said. She looked relaxed in her armchair, wearing navy dress pants and a blue and silver blouse, her dark hair pulled back in a loose bun, with her legs crossed and her hands resting on her thighs. Dr. Amy never took notes, although Ellie assumed she must write things down after the session, but during the session her attention never wavered from Ellie. Sometimes it felt more like a conversation than a therapy session - well, other than the leading questions. "Why do you think that is?"

"Because I trust him," Ellie said. "I trusted him back in high school, and I've seen how he is since he started coming to Stronghold. He hasn't changed."

Dr. Amy had heard all about Michael even before he'd come back to Stronghold. Since he'd come back into Ellie's life, she'd kind of avoided talking about him at therapy for the most part, but this conversation had been inevitable. She needed to talk it through with her therapist. Especially after last night.

"Why not a real relationship then?" Dr. Amy asked, her hazel eyes far too astute. Ellie found her own gaze skipping around the room, something she knew she did when she was feeling uncomfortable with the current topic.

"I've told you before I don't really feel comfortable in those. Not just because of my past but... I mean, I feel like I wouldn't even know how to be in one."

"But you're already stepping into a relationship with Michael, even if it does have boundaries," Dr. Amy pointed out. "He didn't put a time limit on it." Ellie had already given Dr. Amy all the particulars, so her therapist knew the answer, she was just making a point.

"No."

"And there were clauses affecting interactions outside of the club."

"A few." At least, they could. "That just makes sense though, since we see each other outside of the club anyway. Because of our friends."

"This is sounding an awful lot like a real relationship already," Dr. Amy said gently, uncrossing her legs as she leaned forward to rest her elbows on her knees. Her expression was compassionate. "So what are you really scared of?"

Ellie took a deep breath and let it out on an almost sigh. This was what she knew she needed to talk to Dr. Amy about. Something she hadn't realized until last night. Why she just couldn't let go and tell Michael everything.

"I'm scared once I tell him, he'll reject me. Or blame me. Or judge me. Any of those would be too much for me to deal with." She scrubbed her hands on her bare legs. It wasn't too cold in the office, but her skin still felt cooler the longer her appointment ran.

"That's a normal fear," Dr. Amy said, her voice still gentle. "But you told your friends last night, and they didn't react the way you expected."

No... they hadn't. They'd been amazing, actually. Although, Ellie had already thought they'd be more understanding than people in her past. In high school she hadn't told anyone but her best friend at the time, Meg, and Meg had immediately gone into a barrage of questions. Why had Ellie told him maybe? Why had she gotten drunk? Why hadn't she fought him off? - as if Ellie could have easily fought off a man twice her size when they were both drunk. Why didn't she scream? ... and then when the accident happened, Meg said she shouldn't tell anyone else. Everyone was feeling sorry for him, it would look like she was just trying to rain down even more misery on him, bringing it up then wouldn't help Ellie at all. Part of her had still wanted to though and she'd broken down and told her mom... who had agreed with Meg. After asking many of the same questions.

But at least neither of them had ever told anyone else. Ellie's shame had remained a secret.

She'd told her Steve, her college boyfriend - she'd had to explain when she'd panicked the first time he'd tried to get to second base -

but she hadn't given him any details. All he'd known was she'd been raped in high school.

During college she had started to think maybe other women would be more understanding... more of them were having to deal with the reality of drinking, men, and sexual assault. Women were a lot less protected at college than at home. Parties were more expected, drinking was expected, but since Ellie had stayed away from that scene entirely, she didn't personally know - or at least they hadn't told her - anyone who had been through a similar experience. Hearing everyone else's recitation of their own experiences last night had finally given her the courage to say something.

No, none of them had been through anything quite as bad as her experience, and she was glad for that. She wouldn't have wanted them to. But the fact they all could relate, in some way... it had been both heart-breaking and helped give her the courage to share.

"They were amazing," Ellie said softly, smoothing the leather of the couch's armrest with her fingers. It was soft to touch, almost soothing to just run her fingers over it.

"So, you're afraid Michael won't be as amazing."

Ellie let her head fall back against the couch. It sounded so bad when Dr. Amy said it.

"Why would Michael be different?" Dr. Amy asked, after a long moment of silence from Ellie.

"Well, he's a guy," Ellie said, a bit sardonically. Not that men couldn't understand but... it wasn't hard to miss general male reactions to things like sexual assault and rape. They tended to try and straddle the line - no, of course a woman shouldn't be raped, but if she was going to be walking home alone, or drunk at a party, or wearing skimpy clothing after dark, then *she* should have also been more careful. Because, of course, it was still partially her own fault for assuming she should be able to be safe.

She still remembered her own mother's reaction - "Well what did you expect?"

It was a popular refrain in college when an assault came to light, especially if the woman in question had been at a frat party or out after dark. The idea she expected to have a good time and wake up with a hangover, just like everyone else, was apparently just too hard for some people to grasp. It made her so angry. Which, at least was a step up from ashamed and wracked with guilt and self-recrimination.

"Do you think he's the kind of guy who would blame you?"

Ellie stared at her fingers as she rubbed the leather couch's armrest harder. The leather was getting warm.

Under normal circumstances, no, she didn't think Michael would blame her. But under her circumstances?

She'd made some really stupid decisions.

That didn't mean she blamed herself or thought she had deserved what happened to her... but she still struggled with not feeling like she wasn't partially to blame. Felt like she probably should have seen it coming, or at least realized it was possible. Felt like she should have expected everything to go wrong, because she'd already known...

"Ellie?" Dr. Amy's voice had turned coaxing.

"Once he finds out who... he might." Ellie's voice was a whisper, not by design, but because her chest was so tight she could barely get the words out. It felt like she didn't have any air.

"Because Michael knew him?"

"Yes." Because Michael had been her defender against him once.

Lawrence hadn't been the worst, Ryan had definitely taken that title, but he hadn't been great either. She'd been shocked when he'd approached her the year after Michael left, apparently contrite over his behavior the year before and interested in talking to her. It had taken him several months of conversations, notes, and eventually car rides to and from school before she began to trust him. Even then, she hadn't really believed it until Ryan had started teasing her again and Lawrence had immediately shut him down, his arm slung protectively around her shoulder as he pushed his body slightly in front of hers, glaring at his friend until Ryan apologized.

After that, Ryan hadn't bothered her again.

When she thought about it that way and she looked back, she still couldn't believe it had really been Lawrence who had raped her. Meg had certainly had trouble believing it, because she'd been there watching Lawrence slowly coaxing Ellie into a relationship; she'd supported it. But when Ellie thought about the year before and how

Lawrence had helped Ryan harass her... well, her mother's words would run through her head again and she'd wonder how she could have been so stupid.

She'd had no idea what to say to Lawrence, so she'd stayed home "sick" from school for several days. That's when Meg had come over, realizing something was wrong, and Ellie had told her everything. Meg's doubts had only made her want to hide even more.

Then Lawrence was in an accident.

Drunk driving.

Wrapped his car around a pole.

Paralyzed from the neck down.

High school football player's life turned tragic.

Fortunately for Ellie, he'd been in the car with a senior named Christy. Christy had walked away with only minor injuries comparatively - even drunk, she'd put on her seat belt. On the cheerleading squad, Christy had been thrilled with the media attention. She'd told reporters she was Lawrence's girlfriend - and she did a good job of being his girlfriend until she left for college, doing her best to take care of him. Rumors went around the school, students whispering about Lawrence cheating on Ellie, or claiming Ellie had broken up with him at the party and Christy had been there to comfort him...

Ellie hadn't cared what lies people were spreading, she'd been terrified someone might find out the truth, and she just wanted them all to leave her alone. She'd retreated back into her shell, pulling away from everyone but Meg, and during college she and Meg had drifted apart too. She'd focused on school and her art and that was it.

So karma had taken care of him. At first she'd been relieved. There wasn't any possibility of him every hurting anyone else. She didn't have to speak up. Face more doubts, nastiness from people, and possibly no consequences for him, especially in the wake of his accident? No thanks.

And yet, sometimes she wished she had... just for herself. Other times she was glad she hadn't. It just kind of depended on the day.

"Ellie, you know you don't have to share every detail with him," Dr. Amy said gently. Yeah, she did know that. She hadn't really shared any details last night. After getting a good cry and lots of hugs, the other women had all let the conversation move on to Angel's self-defense class and the good it was doing. Something Ellie could attest to. She'd been relieved they'd realized she didn't want to talk any more about it after her initial admission.

"Right..."

But could she really tell him the truth without telling him the whole truth? Even if it wasn't information necessary for him to have, it felt like she was being dishonest. It felt like hiding.

❧ 9 ❧

C lub contract signings were always done in Patrick's office, since it was his club and he was kind of a control freak. That way he knew the boundaries of the various contracts and always had a copy on hand at the club, as well, even though any participants had their own copies. Personal relationship contracts weren't handled through him obviously, but Michael thought he was making the right choice by agreeing to a club contract with Ellie rather than trying to push for a personal one.

She was obviously already nervous just doing this.

Although she looked beautiful. The black PVC dress she was wearing clung to her curves, dipping low in the front to show off a generous amount of cleavage, while its short skirt barely covered her ass. Especially once she sat down. Nearly every inch of her legs was uncovered, and if they hadn't been pressed together he probably could have seen whether or not she was wearing any panties.

Going by how tightly the dress clung to her body, he was guessing *not*.

Her dark hair was pulled into a low side ponytail, the tendrils curling their way down her front and almost into her cleavage, and she'd used a heavy hand with her make-up, making her look goth.

Michael was looking forward to making it run with her tears. He'd start with peeling off her dress and leaving marks all over her body, some of which would be covered when she put the dress back on and some which wouldn't, and work his way around to fucking her into screaming orgasm. Preferably with some tears there too.

"Standard contract, without a time limit, to be ended when either party decides to," Patrick stated, his voice even as he handed the papers over. Michael didn't even need to glance at it, he practically knew the whole thing by heart.

Two blue eyes peeked at him over the top of Patrick's desk as he leaned forward to sign, and he gave Lexie a smile. She spent a good amount of time kneeling beside Patrick while he was working, doing what she could to help him around the office. Lexie winked back at him and then rested her head against Patrick's leg. Almost absent-mindedly, he reached down to run his fingers through her short, black hair.

"You'll have to inform me if either of you would like to end the contract," Patrick said, pushing the papers over to Ellie. "So I can update the records."

Michael appreciated Patrick said 'if' and not 'when.' A small difference in words, but great in meaning. Nice to know he had the big man's support. After all, Patrick had known Ellie for a long time and seen her interacting with the other Doms around Stronghold; an 'if' from him was a big deal.

Triumph filled him as he watched Ellie sign her name, along with a wave of possessive glee. She was his now.

His to torment, his to pleasure... all his and no one else at the club could touch her unless she decided she wanted to end the contract. And he was going to do everything in his power to make sure she didn't feel the need to.

When she set down the pen on the contract and looked up at him, her smile was tremulous, anxious. Michael reached out and took her hand, sliding his fingers through hers and giving her a reassuring smile. She relaxed, just a touch.

"Good girl," he said softly, as Patrick ignored them and handed the contract over to Lexie. More of the tension slid out of Ellie at the praise.

"Make two copies, Pixie," Patrick said, as Lexie smoothly rose from her kneeling position. She'd obviously had a lot of practice at that particular move.

Completely naked and comfortable in her own skin, Lexie beamed at both him and Ellie as she moved around the desk towards the back of the office where the copy machine was. The little silver hoops hanging from her nipples had tiny blue gems on them, which matched the blue base of the plug. The jewel winked at them from between her bottom cheeks as she moved. Patrick always kept Lexie plugged, a practice which Michael wanted to try with Ellie. It was a way of ensuring she'd constantly have her mind on exactly who was in control of her body when she was in the club. Besides, like most sadists, he enjoyed anal sex and he wanted to ensure she was ready for it.

He'd even bought a special plug for her, with a red jewel in the base... Patrick had recommended the website.

Keeping his hold on Ellie's hand, Michael leaned down with his right hand to unzip his toy bag and pull out the plug, still in its packaging. As he straightened up with it in hand, Ellie's eyes widened and Patrick's lips twitched. The sound of the copier started up as Michael placed the package on the desk.

"While we're waiting," he said, giving Ellie a wicked grin, tugging gently on her hand. Not enough to actually pull her out of her seat, but enough to indicate what he wanted. "Over my lap, Ellie."

She gave the plug a wary glance even as she moved. "But... anal play is on my soft limits."

"And I told you from the beginning, I plan to push some of your limits," he reminded her as she bent over his lap. He tugged her skirt up to her hips, his cock jerking at the softness of her body against him and the sight of her completely bare ass now propped up on his leg. Across from him, Patrick leaned back in his chair, his head cocked and watching without comment. "This is one of them. While we're in the club, you'll be plugged."

He ran his hand over her ass, making her squeak and quiver as his fingers brushed over the crinkled hole of her anus.

"You can always use your safe word," he said, but he already knew she wouldn't. She was soft and submissive over his lap, and her protest hadn't been very strong anyway.

Michael sometimes felt like Ellie had been waiting a very long time for someone who was willing to push some of her limits.

Giving him an approving nod, Patrick tossed a small packet of lube across the desk as the copier went silent. Michael tore open the packet, giving Lexie a quick grin as she returned to her place beside Patrick, handing him the copies, her eyes wide with excitement from watching Michael and Ellie.

In her precarious position, Michael could see Ellie was already wet. She might have made a token protest, but she was definitely turned on.

⚜

ELLIE'S BREATH WAS COMING IN LITTLE PANTS OF EXCITEMENT THAT made her want to moan with embarrassment. She didn't even know why she was so aroused right now, she only knew she was.

Because Patrick and Lexie were there? Normally she didn't really get off on people watching her, although she didn't mind it, but this was a much more intimate kind of exhibitionism than she was used to. Or was it because Michael wanted to play with her ass again, a part of her that, because of her soft limits, other Doms had avoided?

Or maybe it was just Michael himself and his confidence, his excitement at signing a club contract with her. The moment she'd put her signature on the page, it had felt like an invisible band tightening around her, but in a good way. She felt secure. Safe.

While she still didn't know what she would tell him about her past, even though she knew she'd have to tell him something eventually, she also knew the contract would keep him from walking away immediately. There were now protocols of behavior in place, at least at the club, and he was honor-bound to follow them - and for someone as honorable as Michael, the protocols might as well be law.

Wearing a plug all the time would be a new experience. She'd already known Michael planned to push her soft limits, but she hadn't realized he'd want her plugged all the time. Just the thought made every submissive bone in her body feel melty. She was going to feel owned, reminded of the contract, for every second they were together in the club with a plug filling her ass. Something which would have scared her off with any other Dom, but with Michael...

He'd bought her a new plug. Not a regular plug either; the silicon plug with its bejeweled base was a special plug. *Her* special plug. No one had ever bought a toy just for her before. Not even Doms she'd played with on a more regular basis or who had wanted more from her than just occasional scenes.

Who knew a man buying her a butt plug could give her such warm fuzzies?

Definitely something to bring up at her next therapy session. Dr. Amy would get a kick out of it. And it would be nice to talk about something *nice*.

Cool, slick fingers probed her anus and Ellie automatically tensed. Michael's warm hand rubbed over her ass as his fingers continued to push at her little star. He kneaded her flesh with one hand while the fingers of his other circled her opening.

"Relax, Ellie, I promise it'll feel good."

She knew it would... it was also just *so intimate*. Plus, the coolness of the lube didn't help, even if the masochist part of her enjoyed the slight discomfort.

"Oh!" She couldn't help the little gasp as his fingers pressed in, stretching her tight ring of muscle. It burned slightly, contrasting to the coolness of the lube, and sending a shiver down her spine.

Michael's fingers pumped gently, working deeper, while Ellie's pussy contracted emptily at the sensation. She moaned, going practically limp over his lap as he twisted his fingers back and forth, stretching and readying her for the plug while her arousal swirled.

"So, you didn't sign up for a private room tonight," Patrick said, his voice conversational, and Ellie nearly moaned just because a normal conversation while Michael played with her ass was just... hot. "Will called in though, Gina's sick, so they're staying home if you'd like the Jail in an hour. I thought I'd give you first refusal."

"I was planning on scening in the Dungeon," Michael started to say, and Ellie spoke up.

"The Jail, please!"

The fingers moving inside of her paused, Michael's body going tense. Not a bad tension, but like a predator, about to pounce. He leaned towards her, and she pressed her palms against the floor, allowing her to turn her head to look back up at him.

"You'd like the private room?" he asked, his voice and expression carefully neutral. He was good at staying neutral whenever he didn't want to push her one way or another.

Warmth filled her as she realized that he might be pushing her soft limits, but he'd planned on scening in the Dungeon because he thought she'd be more comfortable there. Because, other than with him, that's where she'd always scened; he'd planned on pushing a soft limit, but also on stepping back once he had.

But Ellie would rather scene in a private room with him. She'd insisted on the Dungeon with other Doms because it was where she'd felt safest. With Michael, she felt safe no matter what room they were in... and to be perfectly honest, she preferred the privacy with him. Scening with him, with no one else there, she'd felt a lot more like herself than in any other scene she'd ever done.

"Yes, private room," she said firmly.

Well, as firmly as she could when she was bent over his lap with his fingers in her ass. It did kind of ruin the 'putting her foot down' effect. Not that she needed to be firm apparently. A surprised and very pleased smile spread across Michael's face before he straightened back up to look at Patrick.

"We'll take the jail, thanks," he said, and his fingers pumped, spearing her completely and making her gasp and writhe with the suddenness of the renewed movement.

THE REVELATION THAT ELLIE PREFERRED A PRIVATE ROOM WITH HIM was even more rewarding than her signing the contract. He'd figured she'd need a step back after signing, especially since he was already pushing her with the plug... she hadn't objected to previous anal play, but it hadn't surprised him when she had today. He'd been expecting it. Playing in the Dungeon had been his way of making her more comfortable afterwards.

But she didn't need it.

Maybe he was making more progress with her than he'd realized.

He pumped his fingers, sliding them all the way inside of her, and was rewarded with her moan and a shiver.

Patrick's lips curved up in a smile and Lexie was definitely kneeling up farther than she had been before, trying to see over the table. Stroking Lexie's hair with one hand, the way Patrick was looking at his sub told Michael what they'd be doing after Ellie and Michael left the office. Right now, though, they were just enjoying the show.

"Since we're here, Ellie, Patrick and I wanted to talk to you about whether or not you had room in your schedule to do some designs for Marquis," Michael said conversationally.

Her muscles tightened around his fingers and her voice came out as a squeak. "Now? You want to talk about this now?"

"That actually hadn't been my plan, but since we're here..."

The smile on Patrick's face had turned into a grin, and he shook his head at Michael's timing, but he didn't argue. Sliding his fingers from Ellie's ass, Michael reached out to pick up the plug and take it out of its packaging. She shifted slightly on his lap, wriggling into a more comfortable position since he didn't have a hand on her back to help keep her steady.

The curves of her ass were pale and creamy, her dusky pink hole gaping slightly from being stretched by his fingers, and her pussy was soaked. Michael almost wanted to spank her and turn her ass pink... but there'd be time for that later. Plug her now, then they could go hang out at the bar and he could show off his new official claim before they went down to the Jail.

She squeaked again as he pressed the nose of the plug to her rosebud and pressed. When she spoke, she was breathy, but trying to sound normal. Lexie just shook her head at Michael, obviously feeling Ellie's pain at having to carry on a normal conversation while she was having a plug inserted.

"What do you need?" she asked, panting slightly as she strained against the plug's widening area.

"A logo to start," Patrick said, his hand sliding down to the back of Lexie's neck and massaging. Lexie practically hummed her pleasure as she melted against the massage. "And a banner for the website. We'll probably want some help with the actual website design as well. I know you've have some experience."

"Yes..." Ellie's voice was strained, and it wasn't entirely clear whether she was answering Patrick's question, or if she was responding to Michael's stimulation.

Michael watched as her hole stretched, turning nearly white as the thickest part of the plug reached her entrance. His cock jerked as the plug was suddenly sucked into her body, her muscle clasping the indent tightly, so that just the red jewel was winking at him. Fucking gorgeous.

And the noise Ellie made... a cross between a groan, a gasp, and a whimper. It had made his balls tighten. Didn't hurt he already knew he was finally going to be able to bury himself inside of her tonight... if his dick could have thrown a parade, it would have.

Maneuvering her around, Michael pulled her up onto his lap. Her skirt was up around her waist, but neither he nor Patrick were fazed at all. The ponytail her hair was in was slightly disheveled now and her cheeks had turned pink; she had an almost dreamy-eyed expression on her face now as she wriggled against his cock. Wrapping his arms around her, Michael rested his hands on her bare thighs, holding her in place on his lap. Her nipples were hard and the dress did absolutely nothing to conceal them as her breasts heaved, her breathing fast and shallow.

"So a logo and banner?" Michael asked, drawing little circles on her thighs. Ellie leaned back against him, her eyes still hazy.

"Yes, I can do that," she said with a little smile. She blinked, focusing a little more. "As long as you're not just asking me because we're fucking."

Patrick practically choked on his laughter as Michael chuckled. The big man looked surprised and maybe even a little incredulous - even though she was making friends, Michael had noticed Ellie was pretty quiet compared to the rest of the group. While she was occasionally blunt and even sassy with him, it wasn't a side of her everyone else got to see much of. Lexie looked even more surprised than Patrick, but she was giggling too.

"Thank you, Ellie," said Patrick still grinning. "You were the first person to come to my head. I saw the work you did for Andrew. Trust me, you earned the offer."

"Okay then," Ellie said, relaxing slightly, and her smile was brilliant.

"Good, that's settled then," said Michael, lifting Ellie up to a standing position. He bent down and rummaged through his bag. "Just one last thing before we go out into the club."

Straightening up, he held a thin leather collar with a d-ring in one hand and a pair of leather cuffs in the other. Really only the collar was necessary, but he wanted the cuffs too. The collar marked her as off limits, even if she decided to venture into the Lounge area to chat with friends, and the cuffs completed the look even if they weren't needed for the message.

She blinked rapidly and took a deep breath, but didn't try to back away.

Very gently, Michael fastened the collar around her neck while she held completely still, barely breathing. It was just a club collar, but - like the plug - he'd bought it specifically for her and it was made of extremely soft, supple leather. The buckle was silver and he left just enough room for him to slide a finger between the collar and her neck, and that was it.

When he looked Ellie in the eyes again, they were practically glazed over, which shocked the hell out of him. She looked the way she normally did at the *end* of a scene. Soft, submissive, and satisfied.

"Wrists," he said gently.

Again, blinking and focusing on his request seemed to bring her out of her submissive daze a little. She lifted her hands, eyes widening at the softness of the cuffs too.

Okay, so he might have gone a little overboard, purchasing items for her. But he'd wanted to use new things, toys that were totally hers. It had been a long time since he'd had a club contract with a submissive, but it just hadn't felt right using his old stuff. Ellie was special, and he wanted her to know it right from the beginning.

"Is it just me, or was that weirdly hot?" Lexie asked, breaking through the tension.

Ellie giggled as Michael grinned and turned to look at her. Blushing slightly, Lexie just shrugged, only a little abashed as Patrick rolled his eyes.

"Sorry," Lexie said with a shrug. "It was kind of weirdly hot though."

"I'm not going to argue," Michael said easily. Reaching out, he tugged Ellie's dress back down over her hips, hiding her lower body. "We'll get out of your hair now though, with our weirdly hot antics." Now Ellie was blushing as Lexie laughed. Michael gestured down at his toy bag. "I trust you can take care of having my bag in the Jail at the proper time?"

"Yeah, just leave it here," Patrick said, pulling Lexie up onto his lap. There was a gleam in his dark eyes, confirming Michael's suspicions of what the couple would be doing once the office was clear. "Have a good time."

"You too," Michael said, placing his hand on the small of Ellie's back and leading her towards the door into the club. When he glanced back, just before pulling the door shut behind him, Lexie was straddling Patrick and the big man had one hand on the back of her neck while the other slid over the curve of her ass, fingers seeking the base of her plug.

Envy shot through him, along with the hope that he'd one day have the same kind of connection with Ellie.

COLLARED AND WALKING THROUGH STRONGHOLD. EVEN THOUGH IT was a club collar and not like a *collar* collar, Ellie still hadn't thought she'd ever see the day.

It felt good though. The snug fit around her neck was just tight enough she couldn't help but be aware of its presence every time she took a deep breath or swallowed. The same went for the plug every time she took a step. Walking around with a plug inside of her was completely different from anal play during a scene. She felt owned, inside and out... add in Michael's warm touch on her back and it was amazing she was still standing.

The collar didn't go unnoticed either.

Of course, Michael was moving slowly through the club, and not just walking but actually strutting. Ellie found herself smiling at the cocky tilt of his head. Why had she been so nervous about this again? Now that she'd signed the contract and she was here, officially Michael's club submissive, it felt easy. Right.

Especially the recognition. More than one sub waiting in the Lounge gave her a thumbs up. Vicki mouthed the words "Good for you!" at her. Even subs who had been jealous about Michael's constant attention to her smiled at the sight of them.

The reaction was even bigger at the two tables their friends had taken over. They really were *their* friends too. Although Ellie had always been friendly with Lexie and the other submissives around the club, she hadn't really had friends until these girls had started reaching out to her. The friendships had somehow snuck up on her, but it was more apparent now than ever. They were happy for her.

Everyone was there, other than Lexie and Patrick. Jessica was sitting between fiancés, Justin and Chris, with Justin's arm around her waist and Chris' hand on her thigh. Next to them were Hilary and Liam, with Hilary on Liam's lap. As usual, Hilary was wearing her signature pink, making her look like a rose in a garden of leather. Beside them, Jake was there, dressed in dark blue jeans and a black button down shirt, almost blending in with the other dominants. He was definitely an alpha-male, but apparently ultimately vanilla in the bedroom. Rick had his arm slung around Maria's shoulder, his fingers tracing over her skin while she had the distracted look of a sub who was seriously aroused and knew she wasn't going to be getting off for a while.

Adam stood behind Angel, his arms around her, hands resting on her stomach; she'd pretty much given up doing club wear thanks to her ever expanding waistline and now just wore cute babydoll lingerie. Tonight's was black silk trimmed with white lace and looked incredibly comfortable. No longer constantly trapped behind the bar, Andrew was standing next to Olivia, with Kate seated in front of him, much like Angel was in front of Adam. Beside Kate, Leigh was sitting on Jared's lap, his big arm wrapped around her waist to hold her securely in place. Like Angel, she was wearing lingerie rather than PVC or leather. They had more of a Daddy Dom, domestic discipline relationship than anything else, and Leigh preferred to wear lace and satin over leather. Sharon was next to them, without her boyfriend Brian, in an attention-getting black corset which nearly shoved her breasts up to her chin and a black mini-skirt that was just as short and clingy as Ellie's.

"Alright!" Sharon said loudly, holding up her hand for Michael to high-five as soon as they got close enough. "You officially have a new nickname! Magic Mike!"

Angel and Leigh cheered while the others laughed and Michael made a face. He slid onto one of the bar stools, pulling Ellie in between his legs to lean back against him, caging her with his body. The entire time, though, he kept hold of her hand. Ellie relaxed back against him, thankful he was there so she wasn't the center of attention on her own.

"Why Magic Mike?" Michael asked, sounding slightly pained. Sharon was known for giving everyone nicknames. When she'd first started coming to the club, she'd described everyone to Kate using their nicknames... it wasn't until Kate joined her at Stronghold that some of those nicknames had started coming to light. Michael had originally been Master Hell No after Sharon had seen him perform an intense scene (Sharon was so not a masochist).

"Because you have the Magic Penis," Sharon said, in the solemnly earnest way only Sharon could pull off while saying something so outrageous. The reactions around the table were varied. Almost everyone found Sharon hilarious to varying degrees, but a lot of what she said tended to make Hilary blush (Hilary could be kind of a prude), and some of the Doms tried to hide their smiles behind frowns when she was treading the line of being disrespectful. Jake, who seemed to disapprove of almost everything Sharon did, just scowled, without even the hint of a smile.

"I do?" Michael leaned back and Ellie immediately knew he was looking down between their bodies at his penis. She covered her mouth with her hand as she giggled, even more aware of the collar around her neck.

"Yup. Like Kate has the magic vagina." Sharon's gaze swept the group and landed on Jessica. "Or maybe Jessica has the magic vagina, since she's keeping two men satisfied."

"Okay, I'm completely lost," Chris complained. "Although I absolutely agree, Jessica's vagina is magical. Ouch! That was a compliment!" He rubbed his side where Jessica had just elbowed him, while she squeaked as her other boyfriend, Justin, gave her ass a sharp smack.

"They don't need to hear your opinion on my vagina," Jessica sassed, blushing beet red. She wasn't as prudish as Hilary but she could definitely be shy sometimes.

"I'm not sure why we need to hear Sharon's opinion either," Jake muttered under his breath. Sharon shot him a look but ignored him and Ellie couldn't help but wonder what was going on between the two. They tended to rub each other the wrong way but Jake wasn't normally outright rude.

"I read it in a book," Sharon said, almost primly, which made Ellie giggle again. "You know, how the man is a player but then he meets this one woman and has sex with her and then BOOM! He suddenly changes all his ways and wants to commit. Magic vagina. Which means you have the magic penis, because everyone knows Ellie doesn't do any kind of relationships, but then you come along and BOOM! Collared." Every time she said "BOOM" Sharon leaned back a little and threw up her hands in front of her, spreading her fingers like little mini-explosions. It was so amusing to watch even Jake was having trouble keeping a smile off his face.

"How do you know my penis isn't magical?" Andrew asked looking disgruntled as he crossed his arms over his chest.

Sharon patted his arm. "Kate says it makes plenty of magic for her, but there can only be one Magic Mike."

"I'm never going to be able to hear that name without thinking about your penis now," Chris said, making a face at Michael. "Your magical, magical penis."

Ellie laughed so hard she snorted, and she was pretty sure she wasn't the only one.

Conversation turned to Marquis, since everyone was naturally curious about the new club and not everyone had had a chance to talk to Michael or Patrick before now. Angel and Adam, who already knew plenty, and Andrew and Kate headed down to the Dungeon to scene; they'd just been waiting for Ellie and Michael to appear. With how crowded Stronghold was becoming, it was always easier to find a piece of empty equipment earlier in the evening.

Time flew by, until it was suddenly time to go to Jail. Her and Michael's first real scene as a club couple. The collar seemed to fit even more snugly around her neck and her ass tightened around the plug as they excused themselves from the conversation. Her pulse fluttered wildly as Michael took her hand and led her to the stairs.

❧ 10 ❧

As much fun as it had been to catch up with all their friends, Michael was relieved they hadn't had a long wait before being able to head to their room. He was antsy as hell from signing the contract, plugging Ellie, and then seeing her in his collar and cuffs. The need to fully claim her, to mark her so she'd have the evidence of their scene for days, was riding him hard.

The Jail would be good for impact play and he was looking forward to using it to its best advantage.

The Dungeon was crowded, although it looked like the others had managed to find places to play. Michael was extra grateful for Patrick's offer of the private room now. He was not only going to have room to swing the whip, but he was going to have Ellie all to himself. It didn't matter that everyone had been watching her scene with other Doms for months... now she was his.

While exhibitionism didn't turn Michael off, it wasn't something which really got him going either. He appreciated being appreciated for being a good Dom or admiration for his skill with a whip, but an audience didn't arouse him. Since he tried to focus solely on what he was doing, an audience just didn't make a difference to him one way or another.

Being able to keep Ellie all to himself... now *that* definitely did something for him.

When the door closed behind them, it did so with a satisfying click. Some of the noise from the Dungeon still filtered through, adding to the atmosphere, since only the loudest cries and screams were still audible.

Ellie stood in the center of the room, in front of the desk, looking nervous. Behind her, the bars on the cell beckoned temptingly. Michael grinned, which made her shift uncertainly back and forth on her feet. Excitement, anxiety, and just the tiniest bit of fearful antici- pation flitted across her face; just the kind of reaction he liked to see.

"Turn around and move in front of the bars," he ordered. He wasn't interested in actually putting her in the jail cell, but the bars could be very useful. Arousal lit up Ellie's dark eyes before she turned around and scampered over to the bars, moving with a quickness that came from eagerness. "Spread your legs and hold onto the bars in front of you, above your head."

The position made her skirt ride up slightly, the curve of her ass barely keeping it in place. Even from behind, he could see her breath quickening as he approached. She peeked over her shoulder at him before snapping her head back around, as if afraid she'd done some- thing wrong. Michael didn't mind her looking, so he didn't chastise her.

Coming up behind her, he gently placed his hands on her shoul- ders. Her muscles were a little tense, but she quickly relaxed as he kneaded them slightly.

"I'm going to have to search you and make sure you aren't hiding anything from me, Miss Sandler," he said, his voice lighter and more teasing than it should be. This was why he didn't do role-play.

It might be for the best though. Ellie giggled, relaxing further as his hands moved over the backs of her shoulders and to her sides. His fingers stretched to stroke the sides of her breasts as he moved his hands up and down the slick material of her dress; down to her hips, back up to her breasts, slowly moving towards the front of her.

When he cupped the undersides of her breasts, rather than just brushing against them, there was a little hitch in her breath. Michael pressed up behind her, feeling the warmth of her body, and ran his lips over the base of her neck as she leaned her head back against him. Kneading her breasts, he felt her nipples pressing against his palms, through the fabric of her dress.

"Hmmm... I'm not sure, I think I'll need to examine this area more closely for dangerous weapons," he said. "Arms down." Ellie's arms dropped and he rolled the top of her dress down, pulling her arms through the armholes before raising them back up again, placing her hands where he wanted them on the bars in front of her. Then he let his hands glide over her skin, back down her arms to her breasts.

Ellie moaned as he cupped the soft, heavy mounds, his fingers seeking out her nipples and rolling them between his fingers. She squirmed, rubbing her ass against his erection as he pulled and tugged on the tiny buds, teasing her with the light contact.

"Naughty, naughty," he murmured, giving her nipples a hard enough pinch to make her gasp. "Don't worry, I have something to help you stay still."

Going back to his bag, he pulled out a pair of nipple clamps and several short chains, two heavy ones and one very light, thin one. Returning to Ellie, he quickly attached her cuffs to the bars, then he moved around and entered the jail so she was facing him.

Her nipples were tightly budded, her breasts thrust towards him, not quite touching the cool, metal bars of the jail. With her black hair tumbled around her shoulders, enhancing her creamy skin and the pink of her nipples, she looked utterly gorgeous and entirely too enticing.

"I think you're on the wrong side of the bars," she teased, looking up at him with amusement sparking in her eyes.

Chuckling, Michael pinched one of her nipples and used it to pull her forward against the bars. She let out a low moan at the tight pressure on her tender bud, and then shivered as she was pulled against the bars. Leaning down, Michael placed a very gentle kiss on her lips.

He hadn't planned to kiss her yet, until he'd gotten in here and seen her looking up at him with those big, dark eyes, full of passionate arousal. While having bars between them wasn't really the way he'd wanted to kiss her, there was something sexy about it in a fun way. In some ways, it was almost like the wall Ellie had around herself had been made real - and he was sneaking through it. In other ways, there was just something kind of hot about being able to caress her as he pleased, but not do any more than touch. Maybe he had a little streak of masochism in him as well.

The wide-eyed look of surprise she gave him when he pulled away from the gentle kiss without deepening it made him chuckle. He liked keeping her on her toes and doing the unexpected.

"Hold still, beautiful," he said, placing the clamp on the nipple he'd been pinching.

Ellie sucked in a breath at the harsh bite. He'd chosen a pair with fairly tight springs, so they delivered a lot more pressure than the ones he'd used on her previously.

"Good girl," he murmured, quickly placing the other one. He attached the light chain to the base of each clamp, keeping it nice and taut. Now, if she moved too much, the chain would press against the bars and increase the pressure on her nipples, which were already turning a nice, dark pink.

She looked down at them and blinked in consternation as she realized what he'd done.

Michael grinned wickedly. "Now I'm going to finish my search. You should probably stay as still as you can."

Walking back around to her side of the bars, Michael positioned himself behind her and gave her ass a sharp smack.

Ellie jumped and then squealed as her movement made the short chain on her clamps pull tight, stilling immediately as the impact was felt. Her panting breaths as she assimilated the pain had Michael fighting down the urge to speed up the scene. While his cock might want him to hurry along, he wanted as much time with Ellie as he could get. He wanted to make this scene fucking amazing for her.

After all, it was their first scene as a kind-of couple. Hopefully setting the stage for later things to come.

He hooked his fingers under the edge of her skirt and dragged it up over her ass before crouching down behind her, placing the creamy skin of her cheeks right at his eye level. With her legs spread apart, he could actually smell the sweet musk of her arousal, as well as peek between her legs at her glistening pussy. She was soaking wet. Poor pussy wasn't going to get his attention right away though... in fact, not any time soon at all.

His hands skimmed over the outside of her legs and then back up the inside, until he reached the base of the plug in her ass.

"Hmmm... you seem to be hiding something here..." He teased, gripping the base and twisting it.

She moaned, squirmed, gasped, and stopped as the clamps did their job. Michael slowly pulled the plug out, making her tense and relax as her anus moved over the widest part. His cock ached as he pulled the plug almost all the way out and then pushed it almost all the way back in. Ellie cried out as her muscle was stretched, growing and shrinking as he moved the plug back and forth, fucking her tight little hole with it.

Michael's own breaths were coming short and fast as he toyed with her and her arousal increased. "You like this, don't you, Ellie?"

"Yes Michael," she said immediately, breathless with sexual need. She shivered as he leaned forward and actually sank his teeth into the curve of her ass. Not too hard, but not too gently either. Just enough to leave an impression and making her ass throb from the bite. Michael rather liked seeing his mark on her ass.

🕮

HOLY CRAP, HE'D ACTUALLY JUST BITTEN HER!

And Ellie had liked it. It was a different kind of pain than she was used to. Sharp but with pressure, aching but without a sting. Her pussy clenched as he twisted the plug, pushing it almost fully into her as it spun, igniting her nerve endings and making it nearly impossible for her to hold still. If it weren't for the nasty clamps on her nipples, she'd be writhing.

The clamps bit down tightly, new waves of pain throbbing every time she accidentally moved enough that the chain pulled against the bars in front of her. Ellie had always liked predicament bondage and this was no exception, no matter how her poor nipples protested the abuse. The pain slid through her, mingling with her arousal and excitement and making her pussy ache to be filled.

"OH!" A shudder went through her, from head to toe, as Michael manipulated the plug. Somehow it almost felt like he'd hit her g-spot... like, if there was a backside to her g-spot and he'd moved the plug just right. He did it again, and Ellie moaned, her fingers wrapping around the bars and clinging to try and keep herself from moving too much... or her legs from buckling at the intense sensation.

A warm hand cupped her leg, just underneath her ass, as if he was helping her maintain position, as the plug slid snugly back into its home. Ellie whimpered in disappointment as her body fizzed and popped with needy pleasure, knowing her orgasm probably wasn't coming any time soon.

Behind her, she felt Michael's movement as he stood.

"But you haven't checked everywhere yet!" she protested, her lower body spasming in agreement. Even though she didn't think he'd let her cum, she'd wanted his fingers in her pussy... wanted him to touch and stroke her... and, okay, make her cum.

Damn sadist.

Michael just chuckled as he gave her ass a little slap.

"I'll get to it later," he said. "Right now, I'd like to reward you for being such a good girl." Oh, okay. That sounded pretty good. Ellie liked rewards. "What's your favorite impact implement?"

"A leather strap," she said immediately. "Or a rubber one. I like the straps. I can take more of the leather than the rubber." Which was pretty much the case for everyone, so it wouldn't be a surprise to him.

Leather was more thuddy, while rubber could be utterly demoralizing when wielded harshly. Ellie was already feeling high on endorphins right now, so she could go for either. The initial shock, the lingering burn, the throbbing ache... she wanted it so badly. Pain reached down inside of her, stirring her pleasure, fulfilling her darkest desires, and providing an ache which could last for days.

She could hear Michael moving behind her, but unlike earlier she didn't feel compelled to look. In fact, she felt completely comfortable, trusting he was getting a strap to whip her with. It was almost like being in a meditative state; waiting for what came next but without any sense of urgency. Just happily existing, already satisfied with knowing satisfaction was coming. She felt so good, so relaxed, so happy... Normally it took her a while to achieve this state of mind during a scene, but right now she was practically singing her joy in her head.

Yes, yes, yes, yes, yes...

"What's your color, Ellie?"

"Green, Ma- uh, Michael." She'd almost called him Master Michael before remembering he'd told her not to call him that. It felt weird not to do so, but she didn't want to miss out on her reward for something so small.

"Good girl, beautiful," he said, right before she heard the whoosh of air which signaled an imminent blow.

THWAP!

Ellie cried out as the leather seared a stripe across her ass, her body jerking slightly and causing her nipples to protest as the clamps tugged at them. Painful warmth spread like a wave through her body, from the three points of pain through her torso and limbs, making her feel almost woozy.

TWHAP!

The leather hit just below the first stripe, wielded with the kind of precision that made a masochist's dreams come true. A stinging burn that bit deep, thudding against her skin and sinking into her body.

THWAP!

The third blow landed on the undercurve of her ass, making her cry out as the leather snapped against more sensitive skin. The bite was harder, sharper, the fiery pain hotter, surging through her and causing another kind of heat to flare; Michael and the strap was like a blacksmith with his bellows, and she was the forge in which he'd create his masterpiece of agonized ecstasy. The flesh of her ass jiggled as she clenched around the plug inside of her, breathlessly shuddering. If she could have moved to press her legs together, she would have, but even trying would involve the clamps practically tearing off her nipples. The tender buds were already going to be sore for days.

There was movement behind her, and then Michael's hand rubbed roughly over the newly sensitized skin of her ass. Ellie hissed, her hands tightening around the bars she was clinging to, as the sensation swept through her, already knowing it wasn't enough. She wanted more of the leather.

"More please, Michael," she said, letting her need fill her voice. She needed more pain, she needed the pleasure which would follow. She needed him.

"Let's play a game, pretty girl," he said, almost conversationally. "I'm going to ask you questions, and for every answer you give me, you get a taste of the leather."

Even in her pleasure-dazed, pain-needy state, Ellie hesitated. "What kind of questions?"

"All kinds," Michael said, his fingers squeezing her ass cheek tightly, kneading the soft flesh and reminding her how good the pain felt. "For instance, do you prefer dildos or vibrators?"

"I don't really have a preference," she admitted. "I like both for different reasons." It wasn't the answer he was looking for but...

He stepped away.

THWAP!

She shuddered, groaning with pained-pleasure as fire licked across her skin, almost exactly where the very first stroke had landed. Okay, this wasn't so bad.

"Is there a room here at the club you've never used?"

That was an easy one. "Arabian Nights and the Movie Rooms."

Arabian Nights was too much of a romantic room, she'd avoided it on principle. Overall, she was more comfortable down in the Dungeon anyway, although she'd played upstairs in the Office, School Room, and Locker Room. Exhibitionism wasn't really her kink, and she could be a voyeur anywhere, so she'd never been interested in being taped or watching the live feed.

THWAP!

The leather burned and Ellie shuddered as her pain and pleasure mixed into a smooth blend, filling her from head to toe with sensation. Tears sparked in her eyes as the burning grew, the heat of her skin climbing higher.

The questions continued, as did the stripes of leather turning her ass a darker and darker red. He wanted to know what her favorite room in Stronghold was (the Interrogation Room), what her favorite non-impact toy was (clamps... although she almost admitted it was specifically the plug currently inside of her), if she preferred the St. Andrew's Cross or a spanking bench (the cross), and questions along those lines. Every three or four answers, he would step forward and slide his fingers between her legs from behind, either stroking her pussy or tugging and twirling the plug, exciting her arousal even further.

Then, slowly, the questions changed. She barely even noticed, she was so caught up in the way her pussy was quivering needily, the searing heat and deeper ache of her buttocks, and the tears sliding down her cheeks to drip onto her breasts.

"Have you played outside of the club before?"

"A couple of times."

THWAP!

"When was the last time?"

"Years ago."

THWAP!

"Have you ever dated anyone you played with?"

"No."

THWAP!

THE CREAMY SKIN OF ELLIE'S ASS WAS NOW A BRIGHT, BURNING RED. She'd be feeling this whipping for days - which seemed to be what she liked, considering straps were her favorite impact toy. Michael looked forward to seeing her reaction to the rubber strap, which was much harsher. His cock, already rock hard, jerked at the thought of her screams.

She had easily fallen into a headspace to deal with the leather strap, even as he heard the tears in her voice with every answer she gave. Her pussy was soaking wet, swollen to his touch whenever he stroked her, and his cock throbbed every time he touched her, aching to be inside of her. The contrast of the pale skin of her back against the bright red of her ass was fucking gorgeous, and he could feel the heat coming off her skin whenever he moved forward to touch her.

"What's your favorite color?"

Ellie's giggle was effervescent, her answer coming in almost a sing-song manner. "I can't say or you'll stop whipping me."

Michael chuckled. "You haven't had enough?"

She shook her head, peeking over her shoulder at him, her eyes glazed over with lust. The eyeliner she'd been wearing earlier was running down her cheeks along with her tears, and her cheeks were flushed pink. The movement obviously made the chain tug on her nipples, and she squeaked as she whipped her head back around again, but the one look had been enough to tell him where she was mentally. Nearly at sub space and probably not going to say her safe word even if she was nearing her limits.

"Three more questions, Ellie."

"Yes, Michael." Her words were a little slurred, but she sounded so relaxed, so happy... pain and pleasure drunk probably.

"Did you ever think about me after high school?"

"All the time," she admitted, her hips lifting slightly in anticipation of the strap. "You turned out even hotter than I imagined."

He flicked his wrist, catching her on the underside of her ass and enjoying her sharp cry of pain in response. A shiver across her skin as she leaned forward, panting, told him she was probably close to cumming soon. It would only take a stroke of his finger... but not yet.

"Why did you ask me for a club contract?"

"Trust you," she said, her words slurring again a bit.

Second to last stroke. Right across the center of her ass. He heard the sob in her voice as she whimpered and knew they were getting near his limit even if they weren't approaching hers - although he was pretty sure she couldn't take much more of a beating on her ass without regretting it tomorrow. But the stroke was definitely a reward, because he was touched, right down to the center of his heart...

"Why wouldn't you talk to me before the chorus concert?"

"I..." She sucked in a breath. "Don't know how to do relationships and..."

"And?" he prompted after a moment.

But she shook her head, pulling herself against the bars and away from him.

"It's okay, Ellie," he crooned, soothingly. He ran his hand over the flaming curve of her ass, feeling the heat pulsing against his palm. "You earned your reward."

THWAP!

He aimed for the backs of her untouched thighs, and Ellie screamed as her head snapped back, a choked sob working its way out of her throat. The strap had left matching marks on her pristine skin, bright pink and painful. This welt would fade faster, but the initial pain was more.

"Ow.. ow..." she muttered, readjusting her position, taking deep shuddering breaths as the pain worked its ways through her system.

"What color are you, Ellie?"

"Green, Sir," she said immediately, forgetting to call him Michael, but he wasn't going to punish her for the infraction. She was so far gone into the scene, into the pain, she was on automatic. Her bright red bottom pushed out slightly; not much, but as much as she was able with her hands secured to the bars and her nipples clamped and holding her in predicament bondage. By now the pain would be sweet agony, keeping his little masochist's orgasm right on edge. "Fuck me, please... please, fuck me, Sir."

It was the sweetest plea he'd ever heard, and one he was happy to fulfill.

Finally.

This wouldn't make her his unequivocally, but it was a step. Tomorrow she'd be feeling him inside and out. She'd remember how he felt inside of her, how he'd given her pain and then made her scream with pleasure. Sex was part of their contract, but with Ellie it was also so much more. He'd bind her to him with pain and pleasure and everything between them.

Setting the strap on the ground, he undid the front of his pants and let them fall down around his thighs. His cock was aching, the shaft and head an angry dark red, although not nearly as dark as Ellie's ravaged ass. Palming her hot cheeks, he enjoyed her moan as he pushed them apart. They nearly matched the dark red winking jewel seated between them.

He ignored her squeak of distress as he pulled her hips back, lining his cock up with her pussy; the new position would put pressure on her nipples, increasing the pain and the bite right before he removed them and really made her hurt in the best way possible.

"Oh!... oh please..." Her head leaned forward against the bars as he rubbed his cock along her slit, lubricating his already leaking tip, before finding her entrance. The wet heat of her pussy encased the head of his cock like a slick fist, making him groan with pleasure as he sank in, her tight muscles quivering around him. "Michael... it's too much... oh... too much!"

"Shhh," he said soothingly, working his cock back and forth in the tight space, his muscles tense as he fought against the need to go faster and harder. Every little thrust pushed him deeper inside of her, the heat of her ass emanating against his groin, the plug making her tighter than she might have otherwise been. "Be a good girl and take it."

Ellie writhed against him, apparently no longer caring about the way it made the nipple clamps pull. "Oh... oh god... oh please..."

She cried out as his cock slid all the way home, totally encased in the hot, silken clasp of her body. The base of the plug pressed against his groin, the heat of her ass warming his skin. Michael moved his hands up to cup her breasts, kneading the swollen mounds and making her cry out again.

"Oh fuck!"

Then he began to move.

She was slick heaven, her pussy grasping and shuddering around him, like she was fitted perfectly to his cock as he pumped in and out of her. Pinching the clamps open, he let them drop to the floor inside the jail cell as Ellie screamed her climax, brought on by the pain of having her crushed nipples released from their bondage.

Jagged edges of white hot agony flared through her breasts, Michael's fingers stoking the fires as he rubbed and rolled her nipples, increasing the pulsing sensation as blood returned. Ellie writhed with abandon, finally free to do so, as ecstasy shot through her, her pussy pulsing around his thrusting cock, her ass clenching around the hard plug, and pleasure and pain clashing into brutal rapture. Blackness seemed to darken her vision even though her eyes were open as Michael rode her from behind, his hands almost viciously squeezing her breasts, and Ellie gasped for air as the waves of pleasure rolled through her.

He felt huge inside of her, possibly because of the plug, although she knew he was well endowed anyway. Feeling him working his way inside of her, forcing her body to adjust to fit both his cock and the plug, had been too much to bear... and yet she had refused to say her safe word. She'd wanted it. And when he'd told her to be a good girl and take it, in his deep, darkly demanding voice... she'd nearly cum just from that.

It was the release of the nipple clamps which sent her completely over the edge though. Brutal, glorious pain, mixed with the pleasure of being filled to the brim, and her body had exploded with the sensations.

Now she couldn't stop.

Michael worked his cock hard and fast, every thrust jolting against the plug in her ass, making it almost feel like she was being taken in both holes at once... his body slapped against her brutalized ass, making the pain flare like she was being spanked on her already tenderized skin. Her breasts were swollen and throbbing in his hands, her nipples agonized points trapped between his fingers, and with every breath a new wave of tingling ecstasy poured through her. She clung to the bars of the jail, unable to do anything but ride it out as Michael worked out his own needs, satisfaction chasing pleasure at finally being completely on the receiving end of his attentions, the way she'd fantasized about ever since he'd shown up at the club.

She nearly sobbed when she felt him pulsing inside of her, his hands pulling her back against his chest so she couldn't even wriggle as he groaned in her ear, his hot breath panting against her skin. A submissive's pure delight at serving her Dom welled up inside of her, filling her with a sense of contentment which had been missing from every other scene she'd ever done. She'd had sex in scenes before, she'd been praised by Doms before for the scenes she'd done with them, but none of them had ever felt like *this* to her.

She felt completely blissed out.

Satiated.

Almost proud.

"Good girl," Michael breathed in her ear as his hands gentled, his body relaxing against hers, supporting her rather than holding her. She whimpered a little as he gently caressed her poor nipples, sending little shocks of pain through the last shudders of her orgasm, enhancing the pleasure from that small bite.

He'd included a demand to provide after care in the contract and, for the first time, Ellie completely let go and gave all of her control over to her Dom. She just let herself enjoy being picked up and carried out of the room, wrapped in a blanket and snuggled onto Michael's lap, his strong arms cradling her almost reverently. Sighing happily, she nestled in, completely oblivious to the stares around them of people who had never seen her so happily content in the aftercare corner before.

Michael made sure she ate some chocolate and held a water bottle to her lips to drink. She had no idea what the passage of time was like. She felt so woozy, so relaxed... it was like being drunk, except even when she was drunk she didn't let go like this. People came by to chat with Michael and she ignored them, not caring enough to see who they were.

Eventually, he shook her a little. "Ellie, it's time to go, but I don't want you driving home like this. Will you come home with me? Adam and Angel will follow and Angel will take your car to my place before they go home."

"Ooooookay," Ellie said, her head lolling on his shoulder.

When he set her down in the front seat of his car, she fell asleep almost immediately.

⚜ 11 ⚜

The bed wasn't hers.

That was her first thought.

The bed wasn't hers and someone was curled up around her. A big, hard, muscular someone. With a very large cock pressing into her very sore ass.

The night before came rushing back in.

The exquisite pain. The incredible pleasure. Her unusual reaction after the scene.

And now she was in his bed.

She'd *slept* in his bed.

Panic clawed its way up her chest.

Too much. Too much, too fast. Obviously she hadn't been thinking last night.

Ellie never went home with a Dom. She'd only ever once slept in the same bed as another man – Steve - and she'd only done that once. He'd taken it to mean things it hadn't, he'd thought it meant she was getting 'better,' and they'd be a more normal couple. In the face of his optimism, she'd freaked out and pulled back completely, and their relationship had ended. Just like then, she wasn't ready for this.

The need to run hit her hard and fast, and she accidentally

kicked Michael's shin as she flailed, trying to untangle herself from both him and the sheets. The shirt she was wearing seemed to pull, practically choking her. Ellie never slept in baggy shirts with collars, she always slept in a tank top and shorts... it felt like she was drowning in fabric.

"Hey... hey... what's going on, Ell?" he asked, his voice husky with sleep. He placed his hand on her shoulder, a gesture obviously meant to be soothing, but which did nothing to stem her bubbling emotions.

"I have to go."

She could hear the shock and panic in her voice, and inwardly cursed. As much as she wanted to sound normal, she just couldn't. She was too freaked out by how much she'd let go of herself last night.

She'd *slept* in his *bed*. After signing a club contract with him.

Being at the club was safe. There were rules. Boundaries. The expectations were well defined. But now... what the hell was she supposed to do now? How was someone supposed to act the morning after?

Kicking him, panicking, and waking him up was probably not high on the list of "best ways to behave." She managed to struggle to a sitting position, although her legs were still tangled in the covers. Ouch... putting pressure on her bottom made the lingering soreness from last night flare to life.

"Ell, calm down, breathe." His voice had deepened, becoming almost stern, as his warm hands pressed against her shoulders, holding her in place. Between the order, his hands holding her, and the throbbing of her ass, her brain finally stopped flipping out. She took a deep breath as Michael moved around to the side of her.

For a moment his arm curved around her shoulders, and then it suddenly dropped to his side and he took her hand as he sat next to her. Reluctantly, Ellie made herself look at him.

Even in the morning he was beautiful, his hair tousled and falling around his cheekbones, stubble darkening his jaw, and hazel eyes with only half the alertness they normally held. Wearing nothing but a pair of boxers, he looked like the kind of man every woman dreamed of waking up to. Well, maybe not every woman. But Ellie liked that he was lean muscle instead of bulky.

"What's wrong?" he asked, his voice gentle but firm, letting her know he wanted a real answer.

She blushed, averting her gaze in embarrassment at how she'd just freaked out for no real reason.

"I've never do sleepovers," she mumbled.

Michael's fingers twitched around hers and he was silent for a long moment. "Well then, I'm honored."

"I can't do this again." She kept her eyes on her lap, not wanting to see his reaction. Not wanting to see if she'd just hurt his feelings. "This is too much for me right now. I don't know how to do this. I don't even really know how to do a club contract, but I want to try that at least, this is..."

"Ellie." He squeezed her hand as he interrupted her. She still didn't dare look at him but his voice remained gentle. Calm. Soothing. "It's okay. Next time, I'll find a way to get you back to your house or we'll stay at the club longer, or... something. We can talk about it, okay?"

"Okay," she mumbled.

The bed shifted as he leaned towards her and gave her a kiss on the side of her forehead. "I'm going to go get breakfast ready, okay? The bathroom is right across the hall and there's an extra toothbrush in the medicine cabinet. Come on out whenever you're ready."

She nodded, still not looking up at him as he pulled open a drawer on his dresser and walked out of the room, pulling on a shirt as he left.

The second the door to the bedroom closed her head snapped up, and she looked around. The bed she was sitting on was queen-sized with a sturdy wooden frame. Nothing special. His sheets were plain white and the comforter was brown, neither of which matched the dark blue curtains hanging over the single window. Directly across from her was a dresser and she saw her dress neatly folded on top of it, her small purse sitting beside the dress.

Looking down at herself, she could see he'd dressed her in a t-shirt and a pair of his boxers. What was more disturbing was she couldn't even remember him doing so. While she did remember agreeing to go home with him - and it had made sense at the time - she didn't remember anything after being carried out of the club. And she flushed when she remembered that.

It had felt nice. Almost too nice.

Distracting herself, she continued her perusal of the room. There were a few framed play posters on the walls, and she assumed they were shows he'd been in... or maybe just shows he'd been to and really liked? A half-full bookcase in the corner had her getting up to see what was on it. Ouchie... moving hurt a little. Her nipples rubbed against the t-shirt, the soft fabric feeling much more abrasive on the little buds than against the rest of her skin. The bookshelf was mostly scripts. Humana Festival books. A few graphic novels.

And other than that, there wasn't anything else to look at in his room, unless she wanted to explore his closet. Since the door was closed, it just felt a little too nosy. She could move locations to the bathroom but...

For some reason she didn't want to leave this room. It was like a little cocoon bubble of safety. Michael was *out there*. Further conversation was *out there*.

Explanations for why she was such a freak would happen *out there*.

He'd been really nice about it, but he had to have questions. Who wouldn't?

"Ugh... I suck," she muttered as she made a beeline for her purse. Fortunately her phone battery was still half full.

Who to call though? Angel was the first person who popped into her head, but Angel was really close friends with Michael... which was part of why she'd popped into Ellie's head, but the cons might outweighed the pros on that one. Lexie was probably the better choice. Hopefully, it wasn't too early in the morning to call her.

Practically doing a little nervous dance as the phone rang, Ellie almost pumped her fist with relief when Lexie answered.

"Hello? Ellie? Are you okay?" Lexie didn't sound sleepy, so at least Ellie hadn't woken her up.

"Hi, yeah, I'm okay I think," Ellie whispered into the phone.

"Why are you whispering?" Lexie whispered back.

"Michael's in the other room and... I don't know, I guess I don't want him to hear me." Now she felt a little silly, but she'd probably feel even sillier if Michael knew she was calling reinforcements because she didn't know how to handle this situation. It was such a normal situation, she was just a freak who had made it twenty eight years and only had a sleepover with one guy. Well, two now.

"What do you need?" Lexie asked. She wasn't whispering anymore but her voice was still softer than normal. Maybe because she felt weird speaking normally, while Ellie was whispering.

"What do I do?"

"What do you mean?"

"I mean, what do I literally do? He's in the kitchen making me breakfast... do I put my dress back on? Do I stay in his t-shirt and boxers? Do I eat and leave, or am I supposed to stay after we eat? What do I *say* to him?!" Her whispering was getting louder as a new kind of panic gripped her. With every question she asked, her anxiety rose.

She was so in over her head.

"Shh, shh, it's okay," Lexie reassured her. "If you want to leave right after eating, put your dress back on. If you want to stay, you can stay in his clothes. Or you can always just leave right after and steal his clothes if you want to. Stolen t-shirts are the best. What you want to do after breakfast is entirely up to you."

"Okay... but what do I say to him?"

"Just... normal conversation. Ask him about Marquis. Talk about the scene last night. Or go crazy and talk about his apartment and ask him a few questions about himself."

Ellie cringed. What did it say about her that she was way more freaked out about asking personal questions than she was having sex with a guy? Even now, her sore ass and pleasantly sore pussy didn't faze her. That part was great. But she was freaking out about talking over breakfast to the guy who had given them to her.

"You can do it, Ellie," Lexie said encouragingly after a moment of silence. "I know morning afters can be kind of weird, but it's a lot easier once you get out there and start a conversation. Both of you will pretend everything is just fine and totally normal, and before you know it, it will be."

Sounded easier said than done, but Lexie did have a point. Kind of like how Ellie had worked herself up before signing the club contract last night, but once she'd signed it she'd settled down and everything had felt good.

And then everything had felt *really* good.

She was going to be feeling the after effects from last night for days. She wanted more scenes like that. Which meant she needed to get out there and convince Michael she wasn't a total freak. He'd already agreed to take her home after scening at the club, rather than back to his place, so that conversation was out of the way.

She could do this.

"Thanks, Lexie," she whispered.

"Any time, babe," Lexie said. "And you can call me any time, okay? Good luck!"

Hanging up the phone, Ellie took a deep breath. Okay, step one - leave the bedroom. The bathroom was just across the hall. She could totally handle just going to the bathroom. Michael wasn't in there after all.

<hr/>

NOTHING LIKE HAVING A WOMAN PANIC ABOUT WAKING UP WITH him to make him feel good. Michael tried not to let it get him down as he moved around the kitchen, picking up a bowl to crack the eggs into, and setting a pan down on the stove. Eggs, sausage, fruit... that sounded good. He set a second pan down on the stove and turned the heat to medium before pulling open the fridge to grab the food.

It's not personal, he reminded himself.

The fact she was still in his bedroom, rather than already running out the door before breakfast, made him feel marginally better.

She trusted him.

Last night she'd trusted him enough to completely let go and then come home with him, even if this morning she'd woken up and regretted it. Then again, she might not regret it. He'd woken up to her thrashing around, which seemed more like an instinctive reaction than something she'd thought through. Of course, she didn't want to spend the night again now.

Too much, too soon, too fast.

Something he probably should have realized last night, but she'd been too out of it to drive. He wanted to excuse himself by saying he thought it would have been too invasive to take her to her place when she was so out of it, but if he were being totally honest with himself, the truth was he'd wanted her at his. So that's what he'd done.

He heard the bedroom door open, and then a moment later the automatic fan which was attached to the light switch in the bathroom turned on, before the sound became slightly more muted as the bathroom door closed. Alright, so she was still here, which meant he hadn't totally fucked things up. He was just going to have to keep reminding himself to slow down; they needed to move at her pace, not his. Just because the club contract was signed did not mean he should change tactics; if anything, that was proof he needed to stay the course.

The eggs and sausage were almost ready when Ellie appeared in the entryway to the kitchen, still wearing his blue t-shirt and dark blue boxers. The sight of her in his clothes sent a proprietorial thrill through him, and he had to remind himself not to get too excited about it. Her hair was back in a side ponytail, although more mussed looking than last night, and her face was completely scrubbed clean. Last night he'd used some of his leftover make-up wipes to clean off a lot of it, but she'd cleaned off the remnants which had given her adorable raccoon eyes overnight. Good thing he'd still had some of his make-up wipes left over from his last tour, he didn't think she would have liked sleeping with mascara all over her cheeks last night.

"Were you robbed or something?" she asked, leaning against the doorway.

"What?"

"Were you robbed?" she asked again, leaning back slightly to gesture at his apartment. Her gesture took in the couch, television, small dining table, and desk where his laptop rested. "You have no stuff. You have furniture, but no stuff."

She seemed nervous, but like she was trying to be casual, all of which made her look incredibly adorable.

"Since I was always traveling on tour I never really accumulated that much stuff, although I have a bunch of old stuff in the attic at my parents' house," he said, smiling at her. "Does scrambled eggs and sausage sound good to you?"

"Do the scrambled eggs have cheese on them?"

"They can."

Ellie smiled, looking a bit abashed. "I'm kind of a cheese fiend."

"I think I remember that," Michael murmured, grinning as he grabbed some cheddar from the fridge to grate onto the eggs. "You always had a string cheese with your lunch."

She laughed. "I can't believe you remember my cheese obsession."

He shrugged as he grated the cheese onto the eggs and pulled down two plates. "It was cute. Do you want water, coffee, milk, or juice?"

"Just water is good," she said, padding forward into the kitchen to take a plate from him and fill it up with food.

"Forks are in there," he pointed at the drawer. "And fruit, in the basket over there if you want any."

In a matter of minutes they were seated at his dining room table, her with her water and him with his coffee, digging into breakfast. Michael could see how nervous she was, the tension was set in her shoulders, but she was putting up a good front.

"How are you feeling this morning?" he asked, enjoying the way her cheeks immediately heated. "Any bad after effects?"

"No," she said, pushing her eggs and sausage around on her plate, rather than meeting his eyes. "I'm sore, but a good kind of sore. It was a good scene."

"I thought so too," he said, deliberately keeping his voice a lot more casual than he was actually feeling. Watching Ellie squirm was adorable, but he didn't want to push her too much. Still, he'd thought talking about the scene would be easier for her; he'd noticed she was usually more comfortable focusing on the physical. Maybe since the scene was over she wasn't as comfortable anymore?

"So, are you going to start getting more stuff now that you're staying in one place?" she asked, scooping up a forkful of eggs, and signifying an immediate change in subject. Michael decided to let it slide. After all, their contract only extended to the club. They were still going to talk about last night's scene, but he could wait until they were at the club and have the conversation before their next scene.

"Maybe," he said, looking around the space. "I don't really know what I'd get. I could print off some photos of friends or something, that might be nice."

"Also, maybe some end tables. An armchair. Some DVDs," she teased. She was starting to relax a little more. "Something to make this place look a little less like a hotel. Although, hotels usually have paintings up on the walls."

"Yeah, yeah..." He looked around again. "It's just hard to get out of the 'don't buy anything you can't pack or don't want to leave behind' mindset."

"Do you think you'll go back on tour?"

The question of the year. But, ever since he'd volunteered to take on opening Marquis with Patrick, he hadn't felt the same itch to audition. Hell, even before that, he hadn't really been interested. The theater had lost a lot of its flair for him.

"No, I don't think so," he said finally. "I still love to act, but I'm tired of making a career out of it. I want to come home, to the same home, every day. I want to be able to make plans and see my friends in the evenings. I might do some community shows eventually like Angel, but right now I can't see myself wanting even the time commitment. Theater has a way of sucking away my entire life, and now that I've had a break from it, I'm feeling more relief than anything else."

ELLIE WAS FEELING RELIEVED TOO AND SHE WASN'T SURE SHE liked it.

It was silly to feel a stab of anxiety when he hadn't answered immediately about going back on tour. After all, they were just in a club relationship. Yeah, she wanted a real relationship eventually, if she could get there, but she so wasn't ready to make such a big step. Heck, she should have been relieved at the idea of him going on tour and giving her some space, especially if things didn't work out between them, but instead she was just relieved and happy he wasn't planning on going anywhere.

At least Lexie had been right about just coming out here and getting this over with. She'd decided to stick with his clothes instead of her dress, because they were a lot more comfortable (and, okay, wearing clothes which smelled like him was definitely not the worst thing in the world). At first she'd felt incredibly awkward, now this felt so natural it was a little scary.

"Is the cheddar okay?" he asked, pointing his fork at her half-eaten eggs. "It was the only cheese I had."

"Oh yeah," she said, scooping up another forkful. "I love pretty much all cheese. It's hard to go wrong with cheese."

"Are there any you don't like?"

"Mmm... when they put things in cheese to make it taste like something else. Like, fruit or dill or truffle. I don't understand why people feel the need to ruin the cheese flavor." She made a face. "Except bacon. Trader Joe's has a bacon-cheddar cheese that's really good. But bacon is pretty much the exception to every rule."

Michael laughed, his eyes twinkling at her. "Okay, good to know."

Lexie had been right, everything was easier once the conversation was started. She asked him about the posters in his room - she was right, they'd been shows he'd done and particularly loved, either because of the part, the cast, or the play itself. *Laramie Project* was his favorite show he'd ever done, and he'd played the part of the writer, Moises Kaufman, which she could absolutely see with his smooth voice and calming demeanor.

After all her panic about this morning, she was surprised to find she was a little disappointed when breakfast was over and it was time to go. But she needed to get home to Watson and, besides, she shouldn't get used to this. She needed some time before trying this again. Her freakout when she'd first woken up had proven that.

"Do you mind if I wear your clothes home?" she asked, bringing her plate into the kitchen to set it in the sink while Michael started doing the dishes. "I can bring them to Stronghold tonight if you're going to be there."

"That's fine," he said, giving her a small smile. "I plan on being there, although I wasn't planning on scening... we could do something light if you're feeling up to it."

One hand automatically drifted towards her sore ass as she thought it over. Sitting on his hard dining room chairs hadn't done her any favors. Mostly, it had just made her kinda horny again. "Maybe. I'm going to need a little bit of time to recover before another hard scene, but I could maybe do a light scene tonight. If you stay away from my ass."

Michael bopped her on the nose with a soapy finger. "I'm sure I can find plenty of other parts of you to torture, beautiful. Would you be interested in getting dinner beforehand?"

"Um, no... I can't... I um, have stuff to do." She winced at her stammer and the obvious lie, but Michael didn't call her on it. He just kept his attention on the dishes, as if she hadn't made the most idiotic excuse in the world.

"Okay," he said easily, loading a plate into the dishwasher. She relaxed, although her hands stayed in front of her, twisting slightly, and she couldn't help but wonder why he wasn't calling her on it. Wasn't threatening to spank her for such a blatant lie... had she wanted him to spank her? "As for the scene, we can see how we feel tonight when we get there. If you just want to hang out in the club, that's fine too."

She relaxed even more, her hands dropping to her sides, although she still felt a little awkward. Especially since she wasn't sure what she wanted from him right now. Time to get out. Definitely time to get out. "Okay. Um... I'm going to go get my clothes and head out."

"Alright," he said, giving her another smile. It was an understanding smile, but somehow that was nearly as bad as pity right now. Ugh. Why did she have to be such a mess?

By the time she came back out with her purse and clothes, Michael had finished loading the dishwasher. He walked her out to her car and gave her a hug and a kiss on the forehead. For just a second, she thought about what it might be like if she went up on her toes and pulled him down for a kiss on the lips... a kiss like they'd had last night...

And then she regained her senses. That had been during a scene.

Not real life. *You're not ready for a real relationship or intimacy, remember, crazy-girl?*

But her lips still tingled as she saw him watching her drive away.

When she got home, Watson opened one eye, looked at her, and immediately went back to napping.

"Yeah, I missed you too," she said with a sigh.

Dropping her purse on the stand next to the door, she headed back to her bedroom, thinking about the difference between her and Michael's apartments. They were about the same size and had similar layouts, but they were two completely different living spaces. Her apartment was cluttered exactly, but it kind of seemed that way after being at Michael's. She had pictures of her parents, her brother, and her nephew Austin up on some shelves, along with a few of her favorite books. Her entertainment center was filled with DVDs and little knickknacks she'd collected over the years, and she had a ton of paint and photograph prints up on her walls.

Not to mention the amount of Watson's stuff which was spread around. His kitty tower, his kitty box, his kitty scratch post, and all the kitty toys strewn around the floor. Spoiled kitty.

Maybe she should get something for Michael for his apartment.

She made a face.

Maybe she should focus on managing a club relationship before she started doing things that definitely were relationship-relationship.

Rather than changing out of Michael's clothes, she went back into the living room and picked up Watson, who protested the interruption of his nap with a sad little mew.

"Oh you're fine," she said, refusing to let him make her feel guilty. "You can come cuddle."

Despite his protest, he had no problem settling in on her stomach, his orange paws kneading Michael's shirt on her chest while she petted him. She'd make sure to wash Michael's shirt and boxers before going to the club tonight, but she didn't want to take them off quite yet. They were really comfy. That was the only reason, of course. Why bother changing when she was already in comfy clothes?

Made sense to her.

"I can do this," she whispered, stroking Watson's ears as he purred encouragement. "We'll have a club contract. I'll learn how to handle that. And then we'll see where we go from there."

And if the club contract didn't work out, then she would never need to tell him about what happened with Lawrence.... She didn't know which option made her feel worse.

⚜ 12 ⚛

Since there were no open rooms, and Ellie's ass was still sore, they'd agreed not to play again until next Friday. Which really sucked, because watching her tonight, Michael wanted nothing more than to drag her off and play again.

Being in a club-only relationship was harder than he'd thought it would be. While she was wearing his collar and he didn't have to worry about her scening with anyone else, he still couldn't just take her home with him and do perverted things to her there - an option he'd always had in the past with his relationships. She was worth the effort, but it still wasn't easy.

The restriction chafed.

Especially because, despite how satisfying last night's scene had been, he wasn't exactly emotionally satisfied with where they were. After she'd left that morning, he'd ended up going out to Target and getting a couple of things to spruce up his living room, but even while he'd been shopping he hadn't been able to rid himself of the nagging itch on the back of his neck. He wanted more than a club relationship with her, and although a club relationship was the first step, he wasn't sure she wanted more from him.

Or, at least, he wasn't sure she would let herself have more with him. Maybe he shouldn't have asked her to dinner before the club, but people had to eat, right? He hadn't realized a small suggestion of dinner would make her back off so quickly.

And now they were on opposite sides of a bar table, with their friends. Ellie was smiling and laughing and having a good time, but she was also all the way over there. Michael couldn't keep his eyes off of her, especially when she'd squirm on her seat, glance at him, and then drop her eyes as she blushed, and he knew she was feeling the plug he'd inserted as soon as she'd arrived. That or the lingering soreness, which she'd told him she was still feeling, even though her ass was back to its usual creamy color. She'd worn a short flippy skirt with a dark red corset which pushed her breasts up like a shelf, protecting her nipples from rubbing while giving him far too much ivory skin to admire and fantasize about marking.

The collar on her neck gave him the right to do what he wished in the club, but when she'd chosen to sit across from him, he'd decided not to push it and do what he really wanted - which was tuck her under his arm like Jared had done with Leigh, or sit her on his lap, like Liam with Hilary, or stand behind her seat, like Adam with Angel. Fortunately, everyone else was off scening or hadn't made it out tonight, so he only had three couples to compare him and Ellie to and be jealous of.

When Ellie and Hilary decided they needed to go to the bathroom, Angel leaned over and poked him in the arm. Michael looked down at her and raised his eyebrow. He'd been working on trying to get her to remember to be more respectful with him in the club, but it was a work in progress. She had trouble remembering it with everyone though, so at least it wasn't just him.

"Yes, Pest?"

"What's with the pouty face?" she asked, frowning at him as she leaned back against Adam, smoothing her silky purple negligee over her baby bump. "You've been staring at Ellie like you're a sugar addict and she's the last cupcake on earth."

Jared snorted as Leigh started giggling, while Liam and Adam exchanged looks.

"You have such a way with words," he teased a small smile lifting the corners of his lips, even though his thoughts were already whirling. He didn't really look that obvious and pathetic, did he?

"I know," Angel said smugly. "But you didn't answer my question. What's going on with you and Ellie?"

He shrugged, trying not to look or sound as down as he felt. "We have a club relationship, that's all. It's a bit of an adjustment."

Angel cocked her head to the side, her curls sliding over her shoulders. Behind her, Adam gave him a sympathetic look.

"So you want a date with her," Angel said, but not like she was asking, more like she was thinking.

"We should do a group outing," Leigh suggested, giving him an encouraging smile. "Then Michael can try and make it date-like."

Looking down at her, Jared squeezed his arm a little tighter around her shoulders. "No match-making unless Michael actually wants your help."

"Actually, that sounds like a pretty good idea," Michael admitted as he thought it over. "I'd like to spend some time with her outside of the club, to see if we can work our way to more than just a club relationship, and I think the only way she's going to be comfortable doing that right now is with a group."

"Sharon's been wanting to go to the zoo," Angel said brightly. "I'll organize it and make sure we get Ellie to come too." When Adam groaned, she twisted around to glare at him. "And you're coming too!"

"I hate the zoo."

Hiding his own smile, Michael reached out to clap the other man on the shoulder. "Thanks for taking one for the team, man."

"I kind of hate you, too."

There used to be more truth to that statement, as Adam had struggled with jealousy over Angel and Michael's close friendship, but there wasn't even a little bit of bite in his voice when he said it now.

Still, Michael couldn't help but tease him. "Blame your baby momma."

Adam scowled. Although Angel had finally said 'yes' to his proposal, she was still resisting actually planning a wedding. Apparently, she couldn't decide whether she wanted to get married before or after the baby came, but if she kept prevaricating, the baby may end up making the choice for her. It was driving Adam nuts, especially when Angel called herself his baby momma rather than his girlfriend or fiancé. He kind of had a stick up his butt and Michael was a sadist... it didn't matter that Adam was a man, he still enjoyed messing with him.

"We're all going to go," Angel said, flashing a smile around the table. The kind of smile Olivia often used when she was going to be pushy. For a submissive, Angel could be awfully bossy.

Neither of the other Doms argued with her though, and Leigh just looked excited, which meant Jared would definitely be going. Actually, going to the zoo would probably appeal to the two of them anyway. Although they didn't actually have an age-play relationship, Michael saw a lot of a Daddy Dom in Jared and signs of a baby girl in Leigh. A trip to the zoo would be right up their alley; Leigh could act like the excited little girl she sometimes was, and Jared could enjoy indulging her.

A flash of pink out of the corner of his eye made Michael turn his head to see that, yes, Ellie and Hilary were out of the ladies' room and on their way back to the table. Hilary almost always dressed in her signature color, or at least something with pink on it, which made it incredibly easy to spot her in the club. Ellie, of course, wore darker colors when she wasn't wearing black, like most of the other submissives.

The slightly mincing way she walked made him grin, and when she met his eyes and saw his grin she blushed again. Yeah, having her wear the plug in the club was one of the best ideas he'd ever had. Not only did it mean he got to play with her a little every time they were in the club, it also ensured she was thinking about him the whole time they were here.

Baby steps.

Walking around the club with a plug in was a completely novel experience, and one which was making her really regret telling Michael she'd rather not play tonight... but she'd been really torn about whether or not they should play again. After last night and this morning, she'd wanted to, but she'd been scared to; plus she didn't want to lead him on and make him think she was ready to move faster. She definitely wasn't. But she had wanted to play. So she'd decided to leave it to fate.

If there had been a private room available, she would have agreed to another scene, even though part of her was worried it would be moving too quickly. If there was no private room available, she'd ask to wait till next week when they could have one reserved.

Yeah, they could have played in the Dungeon, but that wouldn't be leaving things to fate. This way she hadn't had to endlessly go over all the possible outcomes of playing or not playing and make a decision. Much easier.

"So how's married life?" she asked Hilary as they headed towards the bathroom. Although Hilary was always friendly, they hadn't really spent much one on one time together. Ellie had initially been friend-liest with Sharon before Lexie and Angel started pulling her into their group of friends and inviting her to everything. Now she felt like she was probably closest to the two of them, as Sharon hadn't been spending quite as much time with the group since she'd started dating Brian, a newer Dom at Stronghold who tended to hang out with the other guys he'd had the new Dom class with.

"Good!" Hilary said cheerfully. Fortunately, Hilary was very friendly, even if she was kind of a prude about sex stuff - which everyone loved to tease her about when she was in the club. Her outfits were becoming more daring though; tonight she was wearing a hot pink bandage dress which barely covered her ass and dipped low in front to show off a lot of cleavage. Sometimes she wore corsets or lingerie, but they usually covered more than this dress did. "We've decided to start looking for a house."

"Oh, good!" Ellie said. She felt a little awkward since she didn't really know what to talk to Hilary about when it was just them.

"Yeah," Hilary said, pushing open the bathroom door. Ellie followed her inside. "I mean, we've been pretty comfortable in the apartment, but it's just starting to feel like a black hole for our money... plus I'd like some more space. Every time I go to Jessica's I get house-envy now."

Ellie giggled. Since Jessica lived with two men, they lived in a fairly large house, so she could definitely understand the envy.

"Plus, you know, if babies happen," Hilary said with a wink before heading into a stall. Her voice echoed against the walls and ceiling as Ellie moved into her own stall. It always amused her how girls could happily just talk through the entire bathroom process, ignoring the bodily functions that were happening. "We're not planning on it yet, but I'd rather be settled into a house by the time we are."

"That makes sense."

Geez. Marriage. Babies. Things Ellie wanted and yet...

"So what about you and Michael?" The toilet in Hilary's stall flushed.

"Umm... well, you know, club contract," Ellie said. She flushed her toilet and came out of the stall to see Hilary washing her hands, but looking at Ellie in the mirror.

"Yeah, but you never do those, so it's kind of a big deal, right?"

"Kind of a really big deal to me," Ellie admitted, moving to the sink.

Hilary leaned against the sink she'd been using, watching Ellie as she chewed her lower lip, and Ellie suddenly knew what was coming. She'd told Angel and the others who had hung out after the self-defense class to tell rest of their friends in the group what had happened to her. Probably Jessica had told Hilary.

She'd given them permission because she didn't really want to have to go over it again and again and again, and she'd known it would probably happen eventually if she kept hanging out with all of them. The topic would come up, they'd want to know why she was so skittish - hell, they'd mostly already guessed - and she'd just wanted to get the telling over with. Better they do it for her.

"Is it because of what happened to you?" Hilary asked in a low voice, full of sympathy. "My high school boyfriend tried to push me a lot faster than I was ready to go and I had to shove him off me and practically knee him in the balls to make him stop. It was hard to trust another guy for a while after that."

While, in some ways, it was almost nice to know she wasn't alone, it also killed Ellie that every single one of these other women had a story to tell. One which could never be guessed just by looking at them or seeing how they behaved. It was good not to feel so alone, which was not what her experience had been before this, and to see how they were all in normal, happy, healthy relationships now... but she also felt really sad and angry that they'd all had some kind of shitty experience. There just wasn't any winning with her emotions.

"Yeah, that's some of it," she said, grabbing some paper towels to dry off her hands. Hilary reached out to take her hand as she tossed the paper towels in the trash, giving it a squeeze, and Ellie's heart stuttered a little at the blatant gesture of support. She smiled at the other woman, around the lump growing in her throat. "I've also just never had a normal relationship after that. Well, not that that relationship was normal, I hope. I tried in college, but the only guy who was really willing to put up with all my issues... well, after a while he started getting frustrated with me and... yeah. I haven't even tried since then. I have no idea what I'm doing."

Confessing it felt strangely good. Even though she and Hilary weren't particularly close. She hadn't realized just how much she'd been wanting to share her fears with someone who wasn't her therapist until she'd finally gotten the words out.

"If it makes you feel better, I don't think anyone really knows what they're doing," Hilary offered up, with a smile, as she gave Ellie's hand another squeeze. "I definitely didn't when Liam and I started to get together and I'd been dating for years. But things with him were completely different, and not just because of the domination stuff. The stakes were higher, you know? He was friends with my besties' men, I was really into him from the beginning - maybe more than I'd ever been into a guy - and I just couldn't stay away from him. I think even back then I could see myself having a real future with him, and that was scary. I kept thinking I was going to do something to blow it. But all you can do is take things day by day and see what happens."

"Day by day," Ellie repeated. She smiled, giving Hilary's hand a squeeze. "I can do day by day."

"You're already doing more than just day to day, since you agreed to scene with him next weekend and signed a club contract," Hilary teased.

"I guess, but... I feel safe in the club. Even if it's with a contract. That's the kind of step which feels natural to me. It's all the stuff outside of the club I don't know how to handle."

"Well, you've got us now," Hilary said, giving Ellie a grin as she dropped her hand and turned to inspect her honey-blonde hair in the mirror. "We're good sounding boards. And if you make the mistake of asking for advice, you'll be buried in it."

"Yeah, but that means if anything goes wrong, I can blame whoever gave me the bad advice," Ellie said cheerfully.

Hilary laughed and linked arms with her as they headed back into the main room.

Sliding back into her seat, Ellie could see Michael's disappointment, but he hid it quickly. It still made her feel a little bad. Why wasn't she going around to sit beside him again?

Oh right, because she was trying to take things slowly.

She was wearing his collar and his plug, and the combination had made her feel so immediately submissive and soft inside that she'd immediately tried to shore up her walls by seating herself away from him. Now she was feeling more used to the plug inside of her and the light weight of the collar around her neck... next time they were at the club together, she'd sit next to him. That was a good step, right?

WHEN ELLIE ANNOUNCED SHE WAS READY TO LEAVE, MICHAEL went with her to the aftercare corner down in the Dungeon, the same couch where he'd inserted the plug, to remove it. He cast one longing look at the other occupants of the Dungeon, enjoying their scenes, before leading Ellie by the hand over to the couch and across his lap.

"You know, I could take care of this myself at home," she said, sounding a little breathless and squirming against his legs as he flipped up her skirt.

"You could, but I prefer to do it," he replied, caressing the globes of her ass. The red jewel on her plug sparkled even in the shadowed light of the aftercare corner. It didn't escape his notice that her pussy was wet and swollen beneath the plug, indicating her arousal.

Which at least satisfied some of his sadistic urges, knowing she'd been plugged and aroused all evening.

Smiling, Michael took a firm hold of the plug base and twisted it, making Ellie gasp and shudder. Her back arched as he began to pull, very slowly, and she moaned as the plug pressed against her entrance from the inside, before her tiny hole began to stretch around the fat bulb. The little wrinkles in her rosebud smoothed out and he heard a little cry as her ring of muscle moved over the largest part of the plug.

His cock pressed against her side, although the corset kept her body from feeling as soft and cushiony as she normally did, as he watched the plug slip from her body. The tiny hole gaped slightly after he pulled it completely free, before her muscles flexed and it closed completely. He had to control himself as he wrapped the plug in a small cloth - he'd take it upstairs to clean it after she left - and set it to the side.

"Good girl," he said, smoothing his hand over her backside again before pulling her skirt back into place and helping her to her feet.

Her cheeks were flushed pink, lips slightly parted, and eyes a little dazed, giving every indication of arousal. A satisfying sight.

Michael stood, looming over her slightly, and cupped her chin in his hand so he could bring her gaze to his. "You can play with yourself before next Friday, but no orgasms."

She wrinkled her nose. "Kind of defeats the point of playing with myself."

"Careful, sassy," he warned, releasing her face so he could take her hand again. "You're lucky I don't require you play with yourself but not orgasm. Come on, I'll walk you out."

The way her hand tightened around his when he gave his warning made him think she liked that idea. Michael didn't always indulge in orgasm play, but with Ellie he wanted to. It was one of the few orders he could give her which extended his reach outside of the club – and it also guaranteed she'd be thinking about him. Pleasure came from him. Not only was it more satisfying for him that way, but it was a good method of positive-association training.

When he walked her out to her car, he gave her a kiss on her forehead and sent her off, watching as she drove away. The air was getting cooler at night, with just a little bit of a bite to the chill, so he turned around once she'd exited the parking lot and headed down the street. Even though he was wearing his leathers and a matching vest, his bare arms were definitely feeling the chill.

Instead of going back into the club, he stopped at the front desk where Traci was sitting.

"Can you see if Patrick has a few minutes to talk?" he asked.

"Sure," she chirped up at him with a bubbly smile. Traci was a sweet subbie, but she never played with the sadists. Picking up the phone, she dialed back to Patrick's office and after a quick conversation put the phone back down, still smiling. "Go right on in."

"Thanks."

As usual, Patrick was behind his desk with Lexie sitting on her cushion next to it, naked and looking blissful as she leaned her head against his thigh while his hands stroked through her hair. Michael smiled, he always enjoyed the connection between the two of them. Considering he'd been the one to help Lexie push her way into the club and therefore push Patrick into finally training her as a submissive and eventually becoming *his* submissive, he had a little bit of a fairy godmother feeling about their relationship.

"Everything okay?" Patrick asked as soon as Michael shut the door behind him. "Are you ending the contract already?"

The question was so unexpected, Michael barked out a laugh. "No. Thankfully. I wanted to talk to you about an idea I had for Marquis."

An idea which had been slowly forming throughout the day ever since Ellie had woken up and been upset she was in his bed. Plus, it was an idea which would further serve to set Marquis apart from Stronghold. It wouldn't be for everyone, but that was okay... the people who took advantage of it would enjoy.

Patrick nodded at the chair across the desk from him. "By all means."

Like Michael, Patrick had on his leathers, but he was also wearing a black t-shirt that clung to his muscles. Whenever Lexie's brother Jake came to the club, to hang out with his friends, Patrick's shirt would go on Lexie and he'd stay bare-chested. So far it was a system which seemed to work pretty well. The other guys in the group all thought of Lexie as a little sister, but they'd become used to seeing her naked around the club. Obviously, as Lexie's real sibling, she and Jake both preferred her clothed when he was there.

"What would you think of making Marquis twenty four hours on weekends?" Michael asked. Patrick's eyebrows rose as he leaned back in his chair, running his free hand over the five o'clock shadow on his chin, while Lexie blinked, looking interested in the idea. "We could set up the private rooms so they came as a pair; a playroom connected to a bedroom by an adjoining door. It would take a little more work, but the way the offices were originally set up, I think we could probably get the plumbing set out pretty easily to have a bathroom connected to each room as well. With all the interest in Marquis, the cost of the memberships would cover the extra staff hours, especially if some of the staff wanted to trade time working for time in the private rooms."

"We'll have to go over numbers, but at first glance I like it," Patrick said, nodding his head. His hand came down to rest on his desk, fingers tapping as he thought it through. "It definitely gives Marquis more of the high-end feel that we're going for, to have an overnight option. We include overnights for the full-members of Marquis and have non-full members pay for special occasions..."

"Not having to go home right after a scene would be a big draw," Lexie chimed in. "You might need to limit the amount of nights a member can stay per month. Or some kind of system where they can request a second night and as long as there's a room open, it's theirs."

"Good point," Michael said. "There will definitely be some bugs to work out, but I think it would be worthwhile."

Patrick gave Lexie's hair a little tug. "Go grab the floor design from the file cabinet, please, Pixie. Let's look it over and see what we can come up with."

Feeling incredibly pleased, Michael ran his fingers through his own hair, pushing it away from his face before scooting his chair closer to Patrick's desk. Sure, he'd added more work to his plate, but he really did think it would pay off. It was the kind of thing which would appeal

to a lot of the club members for all sorts of reasons - privacy, conve-
nience, special occasions.

Plus, hopefully by the time Marquis opened, his and Ellie's relationship would have moved forward a little more, but if not... well,
being able to sleep over at the club might make her feel better than
going back to either of their places together. It was kind of like a
compromise.

❧ 13 ❧

The week seemed to crawl by, slower than usual.

Despite what she'd said to Michael, Ellie did end up touching herself, multiple times.

While she was in the shower and feeling hot and frustrated.

While she was in bed, struggling to fall asleep as memories from their last scene ran through her head.

When she woke up in the middle of the night, her pussy throbbing from the dream she'd just had...

She'd had sex with Doms before. She'd had amazing scenes with Doms before. But she'd never had a lingering reaction like this before. Then again, she'd also never been in a club contract or had a Dom tell her she couldn't orgasm until she saw him again. In the past, any control a Dom had over her ended the moment the scene did. She'd expected things to change a little, having a club contract, but she hadn't realized how much it would affect her outside of the club.

It didn't help that Michael didn't exactly stay away during the week either. They weren't talking on the phone, but they still exchanged texts nearly every day. Mostly pictures of Marquis and Watson, but also little conversations about their day or things that were happening. He was the one who told her Andrew and Kate were now looking at houses, which she ended up knowing before Lexie, who seemed both a little put out and highly interested that she was not Ellie's main conduit for gossip anymore. She'd probably be passing on the word to everyone else about how Ellie and Michael were talking a lot outside of the club.

On Thursday, Angel texted her.

Hey are you free next Saturday? During the day?

Ellie automatically glanced at her calendar even though she knew it would be blank. Before the Stronghold girls had started pushing her into going out with them, her main social activity had been going to Stronghold and interacting with people there. Her weekend daytime activities usually involved cleaning house, calling her parents and brother at some point, and maybe going to a Zumba class at the nearby studio.

Yes, what's up?

Oh good! We're taking a trip to the zoo. Sharon's been dying to go. Want to carpool to the metro?

She'd texted back 'sure' before she'd even realized Angel hadn't actually asked if Ellie wanted to go to the zoo. It made her shake her head, but she couldn't help the smile either. Especially because within the next five minutes her phone was buzzing with messages from a group text she'd just been added to.

Jessica: *I haven't been to the zoo in forever!*

Maria: *The weather's supposed to be sunny and in the high sixties, low seventies, but I'll keep my eye on it as it gets closer.*

Sharon: *ZOO!*

Lexie: *Yay! Zoo! I want to go to the bird house!*

Leigh: *Do you think we'll be able to see the new baby panda?*

Hilary: *Omg, I hope so! The pictures are so cute!*

Sharon: *ZOO! ZOO! ZOO!*

Maria: *I think there's usually a line, so we should get there early and head straight for the panda enclosure.*

Angel: *I think we should all meet at the same metro stop so we can ride in together.*

Kate: *Oh, good idea!*

Sharon: *WE'RE GOING TO THE ZOO!*

Olivia: *OH. MY. GOD. I'M GOING TO KILL WHICHEVER ONE OF YOU ASSHOLES ADDED ME TO THIS THING! STOP TEXTING SO MUCH, MY PHONE IS GOING CRAZY!*
Angel: *Sorry Olivia*
Leigh: *Sorry Olivia*
Kate: *Sorry Olivia*
Jessica: *Sorry Olivia*
Hilary: *Sorry Olivia*
Maria: *Sorry Olivia*
Lexie: *Sorry Olivia*
Olivia: *I hate you all.*
Sharon: *Zoo!*

Ellie laughed so hard she had put her head down on her desk and press her hand to her aching stomach muscles.

THE MOST CONVOLUTED PART ABOUT OPENING MARQUIS WASN'T actually the kink part, it was the façade; the front part, where the restaurant and bar would be. It didn't matter that it was going to be small, it still needed to have amazing food and impeccable service; so they'd started looking for staff early and it wasn't going quite as easily as Michael and Patrick might have hoped.

Today they'd come in to Marquis to work in the downstairs restaurant; all the construction was currently happening upstairs. They'd gone over the layout with Luke Davis, the owner of the company doing the renovations. Apparently he had some of the same control issues as Patrick; he'd been there to check in on his crew at least every other day, and something which was to be expected from the way the foreman acted. Even though the place definitely wasn't going to be open for months, it was really coming along, and there was something satisfying about working on location.

It was also a good way to see how the soundproofing was going. So far they'd only heard a few thuds, which was good, because when they'd gone upstairs the second floor had been filled with all the usual construction noise. If they couldn't hear the construction happening, people sitting in a restaurant with music and conversation definitely wouldn't be able to hear the tiniest bit of what was going on above their heads.

"We still have four months till we open," Michael reminded Patrick when the big man scowled and slammed down the stack of resumes he'd just flipped through. He'd been looking for one very specific thing.

"Yeah, and not even a single candidate for an Executive Chef," Patrick growled. "At this rate, I'm going to end up begging Justin to come work for us."

The biggest obstacle was that whoever was going to work for Marquis, even in the front, was going to have to sign a non-disclosure, and Patrick would prefer everyone be at least kink-friendly so there weren't any issues. Michael wanted people to be kink friendly too, but it meant they weren't broadly advertising the positions which needed to be filled. The lack of advertising for positions meant they weren't receiving resumes in the numbers they needed. Although, they at least already had their general manager.

Olivia had actually come to them to personally put in her resume; she was having issues at work with her new boss. While she was incredibly overqualified for the position, they could at least offer her the same salary she was receiving now, plus the perk of full access to Marquis' services when she wasn't working. Patrick had also requested she continue teaching the newbie classes, which she'd happily agreed to.

Michael suspected she just enjoyed torturing the new Doms, as well as getting a feel for each new Dom entering the club. Any Dom who balked at being taught by a woman didn't last through Olivia's class, and that was really for the best.

"Did I just hear you say you need an Executive Chef?"

Both Patrick and Michael looked up to see Luke coming out of the hall to the back, tucking a pair of work gloves into his jeans. Even though he owned LD Construction and Remodeling, Michael had never seen him in anything but jeans and his company's t-shirt. Which made sense since Luke apparently couldn't help but pitch in a hand with the actual construction, which would be a fast way to ruin a suit.

Michael was glad, since he and Patrick were both dressed casually too.

"Are you looking for a second job?" Patrick asked, his lips quirking. Although the rest of Luke's crew didn't know exactly what was going on with the upstairs of the building, Luke had been curious enough (or maybe just controlling enough) to want to know and had agreed to sign a non-disclosure just so he could. They hadn't had much interaction with him, but based on the little bit of conversation both Patrick and Michael generally liked the guy, especially since he hadn't freaked out when he'd been clued into their plans for upstairs.

He'd seemed more intrigued than anything.

"Not for me, but my brother Nick is a Sous Chef at Eva's," Luke said, heading over to the booth. Michael raised his eyebrows. Eva's was one of the top restaurants in the city; some of his theater friends still served there.

Patrick immediately scooted over to make room for him, which would put Patrick between Luke and Michael and keep Luke from looking down on them as he talked. Michael scrubbed his hand over his mouth to hide his amusement at Patrick's subtle power manipulations, but he knew the other man saw it anyway. Fortunately, Luke either didn't notice or didn't mind, he slid right into the booth in the space Patrick had opened up for him.

"So he's looking to be an Executive Chef?" Patrick prompted, folding his hands in front of him and zeroing in on Luke.

The other man nodded. "He's been at Eva's for about ten years now, been the sous chef for two of those. While he loves working there, he really wants to be able to make his own stuff. The Exec there lets him do some dishes, but my brother's ambitious. He's also picky about where he goes; I think a new place he could shape from the ground up would appeal to him in a way other offers haven't." A proud smile flashed across his face. "And I have no doubt he'd be happy to sign a non-disclosure. In fact, it wouldn't surprise me if he ended up wanting to be a member."

Michael and Patrick exchanged a look, and Patrick gave Michael a nod, giving him both his approval and final decision.

"Ask if he's interested and tell him about the non-disclosure,"

Michael said. "If he is, we can set up a tasting and go from there. No promises obviously, but if he's working at Eva's, I'm sure his food will be great. Hopefully our personalities will get along."

"And he'll have to get along with Olivia," Patrick murmured.

Yeah... Michael had a lot of experience working in the restaurant industry from when he was younger. Executive Chefs could be very abrasive. Something Olivia would definitely not tolerate, although hopefully as long as they didn't step on each other's toes...

"There's something else I wanted to talk to you about too," Luke said. "Which will have no bearing on whether or not my brother is hired."

Curious. Michael tilted his head at the same time Patrick gestured for Luke to continue.

"I'd like in as a partner - a silent partner," Luke said, quickly clarifying when both Patrick and Michael frowned. "I don't need to be an equal partner if you two would like to keep control, but I've been doing some research, and I think you two are going to be more successful than even you realize. And I'd like into the club."

"You could just get a membership," Michael pointed out.

Luke shrugged. "I will if you aren't interested in having a silent partner, but I'd prefer the partnership."

"Are you a silent partner in a lot of places?" Patrick asked.

The smile which spread across Luke's face was anything but modest. "I have my fingers in quite a few pies. I like to diversify, and I like success. There are some places where you're cutting corners or choosing lower quality products to save money. Not that the outcome is going to be bad, it's going to be really good, but I'd like to help you turn the final product from good to outstanding. Think about it. Preferably before we start doing any of the tile work in the bathrooms upstairs."

Rapping his knuckles on the table, Luke grinned and took his leave in an obvious tactical retreat. He'd managed to hook both Patrick and Michael's interest, although they were obviously going to have to talk about it.

Still... Michael's mind was already working. Some of the changes they were making upstairs were ending up being pricier than they'd originally planned because of the way they were changing how the third floor private rooms were going to be used. They'd scaled back on some of the plans they'd previously made; Luke was right, they'd still chosen things which were good, but maybe not quite as luxurious. Not quite what they'd initially pictured.

Being tempted with an influx to make everything exactly the way they wanted it... yeah, Luke had known exactly how to tempt them.

THE CLUB WAS ALREADY HOPPING A BIT FOR A THURSDAY NIGHT. Ellie had planned to stay away, rather than torture herself with what she couldn't have since her scene with Michael wasn't until tomorrow, but... Masochist. Plus, if she were being completely truthful, she wanted to see him. And the only safe way she could do that was in the club.

Although, she may have made a mistake. Because as soon as she saw him sitting with Patrick, Lexie, Jake, and Chris, all she wanted to do was run over and jump him. She was so wound up and he looked so good in his leathers, a dark green shirt which hinted at his musculature, and strands of hair brushing against his cheekbones. And when he saw her, his entire face lit up, taking her breath away.

He'd told her he was going to be here tonight, and she'd said she might be able to make it, but she still hadn't expected that reaction from him just for seeing her.

For a moment, it felt like her chest might crush inward on itself under the weight of whatever expectations had made him look like that when he saw her, but she shook herself free as he stood up and obviously excused himself, moving around Patrick to more open space and holding out his hand. Ellie moved towards him, very aware of her steps on her very high heels and the way her wet netherlips slid against each other as she walked. As she came to him, he pulled a small case out of his pocket which she immediately recognized.

Yeah... small chance he'd have left that behind.

The collar was already around her throat since he let her take it home during the week, but he had to be the one to insert and remove the plug apparently. The reasons he wanted to were probably very similar to the reasons it made Ellie uncomfortable... which were also the reasons she was secretly glad he insisted. Andrew had been right about her; she needed to be pushed and she let Michael push her more than she would anyone else.

Probably because she normally didn't care if she pushed a Dom away. With Michael, she definitely did.

"Hey there beautiful," he said, his eyes skimming approvingly over her pleather mini-skirt and silver corset.

"Hello," she said, sliding her fingers into his. Immediately, she felt a little better, a little more grounded, a little less anxious. Was it fair to make Michael her lifeline? Probably not, but it did work.

He turned his head back to the others. "We'll be right back."

"So how was your day?" she asked as he started to lead her towards the stairs.

They headed into the Dungeon while he gave her a quick synopsis of what he and Patrick had been working on for Marquis, including Luke's surprising offer. He'd mentioned the man in passing before, but Ellie didn't know much about him, so she was a little taken aback that Patrick and Michael were considering his offer. Actually, she was more surprised about Patrick than Michael since Patrick was an even bigger control freak than Michael; but when Michael mentioned how, with a third partner, they could do some of the things they'd had to scale back on, she got it. The two of them could have kind of expensive tastes, although with the vibe they were going for in Marquis, it made sense. Especially considering the membership prices.

"We're still looking into him, and we'll probably want a couple more meetings with him, but we're seriously considering it," Michael said. His eyes were alight in almost the same way they had been when she'd walked into the club - with happiness, excitement, and anticipation. Sitting down on the couch, he patted his lap for her to go over it.

"I hope it works out," she said, bending over his lap.

She still felt strange about having totally normal conversations leading up to being plugged... but then, she'd never been regularly plugged before and any anal play had occurred during a scene (if at all).

There was something a little jarring about having a normal conversation while indulging in kink.

"It will," Michael said, with all the inborn confidence of a Dom. Ellie stifled a giggle, and then bit back a moan as Michael palmed her ass.

Her skin felt like it was tingling where he touched her as he squeezed her soft flesh. Like last Saturday, he took his time touching her as he pulled up her skirt. Unlike last Saturday, she'd hadn't gotten off the day before. Or the day before that. Or the day before that and so on. So she was kind of a horny mess right now.

The corset felt tighter than ever as her breasts swelled, and she whimpered a little as his fingers brushed over her pussy lips... such a light touch it almost just felt like a puff of air. Her clit throbbed.

"Have you been a good girl this week, Ellie?" he asked. "Or did you have any orgasms?"

"I was good," she said, wishing he would just hurry up and insert the plug. Being over his lap like this and knowing she wasn't going to get a spanking, or anything else, until tomorrow night was sheer torture. And not the fun kind of torture which she actually liked.

SMACK! SMACK!

Two hard, swift blows to the backs of her thighs, and Ellie cried out as a deep shudder went through her body... the hot, sharp sting felt so good!

"Good girl," Michael said, rubbing his hand briskly over the sensitive skin he'd just slapped. Ellie whimpered. If he just touched her clit, she was sure she could cum...

Instead, his hand moved away and a couple moments later she felt the cool, slick tip of the plug pressing against her rosebud. Apparently the two small spanks had been both her reward for being good, and also additional torture. Her pussy felt like it was pulsing as Michael pressed the plug slowly but firmly into her slightly protesting anus.

As usual, just the sensation of her tightest hole being spread made her feel even more submissive than usual. Michael made the process pleasurable and almost far too intimate. She whimpered as he twisted the plug back and forth as it sank in, stimulating the sensitive nerves in the area. Her inner muscles burned as her ring was forced to stretch ever wider, until the toy suddenly popped inside of her, making her gasp and quiver at the sensation of being filled.

"Good girl," Michael said again, pumping the plug slightly; not enough to actually pull it out of her, but just enough to making her nerve-endings tingle pleasurably.

Then he released it, flipped her skirt back down, took her by the waist to help her stand, and stood up next to her. All the while, her pussy clenched, her leg muscles quivered, and she wanted nothing more than to fall back onto the couch with her legs spread and pull him down between her thighs.

Michael held out his hand. "Let's go join our friends."

She almost whimpered out loud. Looked at his hand. Looked over at the Dungeon. At all the men and women bound or holding themselves in place, gasping, whimpering, screaming, in pain and pleasure. Looked back at him. Saw the sadistic, almost cruel smile spread across his lips.

"Take my hand, Ellie."

Sadistic asshole.

But she did as he said and took his hand.

TORMENTING ELLIE WAS ALSO TORTURING HIMSELF, BUT MICHAEL still enjoyed it.

He'd been thrilled she'd actually shown up tonight. Since he hadn't had anything else to do, and he and Patrick were still thinking and talking over Luke's offer, he'd wanted to come to the club. Both as distraction, and so he and Patrick could continue to share thoughts and ideas about Marquis.

When he and Ellie returned upstairs, Olivia had also joined the group, having finished scening with the sub she'd chosen for the night. Charlie was back in the Lounge area, chatting with some of the other subs. While he and Olivia occasionally played together, so far they'd shown no interest in doing anything but scening with each other. He was a bigger guy, fairly muscular, and preferred scening with male dominants, but sometimes scened with Olivia as well, although

GOLDEN ANGEL

she wasn't the only Domme in the club Michael had ever seen him with.

Keeping hold of Ellie's hand, Michael led her over to the table where everyone was talking. Out of the corner of his eye, he could see her shooting him little glances and biting her lip. She was highly aroused and not too happy about having to wait... and yet even more turned on because he was denying her the orgasm she so desperately wanted. Ah, the dichotomy of being a submissive masochist.

Tonight he didn't give her a choice about sitting away from him. He kept his hold on her hand as he pulled up another bar stool with his free hand, placing it between the only open stool still at the table and Olivia's seat. Ellie sat down without protest, gingerly sliding onto the stool so as not to jostle the plug too much. She gently tugged at his hand, as if testing to see whether or not he would let go.

He didn't.

Olivia smiled at them, the happy, easy smile of a well-satisfied Domme. Her red hair was pulled back in a bun, but it was slightly tousled, and the laces on her leather bustier weren't done up quite as tightly as they had been when Michael had seen her earlier in the evening.

"Hello Ellie, how are you doing?" she asked.

"Good, Mistress Olivia," Ellie said, her smile much more strained than Olivia's.

Across the table, Patrick's lips twitched. Lexie looked at Ellie with sympathy, obviously recognizing the signs of a subbie who desperately wanted more than she was getting. Dressed in a black t-shirt that practically swallowed her up, she was sitting so close to Patrick she was practically in his lap, his arm curved around her waist and resting on her thigh. Next to them, her brother Jake pretended there was nothing odd about his sister's attire as he sipped his beer. Unlike the Doms in their leathers, he was dressed in jeans and a grey t-shirt, but his casual attire didn't stop any of the subs from checking him out. He still had his army crew cut, but even the small amount of black hair made his blue eyes stand out, the same way his sister's did, and his muscles filled out the shirt in a way that made even Michael a little envious. It also always amused him to see the subbies staring blatantly at Jake. They wouldn't dare to stare so brazenly with a real Dom, but since Jake was vanilla and didn't really know how to handle it – since he wasn't interested in the kinds of things which would satisfy the subs of Stronghold – he just tried to ignore them, with varying degrees of success. Sometimes Michael thought the subs might be making a game out of seeing whether or not they could make the man blush.

"We're talking about how all the couples in this group seem to be nesting," Lexie said with a laugh. "Patrick and I are looking for a house, Liam and Hilary are looking for a house, Andrew and Kate are looking for a house, –" strangely, Jake scowled suddenly, "and I think Rick's going to propose to Maria soon. It's making me feel old!"

"Which should make the rest of us feel *really* old," Chris said laughing. Lexie stuck out her tongue at him.

"I just bought some stuff for my apartment," Michael said. "Does that mean I'm nesting too?"

Ellie gave him a sidelong look.

"What'd you get?" Lexie asked, looking interested.

"Just some small furniture pieces, tables, and some decorative stuff. Someone told me it looked like my apartment had recently been robbed, so I figured I'd better make it look a little homier."

"Sounds like nesting to me," Olivia said with a chuckle as Ellie blushed. Michael squeezed her hand. The way she was looking at him was almost awe-struck, as if she was amazed her words had had a real effect on him.

She'd learn. Everything she did had an effect on him.

"It's not nesting," Patrick said, his tone one of a long-suffering man. "Buying a house is just the natural next step."

"Actually, I'm pretty sure most people consider the next natural step to be marriage, but our group seems to do it backwards," Chris said. "Liam and Hilary are the only ones doing it right so far."

"It's not backwards, it's just modern," Olivia said. "We do what we want!"

"Exactly!" said Lexie. "I do what I want! It's the one thing I'm really good at."

Patrick's smile was amused. "It's not the *one* thing."

GOLDEN ANGEL

Jake immediately pointed a finger at his best friend. "I don't want to know the other things."

His sister batted at his finger. "Get over it. It's just sex."

"Oh, so you'd be totally okay with hearing about my sex life?"

"If you were doing anything interesting with it."

"Okay children," Olivia said, interrupting the siblings. She waved her hand at the space between them, making a slicing motion. "That's enough of that. I'm not particularly interested in hearing about either of your sex lives."

"Yes, mom," Lexie and Jake chorused together before catching each other's eyes and cracking up.

Shaking his head, Michael leaned closer to Ellie, just enjoying being in the company of their friends. While he tended to think of himself as an extrovert, their friends were fairly loud. He'd noticed Ellie had a tendency to just sit back and enjoy the floor show rather than trying to join in.

The others made sure they were a part of the conversation without actually putting them in the center of it, and with Michael back at the table it didn't take long until they were talking about Marquis again. Olivia was not thrilled to hear they were thinking about taking on a new partner, one she'd never met before, but slightly reassured when she heard he wanted to be silent. She still wasn't too happy about it though, like any good control freak.

"You realize you're going to be answering to me and Patrick too, right?" Michael teased her.

"Yeah, but I know you two," she said. "I know you're not going to do anything stupid. Or, at least, I know I can stop you if you try to." She raised her eyebrow at him and Michael grinned. Too true. Olivia wasn't just good with a whip, she could flay a man with logic.

"I'm sure you'll be able to handle him as well," Patrick said dryly. "He's got a lot of inner confidence, but he's not an idiot, and he's definitely willing to compromise."

"So not as domm-y as you," Lexie teased giggling. Scowling, Patrick lowered his mouth to her ear and whispered something which immediately cut off her mirth. Probably something about how calling him 'domm-y' wasn't very respectful.

184

"Do you want him as a partner?" Ellie asked, leaning closer to Michael for a more private exchange while the others continued to talk about Luke.

"I want what he has to offer," Michael said, leaning closer to her as well and enjoying her nearness. "I do wish we knew him a little better, but what I do know, I like. We're looking into him, and as long as nothing comes up to indicate he'd be a bad partner, or that there would be serious personality clashes, I think it could work out really well for all of us."

"So do you think he's a Dom?" Ellie asked, probably because Patrick had mentioned Luke wanting membership.

"That's my assumption."

Granted, there were always people who were dominant publicly and submissive privately – Angel being a clear example of that personality type – so maybe he shouldn't be making the assumption, but he was used to the Stronghold Doms who were strong personalities all around. Since Luke was going to be a newbie and had never explored kink before, maybe they could introduce him to Sharon. Michael considered her on the very light end of the kink spectrum, and if Luke hadn't even experimented before, he might fall there as well. Although, that was assuming she and Brian didn't last – he couldn't see them together long term. She hadn't even been bringing him to hang out with the group, which was a pretty clear indication of how casual their relationship was.

"What do you mean she advertised for a new roommate on Craig's List?!" Jake's outraged voice cut through whatever Ellie was going to say, distracting both of them – especially since they'd obviously missed a shift in conversation among the others.

Lexie gave her brother a look, obviously not understanding why he was so upset. "Well, she needs a new roommate since Kate and Andrew are finally moving in together."

They had been taking their time about it, splitting their nights between Kate's apartment with Sharon and Andrew's apartment in his dad's basement. Andrew said they were looking to live in the same general area as his dad so he could still be there to help out with all the things his dad couldn't do.

"First of all, she doesn't *need* a new roommate," Jake growled, looking pissed. Patrick was staring at him with a kind of fascination which sent Michael's thoughts racing as well. "Second of all, if she's going to be looking for a new roommate, she shouldn't be doing so on Craig's List!"

"That's how she found Kate," Lexie pointed out. The smug expression on her face said everything about her intentions, and Michael wouldn't be surprised to know she'd steered the conversation this way intentionally. Apparently, she'd been looking for a reaction from her brother... and he'd provided.

Sharon and Jake had been grating against each other for a while and even though they were currently dating other people, it looked like "annoyed" wasn't the only emotion Jake felt about the diminutive subbie.

"It's not safe!"

Lexie waved her hand. "She hasn't had a problem before, and it's not like we won't be there to look after her."

"She doesn't even need a roommate!"

"Sure she does, otherwise she gets lonely."

"That's not a *need*, that's just being spoiled."

"Well this is going to be interesting," Ellie murmured, watching the retorts tennis ball back and forth between the siblings, and echoing the thoughts of everyone else at the table. Michael couldn't help but wonder if Jake was aware of exactly how much he was revealing by this little scene. Probably not, or he wouldn't be so vehement with his opinion.

Just another eye-opening night at Stronghold.

Getting ready to go to Stronghold with a group of girls was an entirely new experience and a heck of a lot of fun. Being at Stronghold last night had been a lot of fun too, but she hadn't realized how much more fun it could be when Angel had invited her over to get ready with her, Leigh, and Lexie, using the largest of the house's bathrooms to do their makeup and hair. Adam had retreated downstairs where Ellie could hear the faint strains of guitar music as he played, occupying himself while they did their thing. Apparently Patrick and Jared were already at Stronghold working, so they'd decided to have some pre-club girl-time and wanted to include her.

Ellie really liked being included.

Especially since they'd started hanging out with her even before she'd agreed to scene with Michael. She didn't feel like she was just being pulled into their friendship because of him, but it was nice he was there when she hung out with them as a group. It gave her an excuse to spend more time with him, without feeling any pressure to move things faster than she was comfortable with relationship-wise - although her comfort level could change from minute to minute or even second to second.

She could feel perfectly easy in their texting conversation, look forward to spending more time with him, and then suddenly start feeling panicky over how comfortable she was feeling. Worry would creep through her relaxed calm, anxiety sliding between her emotions like an insidious vine, taking over the garden of her mind.

Sometimes she could ignore it, sometimes she couldn't.

"Maybe I should borrow some of your stuff," Leigh said, coming into the bathroom holding up an outfit which looked entirely made out of leather straps in front of her. She looked into the mirror as if trying to see how it would actually cover her. Compared to it, the short lavender miniskirt and white bustier with silver embroidery she was wearing looked almost demure. "Just for funsies."

Angel gave her an incredulous look. "Don't you already have a spanking coming tomorrow if you don't make it to the gym? Do you want to add to that?"

"I'm not Lexie, there's no rules saying I can't wear what I want to the club," Leigh argued, although she was now tilting her head at the mirror as if reconsidering. Unlike Angel, who often went looking for a spanking – although her sexy outfits wouldn't necessarily be the reason for one – Leigh tended to be much more conservative in her fashion, even at the club. She and Jared didn't exactly have a Daddy Dom – baby girl relationship, but there was definitely a little bit of that going on. While she never dressed like a baby girl, her outfits were a lot more conservative than most of the other club goers. The only subs more covered up were the actual baby girls.

"Hey, I wear what I want," Lexie said indignantly. She was currently dressed in blue hotpants with a matching blue bra and a black mesh shirt. Her pale skin glowed against all the blue and black, which matched her hair and eyes exactly. Patrick kind of had a thing for anything which matched the color of her eyes.

"And the second you walk into the club, Patrick takes all or most of it off you anyway," Leigh retorted.

"She has a point," said Angel, leaning forward to put on her eyeliner. Her hand had a steadiness Ellie envied as she deftly swiped the liquid over her eyelid. Ellie never wore liquid liner because she always ended up looking like someone had punched her in the face.

"Why do you want to wear it?" Ellie asked. After all, it was a little unusual for Leigh to want to take off more clothes. While a few of the women in their group of friends were exhibitionists, Leigh, Maria, and Hilary were definitely not. If they played at the club, they played behind closed doors, and while they always looked fantastic, they usually wore less revealing clothing than a lot of the other club members. As Rick often said; they were there to be with their friends more than they were to play. It would be interesting to see what happened when Marquis opened.

Leigh shrugged. "I don't know. I guess sometimes I just feel a little boring next to you guys."

Frowning, Angel's attention immediately centered on Leigh. "You don't think Jared is getting bored with you, do you?" Her voice was filled with disbelief – as it should be, considering Jared practically did back flips to give Leigh everything she wanted. The good thing about their relationship was that Leigh was the same. Their past experiences being in relationships where they gave everything and got nothing in return, made them both incredibly appreciative of each other's efforts, which in turn made each of them try even harder. It was the best kind of relationship spiral to be in.

"No, but I don't want him to either," Leigh said chewing on her lower lip as she shifted back and forth in front of the mirror.

"Jared is not Michael," Angel said sternly, setting down her eyeliner and snatching the leather straps away from Leigh. "He loves you for you. You don't need to change."

"Definitely," Lexie agreed vehemently. "Especially not your style. He likes your style. Marissa used to wear stuff like this just to make him jealous. If the only reason you're going to wear it is because you think he'll like it – don't. I'm not saying he won't like it, but it will bring up a lot of questions."

"Oh."

"Do you want to do something different with your hair or make-up?" Ellie asked. She felt a little bad at how disappointed Leigh looked. Maybe part of her wasn't thinking about Jared getting bored at all, maybe part of her just wanted to try something new. "Or maybe just try one new piece of clothing instead of going straight for the leather bondage dress?"

"I've got an extra one of these," Lexie said, plucking at her mesh shirt. Although Leigh had a serious booty, up top she was slimmer and smaller like Lexie, so she'd easily fit into Lexie's top, especially since it was slightly stretchy. "What color bra did you wear today?"

"Black," Leigh said, a little hesitantly but with growing excitement. "Do you think it would go with my skirt?"

"Black goes with everything," Angel told her. "Go try it on and we'll see how it looks."

※

Michael was standing in the lobby, talking to Jared, when the ladies walked in, followed by a bemused looking Adam. It was cool enough in the evenings now that they all needed to wear coats which covered up their outfits, but as they started taking the coats off, Michael saw the reason for Adam's expression. Angel was wearing one of the low cut silky baby-doll slips she was becoming known for in her pregnancy, Lexie's mesh shirt and shorts were her usual attire, and Ellie looked curvy and luscious in her black corset and tight red PVC skirt, however Leigh had gone off menu.

She looked nervous but adorable, sneaking glances at Jared as she opened her jacket and let it slide off her arms. The lavender mini-skirt she was wearing wasn't unusual in and of itself, but she'd paired it with a black bra and black mesh shirt, making her look like Lexie's taller, more nervous clothing twin.

He tilted his head so he could keep an eye on the ladies while also seeing Jared's expression. Like Adam, Jared looked bemused. Like he wasn't quite sure what to think about his girlfriend's new attire.

While the others were turning their jackets in to Shonda, who was manning the front desk, Leigh handed her jacket to Angel and moved over to stand in front of Jared, wringing her hands in front of her.

"Hey there, little one," Jared said, leaning down to take his kiss. Leigh looked relieved as she kissed him back. She tucked in under his arm, leaning against him as if for strength as Jared straightened back up.

"Hey Leigh," Michael said mildly. "I like the new look."

"Just... trying it out," she said, glancing up at Jared again. He smiled back down at her and she relaxed even further. "I don't want to be boring."

"You're never boring," Jared said immediately, frowning down at her.

"I just meant I wanted to try something different," she said hastily. While Jared was pretty easy going when it came to punishments – all of Leigh's revolved around her health – all of the Doms were pretty quick to react when they thought a sub was saying something self-detrimental. "I always wear almost the exact same thing here."

"And you always look beautiful." The adoring look on Jared's face as Leigh stared back up at him with the same adoring look, made Michael's insides twist with envy.

He turned away, knowing the couple wouldn't even notice, and moved towards his sub, who had just finished checking in. Seeing him coming, Ellie's face lit up. It wasn't quite the same as the adoration shared between Leigh and Jared, but it was enough for now. Michael smiled back at her, his gaze dropping for just a moment to the collar around her neck, which made his smile grow. He didn't think he'd ever get tired of seeing his collar on her.

"Good evening, beautiful," he said, holding out his hand for her to take. Immediately she slid her fingers between his, and the envy from watching Jared and Leigh settled and slid away.

"Hello Michael," she said softly, a peaceful smile curving her lips.

"Have a good time getting ready with all the troublemakers?" he asked, giving Angel a wink. She made a face at him as Lexie giggled and waved, heading towards the door to Patrick's office.

"Yes," Ellie said, her smile widening to an amused grin.

Michael chuckled as they headed into the club. They had about a half hour until the Office, the room he'd reserved for the night, opened up and they spent it at their usual table in the bar area. At first, Ellie seemed nervous he wasn't immediately taking her to insert her plug, but she stayed quiet about it. Michael decided he'd let the anticipation grow. Besides, it would give him a fun reason to punish her once their scene started. Angel and Adam headed straight down to the Dungeon to play, but Kate and Sharon were already at the bar hanging out while Andrew was bartending. Sharon seemed a little distracted – possibly because Brian, the Dom she'd been seeing for a while, was several tables away with his friends, and they both had their backs to each other.

Not that she said a word about it.

Conversation revolved around Marquis, the custom pieces Michael and Patrick wanted Andrew to make for it, and the possible addition of Luke to the partnership – which was looking more and more likely. He and Patrick had scheduled a lunch with Luke on Tuesday to discuss what a partnership would look like in more detail. Which, of course, Leigh, Sharon, and Kate wanted to know all about. It didn't take too long before Jared finished his shift and he joined them as well.

As much as Michael enjoyed talking about Marquis, he was relieved when Lisa came by to let them know the Office was ready. Sitting next to Ellie, holding her hand, and pretending his cock wasn't rock hard had been wearing on him. Especially since, like Ellie, he hadn't masturbated all week.

While he was a sadist, he also liked to be fair. If she had to wait for him, then he was going to wait for her.

Waiting had been a hell of a lot easier when she wasn't sitting right next to him, looking so amazing, her soft skin smoothing under the caress of his fingers, and the subtle perfume she was wearing weaving through the scent of leather and sex permeating the club. With her right beside him, waiting had moved from frustrated anticipation to pure torture.

"Where are we going?" she asked, almost a little nervously, as they headed up the stairs rather than downstairs to the private rooms connected to the Dungeon.

"The Office," he said, giving her hand a little squeeze, and she relaxed. Michael was fairly certain she was relieved he wasn't taking her to the romantic Arabian Nights room, which was a little disappointing, but it was just another reminder they weren't quite where he wanted to be yet.

Baby steps.

After all, she didn't have any qualms at all about coming upstairs with him, when he was fairly certain the only other Dom she'd ventured to the second floor with was Andrew. And only after they'd been playing together for a while.

Once they'd reached the Office, Michael opened the door and ushered her in first, allowing himself a secret grin as he closed the door behind him. Scening with him behind closed doors – and wanting it that way – was like his own little private victory every time he scened with her. When he turned around, she was standing by one of the leather chairs in front of the big wooden desk, watching him with nervous anticipation, her tongue flicking out to wet her lower lip as she stared at him.

"So, Ms. Sandler," he said mock-sternly, raising one eyebrow at her. "I do believe you're in breach of your contract."

Ellie's mouth popped open as he moved forward, obviously surprised. "But... You're the one who decided not to put the plug in!"

"And you didn't say anything," he said as he reached her, spinning her around to face the desk. "But your contract says while you're in the club, you wear a plug. Now, I'm going to punish that naughty little hole of yours, and if I ever neglect to plug you when you first arrive again, I'm sure you'll remind me."

She grumbled as he bent her forward over the desk, but there was a flush of excitement in her cheeks and he was sure she'd be wet when he flipped her skirt up. It only took him a moment to confirm his supposition. Her pussy lips were puffy and pinkly swollen, a thin gloss coating her inner surface. As he looked down at her exposed parts, the little star of her anus clenched, as if in anticipation of the punishment that was coming.

Michael gave her ass a little smack, right down her crease where the skin was the most sensitive, snapping his fingers against her crinkled hole and making her gasp with surprise at the sudden sting. A smile slid across his face. While he enjoyed making a woman scream with pain and pleasure any time, there was something even more satisfying about having a real infraction to punish her for. It just added a little something to the proceedings.

❦

DAMMIT. SHE SHOULD HAVE KNOWN IT WAS TOO EASY WHEN HE hadn't immediately taken her downstairs to insert the plug. Part of her had even suspected she'd pay for it later, but she'd decided to let things play out. If she hadn't, if she'd reminded Michael she'd needed to be plugged, would she have been rewarded instead?

Too late to know now.

He moved around to the other side of the desk – the 'boss' side and pulled his toy bag from underneath the desk and set it on the large chair's seat. Ellie now had a front row view as he rummaged through the toys, building her anticipation. When he pulled out a toy still in its package, her eyes bulged a little.

Seeing her expression, he raised his eyebrow at her again. "Something to say, Ms. Sandler?"

Dammit, why was it so hot when he used her last name like that?

"No, nothing, Mr. Waverly," she retorted.

Calling him by his last name only made this whole little scenario seemed sexier, rather than distancing him the way she'd intended. It was half-roleplay, half-reality... because she really had breached the contract, even though he'd set her up to. Still, she was the one who'd made the choice not to say something about the plug; at the time feeling like she was getting away with something naughty.

Maybe she'd subconsciously been hoping and waiting for him to punish her for it.

Still... he was going to put *that* in her *ass*?

Apparently he was determined to really push her soft limits. But she wasn't going to safe word. She was a little bit apprehensive about the size of the toy, but she didn't want to disappoint him... especially not when she really had earned a little bit of a punishment.

The toy was somewhat reminiscent of a beehive, as if someone had glued a bunch of anal beads with expanding sizes together rather than putting them on a string. The smallest bulge, at the tip, was probably only half an inch in diameter... the fifth and largest one looked like it was an intimidating three inches in diameter. Maybe a little smaller, but not much. It was definitely going to be the biggest thing she'd ever had in her ass and her pussy spasmed in frightened arousal. If anal play made her feel submissive, this toy might just turn her into a little puddle of submissive goo for Michael to mold as he wished.

A thought which should frighten her far more than it did in the moment.

Even more disconcerting was when she realized he'd planned to use that thing on her eventually regardless... since it was sitting in his toy bag, obviously new, and they had a club contract. It wasn't like he would have bought it with anyone else in mind.

Her anus clenched spasmodically.

Michael leaned his hip against the desk as he stripped the packaging away from the toy. "I think a little time with this toy will help you appreciate your plug, don't you Ms. Sandler?"

"Very likely," she said, sounding uncertain even to her own ears. Even while her pussy was creaming with anticipation, and the darker desires of her masochistic side were roused by the size and breadth of the toy, she still couldn't help but be a little anxious. Every so often she was faced with a toy or implement which made her wonder if she'd finally reach her limit for submission and pain... that was how she felt right now.

She stayed in position, bent over with her skirt up, her anticipation building as she watched Michael liberally apply lube to the whole, bulging length of the toy. Apparently he wasn't worried about it coming out, even with a lot of lubrication. Ellie held in a whimper.

When he finally straightened up and began to move back around to her side of the desk, she felt her entire lower body clench.

"Try to relax, Ellie," he said, his voice almost gentle as the cool, slick tip of the first bulb pressed against her anus. His warm palm pressed down on her lower back, making her feel pinned in place – in a good way that made her aware of her vulnerability without making her feel frightened. "This will go much easier if you don't tense up."

"Easy for you to say," she retorted, and then gasped as her sphincter opened to admit the first bulge on the toy, trying to snap shut behind it... but it couldn't, because unlike anal beads, this ball was attached to another. She'd opened easily for the first bulge, the second didn't come quite as easily or as quickly.

Ellie moaned, putting her head down on the desk as her anus burned, stretching and tingling as Michael twisted the toy, firmly pressing it into her and pushing the second bulge into her body. Already she felt as full as she possibly could, and she still had three bulges left.

"Ow... ow... slower, please," she begged as a sharp ache went through her lower back, the burning of her inner muscles increasing as her ring stretched for the third bulge.

Michael's hand rubbed her lower back soothingly as he worked the toy a little, pushing it in to stretch her before letting it slide back so only the first two bulges were inside of her. She panted, feeling her pussy begin to quiver emptily, her inner muscles spasming with growing need as the erotic pain grew.

"Take a deep breath and let it out... push..." Michael said, his voice firm. She obeyed without thinking and gasped, tears stinging her eyes as the third bulb pushed inside of her, making the tight ring at her entrance sting and burn. The submissive position and the feel of her ass being invaded by such a large, implacable object made her feel as though she was melting into the desk. She'd probably obey any order he gave her right now, but it gave her a feeling of freedom rather than fear, of trust and comfort rather than unease. "Good girl."

Warmth slid her through her.

She was being a good girl.

A tear slid down her cheek as he began working the fourth bulb into her ass. Whining noises escaped the back of her throat as her inner muscles were stretched, fiery discomfort focusing all of her attention on that area, even as she felt wetness seeping from her pussy.

"Ow, ow, ow..." she chanted, her breath catching in her throat. She clawed at the desk when Michael twisted the toy, the many bulges inside of her massaging her insides.

"That's a good girl," he said again. "Take it for me."

She let out a gasping cry as the fourth bulge pushed into her. The toy felt so deep inside of her, her poor hole stretched so wide... and she wasn't even done yet. She could feel it all the way up to the back of her throat, pushing at her insides, keeping her stretched ring of muscle from being able to close. It burned continuously, waves of fiery, pricking pain sliding sensuously along the pleasure which was building inside of her. Her nipples felt itchy inside of her corset, and she wished the desk were shaped so she could rub her clit against it, but all she could do was stay in position as Michael finished working the toy into her ass.

Tears dripped down on the desk beneath her, her breath coming as a gasping moan, while the toy pumped back and forth, going deeper, stretching her wider. She didn't see how her poor hole could ever be the same after this. She was devastated, from the inside out, and she was verging on the brink of orgasm as the toy moved back and forth. Her forehead bowed down to press against the cool wood of the desk, and it was so cool against her hot skin that she turned her cheek to it, letting out a cry as the toy pushed hard and suddenly she was so full she couldn't breathe at all.

"Good girl, Ellie, that's all of it," Michael said soothingly, his hand caressing her lower back. His hand slid down to her pussy and he chuckled. "Although you don't seem that upset by your punishment."

Ellie moaned, squirming against his hand as he stroked her tender, soaked folds but didn't venture close enough to her clit for her to cum.

"Please," she begged, her voice a mere whisper as she struggled to suck air into her lungs. Her pussy was on fire in an entirely different way from her ass and all she wanted to do was cum. She didn't know if he'd be able to fit his fingers, much less anything else, inside of her with the toy taking up so much space, but she wanted him to try. She was full to bursting and explosion was imminent. "Please, more..."

His fingers slid around her wet hole, testing the opening but not breeching the entrance. "You obviously love anal, Ellie, why is it on your soft limits?"

"It's too intimate," she confessed, trying to move her hips back, craving more of his touch. "I don't want to do it with everyone." His fingers were so close to her clit...

MICHAEL BRUSHED HIS FINGERS OVER ELLIE'S PUSSY, STILL TEASING her, as his mind raced. His cock was pressing against the front of his leathers, rock hard, but he was too distracted by this sudden realization to really feel the urgency his body was trying to communicate. When he'd decided to use the large, bulbed plug on her, he'd also thought to end the scene with anal sex.

Now...

A sudden reversal of decision. If she'd discovered anal play was too intimate for her to do on a regular basis, then Michael was going to wait. He'd claim her ass when he was actually claiming *her*. Once their relationship was real. Because he didn't want something she considered so intimate that she put it on her soft limits, despite how much she obviously loved it, to become part of their club relationship. He didn't want to diminish the importance of it by treating it like a normal scene.

But he was going to reward her.

Her pussy was as wet as she normally was at the end of the scene, as it had been after her nipples had been clamped and her ass had been strapped. And all he'd done was insert a plug. Granted, it was a big plug, and she'd struggled to take it, but he still hadn't expected quite this much of a reaction.

Michael placed his palm flat against her lips, his fingers curving slightly to press down directly on her clit, and he began to move his hand in a slow circular motion.

Her scream of ecstasy was immediate and deafening, her body shuddering as her fingers clawed at the desk, her sobbing cry rising as he continued to manipulate her pussy lips and clit. His cock throbbed against his leathers, and keeping himself from unzipping and just shoving inside of her to experience the tightness of her pussy as it convulsed required a serious amount of willpower.

Instead, he gritted his teeth and concentrated on enjoying the show of her writhing, sobbing climax. Her juices were soaking his hand, the sweet, musky scent of her body's honey filling the air around them as she came, her buttocks quivering around the thick base of the plug, and her cries ringing in his ears.

He let his movements slow as her orgasm tapered off, leaving her quivering and bent over the desk with her cheek pressed against it. Michael gave her a moment to recover and then he pulled her back by her hips. Her legs were wobbly and gave beneath her, allowing him to ease her onto her knees.

Tears streaked her face, making her makeup run a little under her eyes, and her skin was flushed, eyes almost glassy.

"Open your mouth sweetheart," he said, his voice gravelly with need. "I want to fuck it."

Her lips popped open immediately as Michael unzipped his fly and pulled out his cock. He was achingly hard and he knew he wouldn't last long... but taking care of his needs now meant more endurance for round two. He didn't hesitate to press his cock to her lips and groan as she immediately sucked him in, her hot, wet mouth sliding over his sensitive skin as she tongued the underside of his cock.

Careful not to pull, he slid his fingers through the long strands of her hair and pressed them against the back of her head. He thrust his cock forward, sliding into her throat, and when she didn't gag or try to pull away he let himself go. She sucked hard as he fucked her mouth, his hands pressing against the back of her head, using her mouth for his pleasure.

The glazed look in her eyes as she stared up at him seemed to grow more submissive by the second as she swallowed him, the slight squirming of her body giving away her discomfort from the large plug stretching her ass. She was filled at both ends, and Michael could see the effect it had on her in every one of her movements. Moving his hips harder, he shoved the tip of his cock into her throat, groaning as she swallowed convulsively, massaging the sensitive glans.

His head fell back as he pulled out and thrust in again, this time pressing her lips against his groin and crying out as his balls tightened and exploded... his cum poured down her throat into her belly, her tongue rubbing against the underside of his cock as if trying to coax out every drop.

It was fucking heaven... and they had barely gotten started.

15

B liss. She was feeling pure bliss.
No hesitation. No worries. No tension. No awkwardness.
Just bliss.

Her ass was throbbing around the huge toy, reminding her she'd given herself over to Michael, reinforcing his dominance over her, while her pussy throbbed in an entirely different way as if expressing the rapture which came with submitting. The carpet beneath her knees was soft, cradling her, allowing her to kneel before him as hot cream slid into her. Her pussy lips felt swollen between her thighs, her body craving more from him despite the intense orgasm he'd wrung from her.

There was still pain and pleasure to be had.

When he began to pull his softening cock from her mouth, she followed with her lips, reluctant to let him go completely.

His fingers massaged her scalp. "Kneel back, good girl."

She obeyed, her body humming as the toy in her ass shifted again.

"Would you like a beating, Ellie?" His fingers rubbed against her skin through her hair, firm and pleasurable, making her feel even more melty.

"Yes please."

Her body was bubbling over with pleasure now; she needed the pain to balance her out before she turned into a pile of goo. A craving for the dark burn of a whip rose up inside of her, making her pussy quiver all over again.

"Stand up, beautiful."

Placing her hand in his, she managed to stand on wobbly legs with his help. When she swayed slightly, he stepped forward, letting her lean against him and use his strength as he began unlacing her corset. Ellie wanted to moan again as she nuzzled her nose against the soft cotton of the black shirt he was wearing, feeling the bristles of his hair through the fabric and inhaling his scent. She clung slightly to him as the corset shifted and relaxed around her body, making her feel like she really was about to melt now that the stiff boning wasn't holding her in and upright.

Pulling the corset free of her body, Michael rotated their bodies so Ellie's back was to the desk; she felt the wood press against her bare ass as Michael pushed her skirt down her thighs. The fabric slid down her legs to pool around her feet, leaving her completely naked.

"Can you sit up on the desk?" Michael asked, holding her just above her hips, his dark eyes flickering with anticipation. His pants were still open, although they stayed in place, framing his softened cock with black leather. Ellie couldn't help but flick her eyes over his body, before looking up into his eyes and nodding.

He helped lift her up onto the desk, holding steady as she whimpered, leaning forward as the huge plug pressed up inside of her as her weight came down on her ass.

"Breathe through it," he said soothingly, running his hand down her back, waiting until she was ready to lean back away from him. Her breath came in little hitches as the plug created a deep ache inside of her, unlike anything she'd ever felt before.

"Okay," she said finally through swollen lips, her body fizzing and popping. "I'm green." Michael nodded, acknowledging her placement on the color scale. She moaned a little as she sat upright, but it wasn't a bad moan. It was the kind of moan that started deep in her belly and vibrated out of her throat because her lower body had just clenched hard.

Chuckling, Michael slid his hands from her back to her sides and then up to her breasts, cupping and kneading them gently as she carefully leaned back, placing her hands on the desk to take some of the weight off of her ass - and therefore off of the base of the plug. Her legs were spread so he could stand between them, making her feel incredibly wanton. Even though she wasn't bound, she couldn't move with any kind of quickness as long as she was plugged, and in order to sit comfortably she had to keep her hands on the desk and lean away from him - or her hands on him and lean towards him. It was as effective keeping her in place as ropes or chains would be.

"One day, I'm going to spend a lot of time torturing these pretty breasts," Michael said, his voice almost conversational as he squeezed the soft mounds a little harder. "I'm going to bind them at the base, spank them, and cane them hard enough to give you some stripes for a few days. And then I'm going to fuck them."

Ellie's breath was coming harder and faster as his hands worked her sensitive flesh, ending with a deep groan at the final image his words imprinted in her head. Her breasts, swollen and reddened, striped with welts, with his cock sliding between them while she whimpered and writhed, unable to achieve her own orgasm as he focused on her chest... when he came, the salt from his cum would sting her welts and sensitive skin, only adding to her needy arousal.

"Not today though," he continued. "Today you're too distracted by that big plug in your ass, so I think we'll just stick with some clamps."

She didn't know if she was relieved or disappointed. He had a point after all. With so much of her focus on the massive plug, she wouldn't be able to focus or fully appreciate any kind of attention elsewhere. Everything was going to end up blending together in a delightful symphony of pain, unless he wanted to focus exclusively on her ass this evening.

Which she wouldn't have a problem with.

Although her nipples were now throbbing in anticipation of being clamped. The pair he pulled from his pocket were rubber tipped with adjustable tension. Ellie could see they'd been loosened somewhat, to diminish the harshness. He pinched her right nipple and her lips opened on a moan as she arched her breasts towards him at the plea-surable pressure.

That moan deepened as the clamp bit down on her nipple. The slight burn felt good, but not nearly as rough as she wanted. Then Michael fiddled with it and Ellie felt the clamp squeeze tighter, making her whimper as he turned the tension on the spring up.

"Ow... ow..."

"Tight enough?" he asked, a wicked glint in his eye.

Ellie's nipple throbbed painfully. "Yes."

She let out her breath on a hiss as he gave the screw on the clamp another little turn, tightening it even further.

Sadist. She should have known.

Her other nipple received the same treatment, exactly the same amount of turns, this time without asking her if it was tight enough. The twin points of throbbing pain on her chest made an erotic coun-terpoint to the occasional spasms of her full ass and empty pussy.

"Spread your legs, Ellie." The command made her pussy quiver. The pain now radiating from her nipples as well as her ass had her dripping again. It was slow torment, because she knew Michael wasn't anywhere near done torturing her either, considering he still hadn't delivered her promised beating. He had the look of a sadist who was enjoying toying with his prey, wanting to torture all of her sensitive bits before finally rewarding her with a pain-edged orgasm.

Even though her legs were already somewhat spread, it took a little bit of finagling to widen her thighs further with the huge plug inhibiting some of her movements. Ellie whimpered as she rocked back, not sure if she was doing so because of discomfort or pleasure. Discomfort didn't arouse her masochistic side the way actual pain did, but suffering through the discomfort for her Dom's pleasure certainly appealed to her submissive side... and with such a large plug in her ass making her feel more submissive than ever, her head space was a riot of desire and excitement.

Gently spreading her wet pussy lips apart with two fingers; her pink inner bits glistened under the lights and Michael looked directly in her eyes as he reached into his pocket again and drew out a third clamp. Her clit practically jumped in reaction.

"What color are you, beautiful?"

"Green, Michael," she said, her voice husky, only trembling a tiny bit with trepidation.

He placed the clamp around her swollen clit and she moaned as the tiny bud throbbed in its confinement, the sharp initial pinch around the sensitive bundle of nerves only taking a moment to settle into a more consistent throbbing ache. Then the pressure increased as he turned the screw on the clamp, watching her face as he did it rather than what he was doing. Ellie whimpered, her head tipping back slightly as her thighs trembled with the urge to press together and trap him, to stop the compression of her pulsing clit.

"Enough!" she begged, and then cried out as he tightened the clamp just a bit more before releasing it. The weight pulled on her clit, increasing the pressure, and she thought she might cum just from that if she didn't say 'yellow' first.

Michael gave her the time to adjust, his fingers tracing up and down her legs and sides, circling her clamped nipples and making them tingle without jostling them as she panted through the pain and pleasure, her body quivering and on edge. The clamp on her clit was almost too much to bear, and yet she didn't want to ask him to loosen it either.

Twin tears rolled down her cheeks as she settled into the pain, every part of her body pulsating with the sensations running through her. His cock was starting to swell again and Ellie almost wished he would just shove inside her, just like this, with her legs spread wide, her most tender parts clamped and throbbing... he would rub against her clamped clit and waves of pain would assault her even as his cock filled her with pleasure... or would it, considering how fully her lower body already was?

She wanted it...

But instead, Michael stepped away from the center of her legs, holding out one hand to help her down from the table.

"I want you bent over the table, beautiful, and then you'll get your beating."

A shudder went through her at his words and she reached out to take his hand.

Watching Ellie's movements as she gingerly got down from the top of the desk, her legs still spread for the plug and now also to keep from brushing against the clamp on her clit, sent satisfaction zinging through Michael, straight down to his cock which was already roused from applying the clamps. Her nipples and clit were already more sensitive from having cum once, but she'd taken the harsh bite anyway, seemingly oblivious to the tears filling her eyes as she took in the pain and somehow turned it into her own secret pleasure.

While Michael enjoyed a bit of roughness himself - nails down his back or his lover's teeth scraping over his skin - he'd never quite understood how masochists evolved agony into inexpressible pleasure the way they did, he'd just appreciated the results and learned how to use pain to get them there. It was beautiful to see her flush and pale, to hear her whimpers slide into moans, to watch her take the sexual torment he inflicted on her body, only to turn them into rapturous climaxes.

The slight tremor in her legs and arms would make this part of the torture particularly interesting, since her muscles were already struggling to keep her upright. Michael lowered his head to brush a gentle kiss over her lips as she looked up at him, her fingers tight about his hand, eyes glassy with needy passion. She hummed happily as he kissed her, trying to lean into him, the same way she'd tried to lean forward and keep his cock in her mouth. As before, denying her wasn't easy, but he forced himself to do it anyway... he was in control of the scene and the scene wasn't over yet.

"Bend over the desk, Ellie," he reminded her, his voice practically crooning as he helped her turn around. Her eyelashes fluttered as she turned. Most men probably wouldn't consider a waddling woman to be sexy, but as a sadist who had just plugged and clit-clamped his sub, Michael found her nearly-bowlegged steps fucking hot, because he knew why she was walking like that. In fact, he hoped she would be walking a little like that for the next few days.

When she bent over, exposing her ass and pussy to him, she let out a little gasp as her clamped nipples hit the desk. With her curves and petite height, the only way she'd be able to keep her nipples away from the surface of the desk was if she straightened her arms completely – which wouldn't be easy with her already wobbling from her previous orgasm. Still, she did exactly what he thought she would and straightened her elbows, pushing herself back up and giving him a nice, creamy canvas from her shoulders all the way down to the backs of her legs to work with.

The base of the plug peeked between her cheeks, but he could no longer see the clamp because of her short stature. That was for the best, since he didn't want to accidentally catch it with the flogger. Every masochist had their pain threshold and he didn't think too many would actually enjoy having a clamp accidentally torn off their most sensitive organ. Once she couldn't hold herself in place any longer, he'd either have to switch implements or be extra careful about how he wielded the flogger.

"Good girl, Ellie," he said as he moved to the cabinets and picked out the heavy leather flogger he knew Patrick kept in the office. It would be thuddy against her skin, a deeper, denser kind of pain which would contrast with the sharper bite on her nipples and clit. Once he got her skin nice and sensitive and pink, he'd switch over to the special new rubber strap he'd brought for tonight. It was thin, whippy, and would sting like hell, especially over freshly beaten skin.

Perfect for Ellie.

Standing behind her, he shifted the two chairs seated in front of the desk to give himself more room. He took a moment to admire her creamy backside, that pale ivory expanse just waiting to be painted with streaks, before raising his hand.

The flogger whirred through the air, the heavy falls coming down on her shoulders and upper back.

Thud. Thud. Thud. Thud. Thud. Thud.

She moaned. Michael twisted his arm, drawing back, and snapped the flogger back up against her ass.

Thud. Thud. Thud. Thud. Thud. Thud.

Above his head, a twist, and back down.

Ellie writhed under the leather as it struck her body, her back arching slightly, offering up her ass for more punishment. She moaned, almost continuously, panting slightly as Michael used the flogger over her skin. The ivory of her flesh blushed and then began to darken, turning a brighter, deeper pink as the leather impacted over and over again.

As she moaned and squirmed, her arms trembled, and Michael could see the effort she was using to hold herself up, but it wasn't enough and she slowly began to sink down. He followed with the flogger, continuing his assault on her sensitized skin, as his cock began to swell. Since he'd left his pants open in front, he wasn't distracted by his growing dick, he just focused on Ellie and her dipping body.

He could tell the moment her clamped nipples touched the desk, because she jerked upwards as soon as it happened.

The cool wood would feel especially potent against her sensitive buds, not to mention if she let her weight fall on her chest, her clamped tips would be pressed into her breast flesh, which wouldn't be entirely comfortable either. Especially if she moved at all against the desk, making the clamps scrape over it.

Michael grinned at the conundrum she was facing as he continued to flog her, taking extra care around her ass so none of the strands slid between her legs and anywhere near the clamp on her clit.

She couldn't hold herself totally upright forever though, especially not as her shoulders and ass turned a dark sunset pink and her hips moved with each blow, getting more and more into the rhythm he'd established. The swaying movements were erotic, as she was seeking out the stimulation she needed to cum and was unable to find it. This time when her nipples dipped down to touch the desk, she whimpered but didn't jerk back up as she braced herself on her forearms. The tips of her breasts flattened against the desk and she held herself perfectly still, trying not to move and disturb her clamped buds.

Time to switch implements.

"You said you enjoy the rubber strap, didn't you, Ellie?" he asked, almost jovially as he gave her one last lashing across the shoulders with the flogger.

She shuddered. He thought he heard her whisper 'oh god', but he wasn't completely sure.

Laying the flogger on the desk beside her, he moved around to his toy bag to pull out his new strap. Her face was flushed, eyes glassy and anxious, lips swollen as she watched him. Her eyes widened when she saw the narrow strip of rubber. Only two inches wide, he had practiced wielding it quite a bit this week, knowing it had a seriously nasty bite and not wanting to push her past her limits.

"Three strokes with the strap," he told her, and could almost hear the war going on inside of her head.

Part of her wanted to insist she could take more than three strokes of any implement; another part of her was wary of the thinness of the strap and the fact that she hadn't actually felt its impact yet. Not to mention he'd just flogged her ass to a nice, sensitive, rosy hue and she didn't know how hard he planned on wielding the strap. In the end, she just stayed quiet, her anxiety and desire for more easy to read in her adorably conflicting expressions. Michael just grinned.

He'd start with three. He doubted she'd need more. Or if she could even tolerate more. He was certainly starting to grow impatient. His cock was starting to ache with the need to be inside her, and when she finally looked away from the strap, her eyes went immediately to his dick. She licked her plump lips as she stared at his erection, which didn't help him control his arousal at all.

"What color are you, beautiful?" he asked, folding the strap in half and tapping it against his thigh, which drew her attention away from his cock.

She whined, high in her throat. "Green, Sir."

The 'Sir' came out without thinking, he could tell, so he didn't rebuke her for it. At this point, being a submissive as long as she had been, it was ingrained in her to call her Dom 'Sir', and it was actually a good indicator for him of where she was in her head during a scene. Once she started calling him Sir, he knew she wasn't really focused on what she should or shouldn't be calling him... she was just running on instincts.

Moving back around the desk, Michael admired his handiwork on the areas he'd just flogged. The rosiness of her skin was nicely spread over the entire area he'd flogged, bringing all the blood to the surface of her skin and making her much more sensitive than she would normally be. This was going to hurt.

Grinning, he widened his stance slightly to keep his balance as he set himself just to the side of her, grabbed his throbbing cock with his left hand, and drew back his right arm, holding the folded over strap tightly.

WHAP!

She jerked with a scream, followed by another high cry, as a nasty red welt rose up across the upper crest of her buttocks. The strap had caused her scream; her jerking and scraping her nipples across the wooden desk had caused the second cry she'd made. A double whammy for one stroke.

Giving her a moment, Michael stroked his cock as Ellie shuddered and settled back down, a hitching in her breathing letting him know her tears had started and this time she wasn't able to slow them.

"Do you want me to stop?" he asked, although he was fairly certain he was interpreting her cries correctly.

"No!"

The immediate response let him know he was right on target. Ellie really liked this strap.

WHAP!

The second blow landed just above the base of the plug, across the very center of her fleshy buttocks, and Ellie howled as the two-inch thick line immediately rose on her flesh, parallel to and just an inch below the first. Her body was heaving somewhat now as she writhed in reaction, apparently no longer caring how her nipples rubbed over the desk - or perhaps the pain it created distracted her from the burning line he'd just laid down... or perhaps it felt like nothing compared to the strap's bite.

Michael stroked his cock again until she stilled, waiting and ready for the last blow.

"Last one, Ellie, and then I'm going to fuck you."

"Yes, Sir." Despite her obvious tears, she sounded breathy, eager. Needy.

He flicked his wrist.

WHAP!

Right across her sit spot.

She'd barely managed to scream and start writhing again before he was behind her, his cock pressing into her hot pussy. The fit was too tight for an easy entry, no matter that she was soaking wet, and Michael's balls ached as he drew back and thrust forward, driving himself a little deeper with every push of his cock. Ellie's sobs only spurred him on as she writhed before him, her soft, hot body welcoming him in, the heat rising off her beaten skin only matched by the heat of her pussy as it enveloped his cock.

"Oh fuck... oh fuck.... oh fuck..." She said it over and over, with every thrust he made, with every panting sob for air, as if she was too far gone to be able to find any other words.

He thrust hard, burying himself completely inside of her, and she screamed as her body jolted against the desk, his balls slapping against her clamped clit, and his body rubbing against the welts he'd just decorated her ass with. The scream was half-agony, half-ecstasy.

"Say red if you need to," Michael reminded her, his voice almost harsh with the effort of holding himself still inside of her.

A half-sob was his only response.

Holding her hips tightly in his hands, he started to fuck her from behind.

Deeply.

Roughly.

He pushed her to the limit as he stretched out her pussy, his body bumping against the plug and causing her to jerk in reaction as the large toy jolted inside of her. The ridges of the plug rubbed against his cock through the thin wall between her passages, massaging him as he moved in and out of her gripping sheath.

He could feel his balls knocking against her clit clamp with every stroke, making the tiny organ swell in its confines, and her squirming and sobs increased every time.

Her hard, red nipples would be squashed beneath her, still clamped, throbbing in their confinement, scraping across the table as he rode her hard.

When she started to orgasm, she screamed in anguish as her poor, abused clit tried to expand and couldn't, the tiny bundle of nerves pressing against its constraints.

Michael fucked her harder, his own sadistic passions feeding off of her screams.

SHE WAS LOST IN A MAELSTROM OF EXCRUCIATING TORMENT, buffeted on the winds of rapturous ecstasy, so torn between the two sensations she couldn't tell if she was flying or falling.

Full... she was so very, very full. Full to the brim physically, full of sensations, full of emotions...

Michael's cock moved inside of her, slow and deep. It felt like the plug was thrust into her every time his cock was, until she was so full she could taste the sex in the back of her throat.

The pinching on her nipples seemed worse... harder... as the poor, afflicted buds were moved over the wood of the desk, squashed between her body and the hard wood, putting even more pressure on the taut buds. Although the torment of her nipples wasn't nearly as bad as the sharp pinch on her clit which shot through her with every thrust. It was a sharp pinch that sent her reeling, her pussy quivering around Michael's cock, as pain fought with pleasure, until pleasure finally won... her orgasm expanded, only to be cut through with agony as the clamp seemed to bite down more... which only made her masochistic ecstasy grow.

When Michael suddenly withdrew, pulling out of her grasping pussy as she sobbed through her climax, it was both a relief and a deprivation.

The world spun and suddenly she was on her back, her red nipples pointing to the ceiling, and Michael bending over her as he draped her legs over his arms. She was bent nearly in half as he plucked the clamp off of her right nipple, his cock sliding back into her pussy, and she squeezed down hard around him as she screamed with the sensation of blood rushing back into her crushed nipple. The soft, wet, heat of his mouth helped to soothe the tortured bud, but not enough to ameliorate the pain entirely.

When his body slid all the way home and knocked against her

clamped clit, she was immediately distracted from the agony of blood returning to her nipple as this new stimulation had her seeing stars.

Tears slid down her cheeks and into her hair as he fucked her, sucking on her poor nipple, before removing the other, but she was barely aware as her clit was jolted about, the pressure on the tiny nub almost too intense to bear. Part of her wanted to beg for mercy, to scream 'red'... but she could take it... she could bear it...

And when he finally released her other red nipple and his hand moved down to her pussy, Ellie moaned in denial, knowing what was coming.

"Noooo... please...." She writhed on his cock, her pussy milking and shuddering.

She was riding high on a thundercloud of pleasure, the strikes of lightning assaulting her whenever his body knocked against the clit clamp... but when he took it off it was going to be a tempest of sensation.

"It has to come off, sweetheart," he said.

His dark eyes glinted wickedly, drinking in the sight of her as he opened the clamp and tossed it to the side.

Ellie's nails raked down his chest as she thrashed, screaming and arching, his body over hers, inside of hers, wreaking havoc with her senses as his body rubbed against her agonized clit. He was leaning forward, his chest rubbing against her nipples, every part of her aflame with sweat and sensation, passion and anguish.

She was in the throes of torment and passion simultaneously, and she didn't know if she was flying or falling. Wrapping her arms around his neck, she hung on for dear life as an intense orgasm swamped her, drowning her in sensation, in blackness with jagged edges, in overwhelming explosions throughout her entire body until she lost herself in them.

Just when she thought she might finally scream 'red', she passed out.

MICHAEL'S ORGASM DIDN'T JUST COME, IT WAS PRACTICALLY FORCED out of him by Ellie's gripping pussy as she spasmed around him. He was panting and hoarse, leaning against her just to stay upright as she drained him of his cum.

Just as he was about to collapse on top of her, she went limp beneath him. He didn't quite flop over, but he did have to brace his forearms against the desk to keep from crushing her while he caught his breath.

Even as he did so, he was pushing back a sense of panic as he checked her chest to make sure she was okay, his fingers moving to her neck to feel her pulse.

Fast, but normal.

Breathing, regular.

She was okay.

Just passed out.

Smugness creeped through him. Perhaps not the most noble response, but certainly understandable.

Her orgasm had been so intense she'd passed out.

He'd heard of it happening, but he'd never done it to anyone before.

Even more, he was smug because that was how much she'd let her guard down while they scened together. Not that scening together really seemed to be a problem for her... Sex definitely wasn't an issue between the two of them. Intimacy outside of sex was.

Managing to recover, Michael kissed his sleeping beauty's lips before reluctantly pulling away from her. Unlike in the fairy tale his kiss didn't rouse her, although that worked out anyway. He was able to get himself cleaned up, remove her plug, and get her wrapped up in a blanket and out to the aftercare area quickly and efficiently with the help of the club sub on duty.

This time, he cuddled her and woke her up to drink sips of water until she came out of her scene-induced stupor on her own. She leaned against him, letting him continue to hold her as others came in and out of the aftercare area following their own scenes. It wasn't long before Andrew and Kate were also beside them, Kate looking just as dazed and satisfied as Ellie.

He followed her home afterwards and walked her to her door, leaving her with a soft kiss on the lips, which she seemed happy to accept.

All in all, Michael thought the scene had gone well. So had after the scene.

Baby steps. He was going to baby step his way right into Ellie's heart.

❧ 16 ❧

Why was her alarm going off? It was Saturday.

Groaning, Ellie rolled over to pick up her phone and turn off the alarm, and almost immediately shot back onto her side.

HOLY FUCKING OW.

Everything throbbed.

Her ass.

Her nipples.

Her pussy.

Although her shoulders and upper back felt great.

Holding back a wail, Ellie rolled much more carefully to lean over and grab her phone with its inexplicable alarm.

Oh wait... that's right. I said I'd go to the zoo.

Crap.

Groaning, Ellie turned the alarm off.

Whatever, she was basically awake now anyway, after that painful good morning jolt to her ass.

And Michael's going to be at the zoo.

Ignoring the taunting little voice in her head, she started to push herself up to a sitting position. She hissed as the position put pressure on her sensitive skin. She could still feel the welts from the strap last night. Heck, she'd probably be feeling them for a few days. A sense of warmth suffused her at the reminder, scattering some of the pain and making it more enjoyable.

She wasn't sure if Michael's presence was a draw or a deterrent. While part of her wanted to see him outside of the club, another part of her balked, wanting to draw back and slow down, worried it was too much like a real relationship. Too much pressure.

Real conversations could lead to real confessions...

Her inner demons were silenced - or at least drowned out - by the aches and pains as she managed to get out of bed. One of the many benefits of being a masochist; her physical hurt could distract from her emotional issues. Dr. Amy was occasionally concerned Ellie used her masochism as a crutch, but she wasn't complaining when it helped her shut up the ugly little voice in her head.

Watson protested sleepily as she moved the covers, accidentally jostling his side of the bed. His grumbling mews subsided quickly enough when she left the bed completely to His Majesty, no longer disturbing his slumber with her movements.

Ouch... ouch...

Standing made her pussy lips rub against her sore clit, which still felt swollen after last night's abuse, and reminded her that her ass had been seriously stretched as well. Her nipples were sore and pressing against the soft fabric of the tank top she'd worn to bed; not fully distended, but they were slightly hardened just from jiggling as she moved. Man, he'd really worked her over in the best way possible. Ellie couldn't remember the last time she'd had a scene which had left her with this many delightful little shadow pains and throbbing reminders.

Even as sore as her lady parts were, it was making her a horny.

Although walking kind of sucked.

Waddling was not an attractive look.

Making it to the bathroom, she pulled down her panties so she could admire the marks across her ass. Her skin was still just very slightly pink, although she wouldn't have been able to tell if she didn't have the completely untouched skin of her lower back to directly compare it to, in between the dark welts crossing her cheeks. Those were still so dark pink they were practically red, and Ellie's breath hissed as she ran her fingers across the center one, craning her neck so she could see herself in the mirror.

Yeah, she was going to be feeling those welts every time she sat down for the next couple of days. Feeling it and thinking about how hot the scene had been. Thinking about Michael fucking her into ecstatic oblivion.

It was a little scary how easily she let go with him, but it gave her hope too. She wouldn't be able to do let go if she didn't subconsciously trust him completely. If only she could get her overthinking brain on board with her subconscious, she'd be totally good to go. Well... unless, of course, he ever wanted to talk about her past and what had happened to her, and then if he reacted badly - yeah, there went her brain again.

Closing her eyes, she leaned back against her bathroom counter, hissing as the cool marble pressed against a welt, making her bottom throb painfully and completely derailing her anxious thoughts. With all the hissing she was doing today she was starting to sound like a snake, but it was better than actually shrieking or yelping. Her neighbors wouldn't notice, but it was kind of an automatic response.

Show no pain.

Turning around, she examined herself in the mirror. At least she'd managed to wash off all her make up last night. When she'd gotten inside and seen her reflection, she'd been a little horrified Michael had let her walk around with her melting makeup, even if it was just from the club to her car and then her car up to her apartment.

A little smile curved her lips as she thought about his goodnight kiss. He'd obviously wanted more, but he hadn't pressed. Ellie wanted more too, but... she was glad he hadn't done more than walk her up. Even that had been a big step for her, letting a Dom follow her home and see her to her door. Letting him into her actual space would have been way too much too fast.

"Okay," she muttered to herself, leaning back against the counter and biting back a moan as the pressure increased the throbbing in her ass. "Shower, clothes, breakfast, zoo."

Not necessarily in that order.

IT ACTUALLY TOOK SOME DEFT MANEUVERING TO MAKE SURE HE HAD the seat next to Ellie on the metro, mostly because she'd been talking to Sharon as they'd all boarded the train car. Still, he'd managed by literally tugging Ellie into one of the seats beside him, shamelessly refusing to relinquish his hold on her hand. He'd taken her hand as soon as she'd arrived at the metro station, looking casually gorgeous in jeans and a dark red tank top edged with black lace underneath a cropped leather jacket, and just the slightest hint of a waddle in her walk. Although she'd seemed uneasy about holding hands with him on the platform, she hadn't protested either or tried to move away. She'd just seemed nervous, although her anxiousness had gone away as conversations had started up and no one had made a big deal out of their hand-holding.

Sharon immediately plopped down on the seat in front of him and Ellie, turning around to continue her conversation with Ellie - she'd apparently decided Ellie would make a perfect replacement roommate for Kate and was trying to convince Ellie to come around to her point of view.

"The doorman is always there to receive packages or if you forget your key," Sharon said, her dark eyes bright and cajoling. "It's like having a butler, except he doesn't answer the front door for you."

Jake, who was standing and holding onto the overhead bar rather than taking the open seat next to Sharon, snorted. When Sharon's head whipped around so she could glare at him though, he was looking at the front of the train rather than down at her.

"I think I'm pretty good where I am," Ellie said again, still sounding amused. "I like living on my own."

"When was the last time you lived *with* someone?" Sharon asked, coaxing. "You might like it even more. And I'm a blast to live with. Right, Kate?" The second question was half-shouted across the train, since Kate was sitting several rows back with Andrew and looked like she'd fallen asleep on his shoulder. "Kate? Oh, never mind. What's the use of having a best friend who constantly has all the energy fucked right out of her?"

This time she ignored the derisive noise Jake made. Michael leaned back in his seat, not bothering to hide his grin. Sharon could be incredibly crass, which for some reason seemed to seriously irk Jake, which only encouraged her to be more so. Her nickname for him kept changing, but last Michael heard she'd most recently dubbed him Captain America after he'd rebuked her for cursing.

"How do you know you won't have the same problem with me?" Ellie asked, although unlike Sharon her voice was soft enough only Sharon and Michael - and maybe Jake - heard her response.

Frowning, Sharon's eyes flicked back and forth between Ellie and Michael.

Michael gave her a wicked grin.

She shrugged. "I guess I don't, but since we're good friends and you're not my *best* friend I won't feel quite as neglected if you keep falling asleep when I need you."

"It is incredibly rude to compare friendships like that," Jake interjected, glowering down at her. "What if you just hurt Ellie's feelings?"

"I didn't," Sharon said irritably, waving her hand dismissively at him. Then she frowned at Ellie. "I didn't, did I? Although, if you did move in with me, I'd totally be willing to revisit the question of who my best friend is."

The aggravated noises Jake was making were getting louder. Michael eyed him with amusement. No wonder Ellie was so quiet all the time, just sitting back and watching could be highly entertaining. Although Jake and Sharon were currently the best show in town. In the sideways seat in front of Sharon, Jared and Leigh were curled up around each other, whispering and ignoring everyone else. On Jake's other side, Olivia was sitting in the sideways seat next to Chris, whose lap was currently serving as Jessica's foot rest; Jessica was tucked underneath Justin's arm and the four of them were talking. Behind Justin and Jessica, Liam and Hilary seemed torn between listening to the conversation in front of them or Sharon and Jake's bickering. Lexie and Patrick had no such issue. Patrick was leaning against the window while Lexie leaned against him and they were both watching Jake, who had his back to them or he'd realize just how interested their friends were in what was going on with him.

Behind Patrick and Lexie, Angel and Adam were currently arguing about something, although not very loudly, since they were trying not to wake Kate who was snuggled on Andrew's shoulder in the seats behind them. Since Rick and Maria were directly behind Michael, he wasn't sure where their attention was; and behind them were whatever poor sods had ended up on the same train car as the rest of them.

"So, I get you as a best friend... anything else?" Ellie asked, her eyes sparkling.

The look Sharon gave her was almost of awed respect. "You're kind of sassy this morning, I like it!"

Ellie giggled and leaned against Michael's shoulder. He almost shifted to put his arm around her, but he didn't want her to panic the way she had the last time he'd tucked her under his arm... so he just enjoyed the feeling of her leaning against him, their hands entwined and resting on their thighs.

"Did Michael give you a sass injection last night?" Sharon asked, not bothering to lower her voice as Jake gave her a disbelieving look, which she ignored. Both Michael and Ellie burst out laughing.

"Do you have any sense of decorum at all?" Jake growled down at her.

Across the aisle, his little sister finally couldn't take it anymore. She burst out laughing, and Jake whipped around to finally notice he had the attention of pretty much every single one of their friends at this point - except for Kate who was still asleep on Andrew's shoulder.

"What?!" he barked out.

"De- de- de-" Lexie couldn't even get the word out, she just pointed at him, laughing even harder as tears started to slide down her face.

"What Lexie means is you're turning into a prude, Captain America," Patrick said.

"Don't call me that," Jake snapped.

Rolling her eyes, Sharon pretended she hadn't just stirred the pot, returning her attention to Ellie. "Please tell me you'll think about it?"

"I'll think about it," Ellie said, but her tone of voice indicated thinking was all she'd be doing, making Sharon sigh with exaggerated defeat.

The conversation got a little quieter as the Metro moved along, more people getting on and off at every stop. Sharon started bouncing in her seat with every stop, now chattering about all the animals she wanted to see today and what she hoped they would be doing. When Michael happened to glance up at Jake, he smirked when he saw the other man watching Sharon's excitement, the tiniest hint of a smile curving his lips.

Ha.

Busted.

Jake was lucky their other friends had gone back to their own conversations, since Michael was probably the only person in the group who wouldn't gossip about it. Well, Ellie probably wouldn't either. Her head on his shoulder felt nice, moving occasionally when she nodded in response to something Sharon said.

By the time they reached the stop before the zoo, Sharon had moved herself around so she was on her knees, bouncing incessantly.

"What about you?" she asked Jake, turning her attention to him. His expression was carefully blank, with no hint of the smile Michael had observed earlier. "Do you have an animal you want to see?"

"Do you have to pee or something?" he asked instead of answering her, gesturing at her squirming body.

Sharon laughed, completely unperturbed. "Nope, I'm just excited! Zoo! Zoo, zoo, zoo, zoo-"

She started sing-song chanting, and behind Michael he heard Kate groan. "Dammit, you got her started again!"

Michael was a little distracted, because Ellie was suddenly burrowing into his shoulder, her body shaking although her hair slid forward to cover her expression. He turned towards her, brushing her hair back in slight alarm, only to see her wide grin as she tried to stifle her giggles.

When Sharon farted, Ellie stopped even trying.

"Whoops, excuse me! Zoo, zoo, zoo -"

"Did you just fart?!" Jake looked appalled and maybe just a tiny bit impressed at Sharon's complete lack of fucks to give.

Wrapping his arms around Ellie, Michael dragged her in against him, and they held onto each other as they laughed.

Sharon immediately stopped bouncing and glared. "Of course not!"

"Yes you did, I heard it!"

"I don't fart! I'm a lady! I whisper in my panties!"

Laughter roared out around them because by now the entire train car was paying attention to the ridiculous exchange. Ellie's fingers dug into the front of Michael's shirt as the train, thankfully, ground to a halt at the zoo's stop.

"Oh my god I love her, I love her so much," Ellie whispered to him, wiping away her tears. "My clit wants to high-five her personality."

He officially lost it, hugging her close for a brief second before he released her so they could get up and hurry off the train. He practically stumbled over his steps as he moved because he was laughing so hard. So was everyone else, but not for the same reason he was.

Let all of them enjoy Sharon's loud antics, Ellie was just as hilarious and she chose to share her quiet, wicked humor with just *him*.

The metro ride was not at all how he'd pictured it going, but honestly he couldn't imagine a way in which it could have been more enjoyable.

⚜

Now, in addition to her pussy, ass, and nipples, Ellie's sides and face hurt from grinning so hard.

Sharon was just... everything. She'd immediately noticed Ellie was a little uncomfortable about being so couple-y with Michael on the platform, but before Ellie's anxieties could really start to rear their ugly heads, Sharon easily distracted her. It was one of the many reasons she and Sharon had hit it off so quickly; the other woman didn't mind Ellie's quiet nature and she always seemed to pick up on when Ellie just wanted everyone to act normally around her so she could pretend to be normal.

Well, not like Sharon was totally normal exactly. But it was mostly normal behavior for Sharon, even though some of it might be a little bit more excessive with Jake as an audience.

Michael stepped onto the escalator before Ellie, leaving Sharon to follow her. The other woman, who was as petite as Ellie, leaned forward to hug Ellie around the waist.

"Oh my god, I can't believe I farted in front of everyone," Sharon whispered, looking mortified now that the only person paying attention to her was Ellie.

She leaned down to whisper back. "I thought you only whisper in your panties."

"What else was I supposed to say?" Sharon whispered back. "That asshole pointed it out to everyone instead of just letting it go! He's such a dick!"

And, true to Sharon's personality, instead of letting him know he'd gotten to her, she'd played it off like she didn't care at all.

Maybe that was another reason she and Ellie got along so well. They were alike in a lot of ways.

She hugged Sharon back with her free arm before she had to turn around to step off the escalator, by which time Kate and Andrew had caught up and were distracting Sharon.

Getting to the zoo was both enjoyable and a little surreal. Michael held her hand the entire time and she started to feel like they were kind of a real couple. Everyone was treating them like they were a real couple. Michael was acting like they were a real couple. Heck, she was managing to act like they were a real couple, even if she felt like an awkward fraud and a nervous, bumbling mess.

Sharon's ridiculous antics helped her forget her nerves though. As long as Sharon kept up her rapid chatter, Ellie couldn't focus on whether or not she was ready to act like a girlfriend. She couldn't worry if she was leading Michael on or start feeling panicked about all the different ways this could go wrong when she was too busy laughing at Sharon's outrageous behavior.

It didn't take long before the group started to fall apart once they were inside the zoo. There were three main groups, plus Sharon.

Bringing up the rear were Angel, Adam, Jared, Leigh, and Olivia. Olivia and Adam both seemed to feel the need to read every single bit of information the zoo offered about each animal, which made Angel complain, so Leigh was helping to keep her entertained and Jared just seemed to be along for the ride. It was entirely possible Adam was just trying to get back at Angel for wearing her "Knocked Up Baby Momma" shirt out in public by being slow. If that was his goal, he was definitely on his way to achieving it, but Ellie thought he might just honestly enjoy reading all the facts. She made a mental note never to visit a museum with him.

In the middle, although somewhat loosely strung along, were Jessica, Justin, Chris, Hilary, Liam, Maria, and Rick. Jessica kept trying to move faster but Justin kept pulling her back, while Liam had a tendency to wander and Hilary kept having to drag him back over to where everyone else was. Rick and Maria ambled along, looking far too cutely content.

Leading the way down the paths were Ellie, Michael, Lexie, Patrick, Andrew, Kate, and Jake. Ellie had a feeling Lexie would have been a little slower on her own, but she wanted to give Jake an excuse to be with the front group; mostly because being in the lead group allowed him to be closest to where Sharon was.

Sharon had not at all been feigning her excitement about the zoo. She was like a little kid on crack, and her joy was infectious as she ran back and forth between exhibits, not at all unhappy to revisit one whenever she realized everyone else had fallen behind again. Even Jake's feigned grumpy demeanor couldn't quite hold up against her excitement, and more than once Ellie saw him smiling as he watched Sharon pressing her face up against the glass of the otters or leaning over the fence above the tiger enclosure. He also shifted closer like he was ready to grab her if she fell over, even though there was a safety ledge on the other side of the fence and not even the slightest risk of danger.

For herself, Ellie just enjoyed the strange feeling of being part of a normal couple.

It hadn't been her plan for the day, but it was happening and part of her just wanted to pretend. Besides, it wasn't entirely a pretense. They did have a contractually spelled out relationship in the club. They were friends outside of it. Just because Michael held her hand, was constantly standing close enough their shoulders were touching, and kept giving her little glances and smiles which made her feel all warm and fuzzy inside, didn't mean she had to panic about where things were going.

Helped by distractions from animals and Sharon's craziness, as well as making sure they didn't get too far ahead of everyone else, she was actually able to just stay in the moment and enjoy herself.

"WHAT'S ANGEL DOING?"

The question had Michael turning around. His brain was trying to tell him something important... something about Angel and the zoo. Scanning the crowd looking for Angel, his eyes zeroed in on her almost immediately. Oh yeah. He remembered now.

Angel was sprawled over the edge of the prairie dog enclosure making little clucking noises down at them. He wasn't close enough to hear the noises, but he knew exactly what was going on. He'd visited the zoo with her before, although it was years ago. Looked like some things never changed.

"Come on," he said, starting forward and keeping his grip on Ellie's hand so she came along with him. "We might as well go back and see what Adam wants to do."

"Do?" Kate asked, looking confused.

"She's going to be there a while and I'm not waiting for her," Michael said, gesturing ahead to where Angel was propped. Beside her, Leigh looked highly amused as she watched Adam trying to get his fiancé's attention, with little success. "Besides, I'm getting hungry. We might as well regroup and see if anyone wants food."

"I want food, but I just want to get it from one of the stands and keep moving," Sharon said, catching up with them just in time to hear the end of Michael's statement. Behind her, Jake followed along with a somewhat bemused expression on his face, Lexie and Patrick just behind him. Although he knew the women had plotted this zoo outing to get some extra time for him and Ellie outside of the club - and he thoroughly appreciated their efforts because it really did feel like he and Ellie were out on a date even if it was a group date - the most revealing part of today had actually not been Ellie's willingness to hold his hand and act like they were on a date. Nope, the most revealing part of today had been watching Jake and Sharon needle each other, then observe Jake doing his best to keep up with Sharon while pretending he was doing no such thing, and Sharon running around like a maniac just to see if Jake would follow while pretending she was doing no such thing.

"I'd rather sit down," Ellie said, making Michael smile, because he'd rather sit down with her too.

In the end, Adam was left sitting by the prairie dogs waiting for Angel to get enough of them (Michael assured the other man they'd swing by for them on the way out. Adam hadn't found him very funny, but then Michael hadn't been entirely joking. Angel had a very strange fascination with the little rodents) while Jared and Leigh went to get them food. The others were also going to get food at the stand, but they were going to move on afterwards. Only Andrew and Kate were interested in going and sitting down with Ellie and Michael at the zoo's restaurant. Okay, it was overpriced, but the food wasn't that bad, and Michael was actually glad the others were more interested in continuing to move around the zoo.

Or maybe they hadn't really been and were just trying to give him and Ellie more time together. Andrew and Kate might just be volunteers to act as a buffer in case Ellie needed it.

It ended up feeling like they were out on a double date, which could have been uncomfortable because Ellie and Andrew had had sex in the past, while Kate and Michael had scened together and been intimate during those scenes, but somehow it just worked. Open communication between all of them previously had led to no awkward feelings now; and Andrew was a good enough friend of Ellie's that she was able to completely relax.

On the metro on their way home, Ellie sat tucked under his arm with her back against his side, one hand still wrapped in his as she talked with Maria who was sitting across the aisle from her. It was the moment Michael knew for sure this, she, was what he wanted. More days like this. More time with Ellie like this.

It might come slowly, but for more of this... it'd be more than worth it. And who knew... after today, maybe it wouldn't come as slowly as he'd feared.

❧ 17 ❧

Somehow, Ellie had found herself in a relationship. Sort of. At least, that's what it felt like. Although she tried not to think about it too hard, worried she'd panic or say something and everything would come crashing down.

But as long as she didn't think too much about it, she was happy. Dr. Amy still considered it progress, although Ellie didn't tell her therapist that she felt like a relationship fraud, like she was faking something she couldn't actually do.

Still... it felt nice. And it was more than she'd ever had before.

Michael still hadn't been inside her apartment, and she hadn't been back to his, but they talked on the phone every night now. Not just texts, actual phone conversations before bed. Saying goodnight to him was now part of her nightly routine.

More than once she went out for dinner with 'some of the group' or over to someone's house for dinner, and it just so happened Michael was there too. And since they were both there and liked holding hands and sitting next to each other... well, it just seemed silly not to. He always walked her out to her car and gave her a kiss goodbye, and each time the kiss was a little bit *more*. One of these days it was going to be more than just lips on lips, and the thought made her feel both panicked and excited. Which was ridiculous because they did far more than little kisses at the club.

Ellie was spending every Thursday, Friday, and Saturday night at the club now, even though she and Michael only played on Fridays. That gave them Thursday to flirt and anticipate and Saturday to just hang out at the bar with their friends. Although hanging out was slowly turning into something more like cuddling and flirting.

She didn't have a moment of panic either, although she had occasional bouts of anxiety. Often, Michael helped her turn those aside with a simple touch of his hand on hers. Sometimes she'd shift about and the marks he'd left on her would flare to life or her ass would throb around the plug in it, and her issues would be derailed for another night.

So when he offered to pick her up and take her to Angel and Adam's for Sunday afternoon football, she actually didn't think twice before she accepted. Their relationship had slowly but surely moved outside of the club and she was enjoying it.

The air was crisp, but it was a nice enough day that she waited for him on the steps of her apartment building rather than inside. It really didn't have anything to do with not wanting him up near her space, although the thought had occurred to her too. Hopefully, he wouldn't see it that way.

The grin he gave her when his car pulled up and she came skipping down the steps towards the passenger door said he didn't think twice about it. "So," he said as she got in and pulled the door shut. "Are you ready for some football?"

Ellie laughed and pointed to the Redskins jersey she was wearing. The number on it had sequins sewn on and it was *not* an official jersey. She'd gotten it at Victoria's Secret. "Don't I look ready?"

"I can't tell if Hilary and Jessica are going to love your jersey or find it sacrilegious," he said, shaking his head as he pulled out of the parking lot. Reaching over, he slid his fingers through hers, her hand settling naturally into his. At this point, being with him and not holding hands felt unnatural.

They'd come a long way from this time last year when she'd been avoiding him at the club.

"Why sacrilegious?"

"Because it's sparkly, not a real jersey, and they're weirdly serious about football."

Michael's statement turned out to be a bit of an understatement. Compared to him, she kind of figured anyone could be called serious about football, but he had not been exaggerating. Any impression Ellie had ever had of Jessica being quiet or Hilary being a total prude went right out the window listening to the stream of curses, orders, and screaming demands which were hurled at the television. And that was only the first ten minutes of the game.

She and Michael fled back upstairs to where the more sane members of society were hanging out in the kitchen, eating Justin's snacks as they came out of the oven. The cook in question looked up to see them emerging from the basement and laughed.

"Loud, aren't they?" he asked, dark eyes sparkling with mirth. Sitting across from him at the kitchen bar were Olivia, Rick, and Maria, all of them far more interested in Justin's cooking than in the game downstairs.

"And I always thought Angel was bad," Michael joked as he and Ellie joined the others at the kitchen bar, watching Justin deftly slice herbs and then sprinkle them on top of the bruschetta he was making.

"Yeah, but Angel's always loud, Jessica and Hilary lull you into a false sense of calm before perforating your ear drums," Rick said, dipping a tortilla chip in Justin's homemade salsa before pushing the dishes down the counter towards Ellie and Michael.

"Where's Patrick?" Ellie wanted to know.

The talks with Luke about coming on as a partner for Marquis were going really well and Patrick had invited him to come hang out with the others today. Not that he needed to be friends with all of them, but since many of them would be helping out at Marquis initially, Michael and Patrick wanted Luke to meet them, preferably in neutral territory. Stronghold, where all the Doms felt the need to maintain their authority, wasn't really the best place. Ellie suspected the real reason for the more casual 'meeting' was because of the contemplative redhead sitting at the other end of the kitchen bar, staring off into space.

Although as soon as Ellie asked the question, Olivia's focus immediately shifted to her. The Domme was wearing a black button down shirt, neatly tailored to her curves, with the sleeves rolled up, making her look much less casual than everyone else. Which was probably deliberate, since she knew Patrick was bringing Luke today. Ellie was curious and eager to meet him after hearing so much about him, whereas Olivia looked like she was preparing for a confrontation. She was obviously uneasy with the idea of a new partner in the club, especially one she hadn't ever met and who hadn't met her.

Which Ellie could understand.

Patrick and Michael deeply respected Olivia, as well as trusted her, and the same went for her. An unknown entity might upset the delicate balance the dominants had achieved of respecting each other's authority and not stepping on each other's toes.

"Not here yet," Olivia said in clipped tones.

Maria widened her eyes at Ellie, as if telling her not to open that particular bread basket.

Well, okay then. Ellie was definitely not interested in poking at an on edge Domme. Beside her, Michael gave a kind of resigned sigh, but the expression on his face was one of amusement. He'd told her a lot about Luke, and it was obvious he liked the guy, who had turned out to be pretty easy going even if he was just as confident and self-assured as Patrick or Michael. He also found Olivia's general displeasure over the situation amusing. He'd bet Patrick five dollars Olivia would relax and start treating Luke like one of the guys by the end of this afternoon.

Looking at Olivia now, Ellie was having a hard time picturing Michael winning the bet.

"Do you guys need something to drink?" Justin asked as he finished sprinkling green slivers of herbs on the bruschetta. "I've got sangria and beer in the fridge."

"Ooo, sangria sounds great," Ellie said immediately, as Michael asked for a beer.

The sangria was more than great, it was probably the best sangria she'd ever had. White wine, with just a bit of fizz to it, with pieces of peaches, strawberries, and blueberries floating in it. Even the fruit fizzed when she bit into it, proving it had been soaking up the alcohol for quite a while already.

Leaning against Michael, joining in on the conversation, and laughing at the occasional catcalls and shouts which drifted up from the basement, Ellie relaxed - and ignored the little voice in the back of her head reminding her she wasn't really Michael's girlfriend and none of this was real.

❧

SOMETHING WAS TROUBLING ELLIE, BUT MICHAEL DIDN'T KNOW what or how to fix it.

It had been nearly a month since their first 'outing' together at the zoo and sometimes he felt like things were two steps forward, one step back with her. Sometimes both steps back. Whenever they were together she would start to relax and be herself, and then she'd suddenly tense up and draw back a little. Not just from him, from everyone. Everyone just kept treating her the same until she relaxed again and everything would be fine until the next time.

Michael didn't like to ignore an issue, but he wasn't sure pointing it out would help. Especially since Ellie didn't seem inclined to talk about it.

He just wanted to help her and wasn't sure how.

Maybe there wasn't anything he could do.

But he wished he at least knew what was wrong.

When Patrick finally came in with Lexie and Luke behind him, Ellie perked up again and Michael found himself fighting back jealousy. He knew she was just interested in meeting Luke because she'd heard Michael talking so much about him, but considering they weren't officially dating he wasn't feeling secure enough to be okay with her interest in another man. Especially one as good looking as Luke.

So Michael made sure to stand close beside her as he introduced her to Luke, one hand on her back.

The other man just smiled amiably, shaking her hand and letting go, completely normal and not at all flirtatious or even overly friendly. Smart man.

"Michael talks about you a lot."

"Oh?" Ellie sounded surprised and almost fascinated, which just served to make Michael frown. Why would she be surprised?

"Of course I do," he said, looking down at her. Luke had already moved on to shaking hands with Justin, but his blue eyes were on Olivia, who was sitting back in her chair, arms crossed over her chest, watching his every move. Michael ignored that for now, Patrick could deal with it. "Why wouldn't I?"

She shrugged, her gaze sliding down towards the floor, and Michael inwardly cursed. Dammit, he'd made her withdraw again. Sliding his arm around her shoulders, he tugged her against him, watching her carefully for any signs of panic. To his relief, she snuggled in against him, her hand creeping around his waist almost tentatively. He dropped his lips to her ear to whisper.

"I promise I only said nice things."

Turning her head slightly, she peeked at him. "Yeah?"

He couldn't help himself. He leaned forward the extra couple inches to drop a kiss on her lips.

Slowly.

So she had time to pull away if she wanted to.

She didn't.

Smug but cautious, Michael didn't extend the kiss. "Yeah."

Hoping no one had caught their private moment, Michael looked up again. He shouldn't have worried. Everyone was watching Luke, who was leaning against the counter and trying to talk to Olivia, who was being polite but distant.

Dammit. Looked like he might lose the bet to Patrick after all. Luke was a pretty charming guy. Michael had thought he'd be able to win Olivia over immediately, but it looked like she wanted to be a harder case than he'd anticipated. The expression on her face was reserved, as if she was withholding judgment while she studied Luke.

Neither Rick nor Justin looked entirely pleased at Luke's interest in Olivia. They all knew he'd expressed interest in the club. If he thought Olivia was a submissive, he was going to be in for quite a surprise.

"I'm looking forward to working with you," he said, giving Olivia a wide, warm smile.

Olivia nodded her head. "It's nice to finally meet you."

Her tone said anything but.

"Hey Luke, can we get you a beer or sangria or anything?" Michael asked, deciding to rescue the poor man, who looked like he was trying to think of something charming to say to Olivia. At this point, he was better off being pulled back. Olivia remained reserved, and the more anyone pushed her, the more likely it was she would bite someone's head off. Since they hadn't finalized the deal with Luke yet, Michael would prefer not to lose the man before he became their newest partner.

After the deal was set, it would be funny if he tried to be dominant with Olivia.

She'd hand his ass to him on a silver platter.

"Water would be great, actually," Luke said, turning towards him. As Patrick grabbed a glass from the cabinet, Lexie started telling Rick, Maria, and Olivia about Luke's rescue dog Molly, who was apparently too cute to be believed and the reason they'd been running late. Lexie hadn't wanted to leave the adorable mutt.

"She's a total cuddle whore," Lexie said. "She's like, fifty pounds, but she thinks she's a lap dog."

"And any lap will do," Luke said. "That's actually how she got her name. She's very smart, very sweet, and very needy, so I named her after Molly Hooper on Sherlock."

Beside Michael, Ellie squealed. "My cat's name is Watson!"

Since she remained tucked into Michael's side, he tried not to let his jealousy ride him. It wasn't that hard since even as Luke and Ellie started comparing notes on their pets, Luke kept shooting little glances at Olivia, obviously trying to figure out what she was thinking and what kind of impression he was making. Since her expression remained completely blank, it was really anyone's guess.

"Girls have cooties."

Ellie's nose burned as she nearly snorted sangria. It was kind of potent sangria. But still, listening to Adam very drunkenly, very seriously tell Jake that girls had cooties was hilarious.

Sitting on Adam's lap, Angel was looking a bit ticked off. Possibly because she couldn't get drunk, or possibly because her fiancé and baby daddy had just said she had cooties. "We do not!"

"Yes, you do," Adam insisted, turning his head to face her. "It's proven scientific fact; women have more germs on their hands than men do."

"Probably because men ask us to put our hands in such strange places!"

Adam made a little growling noise, his hand on Angel's belly as he tipped her back slightly to press his face towards her neck. "I'll put your hands in a strange place."

"Oooookay, and Adam's officially wasted," Jake said, laughing as he took Adam's arm to pull him back upright.

He wasn't the only one.

"What the hell is in this sangria?" Ellie mumbled, lifting up her glass and staring into it like it had all the answers. The fruit floated and bobbed, but did not reveal their secrets.

"What?" asked Michael, leaning in closer.

Like he wasn't already super, duper close. Arm around her, legs intertwined, hands held. Pretty much all over her, really. She liked it.

"You like what?" he asked, sounding a little bit more exasperated.

Ellie giggled, and it seemed kind of far away. Like, weirdly far away and disconnected. "Oh my god, I'm drunk!"

"No shit, Sherlock," Sharon said from where she was laying on the floor. Ellie frowned. When had she gotten down there? "What the hell was in the sangria, Justin?!"

On the other side of the sectional from Michael and Ellie, Justin was given his own giggling girlfriend a foot massage. She and Hilary had finally stopped screaming at the television around the end of the third quarter when it became very obvious the Redskins didn't have a chance in hell of a comeback, despite having gone into halftime with a slight lead. Looking up from his task, Justin shrugged.

"Moscato, peach brandy, and fruit."

"Oh my god, there's *liquor* in it?!" Ellie stared at the glass in her hand in a kind of horror. No wonder she was wasted. Which suddenly struck her as funny and she started giggling again. "I didn't mean to get this drunk!"

"Why is that funny?" Michael asked, sounding confused. He'd only had beer. No secretly super strong sangria for him. Ha, say that five times fast!

"I don't know," Ellie confessed, giggling harder, which in turn made him chuckle.

Turning to her other side, she looked at Luke, who was very nice to look at. Not as nice to look at as Michael, but still very nice.

Michael sighed and turned his attention to his soon-to-be business partner as well. "Sure you still want to get involved with this crazy bunch? This is a pretty good look at the kind of people you'll be seeing at a BDSM club, even if we're not doing anything kinky right now."

Luke just laughed. "I'm having a good time. It's kind of nice to see a lot of strong personalities getting along so well."

"I'm not a strong personality," Ellie confessed, her giggles fading away into a little bit of sadness.

To her surprise, Michael's arms tightened around her. "I like you just the way you are, beautiful. And you're stronger than you give yourself credit for."

She snuggled into him, appreciating his words, taking another sip of her sangria. Because it was tasty and she was already drunk so whateeeeeeeeeeeeeever. On the other side of Michael, Luke was looking around the room, taking in all the couples and the non-couples. Olivia was sitting next to Jared and Leigh, chatting with them, while Jake was in an armchair, frowning disapprovingly at Sharon's prone form. If he kept scowling while she was around, his face was going to stick that way.

Ellie giggled again.

Her thoughts were becoming all floaty as Michael and Luke started talking again, so she just sipped her yummy sangria some more and enjoyed being all snuggled up with Michael, just like the other couples in the room.

It felt so nice. It felt so real.

"WATCH YOUR STEP," MICHAEL SAID AS HE HELPED ELLIE INTO THE elevator. She leaned against him, giggling incessantly.

Once he'd realized exactly how drunk she was, he'd stopped allowing her sangria refills and had gotten her some water, but he hadn't realized what a lightweight she was. The damage had already pretty much been done. Still, she was at least an adorable drunk - affectionate and cuddly, although with occasional small bouts of melancholy. Several times throughout the evening she'd made comments, obviously comparing herself to the other ladies present and finding herself wanting.

If she hadn't been drunk, he would have spanked her for it.

Well, probably not really, since Patrick's basement wasn't covered in their club contract. Although, he'd be talking to her about it later. Maybe she'd be willing to renegotiate their current contract to include letting him dominate her for small infractions like that while they were in a group setting...

It was something to think about anyway.

Stopping in front of her door, Michael managed to get her keys out of her purse and open it with one hand, his other arm completely occupied with helping hold her up.

"Come in," she said, jolting forward and pulling him with her. "You should come in."

Almost as soon as he had, an orange blur hit his leg and latched on, needle like claws digging into his calf as big green eyes stared up at him. Michael bit back a yelp of surprise and pain as he stiffened, keeping his body completely still.

"Watson, I presume," he gritted through his teeth as he quickly shut the door behind him. All he needed was to accidentally let Ellie's cat out of the apartment while she was completely wasted.

She blinked up at him, her big dark eyes filled with joy. "He likes you!"

As if to punctuate her sentence, Watson started climbing his leg, little needle claws punching through the fabric of his jeans to scratch against his skin. Since Ellie seemed to be okay holding herself upright while they weren't moving, he let her go long enough to bend down and scoop up the purring cat off his leg.

Damn sadist cat.

Although, the way Ellie was beaming at him, like he'd done something amazing, meant he would willingly take whatever form of "liking" Watson dished out. The little fluffball was a lot cuter in pictures than in person, although that might just be the tingling prickles on his leg talking now.

Watson rubbed his face against Michael's chin, still purring.

Okay, maybe he was almost as cute in person.

"Good Watson," Ellie said, leaning against Michael to rub her cat behind the ears. "You know a good man when you see him, don't you?"

Yeah, Watson was pretty great.

Sliding his arm around Ellie's waist, Michael managed to get a good grip on both her and the cat. "Alright sweetheart, I think we need to get you into bed."

"You too," she said, starting to move. Michael immediately moved with her, dividing his attention between her and Watson - who was still head-butting Michael's chin every couple of seconds and purring like a small motor - as she led him down the hall to her bedroom. It didn't give him much of a chance to look around, but he did get an impression of a warm, cozy apartment with lots of colors and cushions, knickknacks on display, and lots of cat pictures.

Her bedroom was very much the same. The walls were painted a very pale yellow, giving the impression of a sunny room without the yellow being overwhelming, and her bedspread was a light blue with yellow flowers which almost matched the walls perfectly. The curtains on her windows were the same light blue as her bedspread. Above her dresser there was a shelf lined with stuffed animals, but not the normal kind of stuffed animals. They were all octopuses. There was one with a top hat, monocle, and mustache, another red one with an angry little face, another which had a cat head and a bunch of tentacles... Michael didn't really know what to think about the octopussy, but somehow it all just seemed very Ellie. Silly, original, and adorable.

"Come to bed," Ellie said, pulling him along with her.

It probably wasn't a good idea. She was completely wasted. But she was also very insistent. When he hesitated, she yanked at his hand, nearly sending him off balance. For such a tiny thing, she was pretty strong when she wanted to be.

"No sex," Michael said sternly, carefully placing Watson on the bed before laying down next to Ellie. She pouted. Her bed was smaller than his, a double to his queen, and so there was barely any space between them.

Ellie eradicated the little bit of space as she wriggled forward and wrapped herself around him.

Should he try to get her to change into more comfortable sleeping clothes? Not that her jeans and jersey looked uncomfortable... and he was pretty comfortable...

From the way she was nuzzling him, her hands sliding over his chest, it was probably better if they both remained fully clothed, otherwise his declaration of no sex was going to become a lot harder to fulfill.

Wrapping her up in his arms, Michael promised himself he was just going to rest for a bit until she fell asleep. He didn't want to leave her alone when she was this drunk. Before he left, he'd leave her a glass of water on her nightstand and see if he could find some aspirin without snooping too much.

He closed his eyes - just for a minute - to savor how good it felt to have her in his arms like this, so warmly welcoming and content to be there.

❦ 18 ❦

Reality came crashing in with the pressing need to pee, a throbbing head, and a warm arm around her body.

The sensation of heaviness on her body wasn't just from the arm though. A familiar vibrating purr through her chest said Watson was lying on her chest.

Opening her eyes, she had to blink several times as her vision blurred through watery eyes. Her head throbbed. It was way too bright in her room. Sensing she was awake, Watson sat up, pushing his upper body away from her and began washing his face. Turning her head away from him, Ellie saw exactly what she expected to see - exactly what she didn't *want* to see. Michael's sleeping face, here in her bed, in her space...

Despite her head aching, she could still tell from the lack of other aches and pains - not to mention all the clothes on her body - that they hadn't had sex. He'd just *slept* beside her. The way a real boyfriend might do.

What did it mean?

What would he expect it to mean?

What would he expect to change from now on?

Panic welled up, bubbling as something must have woken him up and he stretched and then opened his eyes, his sleep-muddled hazel gaze meeting hers. Ellie just stared at him. She didn't know what to say, what to do, how to act... Part of her liked that he was here, another part of her wanted to scream at him and ask what the hell he was doing here. The last part of her just wanted to close her eyes and pretend to be asleep so he would leave and she wouldn't have to deal with him at all. The last would have been her preferred option, but it was way too late to dissemble now.

"Whoops," he smiled sheepishly, propping himself up on one hand as he raked his fingers through his messy hair. "I must have fallen asleep, I didn't mean to."

Hurt pinged at the feeling of rejection, which didn't make sense since she wasn't even sure she wanted him there - in fact, given the choice between waking up to finding him there and waking up to just her and Watson in bed, she would definitely choose just her and Watson - but reason didn't stop the emotion. Just like reason didn't stop her sudden rush of anger that he had fallen asleep in her bed, invading her space, even if it had been an accident.

"You shouldn't have," she said shortly, her voice clipped, as she grabbed Watson so she could flip the covers up and quickly get out of the bed, holding her protesting cat who was annoyed at the interruption to his morning wash. "You should have left."

The look of sleepy warmth on Michael's face slid away to a more serious expression, tinged with hurt, which just put Ellie's back up even more. Obviously he'd expected her to be okay with him sleeping over, but that just wasn't the kind of relationship they had. They didn't have a real relationship, not outside of the club. Yeah, they'd been spending time together, but nothing beyond that. A few kisses, kisses which didn't even involve tongue, didn't mean she was okay with graduating to sleepovers. Especially sleepovers which were just about sleeping.

While some small part of her acknowledged she should be okay with a regular sleepover, that it was weird she would have felt better if they'd had sex last night and he'd then fallen asleep afterwards, another part of her felt like her abnormal reaction was just another indication of everything damaged about her. Her expectations, her reactions, they weren't normal. She wasn't normal.

Why did she ever think she could do this? Just because she *wanted* it?

Since when had she ever gotten what she wanted without it turning into a nightmare?

She'd wanted a boyfriend, and she'd fallen for Lawrence of all people, until his true colors had been revealed.

She'd wanted her mom and best friend to believe her, to support her, but all they'd done was question her and then tell her it was better to stay silent. She might have come to that conclusion on her own in the end, but she'd still wanted to feel like they would have supported her if she hadn't.

She'd wanted a boyfriend in college, but she'd managed to drive away the one guy willing to try and work through her issues with her.

The only time she'd ever gotten what she'd wanted was when she'd gone to Stronghold and scened with dominants who were willing to give her what she needed, and then she could leave. And now she was fucking that up too, because she'd had to go and want *more* than that. Because she'd decided getting her needs met wasn't enough, she'd wanted to try and be normal, to try and work towards having a normal relationship, even though she was anything but.

It wasn't just the rape to blame. It was her. Other women were stronger, other women moved on and managed to get a boyfriend, have regular sex, be normal... but not her. She'd never managed any of what she'd wanted, she'd hidden away from even trying, and now it was too late. She'd been too messed up for too long, because she'd been a coward, and now she was broken, and Michael was staring at her like he could see all the ways she was damaged, all the ways she was abnormal, and his gaze on her felt like walls closing in around her, trapping her, so she couldn't escape from the truth... the truth was she should have never put her hand in his again, she should have never tried to lean on him again, because she was never going to be worthy of his attention.

"Ellie," he started to say, his voice gentle, his hand reaching for her, from across the bed, but the piece of furniture stood between them as if the divide which had always been there had somehow physically manifested.

"I want you to get out," she said, her voice harsh even to her ears. She hugged Watson, who had stopped mewing and was kneading her shoulder where his paws rested, as if trying to comfort her. "You should have never stayed last night, I told you... I told you I didn't want *this*, I wasn't ready for anything more than a club relationship... I..."

Her voice trailed off as his hand dropped and he stared at her with solemn eyes.

"I know, Ellie," he said, and the gentleness in his voice made her want to scream at him. He was still looking at her, still trying to be patient with her, but still *wanting* things from her, and she felt just like she had in college when she'd tried to have a normal relationship before she'd realized she couldn't, because people in a normal relationships had sex and sleepovers and intimacy. "Sleeping here was an accident and I'm sorry, I just meant to stay until you fell asleep and I must have been more tired than I thought. I didn't mean to push myself on you-"

"Why are you talking to me like that?" she snapped at him, glaring. "I'm not... I don't need soothing, I just need you to leave."

"I just want to make sure we're okay before I go," he said, his eyes looking even more wounded, which made her chest ache even as it made her want to throw something at him.

Stop looking at me like that!

"We're fine, now get out!" Her voice shook and the look he gave her was more firm.

"Ellie, you're not fine and I can see it. Look, I know I pushed too fast, I didn't mean to. I know you're working through some things when it comes to me, and men in general -"

"What do you think I'm working through?" Her voice came out high and shrill as betrayal surged through her. Who had told him? Which of the women she called friends had betrayed her confidence? Angel? Leigh? They were closest to Michael.

The expression on his face said he was searching for the right words, which just made her chest tighten with more suppressed panic, more frustration and shame and misery. He was searching for the right words because she sounded like a crazy person. Because she *was* a crazy person.

"Sweetheart... it's obvious something happened to you. Your hard limits, the way you react to certain things... I know a man must have hurt you sometime in the past -"

Ellie felt like keening as pain burst in her chest, tears burning behind her eyes.

It was *obvious* she was damaged?

Was that why Michael was with her? Because he thought she needed saving, the way she had back in high school? Because he had a white knight complex?

Since he'd returned to the club, he'd been the champion for more than one submissive. Lexie was probably the most obvious example, when he'd been willing to brave Patrick's ire to help the young woman prove she was ready to start scening, but he was always stepping in to help where he thought he could. And there she'd been, *obviously* having issues she needed to work through, *obviously* needing someone she could trust, and he'd stepped up again.

She thought she was going throw up. Her stomach churned. Her head felt like it was splitting open, and not just from her hangover. Hell, she'd been too emotionally turmoiled to even think about her headache again until just now when it hurt so much she wanted to take a hammer to her skull just to let out some of the pressure.

Gone.

She needed him gone. Out of her space. Out of her apartment. Just *out*.

So she did the only thing she could think of to make him go away - she told him the truth.

"Lawrence was my boyfriend and he raped me, okay?" She practically shouted the words at him, taking a kind of malevolent satisfaction in the way his face fell, even as part of her wailed in disappointment. "You left and I started dating Lawrence, because I'm a huge, *fucking* idiot, and I thought I was in love with him, and then when we were drunk at a party, he raped me."

Michael's mouth hung open, his face paling and then flushing and then paling again as he worked through the truth. Through her big secret.

And she felt so empty inside.

"Now get out," she whispered.

Looking almost like a zombie, Michael turned and walked towards the door. His shoulders were slightly hunched, his fists flexing at his sides.

Ellie's tears began to well again at the sight of his back to her.

When he reached her bedroom door, his head turned slightly. Not enough that she could see his face, but enough so she could hear his words.

"I'm sorry, Ellie."

So was she.

She stayed frozen, standing next to her bed, barely breathing until she heard the faint sound of her front door closing. Only then did her tears finally start to fall.

STARING AT HIS TELEVISION SCREEN, MICHAEL BLINKED AS WHAT HE was watching finally started to sink in.

When had he changed the channel to the Home Improvement Network?

He'd probably done it without noticing.

Glancing at the clock, he blinked rapidly.

The time didn't change.

Eight o'clock at night.

He'd done absolutely nothing today.

His stomach grumbled, reminding him he'd eaten nothing today too.

Which hadn't been unusual when he was younger and living like a starving artist, but definitely wasn't the way he lived now.

The pressing needs of his body were enough to bring him out of the fog he'd been lost in.

He went to the bathroom and then the kitchen, grabbing a banana. Ate it. Tossed the peel and opened his fridge.

Incoherent rage, mind-numbing guilt, and the acute sense of help-lessness seeped back in as he stared blankly at the offerings of his fridge. His stomach flipped and the sensation of being hungry receded under the emotional onslaught.

Michael went back to the couch and sat down, leaning back to stare up at the ceiling.

What now?

⁂

POUNDING ON HIS DOOR MADE HIM JERK UPRIGHT FROM WHERE HE'D fallen asleep on the couch. Again. He squinted at the clock on his DVD player, eyes blurry and unfocused.

The digital readout read 8:47.

He only knew it was in the evening because it was dark out. Unless those were rainclouds?

No, it was dark out.

The pounding on his door continued.

"Open up, pretty boy, or we're breaking in!" Angel's voice was stri-dently demanding. "I need to pee and my obstetrician says it's not good for my blood pressure to get too high and I can feel it rising right now!"

Michael's protective instincts kicked in.

His pregnant friend was outside and needed help.

That was something his brain could handle. It was something he could take care of.

His muscles protested as he jumped up from the couch, a twinge in his neck nearly making him groan in pain.

He'd fallen asleep on the couch a couple of times. It had been easier than getting up and going back to his room, to his bed. Although, he'd tried, last night. Being in bed had just made him think of Ellie, though, and he'd ended up back out on the couch after an hour of tossing and turning while his stomach roiled.

When he opened his front door, he nearly slammed it shut again, but Patrick's big hand smacked against the wood.

Angel smirked.

"Pest," he said, with a sigh as he took in the sight of Angel and her reinforcements, his lips curving upwards at the end, and for just a moment he nearly felt normal again.

Then he remembered and it was like being kicked in the gut. Angel frowned at him, her eyes filled with worry. She was bundled up in a puffy coat and jeans, with Adam close behind her, probably ready with an extra scarf and gloves in case she got cold. Beside Adam, Lexie was practically bouncing, trying to see over Angel's shoulders - since seeing over Patrick's would be impossible. All of them had nearly identical expressions of worry on their faces, although Patrick and Adam's frowns were deepening by the second as they looked at him.

"What the hell was that look for? Also, you look awful." She leaned forward and sniffed. "You don't smell great either. What the hell is going on?"

Patrick didn't wait for Michael to answer before adding his own complaint on top of Angel's. "You haven't answered a single text message or email since Sunday, on top of not answering your phone."

Yeah... he'd tried to look at his emails but he hadn't been able to concentrate and he'd ended up just staring at the computer screen. Although he had taken the time to look up Lawrence. He was pretty sure he remembered his parents' saying the guy had been in some sort of horrific accident way back when. Sure enough, Lawrence was a quadriplegic. Which had immediately killed any fantasies Michael had been harboring about hunting the guy down and kicking his ass. There was no satisfaction in beating up a guy who literally couldn't fight back. What had happened to him really was pretty awful, so it looked like karma might really exist. Still, it have him a sense of frustrated helplessness, a lack of justice... and if he was feeling that way, how had Ellie felt?

As for his phone, he hadn't plugged it into the charger when he'd gotten home on Sunday. He'd heard it go off in his bedroom a few times before it had eventually died, but since it hadn't been the ringtone and notification tones he'd assigned to Ellie – although he hadn't really expected her to contact him - he hadn't cared.

Michael ran his hand over his face and nearly winced at the stiff bristles covering his jaw. He couldn't remember the last time anyone had seen him with anything more than a five o'clock shadow. He hated the way he looked with facial hair. The concern in the others' eyes was only growing and he didn't know what to say.

A stiff finger jabbing painfully into the flesh of his stomach had him jumping back with a yelp.

"I'm going to the bathroom and then we're talking!" Angel declared as she marched past him into the apartment.

He glared after her as the others filed in behind her, heading towards his couch. As Adam passed, Michael glared at him too. "You need to beat her more often."

"Probably," Adam agreed. He looked Michael up and down, raising an eyebrow. "On the other hand, in this instance I think she's got the right idea. But we won't make you start talking till she gets back here or we'll never hear the end of it."

Having people in his apartment gave him something to do, and he took everyone's coats and got them something to drink while Angel used the bathroom. He also set out some cheese and crackers, which made his stomach grumble again. Since there was only space for Angel left on the couch, Michael grabbed a chair from his table and dragged it over to sit across from them, muting the television. Being the only one on this side of the coffee table made him nervous so he grabbed some cheese to eat. When the flavor burst on his tongue he suddenly realized how hungry he was. This time his appetite didn't go away immediately. Maybe because he was distracted by the way Patrick and Adam were studying him like a bug, or the way Lexie's leg was jiggling anxiously as she stared at him.

"Have you talked to Ellie?" he asked her, too desperate for information not to.

Lexie shook her head. "She's not picking up her phone either."

His breath caught in worry. Should he call her? Would she even want him to? Probably not, but maybe he should try anyway...

He just didn't know what Ellie wanted him to do and being so unsure was making him insecure. Very unlike him, but he didn't know how to fix it either.

"So what the hell happened with you and Ellie?" Angel asked as she came back into the room, obviously having overheard his question to Lexie. She plopped down on the couch next to Adam, across from the chair Michael was sitting in, frowning fiercely at both Michael and Adam when they tried to lurch forward to help her lower herself down. Eventually, she was going to have to give up some of her independence and allow herself to be helped, but apparently today was not that day. "Tell us everything."

Too defeated to try and put up a fight, Michael did as she ordered and told them everything.

How he'd been pushing her the last month - which they knew. How he'd noticed her uncertainties and anxieties, but kept pushing anyway. How Sunday night he'd let himself be lulled into a false sense of security, thinking things had been going really well with them. How he'd thought her drunken affectionate openness had relaxed his guard, thinking she was more comfortable with him than she turned out to be. How he'd slept over - really without meaning to - without her permission. How upset she'd been when she'd realized he'd done so.

And the worst of it.

He stared at his hands rather than look at any of their faces, his guilt and helpless fury rising up again and making the cheese he'd just eaten feel like it was curdling in his stomach.

"I should have kept in better touch with her, I shouldn't have just let her drift away like I did, I should -"

"Whoa, whoa," Angel said, stopping his recitation of growing guilt. Out of the corner of his eye he saw her try to lean forward and then growl in annoyance when her ever-expanding belly didn't let her. She waved her hands, trying to catch his attention, and, reluctantly, Michael looked up at her. Strangely, she looked more confused than anything else. "What do you mean you should have kept in touch with her?"

"When I left for college," Michael explained, his shoulders hunching against the regret hounding him. "I should have kept in better touch with her. If I had, she would have never -"

"WHOA, hold up," Angel said, a lot louder this time. "Are you saying you think it's your fault she was raped?"

His mouth opened and closed. He looked at the others. Lexie looked aghast. Patrick and Adam were frowning in consternation, but neither of them were looking at him with anything like judgment or recrimination.

"I mean... If I'd kept in touch with her, she might not have fallen for Lawrence's lines... I could have talked to her about him, I could have told her-"

"Stop. Stop right there." Angel pointed her finger at him. "It is not your fault. Not in any way shape or form. Even if you had kept in touch with her, she might not have told you about what was going on with him, and she might not have listened to what you had to say. How can you even think that?"

"Well, Ellie does," he said, even though his brain perked up a bit, feeling that Angel had a point, even though it didn't soothe the raging flood of guilt which had been running through him the past two days. "She even said it, I left and then she ended up dating Lawrence. I knew she was vulnerable. I knew she had a crush on me. And I just let things drift away because being in college was more interesting than a high school girl with a crush on me, no matter how cute she was. But we'd been friends and I should have -"

"Nope, stop." Angel waggled her finger this time and a new emotion finally poked through Michael's self-reproach. Annoyance. "You left for college. People's high school friendships rarely hold through the first year of college. That's normal and natural. It was not *why* she was raped any more than being at a party or any of her choices were why. The only reason she was raped is because Lawrence was a rapist. Period."

Michael wanted to flinch every time she said 'rape' and both Patrick and Michael looked uncomfortable too. Uncomfortable and slightly murderous, so at least he wasn't alone in his feelings.

"I agree with Angel," Lexie said. "And I am ninety-nine point nine percent sure Ellie absolutely does not blame you. She blames herself."

"She didn't do anything wrong!" Michael snapped, glaring at Lexie. Only for a second though, because Patrick shifted closer to his girlfriend, giving Michael a warning look. Feeling a little ashamed, Michael looked away, although at least Lexie didn't look upset at his outburst.

"No, she didn't," Lexie said serenely. "But she feels like she did and it messes with her... sound like something you might be able to relate to?"

When Michael didn't answer after a long moment, his head tumbling through the points Angel and Lexie were trying to make to him, Angel clapped her hands together.

"Okay. You're going to shower and shave, while we make dinner for you, because I can hear your stomach grumbling from here, and then you're going to eat. After that, you're going to call Ellie, and hopefully she'll pick up for you when she hasn't for any of us."

A mutinous response was on the tip of his tongue, but one glance at Adam and Patrick and he swallowed it down. It was pretty obvious what army Angel was going to use to enforce her will upon the proceedings, and Michael knew he would definitely be the loser in that two-on-one scenario.

WHEN HER PHONE RANG AND IT WAS MICHAEL, ELLIE ALMOST picked up.

Because she craved him. Because she wanted to hear his voice. Because she wanted him to tell her everything was going to be fine.

But what if he didn't?

What if he was calling to cancel their contract?

What if he was calling to yell at her for dating Lawrence at all?

Even if he was calling to say her past didn't matter, could she really believe him when it had taken him two days to get to that point? Or was that just her trying to cop out again and being unreasonable, when anyone would have needed time to deal with her confession? Should she pick up the phone?

Just thinking about what he might say, trying to decide how she would respond in each instance, had her panting for air with lungs which were too constricted to really breathe.

No. No, she couldn't pick up the phone.

For the same reason she hadn't been able to pick up the phone when any of her friends had called. Because were they really her friends? Or were they Michael's? Would they be on her side or his? Would they still want to hang out with her? Would she be able to hang out with them when Michael might appear at any minute and remind her of everything she wanted but couldn't have? When he might show up and berate her for her poor choices?

The other women had been sympathetic. They'd been supportive. But then, she hadn't told them about her previous problems with Lawrence. They hadn't known she'd had prior evidence of him being a jerk, of him harassing her.

She always tried to excuse herself in her head, because of how he'd been when he'd started trying to get to know her, but deep down she knew she shouldn't have trusted him. She shouldn't have convinced herself he'd changed. That he was a good guy. That he was a good boyfriend.

Michael knew. Michael knew exactly what a monumental mistake she'd made. And even if he said it didn't matter, would she ever be able to look in his eyes again without seeing that knowledge? Without seeing shock on his face? Without seeing the pale, disbelieving expression he'd worn before he'd realized she was telling the truth?

Ellie buried her face in Watson's soft fur as the tears began to fall again.

She knew she should call Dr. Amy. She knew she should make an appointment.

Tomorrow. She'd do it tomorrow.

And she wouldn't think about how she'd told herself that yesterday too.

THURSDAY NIGHT ELLIE DIDN'T COME TO THE CLUB.

No one had heard from her yet either.

Jake had suggested he go knock on her door and threaten to break it down if she didn't let him in. He'd been mostly joking, but Sharon had practically unleashed the furies of hell on him anyway. A ten minute lecture about why Michael was doing the right thing by giving Ellie her space and letting her choose what she wanted, rather than forcing himself on her, kept anyone else from making any similar jokes.

If he wasn't already half in love with Ellie – okay, maybe more than half if he was being completely honest with himself – he'd probably be worshipping at Sharon's feet.

Even though he was pretty sure he'd have to fight off Jake for a chance with her. He'd decided their sniping at each other was like a really aggressive, slightly angry form of foreplay. Focusing on others who weren't happily paired up let his mind rest a little, distracted him from his own issues. Sharon and Brian had stopped scening together, which seemed to make her even more mouthy with Jake. The two of them were definitely attracted to each other, but neither of them seemed happy about it, was the conclusion Michael finally came to.

They were nearly as fascinating as watching Luke and Olivia circle around each other. Luke had shown up tonight to get a feel for Stronghold, as well as BDSM in general, and he seemed perfectly at home in the club already, even if he was wearing jeans and a button down shirt like Jake rather than leathers. He was also obviously smitten with Olivia who was just as obviously doing her best to have nothing to do with him. Michael found it more interesting that she focused on avoiding him rather than smacking him down. She'd groused some more about him and Patrick taking on Luke as a partner, mostly because he was both a newbie to the scene and unknown. There'd been a rather wicked gleam in her eye when she'd demanded Luke go through the newbie class like all the other Doms before being allowed to play.

Michael and Patrick had agreed.

Luke had agreed when they'd talked to him about it tonight.

They'd told Olivia he'd agreed, although they hadn't told her everything. They were both looking forward to seeing her expression when she realized.

At least it gave Michael something to look forward to.

His head swiveled around as the door to the lobby opened again and another group of people came in.

Still no Ellie.

All he could do was hope she would show up. Hope she'd be willing to talk.

Hope Lexie and Angel had been right. That she didn't blame him. Although if she didn't, he wasn't entirely sure what her problem with him was, but he wanted to talk about it.

Half an hour later, Patrick came out of his office and barreled towards where Michael was sitting, chatting with Luke, a thundercloud across his expression. The conversation between Luke and Michael died as he caught a glimpse of the approaching Dom, and Michael's voice died out. What had caused Patrick to look like that?!

From the way Patrick was headed straight towards him, only two possibilities cropped up – Marquis or Ellie – and since Patrick wasn't even glancing at Luke...

His heart squeezed, and fear and panic seized his body.

"Ellie emailed me a request to cancel her membership to the club," Patrick said as soon as he was in earshot, his voice strangely flat. "Which voids the contract the two of you signed. She sent workups of all the graphics and logo options she's put together for Marquis, said she was sorry she couldn't finish working on them but if we liked them it would be easy enough for someone else to tweak them."

Out of all of that, Michael only really heard one sentence.

Canceled her membership to the club.

A roaring noise filled Michael's ears as pain splintered through the left side of his chest. He didn't even realized he'd stood up until his knees collapsed and he dropped back into his chair feeling incredibly bereft.

She didn't want anything to do with him, to the point where she was willing to leave the club.

"Don't let her," Michael said his voice strained. He stared down at the table in front of him, feeling horribly alone. "Email her back. Tell her I'll stay at Marquis, I won't come here... she doesn't have to cancel her membership to avoid me."

And she'd still be able to get her needs met and be safe while she was doing it. Still be able to see her friends.

To be honest, coming to Stronghold without Ellie there didn't exactly appeal anyway.

"No." Olivia's voice slid through the rest of the club's noise like the crack of a whip, drawing every eye around them. The Domme got to her feet, a steely look in her silver eyes. She pointed at Sharon, Kate and Andrew. "You, you, and you. You're with me." She looked at Patrick. "Don't do anything with Ellie's membership for now. I'll be in touch."

Then she strode towards the door to the lobby, a woman on a mission, expecting Andrew, Kate, and Sharon would be behind her – which they were.

Standing next to Michael, who was too stunned to move or say anything, Luke let out a low whistle. "Damn that was hot." He clapped Michael on the shoulder. "Don't worry buddy, I'm pretty sure Scarlet there is on your side and she's not about to take no for an answer."

It might be a little humbling to know he couldn't take control of his own fate, but for the first time in days, Michael started to really feel a bit of hope.

❧ 19 ❧

When Ellie's doorbell rang, she froze in the middle of putting food into Watson's dish. Was it Michael? The UPS guy? A neighbor worried about the fact that she hadn't left the house in days?

Probably not the last one, people in her building didn't really notice what their neighbors were doing, which was good because otherwise the super would probably be breaking down her door.

She was just starting to feel kind of normal again. Sort of.

Even though she still hadn't called Dr. Amy or left the apartment, but she was feeling almost ready to do both.

Hearing her doorbell ring had triggered her flight or fight response but there wasn't really anywhere to flee to and she definitely didn't want to fight. So she just froze.

Waited to see what would happen next.

"Ellie? Are you home?" Sharon's voice was full of concern. More knocking, a little more firm and insistent this time. "Everyone's really worried about you. Are you there?"

Should she answer? She didn't want everyone to be worried about her, even though the fact they still cared sent a trickle of warmth through her. By now they had to know about her blow up with

Michael. Club gossip was fast, and gossip around the group of friends was even faster. Plus, she'd sent the email canceling her membership.

Which probably explained Sharon's presence at her door. Although, she was still surprised it was just Sharon and not-

"Ellie, I know you're in there. Open the door." There he was. Andrew's deep, firm tone, his Dom voice, a voice she was used to obeying, had her muscles working without thought.

As she moved to the door, a touch of relief trickled through her that the confrontation she'd been so afraid of was finally going to happen. No more fretting over what everyone else thought. No more wondering whose side they'd take. No more anxiety about what might happen when she had to face them. It was finally going to be over with.

That didn't stop the trickle of fear going down her spine as she finally opened the door, and she automatically braced herself - emotionally and physically - for the worst.

Andrew was standing there, his face so full of concern, she almost burst into tears just looking at him. He was in his club clothes, leather pants and a leather jacket over what was probably a bare chest, and she knew just from looking at him that Patrick must have told them all she'd canceled her membership. Next to him, white-blonde hair in a high ponytail, Kate had her hands tucked into a bright blue pea coat, the same concerned expression on her face. Ellie didn't get a chance to see what Sharon was wearing or what her expression was, because the other woman practically tackled Ellie in a hug.

"Don't you ever stop answering your phone again!" Sharon's voice was high and anxious, although not nearly as anxious as Ellie felt when she saw who else had come.

Steely grey eyes pinned her in place. Olivia's tight fitting leather pants, corset, and half jacket did nothing to soften the aura of menace emanating from her. She was the epitome of in-charge Domme on a mission, and Ellie quailed under that hard gaze.

"Let's go inside," Andrew said, putting his hand on Sharon's back so she'd let go of Ellie long enough for Ellie to allow them past.

She retreated back into the apartment, sighing in exasperation as an orange blur zipped down the hall to hide in her bedroom. Sure, the

only other person in the world he wasn't shy with was Michael. That was... just great. It would have been nice to have a cat to hold. Something to put in between her and the others. Like a safety blanket.

Kate, Andrew, and Sharon sat down on her couch, while Olivia took the comfy armchair, looking an awful lot like a queen taking the throne. Ellie eyed the Domme warily. She was well known around the club, both as a mother hen and someone who doled out tough love.

"So are you here to tell me the hard truths?" she asked, using her defensiveness to go on the offensive. Olivia's unblinking stare was unnerving her more than anything else could.

"Oh no," Olivia said, her voice low and smooth. She gestured at the three on the couch. "You get them first. Unless you're uncooperative. Then you get me."

Ellie shuddered. Olivia smiled. It wasn't a comforting smile. Then she sat back, looking over at Andrew as if passing the reins.

"Don't look so scared, Ell, we're just here to check on you and make sure you're okay," Andrew said as Ellie sank down into her other armchair on wobbly knees. "We would have been by earlier, but we were trying to give you space, and since you weren't picking up your phone, we figured that's what you needed."

"You can't just quit the club though!" Sharon jumped in, leaning forward earnestly. She looked upset, reflecting Ellie's own unhappiness about leaving Stronghold. "You need it, Ellie."

"I'll be okay." She inwardly cursed at the absolute lack of conviction in her voice. She was normally a better liar. Even though she wasn't looking at Olivia, she could feel the Domme's gaze, burning into her side.

"Michael's promising he won't come back to Stronghold, so you don't have to quit," Kate said quietly. Unlike Andrew and Sharon, she wasn't leaning forward, she was sitting back against the couch, studying Ellie as if trying to gauge her reactions. "He'll stay at Marquis."

A jump of joy at the thought that she didn't have to quit Stronghold was washed away with despair at the idea of going to Stronghold without Michael there. Of chasing him away. Of being there without him.

"He thinks you blame him for the rape," Kate said, her voice just as quiet as before, but she sliced Ellie to the quick with that simple statement.

"What?! No! Of course not! I just... Of course it's not his fault, how can he *think* that?" Ellie's mind whirled. She hadn't meant to make Michael feel guilty or like she blamed him. How could she when he had nothing to do with it? He'd been out of her life by then.

Sharon answered, rather than Kate. "He thinks because he left, you were more vulnerable. That he wasn't able to protect you, even from afar, because you two lost touch. He thinks if he'd stayed friends with you, if you'd kept talking, that you would have never dated Lawrence."

Pressing her hands against her head, which was starting to hurt, Ellie groaned. That wasn't what she'd wanted. She hadn't meant to make him feel guilty or like she blamed him.

Did some part of her think it was kind of true though? She probably wouldn't have dated Lawrence if she'd still been in touch with Michael. Because she would have been too busy crushing on Michael. Even if she'd gotten over her crush, she would have been too ashamed to tell him she was dating one of the guys he'd had to protect her from, no matter how much it seemed like Lawrence had changed.

But that didn't make it Michael's fault! She'd *never* blamed him.

She'd only ever blamed herself.

Gentle hands lifted her up and the next thing Ellie knew, Andrew was sitting down in the chair and pulling her onto his lap. She immediately looked for Kate; the blonde was kneeling next to the chair, her hand on Andrew's leg, concern on her face as she looked at Ellie. Kate had never been anything but generous with Andrew when it came to Ellie, something which caused Ellie no shortage of guilt. She hated feeling like a burden, and it was impossible not to when she was using someone else's man for her own needs.

"Ellie, do you like Michael?" Andrew's deep voice was firm but not stern, demanding an answer but not judging her.

"Of course I do!" She turned her face towards Andrew's chest, not wanting to look at all the eyes on her. It wasn't as good as cuddling with Michael. Andrew was broader. Harder. Didn't smell right. "Michael's amazing. He deserves... everything."

Andrew's familiar hand rubbed her shoulder. A softer, smaller hand came to rest on her knee. Comforting her. Warming her. Creeping through the defenses she'd spent the last few days trying to shore up again.

These people... it didn't matter whether they were Doms or subs, this group of people didn't leave a wall standing.

"You think Michael deserves everything he wants?" Andrew mused.

"Yes," Ellie said, her voice breaking just a touch as her heart started to hurt again. Michael did deserve everything. Just thinking about him with someone else made her whole being ache, but she wanted it for him. Wanted him to have everything he deserved.

"So why aren't you giving it to him?" Andrew's voice had shifted to a hard demand for information, his Dom voice, insistent and unyielding.

"I- I'm not-" Ellie stammered as her thoughts skittered. She hadn't been expecting a questioning demand from Andrew. Was left scrambling for an answer to his question. "He deserves better than me."

The truth shriveled her and she curled up tighter on Andrew's lap as tears, never far away these days, threatened again.

"You-"

"Ell-"

Kate and Sharon's voices overlapped each other as they both started to protest, both cut off abruptly at Olivia's sharp "Hush."

She curled up even more in Andrew's hold, wishing she could just disappear. Even though he was warm, even though his arms were around her, she felt so small and insignificant. She knew what Kate and Sharon were going to say. That she was fine, she wasn't undeserving, she was just as good as Michael... that was just the kind of people - the kind of friends - they were. But they didn't know. They couldn't see how broken she was inside.

"I don't think I asked what you deserved," Andrew said, his tone deceptively casual. "I asked what Michael deserved and you said everything. Then I asked why you aren't giving it to him. Because whether or not you feel you deserve him, Michael wants you."

Wants.

As in the present.

As in still wants?

Andrew's voice gentled. Softened. "Although, Ellie, you should know you absolutely do deserve Michael. You're a beautiful person, inside and out, and you deserve to be happy. You're not like me. I'm a selfish bastard because I absolutely do not deserve Kate, but I got her anyway, because I'm a selfish bastard who doesn't care that I don't deserve her. She makes me happy, so I went after her anyway."

To her own surprise, Ellie giggled. She opened her eyes, which were just a little teary, and pressed her fingers to Andrew's chest before reaching down to take Kate's hand. Blue eyes full of worry, Kate smiled at her encouragingly. Behind her, Sharon's mouth was set in a line, her dark eyes just as worried as Kate's.

"I think you deserve Kate," Ellie said softly, smiling down at the blonde woman. "Although I'm not sure I deserve either of you as friends."

"Is there anyone you do think you deserve?" Sharon asked, throwing her hands up in the air in exasperation.

Ellie's mouth opened and closed. Her insides seemed to wither again. Was there anyone she really felt she deserved in her life? That she deserved as her friend? She was so grateful to the friends she'd made at Stronghold... she'd always been surprised and amazed they wanted to hang out with her – they insisted on it actually. She'd always wondered why. Did she really think so little of herself that she wasn't even sure she deserved her friends?

She was more messed up than she'd realized.

"Hey, heeeeeeeeey." Sharon pointed at her, frowning fiercely. "Stop thinking, right now. I can literally see you doubting yourself. I'm going to tell you right now, you absolutely deserve us."

"I'm not sure she deserves you," Kate said rolling her eyes, but she said it in the opposite way that Ellie felt - implying Ellie was too good for Sharon. "Definitely the rest of us though."

"Well her deserve-meter is obviously broken," Sharon said blithely, completely ignoring Kate. Ellie wished she had that kind of self-assurance. Sharon gave Ellie a mock-stern look. "You're going to have to use ours from now on and we'll tell you what you deserve."

A rumble of amusement vibrated through Andrew's chest. "Don't you think we should let Ellie figure out for herself that she deserves more than she thinks?"

"She can figure it out for herself, but until she does, she can listen to us," Sharon said. She looked at Ellie again. "And you deserve Michael. Although he doesn't deserve to have you just ghost on him. At the very least, you should talk to him."

Well that was true. Ellie's heart clenched at the idea of having to face him, knowing he knew everything now.

"He's really broken up," Kate said squeezing Ellie's hand. "We've told him not to blame himself, but he's feeling really guilty about abandoning you in high school, and then pushing you too fast now."

He had pushed her kind of fast but he shouldn't be feeling guilty about pushing her... she could have told him no or to back off at any time and he would have listened.

She could have told him no or to back off at any time and he would have listened.

Instead she'd just walled him out. Pushed him away. Cut everything off without even trying.

She'd really messed up, but not in the way she'd initially thought. She hadn't meant to lay it all on him. Or make him feel guilty or like she blamed him. Part of her wanted to spiral into self-recrimination again, but she'd already been doing that, and it hadn't helped - it had just left Michael feeling broken up... for days...

Andrew's hand came down on her ass, hard enough to knock her out of the guilt spiral she'd been about to descend into.

"He was at the club tonight, hoping you'd show up."

"He was?" Strange, that tiny bit of hope lighting up inside of her. She still felt like she didn't deserve him, but she wanted him.

Sharon was right though, he definitely didn't deserve the way she'd treated him this week. She at least needed to undo the harm she'd done, make sure he knew she didn't blame him – had never blamed him. Giving him what he apparently wanted might be a little harder.

Movement across the room made her jump. Crap. Olivia was standing up. Then Ellie saw the Domme's face and the soft smile there. "I can see I won't be needed here. Ellie, don't short yourself.

You deserve everything you want too. And since Michael and you both want each other, that should work out nicely."

With that statement and a quick nod for everyone, Olivia strode to the front door and left, closing it firmly behind her.

"One of these days," Andrew muttered. "One of these days someone's going to get to impart snappy wisdom to her and I really, really want it to be me."

All of the women started giggling at his aggrieved tone. Olivia did have a reputation for setting the couples straight - especially the Doms - when it came to relationships.

But her obvious approval of Ellie, even after everything, broke the last little bit of resistance. Olivia never said anything she didn't mean. She definitely didn't coddle people. Kate, Sharon, the others, even Andrew, they were all kind of softies. Olivia wasn't. The others might try to build Ellie up, just for the sake of building her up. Olivia wouldn't. If she had something to say, she said it.

And all she'd said was that Ellie deserved what she wanted.

"I want to be her when I grow up," Sharon said, still staring at the door Olivia had exited through in a worshipful way. "Can you imagine being so badass you don't even need to be bad cop? It's enough to just let people know you *could* be if they don't cooperate?"

Straightening up, Ellie pushed herself up off of Andrew. It was time she stopped leaning on other men and actually worked for the one she wanted. After all, he'd spent a lot of time working for her. The thought made her heart pound, her mouth dry, and her palms sweaty, but looking at her friends she thought maybe... just maybe she could do it this time.

After all, the worst was over right? They'd confronted her and nothing terrible had happened. They even said Michael still wanted her. They thought she should be with him. Even Olivia thought so.

She didn't have to do this alone, because her friends were there with her. Willing to support her. Seeking her out when she'd hidden away. Because they cared. The same way Michael did.

So now, maybe she should try being worthy of him instead of despairing over how she wasn't.

"Okay," she said, taking a deep breath as she stood, rubbing her sweaty palms on her yoga pants. She didn't feel ready for this... but she also felt a lot better than she had all week. It was time to stop hiding, time to be brave. "So what do you guys think I should do?"

❦

WHEN THE DOOR TO MARQUIS OPENED, MICHAEL LOOKED UP expecting to see Patrick. Or Luke. One of the workers who had managed to sneak out without him noticing. Olivia. Lexie. Pretty much anyone in the world except the person standing there.

She stared at him, looking like a deer about to bolt, and Michael froze in fear of her doing so.

Of course, he'd chase her down - because she'd obviously come to the unfinished club during the day for a reason, and since neither Lexie nor Patrick were there, the only conclusion was she'd come looking for him - but he hoped he didn't have to. He wanted her to come to him.

Maybe needed her to.

Once she did though... all bets were off. When a subbie offered, a Dom took. And Michael definitely wanted.

Ellie's hair was pulled into the low side ponytail she favored, the ends curling on the front of her left shoulder, the dark strands standing out against the deep blue of her jacket. It covered her top, but she was wearing jeans which snugly fit her curves in a way that would give him fantasies about peeling them off of her. She stared at him, shoving her hands into the pockets of her jacket, as if doing so might hide how nervous she was.

When she didn't immediately turn tail and run, Michael silently gestured at the other side of the booth he had taken over. The table was covered with paperwork - not to mention his laptop - but he could push it aside.

His heart pounded in his chest when she obviously gathered up her courage and started walking towards the booth, her shoulders and head slightly hunched protectively. Last night he hadn't totally believed Olivia when she'd said she was pretty sure Ellie was going to reach out to him soon. Today he was just relieved and grateful the Domme was right.

Apparently his friends were also right that she didn't blame him for anything. The expression on her face was full of guilt and wariness; there was no accusation or fear or reproach. She nibbled on her lower lip as she slid into the booth, giving herself barely an inch between her bottom and the edge of the booth. Still ready to flee apparently.

Michael closed his laptop and set it to the side, still watching her closely. There was a little wrinkle in the center of her brow, like she was concentrating on something.

"Hello, Ellie," he said quietly, folding his hands in front of him on top of the table. "What can I do for you?"

"I-" Her head dropped down for a moment and then she took a deep breath before peeking up at him again. There was remorse in her eyes. Unhappiness. Her creamy skin had a pallor he didn't like, notice-able only now that she was so close and he was studying her so intently. A bit of redness around her eyes said she'd been crying. "I wrote out what I wanted to say to you, so I couldn't forget, but now that I'm here it seems so... I mean, I made some assumptions based off what other people told me, but... we haven't really talked and..." Her shoulders slumped again as she seemed to run out of the will to speak, her teeth sinking back into her lower lip.

Keeping his hands still rather than reaching for her was an effort. "Anything our friends told you about me is probably true," he said gently. "I've been pretty open with them, hoping they could help me figure out where I went wrong with you and what I could do to fix it."

That got her attention, and her dark eyes flashed as she sat up straight, indignation clearly written on her face. "You didn't do anything wrong!"

Interesting, how she was so willing to defend him to himself. Michael's lips almost felt like twitching. So she definitely didn't blame him, at least, but... where did that leave them?

"Why don't you read what you wrote," he said, using his acting skills to look calm, even though he felt like he was hanging on the edge of a precipice. She was here. All he had to do was not chase her away again and maybe...

Ellie gave him a little look under her lashes and pulled her hands out of her pockets. In her right hand she was clutching a folded piece of paper, which she stared at as she unfolded it, obviously avoiding his gaze.

When she read, her voice was slightly stilted because she was reading from a prepared script, but it was full of emotion too.

"Michael, I want you to know I don't blame you for anything that happened to me. I never have. Your friendship and protection made my bus rides not just bearable, but fun for an entire year. Drifting apart was natural and it didn't have anything to do with what happened to me. Lawrence spent a long time trying to gain my trust and get me to date him, and even though I should have known better, I fell for it, and that's my fault."

Dammit. He couldn't stand to watch the growing tension in her body, to hear the quiver in her voice. He couldn't just sit here and do nothing. Talking had always made her uncomfortable, sex was where they'd had no issues... Swiftly making up his mind, Michael scooted around the booth, making her freeze in place. At least she didn't run.

Wrapping his arms around her, he pulled her onto his lap, his hands sliding up to her breasts and he squeezed them hard through her jacket. Ellie slumped back against him, the tension sliding away from her muscles at the distraction. He scraped his teeth over her neck and enjoyed the way she shuddered against him. "Keep reading, sweetheart."

While she read, he unzipped her jacket so he could play with her more directly. The shirt she was wearing underneath was a simple, dark red long sleeve shirt with a rounded neckline. His hands went under the hem and up to her breasts, pushing her bra up so he could roll her hard nipples between his fingers, increasing the pressure or twisting whenever her voice faltered.

"I was always scared you'd find out what had happened to me, and I freaked out, because I didn't know how you'd react. I knew I'd been stupid, and I didn't want you to know how stupid I'd been. I haven't had a real relationship, a normal relationship, since Lawrence. I wanted to try, but I think I was always expecting to fail, and last weekend when you said you knew something had happened to me, I just couldn't deal with it. I couldn't stand waiting for everything to fall apart, so I made sure that it did."

Her breath caught and he gave her nipples a particularly viscous pinch, making her shiver. He felt her hesitate.

"Is that it, sweetheart?"

"No, there's more." Her voice was small. Scared. But not in the good way. Michael bit down on her neck again, rolling her nipples and pulling on them until she arched her back in an effort to relieve the pressure. The way she was squirming told him how turned on she was, even as she bared herself emotionally to him.

"Keep going then."

A whine escaped her as he continued to torment her nipples, before she refocused on the paper. Now her words came more haltingly. Unhappily. "You're an amazing man and... you deserve... a submissive who can... give you everything you need... not... not one..."

That was enough of that.

Michael released her breasts and pulled his hands out from underneath her shirt so he could yank the paper out of her hand. The unhappy sub on his lap had hunched in again. Pulling her back against him, Michael scooted her down his lap so her legs were splayed on either side of his, her breasts up for his offering, and her head resting back on his shoulder so she couldn't hide her expression from him.

"Michael!" She tried to fight the re-positioning, reaching for the paper he tossed away.

"No, Ellie, lean back. Safe word or submit." His voice brooked no argument and, heaving a hefty sigh, Ellie leaned back against him, choosing to submit. Her body trembled against his, not quite as pliable as he wanted. Michael ran one hand back up her shirt while the other moved down between her legs to press against the seam over her pussy. Even though she didn't moan aloud, he could feel it through her body. "I don't believe I've ever thought about what kind of submissive I 'deserve', sweetheart, only about what kind of submissive I want. And I thought I made it pretty clear I want you. Do you want me?"

"Yes, and-"

"Hush, sweetheart, yes or no answers." He gave her pussy a little slap. It wouldn't even sting with her jeans blocking the way, but it did get her attention. "Do you believe I want you?"

"Yes."

Oh, she wanted to say so much more, he could tell, but she held back. Followed his order.

"Good girl." This time he gave her pussy a harder slap and her hips bucked upwards, seeking more. "Are you the Dominant?"

"No."

Slap. He squeezed her breast hard, rubbing his thumb over her silky flesh.

"Are you the submissive?"

"Yes." Her voice was breathy.

Slap. Michael's hand moved over to her other breast to give it the same rough treatment. Ellie's little gasping breaths were a sure indication of her growing arousal.

"Do you get to decide what I deserve?"

"No, Michael," she whispered. And then shook herself. "That's what I was trying to tell you, but you didn't let me finish reading what I wrote!"

With a sigh, Michael released her enough so she could sit up. "Okay, sweetheart, you finish reading the letter, but skip to the good stuff. I don't need to hear about what you think I deserve, unless your name is at the end of the sentence."

She gave him a slightly pouty look over her shoulder as she reached for the paper he'd discarded, but he could tell by the way her eyes ran over the writing that a chunk of it was going to go unread.

"Okay... okay, so," her voice dropped back into her reading tone, although it was still tinged with desire. "Even though I feel like I don't deserve you - OW!" He'd pinched the side of her breast hard, enough to hurt in a not-fun way. "It's just how the sentence starts, I promise!" There was just a touch of amusement in her voice though. Michael went back to kneading her swollen breasts, occasionally giving her nipples a little pinch. "Even though I feel like I don't deserve you, I've come to realize I have some self-esteem and self-worth issues which I kept pretty buried and still haven't worked through yet. The others seem to think I do deserve you and you still want me, and if you're willing to take another chance on me, I'd like to try again. I can't promise I won't freak out again, or that I'll be any good at being in a relationship, but I want to try."

Her voice wavered a little with uncertainty on the last sentence. She was breaking his heart. Not that she needed to know how she was wreaking havoc on his emotions right now right now. Right now, she needed reassurance and him to share his feelings - something he'd been reticent to do because he hadn't been sure how she would take it before. But maybe if he'd been more open about exactly how much he wanted her, exactly what he wanted from her - which was a real relationship, then maybe she wouldn't have felt so panicked and insecure about him.

"Oh sweetheart," Michael breathed in her ear. His fingers closed around her nipples. "Now that I know for sure *you* want *me*, you'd have to get the whole of Stronghold to drag me away from you. And there's no way they'd take your side, so you're just shit out of luck on that front."

Ellie squirmed on his lap, against his hard cock, as he plucked at her already sensitive nipples, and Michael bit down on her shoulder again, holding her in place as she panted and whined. But as much as he wanted to lift her up and bend her over the table, that wasn't going to happen. They had the nasty, hot sex down. Now they were going to work on everything else.

NIPPLES THROBBING, PUSSY ACHING, ELLIE FELT FLUSH AND NOT nearly as unsettled as she'd expected to. She'd planned on powering through what she'd written, but once she'd gotten started it had been harder than she'd thought it would be... until Michael had put her on his lap and begun playing with her. Distracting her. Giving her something else to focus on other than her shame and embarrassment.

Now all she wanted was him.

But he was sliding his hands away from her breasts and pussy, pulling her shirt back down.

Ellie squirmed back against his hard cock.

"Uh uh, sweetheart," he said, pulling her off of his lap. But he placed her on the inside of the booth, not the outside where she'd originally been sitting, so her swift sense of rejection followed by the need to run didn't get her anywhere because there was no easy exit. And he'd said he'd chase her anyway... Warmth suffused her, chasing away the rejection. "Naughty subbies who try to push away their Doms don't get easy orgasms."

His tone of voice was easy, almost teasing, but his eyes were serious.

"I'm sorry," she said, slumping slightly again. "I really don't know what I was thinking. I just... I panicked and-"

"It's okay, sweetheart," he said, taking her hand in his. The usual sense of calm swamped her as his thumb swept over the back of her hand. "I've seen you struggling, but since now I know how much you want me -" The cocky grin he flashed her made her want to smack him - "we're going to be amending our club contract. No more running. You can ask for space when you need it, but we're going to work through this together, okay?"

She nodded, even as her stomach twisted at the thought. But it was worth trying for. As Kate had told her - no one was normal, so she shouldn't bother trying to have a 'normal' relationship, she should just have a relationship with Michael, whatever that turned out to look like. "Okay. So now what?"

'Now what' turned out to be him packing up his things and taking her home with him.

Not for sexy times. Nope. Far worse.

They cuddled on his couch and watched *The Princess Bride*. Michael stroked her hair. Made dinner for her. Massaged her feet. And every time she started to pull away emotionally, every time she started to go into her head, he'd pull her over his lap, swat her ass just enough to get her excited, but not enough to give her any real pleasure, and then put her back in the position she'd previously occupied and go right back to doing whatever they were doing, whether it was rubbing her feet or just having a conversation.

She did not sleep over.

But she kind of wished he'd asked her to.

❧ 20 ❧

"Is it possible for women to get blue balls? Because I'm pretty sure I have lady blue balls," Ellie whined to Sharon, pressing her thighs together underneath the table they were sitting at. The music at the club and the conversations going on around them were enough to keep most people from overhearing her comment, unless they were really determined to listen in. Despite her whining, Ellie was in pretty high spirits. She was just also really, really horny.

"Blue labia?" Sharon mused rather than sympathizing, the way Ellie wanted her to. "Blue clitoris?"

Ellie pouted. Sharon grinned and poked her. Ellie poked her back.

Michael was there before it could turn into a poking war, pulling Ellie away from Sharon and onto his lap, where Sharon wouldn't dare to poke her. Nor Ellie poke Sharon, for that matter. The plug in Ellie's ass shifted, heating her lower body even more.

"Bad subbies," he said, his tone wry, although he was definitely amused. Ellie giggled.

In the past two weeks, she'd opened up more than she'd ever thought possible... she hadn't even realized how much she'd held back or withdrawn when hanging out with her friends until they'd all started calling her on it. She'd even started asking them to come over

271

and hang out with her at her place. Angel and Leigh had come over for dinner last week and Sharon and Kate this past week. The others hadn't been able to make it, but she hadn't felt bad or rejected... she'd understood they really were just busy. They'd been too pleased to be invited and too sad about missing out for her to believe anything else. This morning she and Andrew had gone out to breakfast, just the two of them, as friends and he'd been pleased as punch. She'd still worried a bit about what Kate would think, but Andrew had reassured her that Kate was taking the opportunity to spend some time with his sister, and both of them were happy to have him out of the way.

Now, instead of everyone reaching out to her while she remained sheltered but grateful, she was reaching back.

And it was awesome.

She'd already taken the initial steps even before everything had fallen apart - calling Lexie for help with clothes, for advice when she woke up at Michael's, even trying a club contract with Michael - but then she'd stalled out. Tried to take just a tiny step and then stop. But life, people, didn't work that way. She couldn't just stop until she was comfortable and then take another tiny step. Not everything was about her and how she felt about things, she needed to take other people's feelings into consideration too.

Considering how surprised and happy her friends had been to get something as simple as an invitation to dinner from her, she hadn't been doing a very good job of it.

And, even though he'd been careful not to talk about his feelings, she hadn't been doing a very good job of thinking about Michael's feelings either. Everything had been about how he'd made her feel or how she'd worried he'd make her feel. She'd always assumed he'd be just fine without her, but according to club gossip - which was frighteningly reliable - he'd been a bit of a mess.

It felt strange and a little scary to have responsibility over someone else's feelings, but good too. Like she was taking another step into the 'normal' relationships she wanted (even if she really shouldn't be thinking of them that way). And she'd upped her visits with Dr. Amy to once a week while she worked through things. Michael was even going with her to her next visit, just so Dr. Amy could meet him and all three of them could talk about things.

"You are turning into a handful, pretty girl," Michael said, chuckling. He'd started calling her 'pretty girl' lately, almost like a play on Angel calling him 'pretty boy', like they belonged together – although, so far, Ellie hadn't dared to call him pretty boy.

Before, when teasingly chastised, she might have pulled back, feeling the teasing was too intimate, too relationship-y... too much like how their friends in serious relationships treated each other. Now, she just leaned back against him, thrusting her breasts up as she nuzzled her face against his neck. "I have at least two handfuls right here..."

She was still quietly sassy, keeping her remarks low enough only he could hear her, but she didn't think that would change even with her growing confidence. While Ellie was feeling less insecure lately, she was still a naturally quiet person, poking war with Sharon notwithstanding.

"Temptress," Michael growled, slapping her bare thigh and making her moan.

Ellie hadn't had an orgasm in two weeks. Even though he'd given her permission to play with herself to orgasm on her own - since they weren't playing at the club or at home yet - she hadn't. It just wasn't the same. She didn't want her own fingers or even a toy, she wanted *him*. And he wanted to build their relationship first.

Honestly, she was becoming a little impatient.

THREE WEEKS SINCE ELLIE HAD TRIED TO CANCEL HER MEMBERSHIP to Stronghold.

Three long weeks of abstinence and fantasies while they worked on having an actual relationship.

Just this past week they'd started having sleepovers. Real sleepovers where they didn't do more than make-out, much to his cock's dismay.

The sleepovers started after he went with her to a therapy session with Dr. Amy. Michael had liked the therapist a lot and being there had seemed to help Ellie open up verbally. She'd talked about more than just the rape, she'd told him about the aftermath, about the way her mom and friend had treated her. How she'd struggled with trying to have a relationship after that before eventually realizing she could get what she needed at Stronghold without having to put herself at risk emotionally or physically. Hearing all her past and her reasons for her actions actually made it a lot easier for him to deal with his hurt over the way she'd kept secrets from him, from the lack of trust she'd had. She'd sounded awed when she talked about how the other Stronghold women hadn't questioned her or blamed her.

Then, by the end of the appointment, she'd insisted she was ready to try sleepovers, and Dr. Amy had said she thought it was a good idea. Michael might have insisted on waiting a little longer otherwise. The first night she'd been a little stiff trying to fall asleep, tossing and turning and he'd been sure she would call red or yellow - since they'd agreed to institute her safe words for when she needed space or to slow down emotionally - but she'd persisted. The next night had been easier, and the night after that she'd settled right now. Now she was nothing but snuggly.

Snuggly, and somehow her leg just 'happened' to keep sliding up over his legs to rub against his very hard cock.

Little teasing brat.

Michael was certain she wasn't trying to coax him into sex just because she was uncomfortable with where they were at emotionally, which was a relief. She was just horny. He was just worried that if sex was back on the table, she might start regressing.

On the other hand...

Might as well experiment.

Gripping her thigh with one hand, he used the leverage in conjunction with the arm she was pillowing her head on to pull her upright on top of him, straddling him. Even in the darkness he could see the surprise in the line of her body, silhouetted from the dim light coming in through his curtains, could feel it in the way she stiffened on top of him. Waiting to see what he would do.

Michael ran his hands up and down her thighs, teasing the hem of the shirt she was wearing - his shirt, actually. It reached mid-thigh on her because she was so petite.

"Hmmm," he said, frowning. "I'm not a huge fan of not being able to see you at all."

He reached out to flick the switch on his light. Straddling his hips, Ellie blinked down at him as her eyes adjusted, an excited and expectant expression on her face. Well, she wasn't going to get everything she wanted, but she was going to get at least part of what she wanted.

"Hey there, pretty girl," he said, grinning up at her as he slid his hands up her shirt, grasping it and pulling it off over her head. Now she was a naked pretty girl, sitting on top of his cock, which was so hard it could probably break a diamond. "Nice to see you."

She looked a little uncomfortable at his close scrutiny, but in a good way. The squirminess of a submissive under the eye of a predatory Dom. Excited but apprehensive. Unfortunately, he was about to make her feel a lot more uncomfortable, probably in a less good way.

"So now that you're up there, what are you going to do?"

"Do?" she asked, stilling. The wariness in her eyes increased.

"You're the one who was teasing my cock," he said.

The expression on her face turned almost shy. "I was kind of hoping you'd... that you'd um... just take over..."

Michael shook his head, already steeling himself for disappointment. "No, pretty girl. If we're going to have sex tonight, it's going to be vanilla."

The expressions flickering across Ellie's face were too fleeting for him to interpret. None of them looked particularly happy though. Neither was he, since he fully expected to hear 'yellow' or even 'red' and be left with an aching cock for the rest of the night. On the other hand, his inner sadist was going to be well satisfied from torturing both of them.

To his surprise, Ellie leaned forward. Her hands pressed down on his chest, her head lowered, and Michael closed her eyes as her lips met his for a sweet kiss. A kiss which slowly deepened as Michael slid his fingers around her neck, holding her in place.

Vanilla... but ultimately he was still in charge. It was just how he was wired. Not everyone could have kinky sex all the time, and definitely not at the level he liked to play at. Which was why it was some-times fun to explore lower levels, softer levels.

But without the kink, there was an intimacy he was sure Ellie wouldn't be ready for.

Apparently, his brave girl wanted to try. Next time they went to the club, he was definitely going to reward her for her courage. Maybe a spanking when he plugged her. Something enjoyable for both of them without pushing things too far.

She began to run her hands up and down his chest, over his stomach and shoulders, slowly exploring his body with her palms and the pads of her fingers. Michael returned the favor with the hand that wasn't massaging the back of her neck, skimming his fingers over her curves, teasing her with caresses. When he reached her tightly budded nipples, he did give them a hard pinch, enjoying it as she moaned into his mouth.

A little bite of pain was still vanilla for them, especially since he wasn't going to indulge in any real kink.

Only at one point did Ellie slow, and that was when she was sinking down onto his cock while he looked up at her. Being watched so closely obviously made her uncomfortable, but she did it anyway and slowly rode him as they held hands. She hadn't been able to get off though and eventually Michael had flipped her onto her back, pounding into her hard and fast while his teeth scraped over her tender nipples, and Ellie had writhed and cried out for him.

Vanilla. Fun. Satisfying in its own way. And more intimate than he'd thought Ellie would go for.

His girl was definitely getting a reward.

"A SURPRISE WEDDING?" PATRICK WAS STARING AT ADAM LIKE HE'D grown two heads. "That's a terrible idea."

"I like it," Leigh said, surprising all of them.

"I do too," Michael said, although his support of such a crazy idea probably didn't surprise anyone.

Ellie had nothing to say, so she remained quiet. After all, Adam,

Leigh, and Michael probably knew Angel best. Still... a surprise wedding? Adam was taking the control freak thing a little far, even for him. Then again, Angel had been constantly wavering on whether she wanted to get married before or after she had their baby, and they were running out of time on the 'before.'

"I've already talked to her parents," Adam continued blithely, ignoring the comments from the peanut gallery. The rest of the gallery was still sitting quietly, various expressions of amusement and 'oh my good' looks on their faces, arranged on the furniture around Rick and Maria's living room. Angel was out with her mom, but apparently Adam wasn't taking any chances she might come home early to find all their friends there, so he'd called the meeting at Rick and Maria's instead. "We're going to do it in two weeks. The ceremony is going to be held on one side of their dance studio, the reception in the bigger ballroom of their studio."

"Two weeks? The Saturday after Halloween?" Lexie asked, looking concerned. "You're not going to make me skip the club's Halloween party are you?"

"No, you can still have the party Friday," Adam said, sounding a touch exasperated. Lexie looked relieved. "And we're going to do an afternoon wedding, so everyone can still meet up at the club Saturday night. I'll just need help with decorating and getting everything together - and getting Angel to pick out a dress." He glanced over at Leigh.

She gave him a thumbs up. "I already know what she likes. I don't even need her to pick one out."

"Oh yeah, that sounds like a great idea," Patrick muttered under his breath.

Olivia elbowed him in the side at the exact same time as Lexie did on his other side, making him grunt. The Domme gave him a look. "She'll be fine, not everyone is a massive control freak like you."

Everyone cracked up at the affronted and indignant look Patrick gave the redheaded kettle. Ellie covered her mouth as she snickered. She didn't have the loudest laugh by any stretch of the imagination; she just didn't want to draw Olivia's attention in a negative way. Especially since Olivia had been noticeably temperamental lately.

"You... you..." Patrick was actually at a loss for words at Olivia's blatant hypocrisy, which just made everyone laugh even harder.

Adam clapped his hands as Patrick floundered, drawing the attention back to him. "Okay people, seriously, who can help with what?"

As everyone started to volunteer for various jobs, Adam scribbled down notes on a pad of paper. Michael's arm, which was already around Ellie's waist, tightened as he whispered in her ear, sending little shivers down her spine as goosebumps rose. "This is going to be so much fun. She's either going to love it or try to kill him."

Ellie gave him a baleful look. "It won't be much fun if she kills him."

"I said try to," Michael said cheerfully. "If he can't keep her from doing so, he doesn't deserve her anyway."

"Ah. Noted."

The alarmed look Michael gave her after her serene response made her giggle again. His brows came together in a scowl which wasn't nearly as threatening as he thought it was, since she could see the amusement sparkling in his eyes. A little growl rose in his throat as he pulled her closer. "Are you trying to get yourself spanked, pretty girl?"

An imp rose up inside of her, along with a need. Last night at Stronghold he'd spanked her before inserting her plug, for being such a good girl. It had been more frustrating than anything else, especially when they'd returned to her house for more vanilla sex - which was fun and enjoyable, but it still left part of her unsatisfied, even if emotionally she was more satisfied than ever. The needs inside of her were becoming more and more insistent, and he had to feel the same way.

"Maybe, pretty boy," she said, tugging on a lock of his hair.

A light went on in his eyes, sadistic and predatory enough to take her breath away and Ellie quailed as she realized she might have just bitten off a little more than she could chew. Awakened a beast she didn't really have any control over.

"Michael, Ellie, what about you two?"

Michael's fingers dug into Ellie's soft curves as he turned to answer Adam, letting her know she wasn't off the hook.

"We can help set up," Michael said. "And clean up. Who's going to officiate?"

"Sam," Adam said, naming one of Angel's old roommates. Ellie had heard about them but never met any of them. Michael had though, and he jerked in surprise.

"Sam?"

Adam sighed, but his lips curved up in a reluctant grin. "He's apparently a Dudeist and got his certification to be a qualified Dudeist officiant."

"Dudeist?" Maria asked sounding confused.

"As in the Dude," Jake said, as if that cleared everything up, and it did for some of them. Maria still looked confused and she wasn't the only one - Jessica and Hilary also had wrinkled brows. "The Dude. *The Big Lebowski*."

"Oh honey, we are definitely having another movie night," Rick said, shaking his head at his girlfriend. "No *Star Wars* and now no Dude? Your cultural education has been sadly neglected."

Maria snorted. "I'm not the one who had never seen *Clue*."

"You'd never seen *Clue*?!" Sharon was horrified as she looked at Rick, her hands raising upwards as her voice went high and squeaky. "Flames... Flames, on the side of my face."

The meeting wrapped up as it became clear it was devolving into a hangout. Michael took Ellie back to his place, tied her to the bed, and made very slow, gentle love to her. Which actually did quite a bit to satisfy her inner masochist, because she was a begging, pleading mess by the time he actually let her cum. It wasn't kinky really, there wasn't any pain, but his slow pace, his teasing fingers, the constant edging... and the fact that it was the kinkiest thing they'd done in weeks, despite the missionary position, gave her the biggest orgasm she'd had in weeks too.

Laying in Michael's arms, she felt... good. Right. His even breathing as he slept made her feel happy to be cuddled up against him. Happy to know she was going to wake up and be beside him.

Yeah, sometimes things still felt a little surreal. Sometimes she found herself waiting for the other shoe to drop. But now she talked about it. To Dr. Amy. To Michael. To her friends. Even more reassuring had been hearing that Michael and her friends felt the same way sometimes. Like things in their lives were going so well they couldn't possibly be real... right up until they had a small fight or did something silly like squirt ketchup over their white shirt during a lunch meeting (poor Jessica), to remind them that no, it was definitely all real.

Although, Sharon didn't have that problem. She wasn't broken up about her breakup with Brian, but she wasn't really happy about it. Ellie felt bad listening to her friend's sadness about being surrounded by happy couples, because Sharon was amazing and she deserved all the happiness in the world... but as soon as Ellie started feeling actual guilt because she was happy and Sharon wasn't, she made note of it and reminded herself she deserved to be happy too, and it was okay for her happiness to come at a different time than Sharon's.

And she really was happy, other than being super sexually frustrated. Her moments of slight panic and anxiety were becoming fewer and farther between, and she wasn't letting them get in her way anymore. She kept trying. The more she tried, the more the little voices in her head which picked at her, telling her she was unworthy, telling her she was messed up, faded away.

She could really do this.

Running her hand over Michael's sleeping chest, she whispered the words she hadn't dared say out loud to him.

"I love you, Michael."

⚜

"Tonight's gonna be a good, good night," Michael sang cheerfully as he pulled into Andrew's driveway. A good, *good* night.

Ellie was ready.

He was pretty sure she thought he'd been asleep last night when she whispered her little confession – and he had been right on the verge of sleep – but he'd been awake enough to hear her. As long as he hadn't dreamed it, which he'd almost feared he had. But he'd held himself still and waited until she'd fallen asleep before pinching himself, just to make sure.

Awake.

Which meant Ellie loved him. Was even willing to say it, even though she'd thought he was asleep when she had done so. But the more important thing was that she'd confessed it to herself. They'd talked about a lot of things with Dr. Amy during the session he'd attended, and Michael had quickly come to understand a lot of Ellie's anxieties could only be resolved by her. Which was incredibly frustrating for a Dom who just wanted to fix everything, but the best thing he could do to help was be supportive and patient while she worked on readjusting her attitude and responses. She'd also asked him to point out when he noticed her withdrawing. She might need some space or a minute to decide what she wanted to do, but it did seem to help her to have it pointed out. And then they'd talk about *why* she'd felt the need to withdraw at that moment.

The first few times she'd talked about it, she'd seemed almost scared to, like she was afraid he was going to hear what she was saying and run screaming into the night. The more he'd listened, the more he'd just let her talk her way through it, the more comfortable she'd become. Especially after he'd become more open with her.

Told her some of his own worries. His own fears.

Like how he didn't want to push her too quickly. How he worried about accidentally triggering another panic attack. That he was concerned she only wanted him for sex. That confession had sent her into a fit of adorable giggles when he'd forlornly confessed it, practically pouting at her with overly wide eyes. He'd only been half kidding. She'd immediately spouted off a long list of his most attractive qualities, which he'd enjoyed listening to.

Putting his car in park, Michael headed around the side of the house to the entrance to Andrew's basement apartment. Last week, Andrew and Kate had put in an offer on a house just a street away and had it accepted, so now they were just waiting to close, which was happening next week. Till then, Andrew's residence was still the basement apartment of his dad's house.

The door opened before Michael even raised his hand to knock, and Andrew grinned at him. An almost goofy grin on a half-naked man. Andrew's jeans were slung low around his hips, but his entire upper body was completely bare. "Hey man."

"Hey," Michael responded, eyeing Andrew slightly. His grin was a little too goofy for Michael to feel entirely secure when he didn't know why Andrew was grinning.

"Michael!" Kate's voice squealed out from behind Andrew and after a moment she bounced into view, the same kind of goofy grin on her face, and she shoved her left hand into his face. A large sapphire, surrounded by a cluster of diamonds, adorned her ring finger. "Look! Look! Look!"

Michael let out a loud whoop of congratulations, jumping forward to catch them both in a hug. No wonder Andrew had looked so goofy!

"When did this happen?! You didn't say you were going to be doing this today!" Michael said. He would have waited and let the happy couple have their afternoon together if Andrew had.

"It was kind of a spur of the moment thing," Andrew admitted, wrapping his arm around his fiancé and dropping a kiss on the top of her head with a sappy expression. "Come on in, I don't want Kate to get cold."

Since the air was decidedly chilly and Kate was just wearing short cloth shorts and a thin t-shirt, that made sense. Although Andrew's nipples were also getting hard in the cold air, but Michael would let him keep the illusion that he was just doing it for Kate's sake. He stepped inside so Andrew could close the door behind him, Kate practically bouncing as she took a couple steps back but didn't go any farther.

"We were at the mall this afternoon and we went into the jewelry store so I could get my mom a birthday present and when I saw this ring... well, I know it's not the traditional engagement ring, but I just fell in love. So I pointed it out to Andrew and told him that's exactly what I wanted, and I was just kind of joking, you know, but he dropped to his knee right there!" The adoration on Kate's face as she beamed up at him warmed Michael from the inside out. He was damned happy for the two of them.

"I told you when we got together, I was going to marry you," Andrew teased, watching her bounce. He turned his attention back to Michael, grinning. "We're telling everyone else at the club tonight, but since you aren't going to be there..."

"Don't tell Ellie though, I get to!" Kate demanded, pointing a demanding finger at him as her bouncing momentarily stopped. "I'm going to call her first thing tomorrow morning. And don't let her pick up her phone from anyone else. Hide it from her if you have to."

Michael held up his hands in surrender. "I promise, I won't tell her and I will keep her far too busy to even think about her phone." He grinned as he made the promise.

Twenty minutes later - which was far longer than it should have taken since Kate had insisted on putting on real clothes and accompanying them out to the shed, which had taken about twice the time since Andrew had been in the bedroom with her while she dressed since he needed a shirt and the couple apparently couldn't go more than thirty seconds without cooing at each other - Michael was back on the road and headed to his apartment with a gorgeously finished, custom-made piece of equipment in his trunk. Well, half in his trunk. He'd had to put down the back seats to make some of the longer pieces fit entirely.

Fortunately, he'd be able to get it up to his apartment by himself since it was in pieces and Andrew had shown him how to put it together. Ellie was going to be in for a surprise tonight.

⚝ 21 ⚝

Michael had invited Ellie over for dinner before they headed to Stronghold, which wasn't unusual. What was unusual was the secretive smile on his lips when he opened the door and the fact that all of his furniture had been moved out of the way for what looked like a spanking bench sitting in the middle of his living room. The couch and coffee table (which had all sorts of toys laying out on it) had been pushed back against the walls, almost framing the bench, so there was no way she could miss it.

"What's that?" she asked, pointing, even though the answer to her question was pretty self-evident. She was just thrown by its sudden appearance, anticipation and apprehension spiking inside of her since Michael hadn't even hinted that tonight was going to be anything other than going to the club and hanging out with their friends. In other words, nothing different than what they'd been doing for the past few weeks, acting like a vanilla couple.

That bench said something different though, and her body was already fizzing with hopeful excitement.

Strong hands slid over her shoulders, pulling open the front of her coat and tugging it off to reveal the deep red PVC dress she was wearing underneath. Ellie didn't have to look down to know her nipples were already poking through the fabric, indicating her arousal. All it took was just a hint of possible kinky things to come and she was all revved up.

"What's that?" Michael made a tutting noise behind her, his deep voice amused. "What do you think it is?"

Wrinkling up her nose, Ellie danced away from him, already knowing she was going to pay for her next sentence. "Well, I'm not sure, see it's been a long time since I've been on one of those things... or really gotten a close look at one... I seem to have forgo-OH!"

The big bad Dom swooped in and Ellie found herself swept up in his arms, giggling madly at the scowling look on his face.

"You know what happens to SAMs, pretty girl?" he asked, using the popular acronym for 'Smart-Ass Masochist.'

"No, because I don't think I've ever been considered one," she answered honestly, still giggling as she wrapped her arms around his neck. She really hadn't been either. It was only with Michael that she'd ever gotten mouthy, even in the beginning - which was a pretty clear indication how much she'd instinctively trusted him.

"They get punished," he said matter-of-factly, and every nerve ending in Ellie's body cheered in anticipation.

When he dumped her on the bench, on her back, she was surprised. Not just because he'd put her on her back, but because he'd put her down so her head was on the incline and her ass was lower. Michael chuckled as she blinked at him in surprise, pulling her up just enough to yank her dress off over her head. As usual, she wore nothing underneath, and his eyes drank in the sight of her naked body, filled with appreciation.

"Arms above your head," he ordered her, and Ellie complied, almost more curious than she was turned on by what was happening.

It turned out the bench had cuffs which secured her wrists just above her head, forcing her elbows to splay outwards in order to be at all comfortable and completely opening her breasts to whatever Michael wanted to do to them. Oh sure, she'd be able to bring her elbows up in a protective position if she really wanted to, but it wouldn't be comfortable and she wouldn't be able to hold the position for long.

Michael adjusted the incline of the bench so she was tilted back another inch or so, keeping her from sliding right off the bench, and arousal curled through her as she realized exactly how at his mercy she was. Another strap went over her middle, across her ribs, pinning her down to the bench just under her breasts.

"Is this Andrew's work?" she asked as Michael attached cuffs to her ankles, turning her head to look at the glossy wood. She was pretty sure the comfortable padding she was laying on was leather. Andrew made a lot of custom pieces of bondage equipment and she'd heard they could be very... versatile.

"Why, yes, it is," Michael replied with an almost cruel twist of his lips, securing two cuffs to her thighs as well. Ellie squeaked as he pushed her ankles up towards her body so he could attach the ankle cuffs to the thigh cuffs on each leg, splaying her legs wide open and completely exposing all her most vulnerable bits. Then he attached the thigh cuffs to the bench on each side, holding her open. "Very pretty, pretty girl."

Ellie couldn't help but struggle a little, testing the boundaries of her restraints. They didn't go very far. She panted for breath as Michael stood back and watched her wriggle, that same little sadistic smile on his face. The strap across her middle would probably keep her from falling, but she didn't really want to test it by thrashing about too much.

The way he'd restrained her, her pussy, anus, and inner thighs were completely vulnerable and at his mercy. The glint in Michael's eye said he was thinking about all the terrible things he could do to those sensitive areas while she was tied down like this. She didn't know if it was the weeks of nothing but vanilla or her increased trust in Michael, but she didn't think she'd ever been so turned on from so little foreplay.

Really, he hadn't done anything but tie her up and her pussy was throbbing eagerly, her nipples hardened into little buds, and she was sure she could feel wetness trickling down from her folds into the crease of her ass.

"So does this mean the vanilla sex is over?" she asked hopefully.

Michael laughed. "Probably not entirely, sweetheart. I intend to use you hard enough that sometimes you won't want anything more than vanilla sex." Thinking back on some of the scenes they'd done in the past at Stronghold, Ellie could believe it. The ache he'd leave behind during the scenes would be more than enough pain to make more vanilla sex still very satisfying. She didn't want a beating *every* night after all. Michael's eyes swept over her, gauging her reactions. "What color are you, pretty girl?"

"Green." Ellie frowned at him, wondering why he was already asking for her color when he hadn't done anything more than tie her up. "Were you really expecting another answer?"

His fingers reached down to trail over her stomach as he raised his eyebrows at her sassiness. "I wasn't sure, since we haven't done anything particularly kinky outside of the club."

Right. Mingling what they'd been doing the past few weeks with what they'd been doing before... she could see why he was a bit worried it would trigger something. But she felt perfectly safe here in his apartment.

"I trust you."

THREE SIMPLE WORDS, WHICH MEANT ALMOST AS MUCH TO HIM AS the three words she'd uttered last night. It was easier to trust people when she was in Stronghold, where there were protocols, Dungeon Monitors, and her friends. Now she was alone with him, cuffed and strapped down, completely physically helpless, and it hadn't even occurred to her to be worried. It was a beautiful moment of submission, made all the more meaningful by the open way she was looking up at him, waiting for his next move.

"Thank you for your trust, sweetheart," he said softly, moving his hand up from her soft stomach to play with her breast, teasing the hardened bud of her nipple. He pinched her nipple and she moaned in happy arousal, squirming on the bench. Michael grinned. Leaning forward, he took her lips in a long, hard kiss, still fondling her breast, as he kissed her breathless. Then he pulled away and looked down at her naked body.

Time to decorate his pretty girl.

"I have a present for you, but you don't have to accept it right now."

"A present?" She sounded confused, her arms automatically jerking as if to come down and take whatever it was he wanted to give her.

Michael held back his laughter as he reached into his pocket and pulled out the short silver chain. It was made up of tiny silver links, each decorated with a dark, red garnet, shimmering and sparkling in the light. He held it up and Ellie's eyes went wide.

"We'll use your play collar until you're ready for this, but I'm going to start offering it every time we play. There's no pressure to say yes, but I will keep asking until you do say either yes or no."

"Yes."

He froze as his hand had started to lower away. "What?"

A little smile curved her lips, almost mischievous. "Yes."

"This is more than just a play collar," Michael said, frowning down at her even as hope made his heart pound in his chest. "If I collar you with this, you're mine, Ellie. Real relationship, period, full stop."

She pursed her lips, pretending she was thinking, and answered again before he could call her on it. "Still yes."

His hands moved down to place it around her neck. "Once I secure the clasp, that's it. Getting rid of me is going to be three times as hard. I won't back off, I won't let you run away, I'll chase after you until you at least talk to me and tell me why."

This time when she met his eyes, her gaze and expression were completely serious. Open. Tender. "Still yes, Michael. I actually talked to Dr. Amy about this a few days ago. I want this with you. I'm ready. I'm not saying I won't still need help with some of my insecurities and anxieties, but... I think I'll feel more secure when I'm wearing your collar and have a physical reminder that I'm definitely yours."

"Oh, you're definitely mine," he said, possessiveness surging through him. "And now everyone's going to know it."

When the clasp locked into place, all he could do was stare. He kind of wanted to pinch himself again, because this felt too good to be true.

"Are you okay?" she asked, trying to reach for him before the restraints stopped her.

Michael placed his hand on her chest and slid it up to just underneath the collar now adorning her neck. "You know how you say there are times when you think what's happening can't possibly be real and you're scared because you think it's all about to go wrong?"

Her eyes looked a little watery. "Yes," she whispered.

"That's how I feel right now." The moment stretched between them, far too intimate, and he felt like he'd just exposed himself... but all she did was smile up at him. Joyous. Compassionate. Understanding. Michael slid his hand down to her breast. The collar he'd just put on her declared to the world she was his, but now he was truly going to claim her, in every way.

Seal the deal, so to speak.

"You look lovely," he said, his voice full of emotion as he caressed her. He cleared his throat, as Ellie beamed at him, looking completely content. Serenely submissive. "I have a few more items to decorate you with though." Her eyes lit up.

He was looking forward to clamping her nipples and torturing them. After weeks of vanilla sex the little buds would be extra sensitive since she was no longer used to having them squeezed so tightly. Michael looked forward to watching her reaction.

Reluctantly pulling away, he walked over to the coffee table where he'd lined up everything he wanted to use this evening and picked up the pair of rubber-tipped clamps with dangling red jewels, which would match her collar, and the length of dark red bondage rope. When he turned around, Ellie was watching him with wide, excited eyes, her breath coming in fast pants which made the mounds of her breasts jiggle on her chest as she practically wriggled with excitement, easily falling back into the scene. He walked back slowly, giving her time for her trepidation, her excitement to grow. His cock felt about ready to pound through his leathers as he took in the sight of her in his collar; every time his eyes fell on it, it was like his entire body jerked with excitement and male satisfaction.

"If you tied me up like this just to decorate me, I might have to hurt you," Ellie said - teasing him, making it sound like more of a confession than a threat, but it still made Michael shake his head.

"Didn't anyone ever teach you not to threaten your Dom when you're tied down and at his mercy?" he asked as he began winding the bondage rope around the base of her breasts in a figure eight configuration. The soft mounds pulled inward towards each other and then began to balloon as Michael tightened the rope and tied it off. It only took a few moments for her creamy flesh to begin to pinken as the blood was trapped in her breasts. Ellie was panting even more now, her body quivering with arousal from the small stimulation and discomfort, and this time she didn't have the brain power for a sassy answer.

Leaning over, Michael sucked one pert nipple into his mouth, biting down hard enough to make her arch and cry out before releasing it with a pop, and repeating the process on the other nipple. Now the two little buds were glistening, their color a slightly darker pink than before.

Michael held up the clamps. "See? They match your new collar. Aren't they pretty?"

He was probably going to be referring to her collar a lot. Just seeing it on her made him want to whoop for joy. Hold her down and pound into her until she was full of his cum. Wrap himself around her and never let her go.

The little jewels dangled down in front of her and Ellie's glazed eyes met his. "Yes, Michael, very pretty."

"They're going to be even prettier in a minute."

Using both hands, he placed the clamps around her nipples at the same time, easing them onto the tiny buds so the pressure increased incrementally until they were finally completely closed.

"Huuuurts," Ellie whined, although it wasn't entirely a complaint. In a way, she was egging him on, since his Ellie wasn't too often very vocal during a scene until they were well into it. She knew damn well what hearing her whine would do to him.

Naughty girl.

"Good," he said, just for the satisfaction of watching her eyes dilate at the response. "Now I'm going to make you hurt some more."

Not much though. Since she'd shocked him by immediately

accepting his collar, he was changing up his plan for tonight. There was going to be a lot less foreplay than he'd initially planned. Maybe a few stripes on her lovely breasts. A little bit of pain for her pussy.

He didn't want her too distracted when he finally slid his cock into her ass and claimed her completely.

☙❧

For a moment, just a brief moment, when Michael had put the permanent collar around her throat, Ellie had been afraid it would feel like it was choking her. A permanent collar meant so much more than a play collar. It wasn't quite the same as having a collar that was welded shut, and they'd have to have a collaring ceremony to exchange any vows, but both of them knew what it meant.

She was finally, truly, accepting Michael as her Master. As a real part of her life. Not just in a scene, but also outside of it.

They'd done the sexy scenes and club contract, they'd done the reconnecting, dating, and vanilla relationship for over a month now... it was time to merge the two sides of their relationship together. So when he'd offered the collar, she hadn't hesitated.

Was she scared? Yes. She was still terrified of messing this up.

But, like she'd told Michael, she really did actually feel better once the collar was on her. It didn't feel like it was choking her at all. It was more like a hug. A cool, but swiftly warming, permanent hug. The chains weren't tight at all, they looked like a necklace that she could easily wear with everything, and she could feel it encircling the very base of her neck, a reassuring weight which reminded her of Michael's patience and tender care.

As a counterweight to the security and soft happiness the collar gave her, her breasts were becoming sore and achy from being bound so tightly and her nipples were throbbing from the bite of the clamps, to remind her that her gentle lover was also a nasty sadist.

Two sides of a coin, and all hers.

SLAP! SLAP! SLAP!

Ellie moaned as Michael started to spank her breasts, turning the slightly pink mounds a darker pink as his hand batted them back and forth. She could see the arousal growing in his eyes, not just from swatting her tender bits, but also from her vocal response. She'd never really cared before, whether or not a Dom was aroused by what she said or the sounds she made, but knowing Michael was just made her want to make them more - so she could see *his* reaction.

And he didn't disappoint.

The sadistic light flared in his eyes, his hand pausing for just a moment after her moan, as if he wanted complete silence so he could drink in the sound, and she was pretty sure she saw the front of his pants jerk. The large bulge made it clear he was fully erect in his leathers, all large and hard and ready to be inside of her.

SLAP! SLAP! SLAP!

The more he smacked her breasts, the more she moaned, trying to arch her back upwards only to find herself restrained by the strap across her ribs, and the reminder of her immobility just turned her on even more. When he stopped spanking her tender mounds, he gripped one in each hand, fingers digging into the soft pink flesh painfully before easing back just a bit so he could start kneading them. Being so tightly bound, even the massage was uncomfortable, and Ellie gasped and whimpered as her breasts tingled under his firm touch, feeling swollen to three times their normal size.

"Michael... Michael pleaaaaaaase," she begged, panting, as he continued to torment her by playing with her breast and leaving her empty, needy pussy all alone. The upper half of her body felt hot and swollen, coursing with sensation, while her lower half was left throbbing with arousal but completely untouched. She couldn't even rub her thighs together to achieve some kind of stimulation.

"Please what, pretty girl?" he asked, his hands still working on her breasts, fingers playing with the clamps and making her nipples ache, the sharp sensations going straight to her pussy, winding her up like a coil of wire on a spool.

"Please play with my pussy." The plea was heartfelt. She didn't beg to cum because she wasn't quite there yet and she doubted he'd let her anyway. But maybe he'd touch her needy, aching pussy. The collar around her neck shifted as she squirmed, turning her on even more with the reminder it was there. That she belonged to him. "Please, please, please..."

SMACK!

The wet slap had her hips working, pumping upwards as the delicious pain spread through her core. His palm had come down hard on her splayed pussy lips, the heel of his hand spanking her clit, his fingers slapping against her sensitive folds, and Ellie cried out with the sheer, erotic joy of it. It burned, it stung, it felt so *good*.

"More, please, please, please," she begged. If three pleases were the magic words, she'd be happy to do it over and over again.

SMACK!

This time when he slapped down, he didn't just snap his hand away, he slapped and held his hand on her pussy, rubbing her sensitive lips with his palms, stimulating her swollen clit and making her writhe as aching need sheered through her. Her breasts throbbed on her chest as she writhed, trying to rub more of her tender pussy against his hand.

SMACK!

Another slap and hold.

Enough pressure to make her hot and needy. Not enough to get her off. As soon as she thought she might be building up enough friction against his hand, he pulled it away again.

SMACK!

"Please, Michael," she pleaded. "More... more... I need to cum..."

"Oh you're going to cum, pretty girl," he said, his hand rubbing against her open pussy, working its way lower, the tips of his fingers seeking and finding the crinkled bud of her anus. The tiny hole easily accepted a finger, slicked with her arousal, making her shudder at the perpetually naughty feeling of being fingered there. "But you're going to wait until my cock is up your ass before you do."

Her sphincter automatically tightened around his finger, which was working in and out of her ass, fucking the hole - preparing it - as her breath caught. Ellie had known he'd get there eventually. There'd been no mistaking his fascination with her asshole when he'd plugged her every time they were at the club together. She just hadn't realized it would be tonight.

"Is this because I said yes to your collar?" she asked, shivering under his gaze as he watched her with slightly hooded eyes, his finger still working in and out of her asshole, moving much more easily as the small hole stretched.

A second finger began pushing into her as he answered. "Oh yes, Ellie. I told you, you're all mine now and I'm claiming every last bit of you."

Including her ass.

Anticipation and trepidation slid through her. It had been years since she'd had actual anal sex. Only a few Doms had ever wanted to take the play that far and she'd only said yes to the first two before realizing it made her feel too vulnerable, too intimate, too submissive with them. Too much *theirs*. But she was already Michael's, and she wanted it.

"Yes, please," she breathed out. And then wiggled. Frowned. "Shouldn't I be facing the other way for that?"

"No, absolutely not," Michael said, a sadistic twinkle in his eye making her insides curl. His fingers worked harder, fucking her asshole the way he was going to with his cock, making her quiver and shudder. "I'm going to watch your face while I sink my cock into this sweet little ass. I want to see every expression you make while you take me."

A third finger pressed into her and Ellie cried out, trying to arch again, as Michael drove the three fingers into her stretched hole. The burn of discomfort was similar to when he plugged her, but so much more, because she knew it wasn't going to end here. This wasn't just plugging her so she'd remember who she belonged to – he was preparing to claim her in the most base and intimate of ways. There was a reason she hadn't had anal sex in years, but she was prepared to give herself to Michael in that manner.

"Please... yes..." Heat wound its way around her body as she spasmed around his fingers.

SMACK!

The snap of his fingers directly against her swollen clit made her squeal before the tiny nub started to throb.

"No cumming until my cock is all the way in your ass and I say you can," Michael said. "Or I'm going to slather numbing solution all over your pussy and ass before I shove my cock in you, and you won't be able to cum again for the rest of the night."

Asshole sadist!

Ellie clenched her jaw around the curses she wanted to yell at him as she fought back against the threatening orgasm. It was an effective threat, because he'd absolutely do it. All he'd need is a condom and the numbing gel wouldn't affect him. He'd be able to fuck her ass, and she wouldn't get any of the delicious pain or pleasure... and she wanted it. She wanted to feel every inch of him as he slid inside her, wanted the burn and the ecstasy.

Forcing herself to take deep breaths, she pushed away the need to cum, even as Michael continued to pump and twist his fingers inside of her ass. Her clit pulsed in protest, but she managed it.

"Good girl," he said, fucking her a little harder with his fingers and then twisting his hand so he could rub the heel of it against her pussy. Ellie whined, trying to escape the stimulation that was making it so hard to obey him.

"Please, Michael, stooooop," she begged.

The nasty sadist chuckled. "But I thought you wanted me to play with your pussy."

"I changed my mind," she said, shuddering as his fingers probed particularly deep inside of her. "I want you to fuck my ass."

"Well I don't want anyone to say I'm neglecting my pretty sub's wants."

To her relief, after a few more twists of his fingers which had her squealing, Michael withdrew his hand. Of course, that left her completely bereft for a few moments as he stood and began to undo the front of his pants. Her breasts were slowly turning a darker and darker shade of pink, her nipples were already a deep enough red to match the collar she could feel sliding around her throat as she turned her head to watch him. Both her pussy and ass throbbed and tingled, wanting - needing - more. When she and Sharon had been joking about blue labia, she hadn't felt as achy and needy as this. Now, if she hadn't been restrained, she might have tried to sneak a hand down there just to give herself a little of the stimulation she craved.

Michael slid his pants off and knelt on the bench, which thought-fully provided padded ledges in just the right places.

She whined again as he lined his cock up with her pussy and shoved in. Hard.

"Michael!" Her pussy felt stuffed, split open, and shocked by the sudden impalement. With no preparation, he felt larger than usual.

"Don't you dare cum, pretty girl."

She moaned, her arms and legs straining against her restraints as he started fucking her, her lower body trying to escape from the thick cock plunging into her pussy with rough thrusts, making her spasm around him as he pounded into her. The restraints kept her in place, kept her from being able to push him away. Every thrust had his groin rubbing over her clit, sent her breasts bouncing and throbbing with fiery pain, making her struggle against the orgasm circling around her like a vulture, just waiting for a moment of weakness so it could send her flying.

When he finally pulled out, his cock slick with her juices, Ellie was practically sobbing with need and a burning pleasure in her pussy that indicated her imminent orgasm. She gulped air, trying to calm her body, as Michael's cock pressed against her anus. Her muscles burned as they opened for him and she quivered with the intimate sensation of his cock sliding into her ass.

Looking up at him, seeing the intense, almost tender expression on his face, she understood why he'd positioned her like this.

MICHAEL WASN'T OVERLY ROUGH, BUT HE WASN'T PARTICULARLY gentle either, as he pressed his cock into Ellie's ass. Neither of them wanted him to be too gentle. Her face was flushed, eyes teary and glazed with the need to orgasm; the small muscles of her face tight-ened with discomfort as her tight ass gripped the head of his cock. She was all heat and pleasure as he pressed into her, his cock lubricated with the copious honey from her pussy.

Her bound chest, red and swollen, moved as she panted through the pain. Michael slid deeper, not bothering to work his way in so much as he just slowly impaled her body on his cock, barely giving her enough time to adjust before he was pushing her again.

"Ow, ow, ow..." Ellie started writhing again as he reached parts of her the plug never had, the wide base of his cock keeping her sphincter fully open no matter how it pulsed around him.

"That's it, pretty girl, take it for me." Not only would she take it, she would enjoy it. Even with her face screwed up in discomfort, her pussy was weeping fluid.

Maybe he should help distract her. Make taking his cock just a little easier on her.

Michael loosened the bondage rope around the base of her breasts. "Oh no!"

Her ass tightened around him as she thrashed against her restraints, blood flowing back into her swollen mounds as the bondage rope fell away. Thrusting forward so his cock was fully lodged inside of her, he rested there a moment just to enjoy the feel of her ass completely enveloping him and to give her time to adjust - since, once he started to move, he wasn't going to go easy on her. His lack of movement freed up his hands to start squeezing and massaging her breasts, helping the flow of circulation move faster - which just made her wail, especially when the renewed blood flow reached her nipples which were still tightly clamped.

The pain made her ass clench around him, massaging his cock as if returning the favor for the way he was kneading her breasts, except it was all pure pleasure for him. Especially the pained sounds emanating from the back of her throat.

This was the perfect position, because he could admire how gorgeous her collar looked on her while he tormented her and pleasured himself.

Just as she started to relax, as her body became used to the current aches and pains he was inflicting on her, Michael braced his knees on the padded supports Andrew had so thoughtfully put in place, and began to drag his cock out of her ass. Ellie practically sobbed, squirming, clenching, as he pulled away from her sweet heat - and then screamed when he thrust back in.

Playing with her ass had been the fastest way to get her to make noise, to make her come undone - he already knew that - but it was nothing compared to how she reacted to actually having her ass fucked. It was like her entire body had lit up and she'd completely lost control of her reactions, from nothing more than a cock up her ass. His cock up her ass, to be precise.

Because she was his, all his.

"Michael... oh god, Michael, I'm going to cum... I'm going to cum!"

"Cum for me pretty girl," he said, leaning forward so he could plow his cock into her harder, fuck her ass like he did her pretty pussy. "Cum with my cock up your ass."

It was all she needed. She screamed as her ass gripped his cock like a vise, nearly setting off his own orgasm. Her ass squeezed so tight he had to work to thrust his cock in and out, the burning friction becoming more noticeable as the cream from her pussy was wearing off as a lubricant. Of course, the fact he was having to force his cock in and out of her ass now just made her scream louder as the ecstasy rolled through her.

Knowing he wasn't going to last too much longer, Michael opened the clamps on her nipples and let them drop to the floor, gritting his teeth as Ellie's body tightened around him in another wave of orgasm. He pumped harder, faster, as his balls tightened up, ready to pour himself into her.

⊗⁂⊗

In between breathless sobs and the waves of ecstasy rolling over her, there was one immutable, unchanging emotion enveloping Ellie... the feeling of being owned. Michael was inside of her, all around her, hurting her, pleasuring her, and claiming her.

She was finally giving herself over completely to a Dom - not just her body, but her heart and soul as well.

No matter how much her breasts ached, no matter how her nipples burned, or her inner muscles screamed, the most overpowering sensation was that of Michael's splitting her open, the burning path of pleasure as he thrust into her over and over again, and then the flood of warmth as he held himself deep inside of her, his head bowing down to press against hers, his fingers sliding up to play with her collar.

Ellie lost herself in the moment, in the sensations, and just let go, trusting him to completely take care of her. It wasn't subspace exactly, because she felt like she had made a conscious choice to let go.

She felt floaty.

Secure.

Loved.

Especially as Michael's body relaxed against her, letting her softness cradle him. His head moved to the side, resting beside hers on the padded headrest, and she felt the chain around her neck move as he began to play with it. She didn't want to move.

Unfortunately, her stomach growled and then his growled as if answering. Laughing, Michael pushed himself up.

"Alright, pretty girl, I think that's our dinner cue." His eyes raked over her, coming back to rest on the collar around her throat, and the smug pride in his expression filled her with warmth.

"I could eat," she replied with a little sigh, a little sad this was already over.

She shouldn't have worried. The bastard plugged her - to keep his cum in - before releasing her from the bench. Already tender from being fucked, her ass protested being filled again and it didn't make for a comfortable sitting experience while they ate - which of course just got her all revved up again.

More than once she caught Michael staring at her collar with that same smug expression, or her hand creeping up to play with it.

"I hope you're not regretting saying yes already," he said, looking smug when he caught her stroking it again.

"Definitely not," Ellie retorted. A little imp rose up inside of her. Also a little spurt of courage. She wanted to see if she could knock him off balance, but she was also feeling so good, so secure with the collar under her fingertips, that she felt brave enough to say it. "Why would I regret being collared by the man I love?"

Michael choked on the piece of steak he'd been swallowing.

Stared.

Something in his eye glinted.

Ellie grinned.

He practically jumped over the table to get at her, ignoring her squeals that she was still hungry as he carried her off to his bedroom over his shoulder, his hand already palming her ass.

"I love you too, pretty girl."

"This is not how I pictured you saying it back to me," Ellie grumbled into his lower back, pretending to be upset about being carried off like a cavewoman when he'd declared his feelings.

She wasn't upset at all though. Even when his hand came down on her ass.

"I love you, sassy girl."

Ellie hugged him around his middle, squishing her breasts against his back. She didn't think she'd ever been happier.

By the time they got back to their dinner, it had gone cold and Ellie was sitting even more uncomfortably, a dreamy expression on her face which matched the goofy grin on Michael's. Her fingers went back to her collar. There might be some ups and downs along the way, but she knew this was it; this was exactly the happily-ever-after she'd always wanted and never thought she'd get. Now she was going to live it.

EPILOGUE

The look of utter shock on Angel's face as she walked into the door of her parents' dance studio, to be faced with an entire room full of people waiting for her and Adam standing by a gorgeously made altar strewn with flowers, made it very difficult for Olivia to keep from bursting out with laughter. She managed it though. After all, she had a reputation to maintain.

Especially when certain people decided to sit right next to her and invade her space.

Angel looked amazing though.

The white floor length dress she was wearing made the most of her curves while managing to keep her baby bump from becoming the focus of everyone's eyes. She'd been told she was coming to do promotional photos with her parents for their dance studio; she and her mom should be in white formal dresses while her dad would be in a tux. Well, her dad *was* wearing a tux as he held out his arm to Angel, but her mom was wearing a purple formal gown. She came up beside Angel, a white veil in her hands, eyes already brimming with happy tears.

Angel's mouth opened and no sound came out. She looked like she was ready for a photo shoot. Her makeup was flawless, emphasizing her almond shaped eyes and high cheekbones, and her hair pulled back into a pile of curls which looked effortless, but had probably taken an hour to achieve. As her mother tucked the veil into her hair, Angel looked across the room at where Adam was standing in a tux, with Jared by his side, her best friend Leigh opposite him, and Sam in between them (wearing a bathrobe over his suit for some reason), and burst into tears.

Dammit.

She'd really thought she was going to win that $20 from Patrick.

Looking alarmed, Adam bolted past where Olivia was sitting and down the aisle to his erstwhile bride. Across the aisle, standing next to his girlfriend Lexie, Patrick smirked at Olivia. The bastard. She scowled at him.

'She's still here,' she mouthed at the jerk. She glanced at Leigh, who just smiled serenely and didn't look at all worried about her best friend sobbing in the back of her surprise wedding.

Patrick and Olivia's heads both swiveled around to the back of the room - where everyone else's attention was. Well, some people were trying to pretend they were politely looking away. Others were leaning in for a closer look, or maybe to try and hear what Adam was saying to his crying bride. Olivia ignored the little tingle on the back of her neck which said the man sitting next to her was leaning into her personal space. There was no way she was going to let him know how much he was getting to her. He was probably just trying to get a better look anyway. Even if it was none of his business. She didn't know why he'd even been invited.

"It doesn't look like she's going to punch him." The deep, rumbling whisper did naughty things to her lady parts, but Olivia didn't allow any of her muscles to stiffen. She had far more control than that. "I think you might have won the bet."

Arching one eyebrow, Olivia turned her head just enough to pierce Luke Davis with a haughty look. "If I did, I wouldn't need you to tell me so."

It would be pretty obvious if Angel either hauled off and punched her erstwhile groom or ran from the room.

Luke's blue eyes studied her expression, his focus entirely on Olivia rather than Angel and Adam - and she did *not like it, dammit,* no matter how her body responded to his sharp, inquiring gaze, the way it seemed like he was really looking at all of her and trying to decide how best to serve her. She was pretty sure she was assigning meaning to his expression where there was none.

"Yes, Ma'am."

And no, she didn't get turned on just because this incredibly hand-some, confident, alpha man immediately backed down and called her ma'am. That would be ridiculous. Especially since he was probably just mocking her with it. He might be exactly her type physically (so what if she had a weakness for dark hair, light eyes, and an aura of confi-dence?), but he was also going to be her boss soon. Basically her boss. Patrick and Michael had assured her that the day to day running of Marquis would be handled mostly by her and Michael; Luke was just going to be a silent partner... but a partner still meant an owner and she was just going to be a manager.

Being attracted to a man in a position of power over her was unprecedented, so she sure as hell wasn't going to start now. Not if she had anything to say about it. Her body could do what it liked, but she controlled her responses.

Although, she was certainly looking forward to having him join the next Baby Doms class. She'd managed to get Patrick to agree Luke had to go through the newbie class like all the other new members, and she was going to be in charge of the one at Marquis. Lisa was taking over the one at Stronghold. Patrick liked to have Dommes teaching the class, mostly because it practically guaranteed no misogynist was going to make it through the entire course. The Doms had to go through everything they wanted to put a submissive through, so they got to experience whips, floggings, clamps, canes, bondage, wax, the whole gamut. Olivia's favorite day was anal plug day. The plugs weren't big but they certainly brought out the whining.

Could she help it if her particular kink celebrated seeing alpha men submitting? Sure, they weren't submitting to her exactly, since they had an end goal, but it was satisfying nonetheless. She couldn't wait to put Luke through the class.

Couldn't wait in a purely professional sense, that was. Nothing more. Just an opportunity to have the flirtatious, arrogant man under her control for a while. Besides, she might feel like they had more of a balance of power once she'd whipped his ass and put a plug in it, owner of the club or not.

Olivia realized she was still staring into his blue eyes, which were now beginning to look amused. Shooting him another frosty look, she turned away so she could see what was happening.

Grinning like a loon, Adam was now making his way back down the aisle as a weepy but beaming Angel set herself up at the other end of it, one parent on each side of her. Turning her head to face Patrick - who looked like he was torn between relief and disappointment at losing the bet - Olivia smirked.

෴

IT WAS A BEAUTIFUL CEREMONY, EVEN IF IT WAS A LITTLE ODD. SAM only slipped in a couple of Big Lebowski references, including a small sermon on the meaning of "abide," which turned out to be quite touching as he talked about people choosing to abide together, to stay and grow together, all the days of their lives. Angel had cried again.

Jake had a feeling he'd be attending a lot of these soon, including his sister's, if the way Lexie and Patrick were leaning on each other all through the ceremony was any indication. Of course, it didn't hurt that he'd been with Patrick last week when the man had bought the ring. Andrew and Kate had gotten engaged last weekend too. Justin, Chris, and Jessica might not be having a conventional wedding, but it was still happening this spring. He was kind of surprised Rick and Maria weren't already engaged, but he was sure Rick's proposal was coming down the line too. Only Jared and Leigh really seemed uninterested in taking the next big step. Well, not uninterested exactly, just not in the same rush as everyone else.

Not that Angel and Adam had rushed. She'd been making him wait every step of the way. No wonder he'd gotten pushy about the wedding.

Still, surprise or not, she'd been just like every other happy, glowing bride as she said her vows. Several people in the audience had snorted when she'd actually promised to obey, and he was pretty sure at least one of them was her brother. Then again, if Lexie included "obey" in her marriage vows, he'd probably snort too, even though he knew that was exactly the kind of relationship she and Patrick had.

But he really tried not to think too hard about their relationship.

"I now pronounce you, man and wife, you may kiss the bride."

Laughing happily, Angel actually bounced as she jumped forward into Adam's arms. The big guy wrapped himself around her for a long kiss as everyone else laughed and clapped, thrilled to see the two of them finally come together. Jake's own grin felt kind of cheesy, but he didn't bother to hide it. One of the things he liked best about this group of people were their tight bonds and happiness. Sure they had drama sometimes, but it was mostly fun drama.

His eyes drifted over to a curvy little drama queen on the other side of the aisle, who was also bouncing as she clapped. Drawing attention to herself, as usual. It wasn't hard for her, since she was also beautiful, but couldn't she just be happy with the regular amount of attention? Why did she have to go out of her way to be the center of it all the time?

Although her need for attention didn't irk him nearly as much as how all her obnoxious quirks, her lack of responsibility, and her crass mouth still didn't keep his cock from twitching every time he looked at her. She was exactly the kind of woman he'd never wanted, but for some reason his body disagreed with that sentiment. Even worse, she was friends with his sister and all of his other friends, so it wasn't like he could just talk her into bed, get her out of his system, and then peace out. He'd never actually done so before but some of his army buddies had, especially when they were overseas, and it seemed to work for them. This was the first time he'd ever had to deal with a woman he both disliked and desperately wanted but couldn't have, and he didn't quite know what to do about it.

It also bothered him that she riled his protective instincts. She was still looking for someone to be her roommate, putting up ads on Craig's List and other places, attracting who knew what weirdos. There was no reason for it. She was a trust fund baby, she didn't *need* a roommate. She probably just didn't want to live alone because then there'd be no one to pay attention to her.

I could pay all sorts of attention to her.

Jake gritted his teeth. His cock wasn't really talking to him. That was just some bullshit which had started after he'd met Sharon and overheard her having a conversation with her lady parts. Somehow, she'd gotten into his head, and now he couldn't help but think it was his cock talking to him whenever he had an inappropriately sexual thought about her. Which just made him want to bang his head against a wall until he was sane again. Not an unusual impulse when it came to her.

A poke in his side had him jumping. "Our turn to leave, dude," Chris said as Jake shot a glare at him. "Stop staring at Sharon and pay attention."

The seats on the other side of Jake were already empty, because Patrick and Lexie had moved into the aisle to head to the door and the other side of the dance studio, where the reception was going to be.

"I wasn't - never mind."

He didn't have a defense because he had been staring at Sharon, but not in the way Chris had been implying. Okay, maybe just a little bit in the way Chris had been implying. When her mouth was shut, or she was out of earshot, and he could just look at her... well she looked damned good.

Moving into the aisle, ignoring Chris snickering behind him, Jake made a beeline for the door. There was an open bar in the other room and he desperately needed a drink.

HANDS IN HIS POCKETS, LUKE LEANED AGAINST THE WALL, watching the flow of people in and out of the room. He hadn't expected to be invited today, but Adam seemed to feel his place as a partner in Marquis merited it. They weren't friends yet, but Adam expected they would be in the future. At least, that was how Adam had explained it when Luke had expressed his surprise.

A wedding invitation based on the expectation of future friendship.

The idea amused him, just like most of the people in this group of friends did. They were fun and funny, close without being too cliquish, and completely welcoming to him. Well, except for the one person he wanted to be completely welcomed by.

His eyes tracked flaming red hair across the room. Olivia Williams. Long red hair which flowed down her back, reaching just past her shoulders, and wearing a simple black dress, cut low in front and showing off a great deal of her ivory skin, lean muscles, and made the most of her curves. Thirty three years old, manager for Marquis as soon as it opened, faithful Redskins fan, and Dominatrix. Three things which should probably warn him away. He'd been smart enough not to wear his Cowboys jersey going to watch football at a new friend's house in Maryland - no need to piss everyone off right from the start - but it was going to come out eventually. Luke also didn't mess around with people he worked with. Ever. And while he'd always liked bossy women in bed, he knew there was a lot more to being a submissive to a Dominatrix than just enjoying confident women. Some of the porn he'd watched had had his balls cringing rather than his cock swelling...

But none of that stopped him from lusting after the gorgeous redhead. When he'd seen a seat open next to her for the ceremony, he'd immediately claimed it - to her obvious annoyance. But she hadn't moved, because she hadn't been willing to give him that power over her. Which had been hot. Even just watching her walk through a room was sexy. She moved with complete confidence, like she owned the place, and the crowd parted before her as if compelled by sheer force of personality. Despite being shorter, slimmer, and less physically imposing than the Doms, people reacted to her in almost exactly the same way - and those who didn't were treated to a death glare which had them scampering.

Yet she wasn't mean. Well, she was kind of mean to him, in the most polite way possible which was also sexy to him for some reason, but he'd also observed her being incredibly kind. The other women obviously looked up to her, even the more independent ones, and she watched over them like a big sister. She was the one who kept an eye on everyone else, making sure they had everything they needed, with no one stepping up to take care of her needs.

Right now she was handing Angel a glass of water and Adam a beer, so they could have something to drink while being surrounded by well-wishers.

Luke pushed off the wall and sauntered over to the bar. Michael and Ellie were standing in line as well, cuddled up and being almost sickeningly cute. He couldn't help but grin at the sight. Even though he'd only known Michael about a month, he'd seen Michael with Ellie and Michael without Ellie, and he definitely preferred the former. The two of them were good together, and Michael was obviously head over heels for the pretty, petite sub. She was wearing a dark red dress which matched the silver and red necklace on her throat; from the way she kept tenderly stroking it and the triumphantly possessive expression on Michael's face whenever he looked at it, Luke was pretty sure it was more than just a necklace. From the research he'd been doing, quite a few people in the lifestyle wore collars that didn't really look like collars.

As Luke approached, Michael looked up and grinned at him, straightening up with his hand in Ellie's. "Hey Luke, glad you could make it."

Ellie's face was flushed, her eyes slightly glassy, and Luke was a little sad he'd missed whatever it was Michael had been whispering in her ear to make her look like that.

"Me too," he said, glancing around the room again. Olivia was now talking to one of the catering waiters, pointing him towards the tables of food. "So ah... what does Olivia usually like to drink?"

"She's pretty well rounded," Ellie said, her eyes focusing on him as her face lit up with a grin. "Pretty much anything. I did hear her saying she'd like a glass of wine a little earlier though. She usually drinks whites, chardonnays."

"Thank you," Luke said, turning away from the rest of the room. "So... surprise wedding. It came off pretty well."

"Oh really?" Michael asked, looking amused. "You think I'm going to let you change the topic of conversation, just like that?"

"I was hoping."

Michael snorted. Ellie leaned back against him, her fingers coming up to touch her lips as if holding back a giggle. "Good luck. You're going to need it, with both Olivia and the gossip."

Shrugging, Luke gestured for Michael and Ellie to get their drinks since they were now at the head of the line. He then asked for two chardonnays and quickly retreated away from the smirking Michael and grinning Ellie. It wouldn't take them long to turn their attention back to each other rather than him.

As he headed towards Olivia, it didn't surprise him to see the waiter she'd been talking to heading back from the food table with two plates which he took to the bride and groom. They still hadn't managed to leave their current position, since so many people wanted to speak with them, but they now had everything they needed being brought to them. Thanks to Olivia. She was standing off to the side, silvery eyes scanning the room as if looking for anything else which needed to be taken care of.

When her gaze landed on Luke, her brow wrinkled slightly. Then her eyes dropped to the two glasses he was holding, and her lips turned down in a frown even as her eyes widened with surprise.

Stepping in front of her, Luke held out a glass. "I've been told, by a hopefully reliable source, that chardonnay was the way to go."

"You heard correctly," she said, looking almost reluctant to take the glass from him. She did so carefully, keeping their fingers from brushing. "Thank you."

The thanks was almost stilted, her gaze puzzled and a little suspicious, as if she was still trying to figure him out. Luke just smiled and took a sip of his own wine.

"Nice wedding," he said, turning to the side so he was standing next to her rather than in front of her.

"It was," Olivia said, her voice careful and low. "Rather small to be inviting acquaintances, I would have thought."

She always managed to be so polite, even when she was insulting him.

"I would have too, but Adam said we'd be spending a fair amount of time together in the future, so he invited me anyway."

Olivia's lips tightened. "I see," she said, her voice clipped. "I suppose that makes sense."

But she didn't like it at all. For some reason that just made Luke grin even more.

"I hear you're going to be coming to the club soon," she said, obviously referring to Stronghold since Marquis wouldn't be open for another couple of months.

"As soon as I manage to make time in my schedule, yes."

"You're going to have to go through the newbie class first." Satisfaction dripped from her voice.

Luke hid his own smile behind taking another sip of wine. Both Michael and Patrick had been surprised about his choice of which introductory class he wanted to pass through to gain access to the club. They'd then immediately insisted he not tell anyone until it was time to show up for class. When he found the time to. He'd agreed, and now he was especially glad to have done so.

He wanted Olivia, and Olivia didn't want him. Which meant if he was going to get what he wanted, he needed every advantage he could muster. The element of surprise might help shake her up a little bit and give him the in he needed to crack through the armor she had around her. Or she might be pissed as hell, but he was pretty sure he could make that work for him too. Indifference or ignoring him were almost impossible to work with – anger or frustration was much better. She was attracted to him, he could tell, but she was pretending she wasn't. Luke figured it was for all the reasons he felt he shouldn't be attracted to her, but he didn't think he was going to let that stop him.

Of course, he might change his mind once he actually got a feel for what BDSM was all about, but he didn't really think so. At the very least, they should be able to indulge their mutual attraction, shouldn't they?

"I'm looking forward to it," he said, watching Adam and Angel make their way to the dance floor in the middle of the room for their first dance. "Will you save me a dance today?"

"No." It was the rudest she'd ever been to him and yet didn't put him off at all. He just admired her ass as she walked away, heels clacking on the floor.

"IF HE LIKED IT THEN HE SHOULD HAVE PUT A RING ON IT!" SHARON waved her left hand in the air, bumping her hips with Kate - who actually did have a ring on her left hand, and her fiancé and Dom was watching from the sidelines with amusement on his face. A thread of envy slid through her and she took a swallow from the bourbon and ginger - okay, mostly bourbon - she was holding in her right hand. Drinking, dancing, and not spilling was a talent, and she had it.

Sadly, finding a man to put a ring on it was not one of her talents.

A year ago, a lack of a steady relationship hadn't been depressing to her, but watching all of her friends hooking up and settling down... well that was definitely getting to her. She had a few friends back in California who were still single, but they didn't do her much good when it came to having single friends to hang out with. Not that her coupled-up friends here left her out of things. They were really good about including her.

And thank goodness she wasn't the *only* single person in the group. They were definitely dwindling in numbers though.

Dwindling just like her drink.

She looked at it sadly.

"What's wrong?" Kate asked, loud enough to be heard over the music.

"My drink is broken." Sharon held up her empty glass. "I need to go fix it."

The song was ending anyway. She bumped hips and shook her tits at Kate one last time, and then started heading for the bar - why was it so far away?! - as the song changed over to slower. Ugh. Definitely time to get off the dance floor. Although she did have to smile as she saw Michael pulling Ellie onto the dance floor.

Even better, Luke had just come up to where Olivia had been dancing and was now trying to get off, and Sharon was passing right by.

"Are you sure you don't want to dance?" he asked, with a seriously charming smile which made Sharon swoon a little. The man was hot. Olivia needed a dance with a hot guy, even if he wasn't her type. Plus, Sharon was pretty tipsy and wanted to cause some trouble.

"Oh you should definitely dance with him!" she said, 'accidentally' stumbling to push Olivia closer to Luke. The redhead practically fell into him, turning her head to give Sharon the look-of-death. Oopsie. Oh well.

Worth it.

Probably.

Olivia wouldn't ever really be able to punish her anyway, since they were outside the club and what Olivia liked to do inside the club was waaaay past Sharon's hard limits. She sighed inwardly at the thought. It was why she and Brian ultimately hadn't worked out, which she'd known from the beginning they wouldn't but she'd been tired of not having a steady play partner. She'd wanted some intimacy. Unfortunately, Brian wanted more than just rough sex and a little manhandling, something he'd figured out the more they'd played together. It wasn't unusual for people new to the scene to figure themselves out as they played, but it kind of sucked when she already knew what she wanted, it just didn't match up to anyone else. She was too kinky for vanilla men and too vanilla for kinky men. There had to be other people who fell somewhere in the middle, didn't there?

Something knocked against the back of her knee, sending her hurtling forward and into something very hard.

Oops. Make that someone very hard. And not in the hard penis way. Nope. Hard muscles. All over.

Sharon looked up. Blinked. Ah yes. Scowly face Captain America with his usual look of disapproval. But like every good superhero, he'd caught her before she could go sprawling across the floor. Which was like, super hot - or would be if he didn't always have a pinched expression on his face whenever he looked at her.

"How drunk are you?" he asked irritably.

Bristling, Sharon managed to find her footing. "I'm not! Someone pushed me."

She turned her head around to see Olivia smirking at her from where Luke was leading her in slow circles. Sharon stuck out her tongue at Olivia before she realized Jake was still holding onto her and she had more pressing issues than Olivia's revenge.

"You can let go of me now."

"I'm not sure I can," Jake said, still sounding annoyed. "There's a lot of people on the dance floor, it's probably safer for you to just stay here until the song is over."

His big body moved, taking her with him as he swayed.

Holy crap, he was dancing with her!

Sharon peered up at him. He was like a foot taller than her when she wasn't in heels, and even in four inch heels he towered over her. "How drunk are *you?*"

"Not nearly drunk enough for this shit," he grumbled, barely glancing down at her.

He held her tightly though. Securely. Even just swaying in slow rotations, he had a good lead. The kind of man a woman could lean on.

Ah, fuck it.

Sharon leaned. Put her head on his chest, her body swaying against his, just so she could pretend for a moment that she belonged on the dance floor during a slow song, cuddled up next to a man. Her breasts flattened against his hard stomach and she let out a soft sigh.

Pressed so closely against him, she felt him stiffen.

Everywhere.

Oh ho. Well. Wasn't that interesting?

ABOUT THE AUTHOR

Golden Angel is a *USA Today* best-selling author and self-described bibliophile with a "kinky" bent who loves to write stories for the characters in her head. If she didn't get them out, she's pretty sure she'd go just a little crazy.

She is happily married, old enough to know better but still too young to care, and a big fan of happily-ever-afters, strong heroes and heroines, and sizzling chemistry.

She believes the world is a better place when there's a little magic in it.

www.goldenangelromance.com

BB bookbub.com/authors/golden-angel
g goodreads.com/goldeniangel
f facebook.com/GoldenAngelAuthor
O instagram.com/goldeniangel

OTHER TITLES BY GOLDEN ANGEL

CONTEMPORARY BDSM ROMANCE

Venus Rising Series (MFM Romance)

The Venus School

Venus Aspiring

Venus Desiring

Venus Transcendent

Venus Wedding

Venus Rising Box Set

Stronghold Doms Series

The Sassy Submissive

Taming the Tease

Mastering Lexie

Pieces of Stronghold

Breaking the Chain

Bound to the Past

Stripping the Sub

Tempting the Domme

Hardcore Vanilla

Steamy Stocking Stuffers

Entering Stronghold Box Set

Nights at Stronghold Box Set

Stronghold: Closing Time Box Set

Masters of Marquis Series

Bondage Buddies

Master Chef

Dungeons & Doms Series

Dungeon Master

Dungeon Daddy (Coming Fall 2021)

Dungeon Showdown (Coming 2022)

Dad Bod Doms Series

Logan

Henry by Raisa Greywood

Ray by Maren Smith

Faris by Shane Starrett

Black Light Series (Multi-Author)

Defended

Black Light Roulette: War

Masters of the Castle (Multi-Author)

Masters of the Castle: Witness Protection Program Box Set

Poker Loser Trilogy

Forced Bet

Back in the Game

Winning Hand

Poker Loser Trilogy Bundle (3 books in 1!)

HISTORICAL SPANKING ROMANCE

Domestic Discipline Quartet

Birching His Bride

Dealing With Discipline

Punishing His Ward

Claiming His Wife

The Domestic Discipline Quartet Box Set

Bridal Discipline Series

Philip's Rules

Gabrielle's Discipline

Lydia's Penance

Benedict's Commands

Arabella's Taming

Pride and Punishment Box Set

Commands and Consequences Box Set

Deception and Discipline

A Season for Treason

A Season for Scandal

Bridgewater Brides

Their Harlot Bride

Dirty Heroes Collection

The Lady

Standalone

Marriage Training

SCI-FI ROMANCE

Tsenturion Masters Series with Lee Savino

Alien Captive

Alien Tribute

Standalone

Mated on Hades

SHIFTER ROMANCE

Big Bad Bunnies Series

Chasing His Bunny

Chasing His Squirrel

Chasing His Puma

Chasing His Polar Bear

Chasing His Honey Badger

Chasing Her Lion

Night of the Wild Stags

Chasing Tail Box Set

Chasing Tail... Again Box Set

Made in United States
North Haven, CT
17 May 2024

52620501R00200